For L...

INHERITED

Freedom Matthews

Freedom x

OFTOMES PUBLISHING
UNITED KINGDOM

Copyright © Freedom Matthews 2016

This edition published in 2016 by
OF TOMES PUBLISHING
UNITED KINGDOM

The right of Freedom Matthews to be identified as the author of this work has been asserted by her in accordance with the Copyright, Designs and Patents Act 1988.

All rights reserved. No part of this publication may be reproduced, transmitted, or stored in a retrieval system, in any form or by any means, without permission in writing from the publisher, nor be otherwise circulated in any form of binding or cover other than that in which it is published and without a similar condition being imposed on the subsequent purchaser.

All characters in this publication are fictitious and any resemblance to real people, alive or dead, is purely coincidental.

Cover design by KimG Design

Interior book design by Deadpan Designs

For Granddad, who taught me to imagine,

and to

Callum and Ciaran, who aid me in doing so.

THE VISITOR

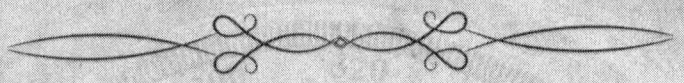

THE OARS HIT the water, and Cherie let out a growl. The long and tumultuous journey had seized her joints, but she didn't slow. As the wood pierced the surface again, she looked skyward. The moon shone overhead, a beacon guiding her forward. How long had it been? Weeks, months, or even days? Yet there it was: land.

Reaching the shallows, she pushed out a weary breath; she had made it. Clambering onto the beach, she collapsed onto the sand, and for the first time in days she was still. Two years had passed since she last touched this place, twenty-four months for her life to come full circle. Desperation had brought her here then, and that same need dragged her back. If this didn't work . . . no, she couldn't think of the alternative.

Tears spilled down her cheeks as she attempted to stand, she swiped them away. This was not the time to cry; there would be chance enough to do that after she completed her task. Composing herself, she stood.

Swaying a little, she pulled in a deep breath and planted her feet.

Before she set off, she adjusted the shawl covered bundle at her breast. The material was grander than the rest of her attire, and tied tightly around her body, creating a sling. With tender hands, she shifted the cargo, her touch so gentle she could only have been carrying the most fragile of burdens. Her forehead creased as she ran her fingertips over the fabric, ensuring nothing had been damaged in her fall.

This was it. She had to move. Throwing back her shoulders and lifting her head, she stepped forward. Her strides did not falter as she crossed the sand. The roads beyond it were silent; every respectable person was asleep. Keeping to the shadows, she danced amongst the inky darkness. Her soundless footfalls troubled no one as she wound through the side streets and alleyways. She didn't trust the quiet, and her wary eyes searched every darkened corner for imagined ghosts. With a quickened pace, she reached the stable yard, her breathlessness disturbing its occupants. The startled neighs had Cherie tripping over herself. Colliding with a wall, pain shot up her arms. Stopping to examine the scrapes, she leaned against the cool stone. Her breath hung in the air as she tried to settle her pounding heart. Not far to go, she thought, setting off again.

Rivage had been a picturesque village, once. Yet as Cherie dodged around broken glass and eyed the frail hinges of barely usable shutters, she remembered the glory the houses once appeared to possess. Focussing her melancholy elsewhere, she ducked beneath an archway and was greeted by a small weather-beaten bridge. The sight stalled Cherie's progress, and she skittered to a stop. Crossing this wooden pathway meant her life would be forever-changed. Cherie's return would not be welcomed but she knew there could be no other choice, she needed help, and across that bridge was the only place she could find it. Her heart was racing with the fear of what she would find on the other side, but she knew that despite her misgivings she would carry on.

Resolute in her choice, she stepped onto the worn bridge, flinching as the damaged wood let out a creak. Was that the sound of regret? She brushed the thought aside. She hadn't come this far to let trivial demons chase her away now. Cherie ploughed on, trying to ignore the building tension within.

A few strides later, she reached the other side. As the surroundings attacked her senses, she released a pent-up breath. Bittersweet memories threatened to overwhelm her as she took in the view. The clear contrast between the broken village where she had walked and the opulent one in which she now stood was immense. A sign nailed to a post read 'Quart de Plaisir.' She gave it little attention as she passed by.

The streets were alight with colour and sound. People were everywhere. As Cherie stepped onto her home turf, a smile bloomed, erasing all traces of tiredness. Singers and musicians cluttered the pavements, their outfits draped like silken shawls. Nothing had changed in her absence; the inhabitants of the underworld remained just as talented and dark as she remembered.

"Welcome back, *Ma Cherie*" A handsome, long-haired fire eater winked.

"*Merci*," she replied as the man swung a lit orb over his head. The crackling flame licked at his skin before extinguishing completely.

Awed by the performance, Cherie stepped back. So captivated by the display, she didn't notice another entertainer at work until she collided with him. She spun, her heart in her throat, as the juggler's arms lurched forward. His ornaments tumbled from his hands. Without missing a beat, he leapt into the air, spinning once, before landing beside the fallen objects. Picking them up, he hurled them one by one, making the blunder part of his act.

The audience cheered, impressed by his expertise. No amount of praise or money could dampen the warning in the juggler's gaze, however. Cherie's apology died on her lips as she dove amongst the crowd, putting as much space between herself and the juggler as she could. In her false sense of confidence, she had forgotten the edge that came with the entertainers of the *Quart de Plaisir*.

Pushing her hair over her face, Cherie wound her way between the performers and their patrons, hoping to remain unnoticed. Despite her best efforts, she was recognised. Folks either acknowledged her with kindness, as the fire eater had done, or shrank back into the shadows... As she made her way across the square, her self-assurance grew; the wait would soon be over.

Cherie paused on her journey, stopping to gaze at a large sculpture which stood in at the central point. Though Cherie had seen and walked past the statue many times, she hadn't ever truly taken in its form. The figure had been moulded into the shape of a pirate and his lover. Their passionate embrace, cased in iron, represented a forbidden love that had tears blurring her vision. Cherie turned away, so overcome by the image. Returning to her task, she stalked across the square. The châteaux style house she headed for was alight. People crowded it, spilling out onto the porch and beyond.

"*Mon Dieu*, is that a ghost? Cherie, we never thought we would see you again."

A woman, dressed in little more than fancy undergarments, left the man at her side and rushed down the porch steps.

Not stopping to greet her friend, Cherie spoke in a rush, the words tumbling out, "I need to speak to Hans I have a favour to ask..."

Her desperation must have been obvious, as the woman grasped her by the arm and all but bundled her through the main entrance. The crowd parted as the two of them charged into the hall. The jangly piano and crowd noise pounded in Cherie's head as she rushed to keep up the pace.

As they climbed ever upward, each floor was overrun. Men of every shape, size, and class drifted amongst scantily-clad women. All were too immersed in their own worlds to notice the hurriedness of Cherie and her friend.

Reaching the final landing, Cherie stopped to catch her breath. An eerie silence greeted her—which didn't help her nerves. As they continued along the corridor, Cherie noticed each of the door handles were decorated with multi-coloured scarves. These rooms were occupied. Cherie forced herself to breathe; the action brought forth the heady scent of cheap perfume and stale liquor. This all-too-familiar aroma only increased her stress.

"Good luck, *mon ami*," her guide whispered, stopping before the final door.

She squeezed Cherie's hand and kissed both her cheeks, leaving her to confront the demon alone. Cherie stared at the flawed oak before her. Splits and whorls tarnished the finish and represented what lay behind it. As her gaze strayed to the brass plaque, nailed amongst the defects, self-doubt welled up inside her and she pushed away a wave of nausea.

'*Agréable, rien de plus que le plaisir.*' 'There is nothing more pleasing than pleasure,' was engraved into the metal. Cherie recoiled. To most, this phrase was harmless, but nailed to this door gave its meaning a sinister flair.

Pulling in one last breath, she locked her nerves away. No turning back now. Gripping the handle, she stepped inside. Her heart thudded in her chest as she came face to face with her fear. He hadn't changed, though Cherie never doubted he would. His tall, lean frame stretched out on a chaise, and his soul-searing blue eyes could not be hidden by his long, curly hair.

"Well, well, well. Look what the *argent* dragged in," he said.

His lips twisted around a cigarillo as he nuzzled a young girl draped across his knee. "Returning to your duty, mon canard?" He blew a smoke ring, his bright eyes unwavering. "I'm sure we could find room for another *femme de chambre*."

Cherie did not cower at his sarcasm, though her entire being begged her to turn and run. She wouldn't bow down to his cruelty or make her escape; she had to fulfil the reason for her return.

"Hans…" Before she could continue, the shawl at her breast began to squirm, and the cry of a child echoed throughout the room.

CHAPTER I
THE NEWCOMER

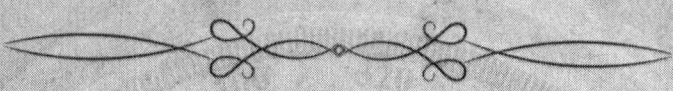

18 YEARS LATER

THERE WAS A flower in the water. Red petals with a yellow centre, it stuck out amongst the darkened waves. The tiny floating flora was what started it all. Life aboard the Wilted Rose had been somewhat simple until then.

Where had the blossom come from? We hadn't caught sight of land in hours. We had left a very welcoming seaside town, just after midnight, some of us a little tipsy and all of us in need of sleep. Although my crewmates had drifted to their respective cabins, I had stayed up to see the sunrise. As the weak light filtered through the clouds, the unusual object had jolted me from my reflection.

Scanning the skies, I sought our resident bird – Caw. Not seeing him, I let out a whistle. His squawking reply had me looking over my shoulder, towards the helm. From first glance, Caw might have been called a parrot, had he not looked so strange. He held the vibrant colours of one, yet, his size, tail, and wingspan were greater. With a graceful swoop, he glided over my head, circling once before landing beside me on the guardrail.

"Could you fetch me the flower, perchance?" I asked.

With an earnest nod of his head, the creature rose into the air once more. His long talons grasped for his prize with gentleness. Soaring upward he flew past me, dropping the cargo into my outstretched hands.

"Thank you." I called as the bird returned to his perch.

"Caw, this gift has come from a man of great kindness. A new comrade awaits your arrival, caw!"

The creature's words were clear and strong.

What did Caw mean? Were we getting another comrade? Putting the thoughts aside, I examined the delicate flower, the soft petals were damp but the striking bloom had not lost its lustre.

You could say I was once a striking bloom. Despite being only seventeen, my youth had waned. There was no innocence in my wary gaze, for I'd seen far too much already. Though I was born Valencia Roux, here aboard the *Wilted Rose*, I was simply known as Lennie. I had arrived aboard the fabled ship, a beaten and terrified teenager. Four years had passed since that day, and the skittish girl I once was, had transformed into a feisty sword-wielding pirate. I was the only woman aboard our cursed vessel and though I sometimes missed female companionship, being 'one of the boys,' was just how I liked it.

As I continued to stare at the damp blossom, somewhere behind me the sound of footsteps echoed in the morning silence.

"You're up early, did you even go to bed?"

I turned to find Butch looking worse for wear and leaning on his mop. He stepped to my side and peered down at the now petal-littered sea below us. His blond hair, well in need of a trim, covered his youthful face. Butch was the baby of our crew, barely sixteen. Though we teased him he took it all in his stride.

"I did manage a few hours" I lied, swinging my legs over the rail. "Enjoy yourself last night?"

I reached up to push his fringe from his face, he grinned but swiftly stepped out of my reach; the movement made him wince, and I caught sight of his blood-shot eyes.

"What happened to you?" Butch countered. "We lost you after one-eyed Jack's."

"I watched the people dancing on the beach." It was a guilty pleasure of mine, something I'd enjoyed doing in my previous life, before the *Wilted Rose*.

"If you'd wanted to dance…"

"No, of course not," I said. My reply slipping out too quickly. Pasting on a smile, I tried again. "The racket you and the others were making was enough to keep me entertained."

Forcing my attention back to the flowers, I watched the water overpower them. One by one, they sunk. Butch was staring at me, I could feel it. I was sure he hadn't believed a single word I'd said. Besides Ned, it was only he, out of all of the crew that could see through my 'tough-broad' persona.

After a long pause, Butch chuckled. "Well the offer still stands, charity does begin at home after all."

With a roll of my eyes I swiped at him. Butch danced out of reach, his fists raised like a boxer.

"You've got to get up earlier to catch me," he said.

"You were lucky, I don't usually miss."

Our banter was disturbed when the helm began to spin with a terrifying speed, and the ship shuddered beneath us.

"Did you feel that?" I asked.

Before Butch could answer the entire vessel turned clean on its axis. Almost losing my footing I grabbed for the rail.

"What the devil happened?" Captain Rourke was breathless as he arrived at the helm. The wheel spun with a force so strong he couldn't even attempt to control it. His feather topped hat was set askew as he fought the whirling wood.

The sails billowed as the ship picked up speed. I jammed my hat onto my head squinting through the sea spray. After a rocky start, the turbulence eased enough for Butch to race up to the crow's nest. With an experienced eye, he scouted for land.

As we journeyed on, more of the crew began to emerge, the first of which was Davy. Of African descent, his skin had been the cause of as much discrimination as my gender. Despite this, he was the calm in our very spontaneous lives – the man we all relied upon to ease any tension. As he stared northward he showed no sign of panic, even with the ship racing through the waves.

With one hand shielding his dark eyes from the glare off the sea, he used the other to cup his mouth. "It has to be another heir."

"You might be right." I called back.

"Nice day for it." Rupert strolled across the deck, his red hair tousled, shirt untucked and his hands thrust deep into his pockets. He was infuriating.

"Yes, Davy and I were just thinking about heading below for a spot of tea," I said mimicking his mocking tone.

"It's a little choppy, we don't want the sandwiches to fly overboard." He winked, nudging me with his shoulder.

As the ship raced on, I stayed alert eager to see what was waiting for us when the anchor fell.

"Where do you think we're headed?" I asked.

"If I've been woken from my beauty sleep for nothing, I will not be best pleased." Rupert ran a hand through his vibrant hair, mussing it further.

"And we wouldn't want that," I mocked.

The redhead scanned the water, his jovial face turning serious. "If it is an heir, it can only be Caleb's son."

"Could there really be more of us? It's been a long time since we found anyone," I said.

"We have to believe, Lennie." Ned, the eldest member of the crew, spoke with a firmness. I immediately straightened at his approach. Though he was barely twenty years older than the rest of the us, Ned was grey and scarred. His flawed face held one good eye and a wooden replacement, which saw much more than it should. He was the father-figure on our ship and I adored him.

"You must remember there are three heirs still missing, if Rosa senses one within reach, she will not stop to ask us." His gravelly voice and knowing tone put an end to our speculation.

It had been a few years, since we'd had a new crewmate. Davy, Butch and Rupert had all arrived in quick succession. It would be nice to have someone new to add to our unique family. What would they be like? Would I finally have a fellow female to spend time with? How would they take being cursed? Each of us had reacted differently.

"Land ahoy!" Butch cried, sliding down the mast with practised ease and awakening me from my thoughts.

The anchor crashed into the seabed and we gathered at the rail, pushing and shoving to get a better look. Butch and Rupert vied for the spot in the centre, but I slipped between them. My shin caught Rupert's boot on the way, and with a curse and a laugh I turned to see the reason for our hasty detour. He was tall and broad, with dark hair and swarthy skin. His handsome face held obvious confusion as we came to a stop in the shallows. He held a book in his hand, which he was using to shield his eyes from the sun. As the ship blocked the glare, he lowered his arm, to reveal one very distinctive feature.

His eyes were blue. Not just blue, they were cerulean. Bright, clear and exactly like Hans'. I hadn't see irises that colour in four years. In the newcomer's tanned face, they were unavoidable. I swallowed my shock, as the captain vaulted the rail.

"What is this? Who are you?" The man's tone was affronted as he glared at the mismatched band of pirates gawping at him.

"Greetings, I am Brandon Rourke, Captain of the *Wilted Rose*."

Before the captain could speak further, the newcomer discarded his book and raised his sword.

"You have no right to drop anchor here, this is the property of, Sir Henry Davenport." His rich voice held suspicion and indignation, rather than curiosity. Despite the gentleman's size and anger, the captain did not quail.

"Has anyone ever told you of the Eight Brothers?" Captain Rourke asked.

"No. I cannot say they have…" the man hedged, his sword never wavering.

I gripped my own, the elaborate handle winding up my arm. Though this man could help us in our journey, I wasn't about to let him get that sword into the captain. For good measure, I pulled the dagger from my boot.

"It all begins with what is beneath your sleeve." Captain Rourke's words held a challenge, but his tone was gentle. I knew the next step was for the newcomer to reveal the brand which marked us all as equals. Equals in a curse.

This was how we heirs identified ourselves, by the marking on our wrists. Just like the flag flying over the ship, each cursed heir wore a tattoo, depicting a skull and crossbones entwined with a wilting rose. The skull of my own mark smiled up at me, the vibrant red petals of the rose, dropped further beneath my rolled up sleeve.

"You have all the proof we need." The captain sounded pleased by what he had found.

I glanced down, sure enough the twin of my own brand was there upon the newcomer's wrist. The man in question was frowning, as he clamped a hand over the mark.

"What does this all mean?" he asked glancing towards the ship and back again. He'd lowered his sword but his knuckles still showed white as they clenched the handle.

"You, friend, are one of us: an heir to the Curses of Eight, and the offspring of a brother – the brethren who were sent to sail aboard the *Wilted Rose*."

"I'm cursed? How? Why?" His questions tumbled out quick succession; all of his previous bluster was gone.

"Our parents failed to end the enchantment and we are, unfortunately, paying for it. We feel, as a group, we could convince its creator to end the curse."

"Who cursed us?"

"Well, in the simplest terms, a faery queen known as 'the Sorceress.'"

The newcomer blinked at the answer but asked another question, "How many of you are there?"

"Eight, but you're the sixth we have discovered."

"What does this curse entail? Where are the other two? What do you want with me?"

"If you would join us, we can take you to someone who can explain the curse to you."

The captain spoke with care. If we wanted even a chance to end the curse, we needed the newcomer to join us.

"We are still in search of the remaining heirs, we can only guess their location or if they are even still alive, and in answer to your final question, very little. All we require is your presence. We feel that if we reunite, we can convince to Sorceress who cursed us, to end it."

The man sheathed his sword. "Strength in numbers."

"Something like that," the captain replied.

"And I can leave at any time?"

"As much as we need you, we wouldn't force you to stay."

The newcomer paused in his questioning, pursing his lips he turned his head to one side, and looked up at the ship. Our eyes met and with a gasp I stepped back. The look hit me like a sucker-punch they were so blue. Butch glanced my way, but with a shake of my head he returned to his staring. Pulling in a long breath I concentrated on the conversation below.

"You call us heirs and have mentioned our parents, what happened, how did they fail?" The newcomer's voice was soft, his gaze flickering back towards me once more.

"According to our sources they were selfish, they ignored the warnings of the curse and defied the Sorceress, we are the product of that rebellion and all that remains. I guess you could say we're paying for their defiance." There was a hint of bitterness in the captain's tone but he covered it well.

"So there were no survivors from the original crew?"

"As far as we know, there were none," the captain confirmed.

The newcomer nodded. "My uncle and I have been searching for my mother for many years. She promised when she left me here, that she would return."

"Although there is a slim chance of finding her, if we can aid your search, we'll do it," the captain promised.

We'd all felt as the newcomer had. If I had a chance to speak to my parents, to learn from them, to know them, I would jump at the chance. Despite myself, I felt a camaraderie with the newcomer.

As the captain continued to answer questions, I stepped away. Seeing that second flash of blue had shaken me, it dragged up memories of things I had long since buried. Brushing the hair from my face, I caught sight of my hand. Specks of red dotted my palm and the echoing memory of screams flooded my ears. My heart quickened but as I turned my hand over and back again, the imagined vision disappeared. Swiping it down my leg, I composed myself, just in time to see the captain lead the newcomer aboard.

Not wanting to look into the newcomer's eyes again, I concentrated on his feet. He wore expensive leather boots. The brass buckles were dusted with sand and held no trace of wear.

"I...I am Nathaniel Davenport-Lee," he stumbled, surrounded by expectant crewmen.

"Welcome aboard," Rupert said, breaking the awkward silence with a slap on the man's back.

Butch thrust out his hand in eagerness. "So pleased to meet you."

As they continued to welcome the newcomer, I took in the fine material of his tailored suit. In my hand-me-down britches, shirt, and jacket, I felt anything but proper. This was a man of money and standing. In any normal circumstance, I'd be in linen and lace. I wrapped my arms around my middle, sighing in reproach.

The crew continued to fawn over the tall man in buckled boots. Ned caught my eye as he rocked back and forth on his heels. With a wry smile, he regarded the newcomer, his good eye travelling up and up. The man was almost a foot taller than everyone else. Ned winked, and even in my dark mood, my lip twitched.

"Ain't this is grand? There are six of us now!" Butch was breathless with excitement as he flung his arm across my shoulders.

"It depends on what you class as 'grand,' I suppose."

"Come on," he cajoled. "There are only two more heirs to find."

"Hurrah," I mocked waving my hands.

Butch didn't notice my sarcasm as he wandered back the way he'd come. With a shake of my head, I set off in the opposite direction; I paused at the stairs to take one last glimpse at the group.

This is a mistake, I thought, as my gaze once again clashed with the newcomer. I swallowed back a sliver of fear and fled.

WHAT GOOD HAD it done, hiding alone? The light had faded from the porthole, and stars now glittered amongst the blue-black sky. Hours had passed while I'd remained shut away, and though most of the time was spent arguing with myself, all I'd discovered was there were no answers to be found.

The eyes of my past, and those of the newcomer were not the same. My reaction was entirely irrational. But how many people held irises as bright as a summer sky? Just thinking about the colour made my body turn cold, and caused long faded injuries to ache.

Thumping the mattress, I watched the dust mites float in the moonlight. I couldn't hide forever. The ship wasn't big enough, and I wouldn't again spend my life afraid in the place I called home.

Though doubt lingered, I rolled out of bed and made my way along the ship's passage. Voices drifted from further down the ship and light shone out from the open saloon door.

"…there they perished, eight men and women. We are all that are left."

The captain finished speaking as I stepped over the threshold. There was only one space left at the table, which just so happened to be opposite the newcomer. His hopeful expression almost had me smiling in return. I chose instead to ignore it, deciding to dissect the flaws in the scarred table. Ned took hold of my hand; his rough skin was a comfort as he brushed his thumb back and forth.

"Now!" Captain Rourke barked, slapping the table to gain our attention.

I turned to look at him, and from the corner of my eye I saw the newcomer do the same. Pushing aside prickles of awareness dotting my skin, I concentrated on the captain. Our leader's expression was firm as he eyed the newcomer once more.

"With an uncle such as yours, you are no doubt used to being of high rank and standing. People jumped at your every command and you could demand of them what you wished. Here, that is not tolerated. We are a team, we help, aid and support each other."

The newcomer nodded, his solemn expression never wavering. "I understand, sir."

"There is not much of a class system or hierarchy aboard the *Wilted Rose*." The captain continued. "This is a ship of equals. Pay no mind to the colour of Davy's skin, Butch's youth, or the fact Lennie's a woman. We are all the same."

The newcomer dipped his head again, glancing to me before returning his attention to the captain. My heart caught in my throat as the blue flashed in my direction. He was obviously curious but my reaction to his stares did little to endear me to him.

Captain Rourke sat up straighter, his narrowed eyes widening a little. "I hold the highest rank on board. I'm here to guide and to counsel. Ned is my second in command; his seniority gives him more knowledge than the rest of us, and he's to be respected. I'm not a tyrant, though I must warn you, if I have to enforce my position, it won't bode well for you."

INHERITED 🕸 21

As he finished, the captain leaned back in his chair, awaiting a response. The newcomer watched him for a moment before replying.

"I understand, sir. I will not use my 'high-class' status, to throw my weight around. I am but one of many on this quest."

"Good." The captain smiled in approval, his kind countenance returning.

"Well, now you know all about us. What about you?" Davy dragged a tankard of amber liquid across the table.

"I am not sure where to begin." The newcomer's voice held a deep and lilting timbre.

I couldn't help leaning closer, curious to hear his story.

"Perhaps try at the start, my friend?" Rupert winked. "Everyone has their own dirty little secrets."

The redhead's gaze flickered in my direction before he grasped a bottle and took a swig. I glared back at him. There was no need for the newcomer to know anything of my 'dirty little secrets.' Rupert just raised an eyebrow at my expression and continued to drink.

With a smile, Nathaniel began to speak.

"I have lived near the ocean my entire life." He began, his voice the only sound in the room. "My mother left me with her brother when I was six months old. I have fought to never take my privileged upbringing for granted. I look to those of more diminutive standing for guidance and advice, rather than listen to those who have yet to experience such things." He paused looking up. "Although I prefer books over battle, I am learned in the art of the sword. I also do not let others assume my responsibilities, hence the reason for my being here." Nathaniel stopped his eyes roaming over his audience. "I have so many questions, yet I just don't know how to ask them."

As he spoke, his gaze lingered upon me. I shifted in my seat, I wasn't used to so much attention. I was just part of the furniture to my other crewmates. Hunting for a distraction, I spied the mismatched bottles on the table and reached for one. Wanting to shock the gentlemanly newcomer, I clamped my teeth around the cork and yanked. It released with a satisfying pop that had my lips lifting in a smirk. Without pride, I spat it onto the floor and drained a hefty portion of the liquid. Wiping my lips on my sleeve, I winced as the burn hit my throat – it was the good stuff. I glanced at the newcomer from beneath my lashes, my attempt had worked, his eyes were wide, his mouth a little slack. I could steer his attention away yet.

*"**LIE STILL!**" **HIS** hand met my cheek, and the sound rang through the room; silent tears drenched my face as I did as I was told. "There, that wasn't so hard now, was it?"*

The hand which had struck me now caressed the reddened skin; I turned my face away as he trailed his touch lower. I clenched my eyes together and prayed for morning.

"No!" I wrestled with the covers as tears fell, unchecked, down my cheeks. The night terror had seemed all too real; the sting of his slap echoed on my skin. Annoyed at my weakness, I bundled myself in blankets and padded barefoot to the deck.

Mist clung to the sails, cooling my fevered skin and obscuring the stars. I wrapped my fingers around the helm; the thrumming energy within the wood helped chase away the nightmares. The wonders of a bewitched ship meant the *Wilted Rose* navigated itself, it allowed me to relax while the lull of the waves soothed my frayed nerves.

I settled upon the steps leading to the quarterdeck and sighed as the cool breeze lifted the damp hair off my face, taking with it the remainder of my tears.

"Could you not sleep either?"

I froze; the newcomer was propped against the foremast, his tousled hair falling across his face. He pushed himself off his leaning post and stepped forward. I retreated, tightening the blanket around me as I stumbled down the staircase.

"Well?" he urged inching closer.

I reached the bottom step, and without answer, I ran.

CAW'S CRY ROUSED me at daybreak. My sleep had been fitful, filled with terrible memories and the image of sky blue eyes.

"Awaken into greatness, for a new adventure beckons."

I chuckled as Butch's voice sounded above me, along with a hefty stomp through the ceiling. Wandering to the galley, I met no-one. Used plates crowded the surfaces alongside an over-stewed pot of tea. Deciding against adding to the chaos, I snatched an apple and made my way towards the deck.

Despite the newness of the day, the sun blazed warm and bright. Reaching the top of the stairs, I pulled the brim of my hat down, shielding myself from the glare. Most of the crew were crowded around the table, their shoulders hunched and their hands filled with cards. The captain stood stoic and straight by the helm.

"What do you think of our newest member?"

Davy's hand on my shoulder, along with his words, jolted me. I'd expected him to be with the rest of the group.

"I would say I'm indifferent to him." I nodded, happy with my succinct answer.

Davy however, cocked his head, narrowing his eyes.

"Yet..." I continued, knowing he expected more, "shouldn't he act a little strange, for he's a stranger after all?" The blasé remark had Davy cackling; it drew curious glances from the players at the card table, including the newcomer. With a shake of my head, I ventured towards the captain. He stood considering the view. I joined him, but the tame ocean did little to calm my agitation. After a few moments he shoved back his hat, his rugged face drawn as he peered down at me.

"Would there be something troubling you, sailor?"

"May I ask what the agenda is for today?"

His lips turned upward as he leaned in closer. "I thought we would introduce our newest man to Rosa."

CHAPTER II
ROSA

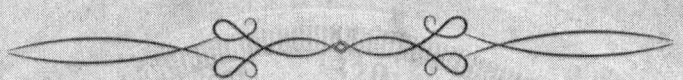

ACCORDING TO FOLKLORE, Rosa had been the first captain of the *Wilted Rose*. After succumbing to pain and loss, the Sorceress (the creature responsible for our curse), bewitched Rosa turning her into the figurehead of our fabled ship. After the original cursed eight had died, she was banished to a cove in the middle of the ocean for her failure. The wooden woman was our higher power, and the only link we had to the Sorceress. Visiting her was almost like coming home, she was a warm and mothering creature, who we all looked to for advice.

The pace of the vessel grew, and the salty air whipped at our faces as the sails billowed like patchwork clouds. The calm water added no trauma to our travel, and as the sun set, we closed in on the cove.

The cavernous opening beckoned the ship forward. The tension, tying my body in knots, eased a little. At least here I would be distracted from the newcomer. The man in question gawped as Butch pointed out the candles, which burned in elaborate brackets, lighting the path as we travelled deeper into the catacombs.

"At last." Ned's words stilled the hubbub of the crew.

We gathered around him as the anchor dropped into the sandy shallows.

"There's no need for fear," Butch whispered.

The newcomer's tanned skin was pale in the lowlight.

"I have too many questions, they are overriding any fear," he said clambering down the rope ladder.

The captain led the way to the inner chamber. Following in his wake, I trailed a hand along the stone walls, my fingertips finding the carved images decorating them. Beautiful roses of every variety greeted my touch. Someone had carved newer scenes of couples in romantic embraces above the archway. As I stopped to take them in, a pang of longing hit me.

Between Hans and the curse, romance and all that came with it, would never be an option for me. I couldn't afford to feel pain or loss, that could be the difference between life and death, so I chose determination. This curse would be ended for my fellow crew however. I would ensure their lives would be whole, no matter the cost to me.

I'd held up the procession and my brethren passed me by. Butch patted my arm as he followed them and I nodded in acknowledgement. Sighing through my reverie, I turned from the artwork and wandered after the others. They had already taken their seats; some chose the carved boulders and benches, whilst the rest lounged on the stone floor. Winding between them I stopped beside a rock pool, taking a seat at the water's edge. At its centre was a raised stone platform.

Feminine in shape, a wooden figure stood atop the plinth. She looked to be sleeping as she leaned against a boulder. The tanned wood had been whittled using such skill the sculpture looked as if it could have been breathing. Her hair fell across one eye, half-covering an emblem painted upon her forehead. In her hand, she held a single carved, wilted rose.

"Rosa, we bring news." Captain Rourke had doffed his feather-topped hat as he perched upon a bench. His gaze was trained on the still form above him. "May I present to you Nathaniel Davenport-Lee.

The rose wielding figurehead lifted its lids.

"Congratulations." Her melodious voice filled the chamber, and her wooden limbs came to life. "Son of Caleb, come forward. Let me see how you have grown."

The Newcomer, Nathaniel, straightened his shoulders and followed the request. His feet stopped mere inches from where I sat, his hands clasped behind him.

"A lot has changed for you," Rosa noted. "Are you ready to join your comrades?"

Nathaniel cast his gaze upon each crew member in turn. I saw nothing in my friends faces but hope. He left me for last. Like a fly caught in a spider web I was ensnared by his gaze.

Turn from him! My mind yelled, but I couldn't. His blue eyes were so vivid; even in the candlelight they didn't lose their intensity. I saw so much in that gaze. My own hopes and deepest dreams were reflected back at me. Blood pounded in my ears and my face heated. At last he blinked, and I was free. What had just happened? I shook my head to rid the errant thoughts dancing through my mind. When I had composed myself, he was speaking.

"I do wish to know more of my parents, how they lived and died. Perhaps here, amongst you all, will be the best place to do that." Nathaniel's words were careful.

Rosa pulled her floral token to her chest. "Keep your heart close, dear Nathaniel, for nothing will bring you comfort should you leave it with another."

Nathaniel stared. He was now bound to the ship, committed as we all were to ending the curse.

"What does this mean?" Nathaniel wheeled around to the captain, who came to stand beside him.

"It means that you cannot profess love, doing so will mean death to your beloved."

Captain Rourke's tone was gentle, yet Nathaniel stepped back as though he had been struck.

"This is what I am to agree to?"

"No," Ned said. "You're cursed whether you're with us or not."

"So there is no choice? As you said, you cannot force me to stay, yet I can never leave." He threw his hands up in exasperation, shaking his head.

"We all feel that way; you're not alone in this," Rupert said.

"That brings little comfort at this moment." Nathaniel snapped. "I have so many more questions, will this never end?"

"Ask us, we have all stood where you have, brother." Davey's tone was pleading.

"How are we cursed? I do not recall encountering anything mythical, at least not until today."

"We were born with this curse, it runs in our veins." It was Butch's turn to answer. His sleeve was rolled up, his decorated wrist on show.

"Our fathers had this curse placed upon them; they never fought to end it and that was their downfall. We are fighting to complete what they had no inclination to."

"How do we end it?" Nathaniel asked.

"We don't know," I said.

"You don't know?" Nathaniel accused rounding on me.

"We hope that if we can reunite all eight heirs, we can convince the faery sorceress who created the curse, to end it," Captain Rourke explained.

"Do you think she will do it? If we can find the remaining two heirs, would she end it?"

"We can only guess." The captain shrugged, though I wished he'd have said something more profound.

"Son of Caleb, you will do better to remain with your brethren. They will help you with this burden, just as they have done with their own," Rosa said her tone firm.

"How long have you been searching for these heirs?" Nathaniel directed his question to the figurehead.

"Since you were all hidden, we have slowly found you and there are only two that remain missing."

"Do you know where they are?"

The wooden woman shook her head; she pressed her lips together before she replied.

"We have knowledge of perhaps one child; the second child's mother disappeared before she gave birth."

"This is madness." Nathaniel shook his head. "A wild goose chase."

"Would you rather we remain cursed, to be forever at the mercy of someone else's rules?" The words burst out of me. I was standing now, anger causing me to shake. With a frustrated growl, I turned away from the gaze of his vibrant eyes.

I pulled in calming breaths only to freeze as a hand touched my shoulder. I stared at it, waiting.

"I do not mean to offend you, Miss but how did you find me? How are you to find the others?"

Refusing to look at Nathaniel, I concentrated on the carvings upon Rosa's plinth.

"We didn't find you," I said. "Rosa's the one who navigates the ship."

"So it was you who found me?" Nathaniel said, directing his question back to Rosa releasing me.

"Finding your fathers journal caused your brand to appear, this triggers the enchantments on the ship. The *Wilted Rose* found you, son."

Each word from Rosa was direct and matter of fact, as though nothing she had said was unusual.

"And this happened to everyone?" The nodding heads of the crew seemed to appease him as he unfurled his fists.

"I have much to learn, I know this now," Nathaniel said, his anger waning. "I will take this journey with you. I have always longed to know more of my history; this may be the best way to discover it."

"You don't have to like this," Rupert said, reaching up and patting him on the back. "It does get easier."

Though Nathaniel made me uncomfortable, I knew we couldn't afford to lose him. The uneasy part of me was overridden by the relief of his reluctant agreement to join us. I looked to Rosa, a smile lit up her unusual face.

"Thank you for your acceptance, son of Caleb. You will soon discover how your parents perished. Be sure it does not happen to you."

"I will endeavour to complete the task my parents were unable to," he vowed.

"That is all I can ask. Yet saying three simple words could end it for you. Those three words could destroy all of us. Remember that." Her dark eyes were serious as she spoke.

"I cannot profess love..." Nathaniel paled as the new found information settled. He stepped away from the figurehead, his shoulders sagging.

As he walked by, I was overcome with emotion; the urge to comfort him almost made me reach out. Instead I threaded my fingers together. The thought of even attempting to ease his pain had my stomach turning upside down. Though guilt-ridden, I remained where I was, unmoving. Why did I feel such a pull towards him? He was broad as he was tall and made me remember things I wanted to forget. There was also the little thing called curiosity. A tiny part of me wanted to know him. I saw something in his eyes, beyond the familiar colour, and I wanted to discover what it was. That terrified me even more.

"Do you bring me any other news?" Rosa asked, drawing my steady focus from Nathaniel.

"We managed to aid a few sea dwellers upon the Spanish coast last month," Butch said, twirling his hat in his hands.

"Ah..."

"Yes, they were finding the waters rather choppy for their liking, but we managed to get them ashore."

"It sounds like a successful job. Well done, men." Rosa's tone was clipped and formal, but her smiled showed her approval.

"Don't forget the burning vessel in Burr Creek," Rupert said.

"Oh yes, I recall such a task.... All came well in the end?" Rosa's question was aimed at Ned, who nodded.

"The legacy of the *Wilted Rose* continues on, and for that I am glad. Just because we are a cursed ship does not mean we should lose our origins."

"Origins? Of where does the ship originate?" Nathaniel's whispered question echoed off the cavern walls.

"The *Wilted Rose* was used, at least in Rosa's day, as a ship to aid those troubled by the sea." Ned's reply had the wooden woman smiling in agreement.

"Any sign of Hadnaloy as of late?" she asked, returning to business.

"None yet," Davy said. His curt response and clenched jaw put me on edge. Davy was usually the calm one, Hadnaloy always set him off.

"Be sure to keep a weather-eye out for her." She tilted her head towards Ned as she continued. "Remember, the children of Roberto or Edmund are out there, I can feel their presence, just as I could many of you. Keep a steady watch on the water and I shall lead you to them, when the time comes. Having all eight of you together will ensure our chance of success. Keep safe, and return to me soon."

With her last words resonating through the cove, Rosa resumed her statue-like position; the stillness of her presence signalling the end of our meeting.

"Come on, Nathaniel, I'll race you." Butch tapped him on the arm before speeding off. The sound of his boots vibrated through the cove as Rupert and Davy joined the race following close behind. Nathaniel turned to the captain.

"It would not hurt to run it off," the captain advised.

Nathaniel nodded before he raced off through the entry way and back towards the ship. The captain winked at me as he stepped through after them.

"I won't be long, sir," I called at his retreating form.

"Take your time," came his reply.

Nodding absently, my gaze strayed to the wooden woman. I had always sympathised with Rosa, being trapped as she was, not only within the stone walls but inside her wooden shell. For Rosa was once human a long time ago.

As I made my way back to the ship, my mind was on the figurehead. All the trials, sadness, and horror the bewitched lady had been through hadn't made her evil or bitter. She had channelled her pain, fighting hard to find a solution to our happiness.

Could I ever be so strong? To take all the pain I've felt and turn it into a positive outcome? The thoughts wove in and out of my mind as I passed beneath the arch and into the candle-lined walkway. My fingertips returned to the stone wall, I could hear the boys further down the passage, their jokes and laughter echoed back towards me. I smiled, glad for my moment alone, I needed to think.

When I had joined the *Wilted Rose*, there were only two others: Ned and Captain Rourke. Yet, when the three boys, Butch, Rupert and Davy had appeared, I felt as though I'd inherited brothers. My stomach hadn't erupted in butterflies, nor had night terrors invaded my sleep. What was so different about the newcomer?

I was still none the wiser as I stepped into view of the fabled ship. I faltered in my approach. Nathaniel stood waiting; the colour had returned to his face, and a more genuine smile played across his lips. He said nothing as he motioned for me to climb the rope ladder first. Finding the rungs, I pushed myself up towards the rail, my hand just missing it's hold.

"Here, let me help you." He grasped hold of my foot, pushing me upward.

The shock of his touch caused me to misjudge my landing. I flailed, arriving on the deck in a heap, my entire body weight landing on my ankle.

"Ah!" I yelled yanking off my boot and glared down at the offending body part as it swelled.

"What happened?" Butch asked grasping for the injury. My hiss of pain had him removing the pressure.

"The newcomer decided I needed help," I muttered as Nathaniel landed beside us.

"Oh my goodness. Are you all right?"

"Yes, I'm wonderful. I felt the deck was the most apt place to take my leave." My voice dripped sarcasm.

Clenching my teeth against the pain, I got to my feet. I wobbled and Nathaniel attempted to approach me as I glared in his direction, he paused.

"I wouldn't," Butch warned.

"Stop crowding me." I grumbled shoving Butch away.

Forcing my weight on one foot, I struggled towards my cabin. I refused to lean on Butch. He hadn't taken my hint though because he hovered close by, his hands outstretched as he followed beside me.

"You'll need to rest it," Butch said as I collapsed onto my bed.

"I never would've thought of that. Thank you, Butch." I glowered at him, reaching for the draw beside my bed. My fingers grazed the handle, not quite reaching. I couldn't stop the growl escaping from between my teeth.

"I only meant to help." Annoyance flickered across his face as he stepped further into the room. Flinging open the draw he pulled out a bandage.

"I don't need –"

"–Shh," he interrupted. Ignoring my protests, he soaked the linen in the wash bowl before returning to me.

"Look at how well 'helping' turned out the last time," I dead-panned, pointing to my ankle. Guilt crept though my anger as I spied his drawn features.

"Thank you," I offered.

"I'll let you patch yourself up," he said, tossing the bandage to my unsuspecting hands. He headed for the door not sparing me a look.

"Butch…" I waited, hoping my friend would respond.

"Yes?" He stopped, reaching for the handle.

"I do appreciate your help, I'm just –"

"I know."

Butch smiled, though something close to sadness and pity lingered on his face and that was the last thing I needed to see. I turned my attention to the porthole. We were moving from the cove and heading out to sea. The silence stretched and soon the door clicked shut. At Butch's departure I let out a long-held breath. The bandage was cool, as I clutched it in my fist. Unravelling it, I wrapped it around my swollen ankle. Biting my lip against the pain, I secured it the best I could, before tugging off the other boot. Still irritated at the nonsensical injury, I launched the item without thought.

"You missed."

With a gasp I turned towards the door. The newcomer was stood in at the threshold, a wry expression on his face. How had he opened the door without my noticing? I narrowed my eyes at him, pursing my lips at the audacity of his being there.

"What do you want?" I snapped, angry at myself for not hearing his arrival and fighting my new friends – the butterflies, who had erupted in my stomach the instant he'd spoken.

"May I?" He asked, gesturing to show he wanted permission to enter. I nodded in reluctance and he walked further into the room, setting a tray of food on the table.

"I came to apologise; my manners overtook me," he said.

Without invitation he sat down beside me. I held my breath as his thigh bumped mine.

Leaning closer to the bedpost, I urged myself to breathe. There in the dimness of my room his closeness felt far too intimate. I couldn't see his vibrant eyes that at least would allow me to guess what he was thinking, and the not knowing scared me.

My thoughts were so conflicted. He irritated me, he'd caused so much anxiety in my usually strong and unfettered life. If he was some passenger we'd picked up along the way, I could avoid him until he was left on some new adventure. Yet, if the curse was to be ended, I needed him, and begrudgingly that was the worst part. For needing a man with eyes resembling the sky, I had done once already. And it had not ended well.

Focusing on anything but his most prominent features, I found myself watching as he clenched and unclenched his fists. The gesture showed nervousness and despite myself, I found it endearing. My palms itched as I fought the urge to still them.

They were working hands. Calluses and rough skin covered his long fingers and wide palms. His knuckles too seemed worn, as though he'd fought. A signet ring shone from one finger, heavy and gold. Ink also stained the inside of his left index finger and thumb. What was that from? Did he write? My imagination ran rampant at the thought of our palms pressed together. Would my fingers feel dainty surrounded by his?

I pushed the dangerous thought aside. In its place other questions arose. What did this high class boy know of work? Why were his hands so rough? The thoughts vexed me just as much as the fall. My anger flared again and I wrenched myself away.

"Just so you know, no-one looks after me here," I said breaking the silence. "I'm not the weak link, nor am I considered a second class citizen because of my gender."

I tapped at the brim of my hat to see him better. "I pull my own weight and fight alongside my fellow crewmates. I don't run and hide when the hard times come."

"The captain already made that loud and clear." Nathaniel said, as he lifted his palms in surrender. "You are a liberated lady."

Just as with Butch, I turned to the darkened porthole; the fight had gone out of me as the pain in my ankle increased.

"I'm simply Lennie," I murmured. Nathaniel thankfully took the silence which followed as his dismissal, leaving me to brood alone.

DAWN BROKE THROUGH the porthole, and light spilled into the cabin. I whined at the intrusion. My swollen ankle throbbed as I dangled it over the side of the bed. Unwinding the bandage, I found a large purple bruise covering my skin.

"Perfect," I muttered. Hobbling across the room, I doused a fresh dressing in cold water. Keeping the weight off my foot, I slumped back on the bed to apply it.

"Morning Limp."

I bit my tongue as Butch peered around the door.

"What do you want, besides to laugh at my ailment?"

"To give you this," he crossed the threshold, a tankard in his hand. The odour coming from the cup was enough to turn my stomach,

"There's no way—"

"—Ned made it, he said it would ease the pain."

I pushed the foul smelling concoction away with one hand, whilst covering my nose with the other.

"It reeks."

"Do you want to get better?" Butch thrust it at me again, forcing it into my hand. I huffed pursing my lips as I took hold of it.

Though the metal container was warm, no steam rose. Staring inside I grimaced, the liquid was thick and dark and an object floated on the top, moving as though it were alive.

"What is this?"

Butch shrugged. "A painkiller, I think?"

"Drink it." Ned appeared, two walking-canes were shoved under his arm. "It is an elixir to heal."

"It smells," I whined.

"So do half the crew, but do you hear anyone else complaining?"

"Ned…"

"Do you want to use your foot again?"

"Yes,"

"Bottoms up!"

Knowing I wouldn't win the argument, I clamped my nose and chugged.

It's strong ale, nothing more. My mind raced through countless different excuses until the last drop was gone. Wiping my lips on my sleeve, I pressed my hand over my mouth. I was sure I'd see a repeat of it any second. "We will let it settle, then Butch and I will get you on deck."

"What use would that do? I can't graft today." I lay down; the movement caused my stomach to churn.

"Come on Lennie." Butch gripped my hands and pulled me upright once more, "lean on me."

Using all my strength, and with much cussing, I made it onto the deck with Butch's help. He was so attentive, setting me up at the table alongside a book, and another tankard of the vile brew.

"I think you'll be alright for a while."

"More than alright, thanks Tobias." My young friend stilled as I used his real name. He looked up at me, a small smile playing on his lips.

"No problem." As his face flushed he turned to join the rest of the crew, who had already started working.

Opening my book, I scanned over the first page but my attention couldn't be held. For right in my eye-line was Nathaniel. He seemed lost following the crew about until they set him a task.

"Could I be used in the armoury? I was able to assist at home." Nathaniel asked about an hour later. My head shot up, the armoury was my domain.

"I think it will be fine for today," Davy said.

"I promise I am qualified, our guards were quite pleased with my work."

"As I said, it'll be fine." Davy winked as he passed by my station.

"Why are you so puzzled, son?" Ned said his arms were weighted down by the books he carried.

Nathaniel hovered, looking out of place once more. "My role has not been allocated quite yet."

"No? Well you did just arrive, boy, once you have been here awhile, we will find where you are strongest."

"But—"

"I heard you, I'm sure you're more than able to take care of our weaponry, you just need to prove yourself. You've not been here long boy, settle in and then you'll find your place."

The older man set his load down on the table beside me. Hiding behind my book, I tried to cover a smug smile.

"Lennie here is our gun keep and no-one is to clean or even touch our inventory until she says so."

"I hear you, sir." Nathaniel nodded as I peered over my tome. Blue eyes caught mismatched ones. "If I may be so bold, Miss Lennie?" His voice was soft and I couldn't look away.

"Yes?" My reply was faint, and I coughed to cover it. "What do you want, newcomer?"

"Could I be of use? What I mean is..." He floundered for a second and I threw a withering look to Ned. The older man's responding glare told me to be patient.

"Sorry, but as I am the one who caused your injury, I would be honoured to show my remorse, by taking over your duties – If you would allow me to do so, of course."

Nathaniel's formal address and apparent guilt softened my annoyance. No one had ever spoken to me in such a way. It was a little flattering; I wasn't going to give in though.

"Thank you for your kind offer." I began, with a shake of my head. "However, I rarely allow the others to help me with my work; to hand it over to you would be unfair."

Pleased with my response, I picked up my book and returned to its pages. With a curious eye however I peered over the top of my novel. He caught me, his eyes locking with mine. After a second of staring he broke our connection, returning to Ned.

"There must be some occupation I can aid in? I cannot be content in doing nothing whilst the rest of you work."

Ned frowned a moment, contemplating the request. With a nod he replied, "Of course not, follow me."

At their exit, I discarded my book. Sliding my sword from its sheath at my waist, I ran my fingers along the blade. Catching my reflection in the glinting metal, I frowned at the tousled waves which fell around my face. Why did Nathaniel keep bothering me? Was it because I was the only woman on board?

"Put it away or use it."

I chuckled at Butch's threat. Flipping the sword in the air I caught it with ease.

"Show off," he muttered swabbing at the wood around my chair.

"Is there any way you could do me a favour?" Butch stilled, leaning on his mop.

"What would you have me do?"

"Go and get me-"

"– a few bits from armoury so you can work?"

"Am I that predictable?"

"No, I just know you too well."

My smile was sheepish as I stowed my weapon. "Would it be too much trouble?"

"Of course not, anything to stop the newcomer from taking your job." His grin was boyish, a rare occurrence for the youngster.

"DO YOU NEED anything?" A grease stain decorated Nathaniel's cheek as he returned. Ignoring his question, I cracked open the rifle in my hands and blew down the barrel. Nathaniel stood waiting, his shadow blocking my light.

"I'm fine," I said snapping the gun closed.

"Perhaps you would require another cold bandage, a beverage, or something to eat?"

"I know what you're doing."

Nathaniel stopped his fussing and looked me square in the eye. A shiver ran through me but I ignored it, returning to my work.

"Yes you were at fault but I don't need your help." My tone was gruff but no less polite, pushing out a breath, I wiped a cloth over the metal.

"That may be, but I will not give up," he said with a cocky smile.

As he walked away I clamped my jaw shut. How dare he? Who did he think he was? He must have been taking pointers from Rupert. The handsome devil was attempting to use his charm and my traitorous body was reacting. Darn the butterflies – my stomach was dancing with them.

"Give him a chance," Ned said, as I frowned at Nathaniel's retreating back. "I know you have issues with men of such ilk. Don't tar them all with the same brush."

Ned was right of course, though the lingering need to avoid Nathaniel hadn't disappeared, I didn't want him near me. There was fear that had settled, right down to my core, a fear I'd not lived with for four years. Since boarding the *Wilted Rose* the only thing to scare me was the ship's enemy – Hadnaloy. The idea of fearing someone in my own home did not bring comfort. I'd done that before, I didn't want to repeat old stories. I knew how they all ended.

"You've had enough for today, Hop-along." Butch teased breaking me from my thoughts.

"I think you're right."

Taking hold of his outstretched arms, I attempted to stand. Pain shot up my leg as I put a small amount of weight on my injured ankle. A single step, then another, I bit back a curse but I'd known worse pain. Awareness prickled up my back and I turned to find Nathaniel. His concerned expression propelled me away from him, I didn't need his pity.

Reaching my cabin, I threw myself onto the bed. My whole body was spent, even after such a short journey. I hated feeling so weak.

"Comfortable?" Butch asked, as he grabbed a blanket and laid it across my legs. I fought the urge to kick it off.

"Of course, this is paradise." I said not hiding my derision. Rolling my eyes I smiled through my disgruntled mood.

"You can't be that bad, you're still mean." Butch grinned, not taking offence this time. "It wouldn't hurt you to let us help."

He didn't look at me, he busied himself straightening the books beside my bed. I knew he wasn't just talking about my ankle.

"Old habits are hard to break." I offered.

"Sure," Butch agreed. "But you do know I'm here for you."

"Of course." I said as my friend headed out the door.

Once I heard Butch's steps fading down the galley, all my bluster flew over the threshold behind him. My well placed façades crumbled and I broke. The strain and tiredness I'd been ignoring, shook my body. My breathing came out in short, sharp bursts as I fought the sobs. Thoughts attacked me like pellets, hitting the places which mattered the most — head, heart and soul. Curling onto my side, the coarse fabric muffled the sound of my tears.

"Oh Lennie!"

In my woe I failed to hear the door open. Before I could protest I was gathered up in a cocoon of two strong arms. The large body swallowed my petite frame, as it rocked me back and forth. Resistant at first, I stiffened. Yet the soothing timbre of the voice, and the gentleness in which I was held, had me sagging against the warm body.

I refused to acknowledge who held me, though I was sure I knew who it was. Instead of dwelling on it, I nestled closer. I hadn't been comforted in such a way since childhood. Pulling in his scent, I was surprised to find not the stale perfume or putrid alcohol of my past, but the earthy aroma of masculinity, fresh parchment, and even ink.

It was a while before I could contain my sobs, small hiccups jostled us and though drained, I was over the worst. Once I'd stopped shaking my comforter lessened his hold. With gentle hands he brushed aside my damp hair, but something lingered on his face which made the unease return. His sky blue eyes held so much.

As he sat before me, his face morphed into someone different, though the eyes remained the same. The hair was long, fair and curling, the skin held sun damage and stubble. Accented threats spewed from his hard mouth and I shrunk away from him.

"Lennie?"

I blinked away the vision as Nathaniel's voice broke through. I knew fear was emblazoned across my face. He stared down at me, confused.

"What is it?" he asked searching my face.

"No, please," I pleaded, burying my face into his chest. He held me, whispering soothing words over my head. I clung to him, demanding affection I'd never wanted or needed before.

"It's all right," he murmured, his large but gentle hands running soothingly through my hair.

Comforted again, I looked up at him, in the dim light he no longer looked like the man from my night-terrors.

"I'm here Lennie, no-one can hurt you." He smiled, his reassuring tone almost had me believing him.

"It's a nice thought," I said looking down.

I was still in his arms, his warmth and heartbeat so close. With a finger beneath my chin, he lifted my head to face him.

"Don't turn away from me, please, you have nothing to fear."

I wanted to turn away, to run as far as I could, I really did. Yet so many things fought against it. The curse, my past. Once he knew of my background, he wouldn't be so determined to have me so close, or even worse he'd want to be closer still.

"Lennie, stop over thinking things." His soft words held pleading.

Traitorous tears fell, in silence, down my cheeks. He brushed them away and I pressed my face into his hand. I looked back into those bright eyes and saw my longing reflected back at me. At that moment I didn't care, I yearned.

"Forgive me?" I begged and pressed my lips to his.

It was over in a second, just a whisper of a kiss. Yet when it was over mortification, terror and fear overwhelmed me. Deep down, I wanted more and that was even worse.

Nathaniel coughed into the silence. "I had best be going."

Disentangling me from his arms, he set me back on the bed.

"Do not forget to rest," he said, leaving without a backwards glance.

There in the short sound of his exit, I had unlocked some of my confusion. I was not only fearful of what Nathaniel Davenport-Lee represented, but of what he could mean. Plain and simple I was scared of the hope he could entrust to me, and of the attraction I felt. The thoughts did not ease any of my tumultuous feelings. I was not wrong. He was dangerous, for I wanted him. Him and all the dreams I couldn't have.

CHAPTER III
SKIRMISH

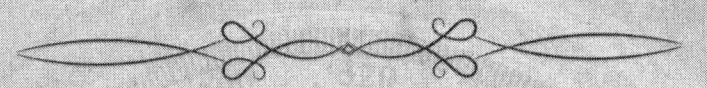

DESPITE MY OWN troubles the *Wilted Rose* hadn't stopped for a second. Supplies were running low and Butch had scouted land, off in the distance. We hadn't ventured far from Nathaniel's homeland of England, and the beauty of being aboard the *Wilted Rose*, meant you never quite knew where we'd drop anchor or what sites we would see. Each day was an adventure and without the captain's map we'd be lost.

Beyond the harbour, women tended their gardens and hung out washing, whilst fishermen sat awaiting their catch. Small working boats littered the waters' edge and at our approach, heads turned.

Getting closer, the hope of welcoming townspeople faded. Their smiles and bustling stopped. Their stares and accompanying glowers had me staring at the heavens. *Here we go again.*

"Why are they so hostile?" Nathaniel asked as we docked beside the once merry fishermen.

A wizened sailor spat, sending his missile over the guardrail.

"Return to where you came from!" He bellowed.

A woman, not much older than myself, approached the dock. Her bare feet were dirty and in her hand she held dull coloured objects.

"There's no room for you, blaggards!

With great aim she tossed a piece rotten fruit at Davy. It split as it struck him, the juice dripping into his eyes.

"We are naught but demons and thieves to them." Davy's words came out low and bitter, his body shook as he stared over the heads of the narrow minded townsfolk.

"Whore!"

I turned to find another of the fishermen pointing his crooked finger my way. With clenched teeth I grasped Davy's elbow. The word hit me but I refused to acknowledge it. It wasn't the first time and it wouldn't be the last.

"I pity them for their narrow minds, for ours are more open despite our trials," Davy said turning on his heel.

"You sir, have no right to judge," Nathaniel cried.

My thoughts were pulled from Davy, as Nathaniel yelled over the rail. His face reddening as he thrust his fist in the air.

"You have no rights at all," came the reply from dry land.

Turning away from the scene, I hobbled back to my chair. Nathaniel and I hadn't spoken much since the night he'd consoled me. Brooding had become my past

54 FREEDOM MATTHEWS

time and I hated feeling so conflicted. I felt changed. It was as though realisation of my weakness, my fear, made me different, more vulnerable somehow.

"Perhaps we can last a little longer eh, captain?" Ned said as more fruit flew.

"I think you might be right," Captain Rourke agreed.

"Come, Nathaniel. Do not make it worse for yourself." Ned handed him a handkerchief.

"I just do not understand some people," Nathaniel said swiping the rotten juice from his face.

"Just as Davy said, we're nothing but rogues to them," Rupert explained.

"In your case, they'd be right," Ned deadpanned as he followed the captain towards the helm.

We were once again sailing onward, the dark glares and heckles had long since passed and nightfall would soon be upon us. Sat at the card table, I buffed the blade of my weapon. The fading light made the task hard, but I was merely keeping my hands busy. Tucking away the sword, I stared out to the retreating land and darkening waters. Rupert tusked at the sight. Shuffling his cards and taking a seat, he dealt me into a game.

"Don't feel that way," he chided placing down my last card.

"Excuse me?" I asked, spreading them out in my hands.

"You shouldn't waste your time on guilt, especially when it's unfounded."

"Who says I feel guilty?"

I shifted the small pile; not liking the way the conversation, or my handful of cards, were going. Since my injury, the well-ordered control I'd cultivated had been lost. I'd even had to relinquish my hold on the armoury, letting the boys take on the jobs I relished.

"No one has to say anything. It's written on your face. Each time Butch swipes a cloth over a blade, when I clean the cannons, or Davy takes his turn with the gun cabinet."

I couldn't stop the pout as I concentrated on my hand. It was true. Though I was thankful for their assistance; I knew I couldn't rest until I could work alongside them again.

"You'll be better before long, and whipping us all into shape." Rupert assured, setting down a card.

"I hope so," I said, taking from the deck.

Damn! These cards were not on my side today. The sound of heavy footfalls snagged my attention. My dud hand went ignored as Nathaniel passed the table. My face felt warm and a new wave of shame swelled in my fluttering stomach. I had kissed him. I was a fool. Would he tell the others of my weakness? In all my young years I had never acted in such a way. I had never been so forward before whatever my past may be!

Returning to my cards, I almost growled as my fingers shook. Rupert hadn't failed to notice, his brows knitted together as he spied my unease.

"Are you all right?"

He reached out, wrapping his roughened hand around my wrist, stilling the tremors.

"Of course I am. Are we playing, or am I just wasting my time?" My terse reply had the crease between Rupert's brows deepening.

"All right, we can just play."

He let me go and set down another card. I placed a few of my own, though quickly I became distracted again. Nathaniel was leaning over the rail; the light breeze lifting his dark hair as he stared out to sea.

"What caused this?" He pointed down at the water below him; it looked as though someone had upturned a bottle of ink.

"We should tell the captain," Rupert muttered.

"Why?" Nathaniel asked.

"The dark water means that Hadnaloy and her cronies are not far from here. It's her little calling card." Rupert spat out the name as he picked from the pile before him. His cheek twitched as he pretended to concentrate on the game.

"What is a 'Hadnaloy'?" Nathaniel asked as he took a seat. "I remember Rosa mentioning the word, but she never explained it."

"Hadnaloy happens to be a sea-witch, and not a great fan of ours." Davy said joining us.

His brow furrowed as a small shiver rippled through him. I pressed a hand to his shoulder and he smiled in thanks. None of us liked to talk of the wicked creature. It felt like a bad omen.

"What did we do?" Nathaniel asked, staring around the table.

"She and Rosa have a long standing feud," I replied trying hard not to be affected by either the darkening water, or Nathaniel.

"I'll go forewarn the captain," Davy offered. With a salute he raced below.

I couldn't concentrate anymore, the cards I held swam before me.

"I fold," I said throwing them onto the scarred wood.

"That wasn't much of a game." Rupert conceded, gathering the deck and shuffling them once more.

Ned appeared holding a useless boot under one arm, we all gazed up at him expectantly.

"Come on; let's get rid of this bandage," he said, his good eye on me.

"Are you sure?" I asked.

Rupert's expression screamed, 'I told you so' and I rolled my eyes.

"Of course, come on girl, you're stronger than you know." Ned smiled as he pulled off the cloth. With gentle hands he prodded the still-bruised ankle.

"Move it about a bit, my girl." He suggested.

Though a little stiff, I turned the ankle, pressing my lips together at the discomfort.

"All healed."

"Thank the Lord!" I cried my fist reaching into the air.

Ned handed me my boot and I pulled it on, it felt strange to be wearing two again. I took a few small, albeit wobbly steps.

"It's as good as new." Though there was still a little ache, it was something I could live with.

"Well then child, we can put you back to work." Ned's smile was joyous.

Rupert stood tossing his cards. I frowned at the redhead as he pushed away from the table.

"I'm done. Fancy crossing blades? I'm in need of practice. None of us wanted to even attempt it without your full supervision."

Rupert's words were accompanied by a wink. He was teasing me, the seriousness was over.

"Of course, that sounds like just the thing I need," I replied.

The sword at my hip had lain redundant during my convalescence. My fingertips traced patterns upon the tooled metal of the hilt. I'd missed using it and a small skirmish couldn't hurt. I wanted to do more than play invalid anyhow.

"Mind if I join you?" Davy said, breathless with his hasty return.

"Of course, follow me fellers."

Leading the way towards the quarterdeck, I couldn't stop my grin. I was back. This was my forte, swordplay and fighting. It was all I knew, the rest I just guessed at.

Sitting atop the rail, I let my newly-healed ankle swing to and fro.

"Show me what you can do," I called.

The men smiled in unison as they yanked their weapons from their belts, without preamble they crossed swords. Both were evenly matched in skill. Their youth, fitness and trust in each other, allowed them to manoeuvre with speed and confidence. There was no possession of fear or doubt.

Davy spun; his blade almost grazing Rupert as he lunged forward. Rupert didn't falter; he wielded his sword over his head with a flourish, swiping it through the air

"Well done," I praised leaping off the rail. "Davy, you need to steady your feet when you turn."

He nodded, trying the move again.

"That's it," I said as we shared a smile.

Stepping beside Rupert, I thrust out my sword so it was parallel with the ground.

"You need to improve your form. Straighten your arm as you bring your sword down, it'll keep your balance and you won't throw out your muscles."

We attempted the move together, bringing our weapons through the air.

"Wonderful," I exclaimed. Flipping my blade, it landed in my hand without trouble.

"Where did you learn to do all that?" Nathaniel asked as he stepped out from his hiding place.

"It comes naturally," I said shrugging as I sheathed my sword. My palms had grown slick and I hoped my face didn't look as warm as it felt.

"That's interesting," Nathaniel said grasping for the sword at his hip. I eyed him, only having seen him unsheathe it once before.

To everyone's surprise Nathaniel snatched the hilt from Rupert's hand and began to juggle them; a superior look upon his face. The blades crossed and looped around each other as he made them dance. Rupert and Davy gaped at his ability but I was far from impressed. Where I had grown up, sword jugglers were a ten to a penny.

Stepping around him, I counted the rhythm of his throws. One, three, five, seven... Thrusting out my hand Rupert's sword fell within easy reach. Nathaniel let out a yelp, as the other one crashed to the floor.

"Parlour tricks do not equate to skill, newcomer," I stated.

Handing Rupert his weapon, I spun on my heel. The silence that followed me had me feeling a little more smug.

My hauteur didn't last long, the captain had returned to the deck, a frown drew creases across his face. Ned beside him too looked worried.

"Gather 'round, men," Captain Rourke ordered.

Rupert, Davy and Nathaniel all came to stand with us. Butch was the last to arrive. He raced to our group, his hair mussed from sleep. He bounded to my side. A broad smile lit up his face as he pointed down at my booted feet. Before he could speak the captain addressed the group.

"Right then, Davy informed me a while ago that the sign of Hadnaloy has appeared in the water. After much thought and deliberation, Ned and I feel we should pull guard duty. This is risky territory and until we're out of the worst of it, I want us all to keep a weather eye." With a nod, he wandered to the wheel. Touching a hand to it, he looked northward. "Go get yourselves kitted up, men. We shall arrange positions next."

"Guard duty?" Nathaniel asked as the group around us jumped to action.

"We take turns watching over the ship, we're on high alert, sailor." Ned explained as I led the way to the hold.

The bottom of the ship was home to a brig, some of our supplies and the armoury. I dove down the stairs towards it. Wrenching open the door of a large cabinet, I pulled out a number of guns, sabres and other weapons, hurling them at the crew who had followed behind me. Spying blemishes upon the metal I let out an audible groan. I'd been away too long.

"If you want a job doing...." I muttered. They had obviously tried to take on my role, but the care or inclination hadn't been there.

"You can clean them once we're done," Butch chided, pushing a dagger into his boot, Davy and Rupert belted their holsters failing to hide their smirks.

Reaching for a pistol, I held it out to Nathaniel. "Can you handle one of these?"

"A little," he replied.

A haughty expression crossed Nathaniel's face as he reached for it. The gun hovered between us and I glared. This was not the time for him to be cocky. His impatient beckoning almost had me refusing to hand it over. I knew time ticked on and pushing out an over-exaggerated sigh, I thrust it at him.

"Be sure not to blow a hole in your foot," I warned, throwing ammunition over my shoulder, along with a holster. His chuckle raised my ire but by the time I had turned, he was gone.

As I reached the deck, Butch was already stationed in the crow's nest. Below him, the captain oversaw the helm. Davy and Rupert were close by, their hats shoved back so they had the best view. I couldn't see Nathaniel, perhaps he'd been despatched to man the canons below. A slight niggle of worry befell me. Did he know what he was doing down there? Men had been known to blow off a limb – not that I cared or anything.

As I lingered upon the quarter-deck I tapped out a rhythm upon the hilt of my sword. Beside me, Ned stared further out to sea, his wooden eye held clear sight of the situation.

"Keep calm," he murmured as I let out a shaky breath. Caw, his feathered companion, swayed upon his shoulder. The bird's beady eyes blinked at me as I looked his way.

"Caw, never fear what cannot be loved, caw," cried the creature.

Did he mean my situation? I stared up at the bird. No, he'd meant Hadnaloy. My paranoia had to stop, I couldn't go on fretting, it wasn't healthy.

"Thank you," I whispered reaching up to stroke his coloured feathers.

"Nathaniel is downstairs; perhaps you should see if he's in need of any help. I don't think he's had much experience with cannons." The captain suggested.

"I did think about that," I said. Though I was hesitant to go. The last time we were alone, I'd made a fool of myself.

"Though, wouldn't one of the boys be better suited?" I stopped myself. The cannons were part of the armoury and I was in charge of that. It had to be me. I turned to Ned, opening and closing my mouth. I had no other excuse to stay above deck.

The older man chuckled. "If there is any sign of action, I'll shout for you."

With a wave in thanks, and much reluctance, I headed towards the stairs.

The candles burned low, casting shadows into far reaching corners. I felt unseen eyes watching and it did little to calm my unease. The ever present stomach-filling butterflies flapped their wings in rhythm to my increasing heartbeat and bubbling annoyance, which refused to settle. I pressed a fist to my stomach as I travelled further into the depths of the vessel. It wasn't long before I found Nathaniel. He'd settled beside one of the many cannons lining the hold. He was hunched over a notebook whilst another rested upon his knee, scrawling script and drawings filled the pages on view.

"It looks like you're busy down here..." I muttered as I leaned against the door frame. Nathaniel's head shot up, connecting with the low beam above him. His eyes clenched tight as a curse burst from him.

"I'm so sorry." I cried.

All of my false bravado and fear was forgotten as I raced towards him. There was no hesitation as I touched the spot he'd hit. A small hiss crept from his between his teeth as I continued to examine his injury. I could feel the beginnings of small lump forming beneath my fingertips, but at least there was no blood.

"I will live," he said, reaching for my wrists, trapping me.

At his touch, I pulled in a sharp breath. The fluttering creatures in my stomach almost took off. Our eyes met, and I looked away, my heart pounded far too quickly and the memories which threatened to resurface had my lips quivering.

"I'm fine, look at me," He urged.

Though reluctant, I returned his gaze briefly. We were so close I could feel his warm breath on my face.

"I came down to check on you and the cannons, now you're hurt." Remorse coloured my tone. I'd done it again, I'd been foolish.

"Well I would say we are about even then," he teased.

His voice was intoxicating and I slid out of his grasp. Being so near to him could prove fatal. I pasted on a smile as I stepped out of his space.

"Then again…" I said, crossing my arms. Pacing the room, I stared at my boots. Yes, boots were safe, blue eyes, not so much. "I lost the use of my foot for a good few days, you on the other hand, a speck of sense or two. Not a fair trade in my estimation."

I risked a look in his direction, Nathaniel's smile was playful. He stepped forward and I stopped.

"Lennie, we should talk—"

"— Lennie! Nathaniel!"

Whatever Nathaniel was about to say, was lost to Ned's cry. I raced to the deck, my fingers hovering over the hilt at my hip, ready for what awaited us.

Reaching the deck, I yanked my blade from its prison. Yet, there was no battle, only the group converged at the helm. The once jet black water now sparkled in turquoise clarity all around us.

"Are we home free?" I asked, sheathing my sword once again. Beside me, Nathaniel skidded to a stop.

"For the most part, we just need to remain vigilant," Ned said.

"What happens now?" Nathaniel gingerly brushed the top of his head; I tried hard not to mimic his wince.

The captain lifted the brim of his feather topped hat, glancing towards the horizon.

"We continue to be on our guard, and keep on the lookout for unusual activity on the water," he said.

"That doesn't mean Butch and his swan dive…" Rupert teased.

Rupert poked out his tongue and nudged Butch, whose face turned red. The memories of Butch's tumble played out in my own minds-eye, causing my own chuckles. The boys continued to banter around me, hurling abuse at one another.

"Should I ask what happened?"

I gasped in surprise as Nathaniel's voice sounded beside me. His breath ticking my ear.

"Oh sorry Len," he said, reaching out to steady me as I stumbled.

Stepping away from his touch, I headed to the rail. I tried to smile, covering my reaction. Talking about the boys would steer his attention from me, straightening I began my tale:

"Butch had only just come aboard, all the boys had barely arrived really. Butch had been fascinated by the crow's nest from the moment he'd stepped aboard, and one early morning he climbed the mast. He told me later, it had called to him and once he'd made it, he'd grown cocky. He decided to mark his victory with a jig upon the lip of the nest. We were all asleep – that was until an almighty splash sounded We raced to the deck to find this child bobbing up and down, swallowing half the ocean as he tried to get back on deck.

Rupert and Davy pulled in the rope ladder of course, the poor kid took over two hours clamber up the side of the ship without any help."

"He fell? Why did no-one help him?"

"Face first bless him, I don't think he was dry for a full week afterwards." I let out a full laugh, the first in a while. "Ned and the captain felt he'd learn from his mistake if he managed on his own. We would have helped if he was in any danger, he was more embarrassed than hurt."

"You are very fond of those boys." Nathaniel said.

My laughter stopped. "Yes, they're my family."

I turned to watch the boys in question. They had moved on from the banter and had begun to spar. Davy stood between Rupert and Butch as he outlined the rules in a low voice.

"What on earth are they up to?" Nathaniel frowned as he shifted uncomfortably beside me.

"Passing the time, there's only so much to do when the ship sails itself."

Davy caught my eye gestured for me to join him. Excitement replaced my nervousness as I jogged over, leaving Nathaniel behind.

"Fancy a scuffle?" Rupert winked as he sent a right hook at Butch. The youngster ducked out of reach, giggling like a cheeky school boy.

"Why not?" I replied, rotating my shoulders.

Davy grinned pulling rags from his pocket and tossing them at me. While he strapped make-shift protection to his hands, I swaddled my own. Some may have called them dainty or feminine in the past, but in my four years aboard the *Wilted Rose* I had acquired some well-earned calluses and flaws. I was proud of them; they were part of my journey, a badge of honour for what I had achieved and what I was capable of.

Finished I flexed my fingers, ensuring they had full range of movement. Just to make sure, I pounded each fist into the opposite palm.

"There is no way that she is fighting," Nathaniel cried in disbelief.

I glanced across at Nathaniel stood beside Ned.

"Just as the captain told you, we don't judge people by their gender, colour or class here, son. Lennie's tougher than us all, you'll soon learn that," he explained.

With Ned's words ringing in my ears, I turned back to Davy. Standing toe-to-toe we bumped fists. He, unlike Rupert, wasn't bolshie or quick to quip. His eyes didn't hold teasing nor did his lip twitch in mocking. Davy was solid and stable; his lean and lithe physique gave me prudence to learn more.

"Ready?" he asked.

"Ready."

"Alright then, come on." Davy motioned me forward and we began.

Bouncing on the balls of my feet, I cleared my mind. Counting down from ten, I began to jab. The sound of my fists connecting with Davy's open palms satisfied the animal living deep inside me.

Left, right, left right. Ducking and diving, spinning and sliding – all the natural abilities I had discovered with my sword were equal with my fists. My childhood, at least the latter part, had been filled with people taking jabs at me. This gave me the fire to hit out, to make me take back some control of the situation which had threatened to swallow me whole. It hadn't, and that was thanks to the fight within me.

Davy soon raised the stakes, his clenched hands swiped at me as I pounded harder. I felt the fire in my stomach build from a low blaze to an erupting volcano until I was sweating, it dripped off my face and soaked my back. A deep, feral growl slipped between my teeth, and my punches became erratic. My eyes narrowed into slits and my opponent morphed from the calm and quiet Davy, to a large, overbearing man with long curly hair and irises as blue as the sky.

"I took you in when no one else would. You could have been fodder for the work 'ouse but I gave you a roof over your 'ead and beautiful clothes to wear. This is the least you can do. You owe me."

The thick, accented voice battered me like a hammer, causing my growls to break into cracked screams. I did not falter in my attacks, if anything I was more ferocious. Pounding face, body, I didn't care. My opponent wasn't fighting back, if anything they were trying to prevent it. That just made me angrier and in my fury I yelled.

"Bastard!"

"Lennie, enough."

The present came into focus with sharp slap, sweeping away the past I had been fighting. Tears continued to pour as I rested my forehead against Davy's chest. As my hiccupping sobs shook my body, held me My pounding heart and raw throat scratched as I caught my breath. Clasping a hand to my mouth I rushed to the rail, putting an end to my churning stomach.

"Come on child, settle yourself," Ned said.

Brushing a hand over my shoulder blades, he offered me a flask of warm liquid. I couldn't help myself, I sniffed at it before taking a long drink.

"I'm sor–"

"–Now, now, don't even attempt to speak, just drink," Ned admonished.

As my heart rate slowed I gathered my bearing's sliding to the floor. Davy stood a little way off, his dark skin showing signs of a swollen eye. His lip was split and dripping blood down his chin. Rupert was offering his handkerchief as Butch as rustled up a tankard from somewhere.

"Oh, Davy! I'm so sorry."

"No harm, no foul." Came my friends muffled reply. "Remind me never to get on your bad side."

"I don't know what came over me."

"Don't worry, Len, we all know." Davy paused. "We all know what you've been through. If a split lip is all we get, then we're bloody lucky."

He attempted a smile. Tears filled my eyes once more, he was being so nice, even after what I'd done to him.

"Least you can say you were beaten by a damn good fighter," Butch said.

"We would all say that," Rupert agreed.

"Go clean yourself up boys. We'll join you in a while," Ned said, waving them off.

They all followed his request – all except Nathaniel, who hovered beside the foremast.

Ned urged me to drink more of the warm brew. Lifting my hand to wipe my face, I found my fingers stiff.

"Here, let me," Ned said as he gently untied the bounds. My knuckles were a bloodied mess. Purplish bruises were beginning to show beneath the grazes and my fingers felt numb.

"How did this happen?"

I gaped at the damage I had done. Blood trickled down my fingers, Davy got off easy, I could have killed him. *It wouldn't have been the first time I'd killed*. I pushed the thought aside, there was enough bad blood without those memories resurfacing.

"You got carried away I fear," Ned said, dabbing my cheeks with the soiled material of my bounds.

"I saw Him, inside my head. I heard his voice and it was all over." The revelation came out on a whisper as I clutched Ned's flask.

"He cannot hurt you anymore; you of all people should know that."

"I do," I assured.

Turning the flask upward, I drained what was left of the liquid. Discarding the flask, I came face to face with Nathaniel. His concerned expression mixed with his all too familiar eyes, sent shivers down my spine.

"I need something stronger, excuse me," I said as I made to stand.

Ned grasped my elbow as I stumbled.

"Do not indulge too much child, for I believe what you need is about to emerge upon the horizon."

The older man pointed eastwards, the sun was about to set but through the burnished yellows, was the sure sign of land.

"I think you're right." I agreed.

WITH THE UNMISTAKABLE sight of people, lights and their welcoming sounds, the Island of Plenty beckoned like an old friend. By nightfall we would be enjoying the delights the stopping place had to offer - with no fear of flying fruit.

"Blast! That was the last of it," Butch complained as he finished the final bottle of rum.

"That can't be true, surely?" Rupert said snatching it from him and turning it upside down. Nothing ventured out of the opening.

"It's not all bad," Davy said, draining the last of his bottle. "We'll be stocked up soon enough."

"Let's hope," Butch grumbled, grasping the useless bottle and disappearing downstairs.

"Wonder what the sport will be?" Rupert sighed flipping the queen of hearts between his fingers.

The question had me smiling from behind my book. Of course Rupert would want company.

"What do you mean 'sport'?" Nathaniel asked, putting his own book down.

Burying myself within the pages, I kept my ears pricked. I was intrigued to learn more of our newest crewmember.

"Women, my dear man, someone to pass the time of day with, or should I say night." Davy winked at him but Nathaniel still looked clueless.

"What is Lennie, a bullfrog?" Nathaniel exclaimed, his hand flying upward.

Neither Rupert or Davy could contain their laughter at that — even I sniggered aloud. Rising from my seat I strode over to the table, my damaged fingers resting between the pages of my reading material. Leaning against the back of Rupert's chair I tapped his hat with the book cover.

"What our dear red-headed friend wants, I sure as hell wouldn't like to give."

I felt a spark of triumph when Nathaniel blushed. *I shouldn't goad him*, I told myself. He could reveal more than I'd like him to, and these boys already knew more about me than was proper.

Biting the inside of my cheek, I took a seat amongst them and returned to my novel. The story didn't grip me like it had before, and my mind returned to Nathaniel. What were his small pleasures? He didn't partake in the excessive drinking, nor did he speak of female companions like Rupert or Butch. I'd seen him reading more than once; but what was that compared to the taste of ale or the want of a partner? Or had I been around Rupert too long? Although I'd like to, I didn't have the courage to ask.

Reading over the last page again, I found a passage that struck me. A woman had just broken down in front of the man she loved. In turn he had avoided her. If only I had been so lucky. Since my sudden outburst during the sparring, I'd noticed the boys glancing at me, concern clouding their expressions. Were they worried I'd lost my mind? That I'd turn on them like a madwoman? Or were they truly worried about my wellbeing?

"How did the island acquire its name?"

Nathaniel interrupted my brooding as we eased ever nearer to our destination.

"It's a place where we and many others seek refuge, comfort and nourishment. With its plentiful bounty, we're well catered for and we can stock up for our next adventure." Ned said.

"And a large enough bookshop to tempt even Rupert to read." Butch grinned.

"Bookshop you say?" Nathaniel appeared somewhat lifted by the talk of such a place.

He closed the book in his hands, lifting another he caressed the spine. We had many books in the saloon, and from the title, I could see I'd read the one he held. Yet, I'd never treated it with such reverie.

"It helps retain the binding," Nathaniel said.

I blinked, I'd been caught.

"I've never seen anyone do that before," I murmured.

"It comes with loving books I suppose," he said as he ran a hand down at the yellowing pages. "You want to keep them safe from harm, yet crave to know all of their secrets."

"Like a woman then?" Rupert quipped nudging Nathaniel as he stood to leave.

The interruption saved me from having to respond. I couldn't help but be drawn to the way Nathaniel's lilting voice spoke with such affection for something I adored. Novels and stories had always been my escape. A way to run away when I wasn't able to. I agreed so wholeheartedly with Nathaniel's sentiments. It caused the butterflies to dance again.

"Why is he always so vulgar? Women should be respected." Nathaniel's tone held annoyance. All at once the wings stopped beating.

"He prevents us all from drowning," I said shortly.

Leaving the table, I stood at the rail watching the fancy twinkling lanterns strung up across the island. They surrounded the beach and wove between the buildings beyond. It had been many moons since our last visit. I loved the history, the stories and the entertainment it provided. There had been at least three brawls upon our last trip, though I hadn't partaken. Ned and I had been holed up in the tavern, poring over our purchases and people watching.

There was a bitter-sweet tinge to our arrival, however. The Island of Plenty hosted a mixture of patrons of all colours, creeds and classes. This bustling and forthcoming atmosphere reminded me of a place I would be glad to never see again. My hometown. The Island of Plenty was more of a safe haven, a spot free of pasts which were best left within memories. Though the similarities were there.

"Why so solemn?" Butch tapped my shoulder, jarring me from my daydreams.

"Nothing to trouble yourself over," I assured, turning away from the island.

"It won't be long before we drink our fill and beat every card game the tavern has to offer."

"Here, here!" I said, not trying to hide my smile. Butch always knew what to say to raise my spirits.

"Come see this," Davy shouted.

The tone of our crewman's voice stopped our stupid grins, and had us both running. Davy was still as he concentrated on the large craft which approached us on the starboard side. It wasn't as ancient as the *Wilted Rose*, but there was a definite decay and neglect which clung to the sails and woodwork like mould.

"I should've spotted them earlier," Butch said as we reached them.

"Weapons ready," Captain Rourke commanded.

Nathaniel frowned, pulling out his own blade.

"Are these people we know?" he asked.

"The flag is somewhat familiar," Ned replied as he narrowed both eyes towards the darkened material. As the moonlight hit it the image became clearer. A helm crossed by two swords.

Anxiety rose within me as the looming vessel sailed ever closer to our own. Why were we still floating aimlessly and not headed for land? Darn the cursed ship with a mind of its own! I hadn't failed to see the second flag upon the mast. Skull and crossbones, the pennant more commonly used by the pillaging and attacking variety of pirates. For that's what this boat appeared to be, a genuine pirate ship. We had come in contact with folks such as these before; it hadn't ended with a drink at the nearest tavern however. I turned to Rupert and his apprehension was evident by his shifting feet and clenched teeth, his sword turned in his hand.

"Stay vigilant; any sign of aggression do what you must," the captain ordered.

Releasing my sword from its sheath, I held it downward. The weight of the blade and roughness of the handle was all I needed. The taste of battle was enough. I needed to go to work.

Looking to my left, Nathaniel held the hilt of his sword with such force his knuckles protruded.

"Whatever you do, don't show fear, they can smell it, remember that and you'll be fine," I advised.

Nathaniel's eyes never strayed from their target, but he nodded to show he'd understood.

"What's your purpose?" Captain Rourke called, as the opposing ship stilled. There was silence aboard, even their lamps were dim.

"What say you, stranger?" The captain tried again. "We mean you no harm, we're merely curious of your approach, are you in need?"

A cloaked figure moved amongst the shadows, the only sign of life aboard the mysterious ship. There was a pregnant pause before the figure responded. It didn't speak at first, but hummed a few bars. The eerie tune chilled me, what was it doing? My skin dotted with gooseflesh as the notes turned into the words:

"Yo ho, yo ho, no pirates left for me. We pillage, we plunder, we pull people under, what a pirate I must be!"

This was no shanty, derision and dull mocking filled the figure's gravelly tone, the quiet of the ocean allowing his dark voice to echo across the void. I shivered at the lyrics. This song held a warning, I could feel it. My hand touched the hilt of my sword, ready for what, I didn't know.

"Yo ho, yo ho, a cannon does blast free!"

So ensnared by the strangeness of the song, I yelped as the opposing ship opened fire. My crewmates cried with me as they scrambled for their weapons.

"Aye, boys, to the cannons!" Captain Rourke bellowed, his orders sharpening our focus.

Davy and Butch lurched towards the stairs. Who were these people and what did they want? The ship shuddered beneath me, as our own fire echoed in retaliation.

Smoke filled the air but without hesitation I raised my sword and dove into the melee. My crewmates darted across the deck as the opposing ship's crew swung across the short gap on ropes. A few never made it, for Rupert and Ned's gun's filled the air with the scent of gunpowder.

Those that did make it swarmed our ship, their numbers far greater than our meagre seven. As Nathaniel and Captain Rourke slashed their swords through the ever increasing enemy, I set about cutting loose our rivals ropes. Those who did arrive on board, were dealt with a thrust of my sword and a hefty push, leaving them to disturb the fish.

A sharp pain hit my shoulder and I spun, a large man was grinning back at me, his yellow teeth clenched as he waved his now bloody sword. I raised a brow, dancing around him, mocking his limited movement and ignoring the pain of my injury.

"Keep dancing, little beauty, there'll be no chance to in hell!" he hissed as I scored his face with my blade.

"Wench," he spat, crossing his sword with mine.

"Now, now, there's no need to call me names," I sang, spinning behind him, and slicing a hole in his shirt. Now we matched.

"You'll be getting more than names when I'm through with you." His sword pushed forward with yet more clout but I simply stepped out of the way. His size was no match for my light feet.

"You need to catch me first," I teased, touching the tip of his blade with a finger and giving him a wink.

"I'm done with this," the man said in exasperation. We crossed blades once more and as our hilts met, he curled his lips into a sneer. Perhaps I'd pushed my luck in teasing him, as before I could contemplate his next move, he launched himself in my direction. With his bulk, I couldn't hold him off and we hit the floor hard, my head colliding with the deck.

The pain clouded my vision for a moment but as he pounded at my body, I returned the favour. Though my fists were far from healed, I punched, kicked and bit out at him. He too gave his best, punching my face until I spat blood – darkness began to edge it way around my eyes and if I didn't think fast, I'd be out cold.

"Lennie!" Butch's voice rang out through the hubbub, and soon the weight was pulled off me. Skinny, youthful Butch hefted the giant over the rail, but he managed to catch hold of it, begging for mercy.

"Out of options now aren't you?" Butch growled.

"Please, please, no!"

"I hope your next life is a better one." Butch's cruel epitaph was the last words the big man heard, for my friend shoved the devil over the rail.

"Are you alright?" He asked turning to me.

"Don't worry about me, let's finish these off," I said sucking in a breath, the wretch had winded me. Swiping my face with my sleeve, blood stained the fabric as I pulled it away. My hand shook as I stooped to pick up my sword. Straightening I pushed out a breath.

Davy slammed into my back as another rogue vaulted the top cannon. So much for breathing properly.

"Cover me!" Davy cried thrusting his sword at one of the three opponents he was battling. I duelled the man at his left. He managed to nick me across the face but I retaliated with a swipe at his arm. With a cry he retreated.

Beside me, Davy had finished off another, stomping a boot to the fiend's chest in order to free his sword.

One man remained before us, his toothless grin riling me

"So you thought you'd trade your dolls for swords little girl?" he spluttered.

I narrowed my eyes at him, anger making my blood boil.

"Lennie, he's not worth it."

Ignoring Davy's protests I raced towards the blaggard, my sword aloft. His eyes wide with shock were the last I saw before he was sent overboard.

Cleaning off my sword, I hunted for my crewmates. The captain was holding up well, though his feather topped hat was missing. He turned to another rival, slashing his sword through the air making little work of the fight.

Heading back to the rail I struck more ropes, the sound of cries and the inevitable splash became a satisfying sound. Men were everywhere, we were outnumbered and I was afraid for my crewmates. As I rallied myself to return to the throes, I heard a shot not too far away. As the smoke began to clear, I could see Nathaniel was the culprit.

"See, I'm an old hat at this," he cheered. He paused however, staring at my face. Stowing away his gun, he stepped to my side. With gentle hands he touched my battered face. My left eye was swelling and I knew more than one wound marred my cheek.

"It's nothing," I said. "Let's get these bastards off our ship!"

He nodded, pulling his sword from his sheath.

"Take care of yourself, Lennie, see you on the other side!" he yelled, hurrying back into the fray.

"Stay safe!" I called after him, though my voice was drowned by the noise of the battle.

As I watched Nathaniel fade into the crowd, a battered Rupert appeared. His shirt was ripped and an oozing wound soaked what was left of the fabric.

"Lennie, go and relieve Ned." His breathless demand came as he lifted his gun. I didn't wait to see his success, but I heard the shot meet its mark as I raced between the battling hoards.

Ned was close to the helm, battling two men half his age. As I propelled myself forward, a whistle sounded and I spun.

"Someone with such a face should not be fighting my crew; she should be in my bed."

Across the void, a single darkened figure stood manning the opposition's boat. It was the shadow from the other ship, the lone instigator of this war. Anger bubbled from my every pore as I made for the rail. Growling with pure hatred, I muttered a curse.

Before I could grasp one of the few remaining ropes left by our rivals, someone had hold of me. Their fingers biting into my arms as I struggled.

"Bring her to me." The shadow yelled.

"Let me go!" I demanded, elbowing the wretch in the stomach." His grunt told me I hit my mark. He didn't loosen his hold much, one arm was wrapped around my waist, my arm caught. As I struggled, I kicked out, my free hand punching and scratching the best I could.

"Boys! Butch! Ned!" I hated calling for them, but I needed their help, there was no other way. Despite my fighting prowess, this blaggard's strength was just too much for me. I wouldn't give in though, I wrenched my body forward, freeing my trapped arm. With more range of movement, I began a two fisted onslaught. To my frustration the punches bounced off him like flies.

With the battle raging around me, no-one could come to my aid. Distracted by their own rivals I was alone in my fight. My screams did bring others, however. Men from the opposing ship came at me from all sides. Each of them dull eyed and sallow skinned. My damaged hands were bleeding as I threw blow after blow, but I was no match for them.

I screamed, kicking, biting and punching. I even gave a swift head butt but they didn't release me. Soon the others converged, clamping my arms and legs. Once I was truly immobilized, a gag was fastened.

Making myself into a dead-weight was the only trick I could think of, and though I'd landed a few more good shots with the back of my head, my quick thinking was in vain, for my last sight was the hilt of my own sword as it headed for centre of my forehead.

The world went black and I knew no more.

CHAPTER IV
LOST & FOUND

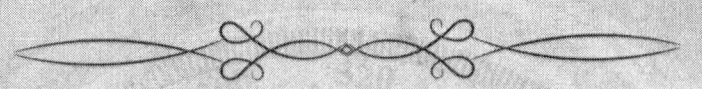

THE SMELL WAS rancid, like dead fish that had lain untended for days. Blinking through the pain, I searched for the source of the odour. It was difficult to concentrate, the throbbing in my head overpowered almost everything and all I wanted to do was drift off again. Pushing aside the hurt, I fought to keep my eyes open.

Darkness greeted me, though a glimpse of dim light filtered in from a half-covered porthole. My hands and feet were bound and each movement caused further pain. The dirty rag my captors had tied, cut deep into my face and added to the aches and sharp stabs which coursed through my tired body.

Sobs threatened to escape, as my head whirled like a spinning top. Panicking was futile – it wouldn't help matters. my stomach rolled with a mixture of the stench and shock, my throat closing around dry heaves.

After a moment the nausea subsided I stared around me. Rolling onto my side, I spied a body. Squinting in the half-light, I could just make out the dark hair and large build of the newcomer – Nathaniel.

Blood seeped from a cut at his temple, yet he stared straight at me, alert and conscious. Seeing I was awake, he shuffled closer. Reaching my side, he pressed his forehead to mine. I closed my eyes, savouring the connection. I wasn't alone. We would get out of this. Together.

"You did what? Those are your siblings Macrucio, they are not the enemy!"

A woman's voice echoed above us. The words were clipped and shaky, whoever she was, she was furious.

"They too are under the Sorceress' spell." The woman continued. "You hold far too much trust in Hadnaloy than you should. She will not help you, these people will." Her voice had taken a harder edge, as though she had spoken through clenched teeth.

"Do you, in all seriousness, believe that?" The reply came from a man. His rolling Spanish accent was familiar.

"If we released them they would murder us. Is that what you want?" He spat.

"I know in my heart they are my family"

The male voice laughed, mocking her sincere admission.

A small sense of relief crept amongst the fear festering within me. Whilst six of the heirs had been squirreled away by their parents, there were two whose whereabouts were unknown. One had been abducted, the other lost.

Something deep inside me knew that these were those two heirs. It seemed all too obvious now that Hadnaloy had been behind the disappearances. Without quite meaning to, Nathaniel and I had stumbled upon the missing heirs to the Curses of Eight.

Whatever happened now, I had to gain their trust and return them to the *Wilted Rose*. If I was injured in the process, Nathaniel would be able to aid me in my return. It wouldn't be ideal, but it would help the cause, and there would finally be a full house aboard the ship.

The angry woman seemed to grasp the idea of getting the heirs together, she wouldn't take much convincing. Yet the man, would he be harder to coerce?

My past had prepared me for circumstances such as these. There had been a time when I could have had anything I'd wanted from the male species. No matter how much it repulsed me, I would have to put my old wiles to use if the man proved difficult.

Footsteps sounded above us, and it wasn't long before the door of the brig opened with an ominous creak. Light flooded the room and I pushed my face into the roughened wood beneath me. From the sounds of footsteps approaching, I was sure more than one person had entered.

There wasn't much time to find out as I was hauled to my feet. I glared up through my lashes at the faceless brute that snatched at my arm and dragged me around like a ragdoll, whilst Nathaniel grunted beside me as his own captor yanked at his binds.

"Why are we here?" Nathaniel asked, muffled around his gag.

The answer to his question was a swift knee to his stomach. I made to speak but my captor raised his hand, threatening to slap.

I bit my tongue. I wanted to fight, to kick out, yet the cold hard barrel of my captor's gun launched me onward, and stopped any back-chat. My aching body and pounding head protested as we neared the source of light. We were on our adversary's boat. The worn wood beneath my feet and the heady stench of neglect was everywhere.

"I do adore punctual guests."

It was the shadow. The man who began the battle, and the Spanish sounding gentleman who I'd heard from below. He was the same fiend. Our captor.

I could scream, why did I have to need these people? Damn it! This man could very well be one of the heirs we needed and he'd almost destroyed all we'd held dear!

He was tall, though not compared to Nathaniel, with long jet hair falling around his face in uncontrollable waves. His olive skin highlighted his dark eyes; which were as black as a starless sky. He would have been moderately attractive or even handsome, had his mouth not been curled into a menacing sneer.

He came towards me, his fingers biting into my arm as he gripped it tightly. His warm breath brushing my temple as he pulled in my scent and I fought against urge to kick him.

"A fine flower…" he crooned.

His hand slid down to my waist as he cupped my hip, nestling himself closer. His body pressing into mine. I clenched my jaw; I knew it wouldn't do Nathaniel or me any favours if I reacted. From the corner of my eye I could see Nathaniel struggling in his hold. He growled, his face reddening as his bright eyes flashed with contempt. I couldn't place the intensity of his anger, but it wasn't helping our cause either way. I tried to shake my head but it was too late, the man caught him.

"Well, well." The loathsome man said, grinning at his crew. "We seemed to have ruffled a few feathers."

As he nuzzled at my loosened hair, I fought away images of other men. Their faces pressed into my neck, their scents overwhelming me almost making me retch. I stopped my thoughts. I couldn't return to that time, even in my mind. I would be lost.

I began focussing my attention on the different shades of wood which made up the ship. Opposite, the worn timber held whorls in the shape of eyes; they looked back at me, owlish and bland.

"Leave her alone!" Nathaniel's words were muffled by his gag, but they were no less plain.

Not releasing hold of me, the dark haired man – Macrucio, reached out and patted Nathaniel's cheek with a mocking smile. As he did, I caught the flash of a mark on his wrist.

"Now, now, you will have your turn soon enough." Macrucio said.

His crew cheered in anticipation and I knew what would happen, even before the olive toned hand gripped my shirt.

"Let them go, Macrucio, I will not play your games, not today." A strong, clear female voice called behind us, stalling his work.

Macrucio flexed his fingers against my skin but still he didn't loosen his hold.

"Claudette," he muttered, "This is none of your concern."

The woman was tall and willowy with long, pale blonde hair which tumbled in curls down her back.

"Oh that is where you are wrong." Claudette replied. "Let him go free." Her voice was curt as she pointed.

The two oafs who restrained Nathaniel did as she asked without argument. Claudette strode forwards, a triumphant expression lit up her face as she approached.

Reaching the group, the woman stroked Nathaniel's face. "What fine eyes."

Her stare was hungry as she traced a finger along his neck, before continuing her trail down his chest. Macrucio stiffened beside me, I could understand his tension. Anger mixed with something much more potent, had me balling my bound hands into fists.

Claudette continued to circle Nathaniel, her full lips curled into a seductive smile. With a lift of a long finger, Nathaniel's hands were freed. Before I could question how she'd done it, the gag was removed and he was murmuring his thanks.

"Now let her go." Claudette's words were slow and precise. Despite all of the bravado and charisma Macrucio wielded over his crew, he visibly deflated in front of this woman.

The soulless eyes of my captor were narrowed as they held Claudette's. The fair haired woman raised her left index finger as she moved closer. Without breaking his stare, Macrucio trailed his hand down my body before shoving me away from him, and into the waiting arms of Nathaniel.

"Are you all right?" Nathaniel whispered as he removed my bonds.

"Yes," I gasped tugging off the gag. Despite being free, my gratitude was dimmed somewhat by the strange emotions raging within me. I couldn't place them, but they were fierce.

"Does that belong to you?" Claudette asked.

Turning back to our captors, I spied my belt, fastened around Macrucio's waist. The worn but detailed tooling of the leather and the large brass buckle were definitely mine.

"Does it?" Claudette questioned again.

With an aggrieved sigh and a roll of his eyes, Macrucio unbuckled the belt and tossed it at me. My sword was still secured in the sheath and the knife hadn't been removed from the lining. Before either of them could change their minds I quickly pulled it on.

"Now we have finished with this nonsense." Claudette sniffed. "It is time we made our guests more comfortable. When my door closes, I will not be disturbed."

Claudette's stare had not wavered from Macrucio's, yet the men who'd dragged us onto the deck stepped back. Minutes passed before Macrucio's patience waned and he looked away, but she remained staring at him for a moment, her lips drawn in a thin line.

"If you would follow me please," she said, turning to us. In my hurry to be free I hadn't noticed, but this woman held unusual eyes. Sparkling and bright, they were a distinct shade of lilac. If Ned's teaching were anything to go by, this woman held magic. Fae magic.

Claudette shot one last glare in Macrucio's direction, before motioning for us to follow. Despite my earlier misgivings, I was curious.

"Shall we?" Nathaniel asked offering his arm.

"Let's," I replied, taking it.

We were led below deck and into a large cabin reminiscent of the saloon aboard the *Wilted Rose*.

"Please take a seat," Claudette urged.

The rough and neglected exterior of this ship was nothing compared to what awaited us below deck. Elaborate drapes hung from one large picture window and several portholes. Delicate tables, holding vases of flowers and countless feminine knick-knacks stood beside overstuffed arm chairs and sofas.

Two armoire's flanked a large mirror and dressing table which covered one wall. This table was covered with all kinds of lotions, potions and beauty products. The entire room was a mix between a boudoir and a royal bedchamber. If I squinted and added the intoxicating aroma of stale liquor and perfume, I'd be back within the confines of my childhood home.

Taking the lead, Nathaniel sat upon a velvet covered chaise and pulled me down beside him. Our bodies collided on the small seat and I covered my gasp. With my face growing warm, I crossed one leg over the other, creating a space between us. The close proximity seemed all too intimate in the sweet smelling room. Claudette coughed into the silence which followed, and I looked up to find her perched upon an ornamental desk, swinging her legs like a child.

"I'm Claudette by the way."

"I'm Nathaniel and this is Lennie." Nathaniel said, introducing us both.

"Pleasure, I first wish to apologise, capturing you by force was never my intention," she said, her pretty face pinched in worry. "When Macrucio spoke of the *Wilted*

Rose, I was eager to meet you all. I never dreamed he would harm any of you... are you hurt?"

Staring up at Nathaniel, I spied the drying blood at his temple. I held my breath as his hand brushed across my bruised forehead and came to rest upon my cheek. The soft pad of his thumb touched the welts the gag had made and I fought back a wince.

As I scanned his features, I realised this was in fact the first time I'd truly looked at him. During his time aboard the *Wilted Rose*, I had concentrated only on individual parts of his person at a time, his eyes, hands, hair, and even his manner. Taking in the entire view I could see he had a kind, but roguishly handsome face. But now, being so close, I could see the faint lines around his eyes and mouth, he must laugh a lot... My gazed lingered on his lips, their softness showed in his tender smile. Without thinking I moistened my own.

"Nothing we cannot handle." Nathaniel's reply jolted me back to the present.

"I'm sure." Claudette replied wryly. Still swinging her legs, she pushed her long hair off her face, revealing a brand on her wrist.

"So, I was right," I exclaimed.

Claudette eyed me with suspicion. "What, may I ask, were you right about?"

"That you must be Edmund and Rosetta's lost child. We knew Caleb's heir was a boy," I said, gesturing towards Nathaniel. "We also knew Macrucio was taken by a sea-witch, from eyewitness accounts." I said as Claudette nodded. "It's strange, Rosetta fled pregnant, no-one knew when or what gender she bore."

"You know your history well." Claudette smiled, her guarded expression gone. "From the information I have cobbled together, I have discovered I am the daughter of Rosetta and Edmund Pearce. I was abducted by Hadnaloy around the age of three – my mother had already perished, my father was missing and I was living with relatives. Hadnaloy wanted her own heir, someone to continue her work and apparently I seemed the best choice."

Claudette then turned her arms upward, to show us her tattooed wrists. One held the skull and crossbones of the *Wilted Rose*. The other resembled the flag which adorned the mast above us. A helm with two swords crossed through it.

"Hadnaloy poured some of her magic into me. And so as I grew, so did my abilities. She needed someone as cold hearted and evil as she is. She had managed to change Macrucio from a thoughtful, brooding boy into what you see today, after all, so why not me?" A muscle worked in Claudette's cheek as she clenched her teeth. Was she still annoyed at her crewmate or just her mistress?

There was a shift in Claudette as she stared off into the distance, her bright eyes clouding over. "The only trouble being, I was born out of love. I was neither cold hearted nor evil. As Hadnaloy described my destiny to me, even my young mind knew it was wrong."

Claudette spoke as if to herself. "I vowed to her I would use my abilities for good, nothing more."

She blinked, looking at us as if she'd forgotten we were there, a solemn expression marred her delicate features.

"How did Hadnaloy feel about that?" I asked, moving to the edge of my seat in anticipation.

"As you can imagine, she was not best pleased." Her fingertips brushed across a scar on her cheek, the only flaw on her beautiful face. "I am one of her rare failures, you see. Though she is a determined creature and feels I will grow into her likeness in time. Even if I never succumb to her ways, I am one of the cursed eight, after all... that is something she can use, I guess."

"You don't sound convinced," Nathaniel said, as he too moved closer. All his attention on the fair haired woman. The atmosphere crackled between them as the pause became a long drawn out silence.

The strange feelings returned within me and this time they had voices. They snarled in my ear as I bit the inside of my cheek. *She has nothing more to hide than magic. You are nothing compared to her. Beautiful, feminine, she is a perfect match for him. He'd never look twice at a harlot, he's a man of good breeding.*

"So you're a prisoner?" I said breaking the silence.

Claudette pressed her lips together, turning her attention to me.

"You could say that. Macrucio is here by choice, he is blinded. His adoration for her prevents him from seeing through her lies. He has been clouded by her charm for many years. To him she is mother, leader and saviour." She pulled in a ragged breath before continuing. "I am not fooled however; her mind games do not work on me. I am cursed twice over you see. Not only am I heir to the Curses of Eight; I am heir to Hadnaloy's empire. Her power, this ship and the lair below it will be mine once her last breath is exhaled. In that she cannot control me as she does Macrucio."

"Control?" Nathaniel's question came out hoarse.

"Hadnaloy has great power, not only magic but in manipulation. Macrucio thrives off it and what she bids he will do in order to retain his place as her second in command- it's a vicious cycle. This means however, that when time comes to inherit her empire, Macrucio will be lost. The dedication he has shown her will no longer put him as her second but mine. Our relationship is different. Despite my power, we see each other as equals and our crew also see that in us. Though perhaps they are a little more frightened of me…" she smiled something close to smugness coloured her tone. "You see, once Hadnaloy is finished, I gain all of her power and step into her role – whatever that is."

The flippant way she spoke of her mistress' demise and the pride in her own power set my hackles on edge, was she warning us? As Hadnaloy's heir she couldn't be trusted, no matter how dear to the cause she was.

"You seem wary, sister." Claudette turned her head to one side gazing at me speculatively through her pale lashes.

"You can't blame me, surely?" I challenged, not breaking our connection.

"Now, Lennie," Nathaniel said. "Claudette hasn't given us any reason to fret, if anything she saved us.

His words held truth, but I wasn't feeling too ready to trust her yet.

"But she is Hadnaloy's heir." I countered

"I can understand your concern, I would too if I were in your position, but as your friend here put it, I'm a prisoner."

Claudette touched a finger to her own skull upon her wrist. "Because of our lineage and our skills, Hadnaloy has kept us to do her bidding; there is neither care nor kindness in her approach. We are slaves, chained to her will and forced to do as she demands."

"Can you not escape?" Nathaniel's question mirrored the one I was about to ask.

"I have tried, more than once." Claudette turned her elfin face downward. She linked and unlinked her fingers. It was there, on her forearms I could see scars, pale and stark against her skin. This girl had known abuse, just as I had – I wondered what her story was. Did she have night terrors and flashbacks just as I did?

"I couldn't bear to leave Macrucio, he and I have a closeness, a bond and to be without him…" She bit down on her lip, looking back up at us tears fell down her cheeks.

"She knows my weakness and uses it well, he's the one thing she has to manipulate me with, my Achilles heel." A sob ripped from her but with a sniff she continued. Anger now laced her tone. "I hate him for doing that to me, for making me care for him, to be my ally, friend and more, but I hate myself more for letting him."

And thus, in one short sobbing sentence she had unearthed my entire ethos. Love killed. Perhaps not literally, but metaphorically. My heart softened a little for the weeping woman before me for these were no crocodile tears.

"Forgive my frankness, but if you're as against Hadnaloy as you hint, why hasn't she disposed of you and started again with another child?"

Dabbing at her face with the hem of her dress, Claudette replied, "I do not flatter myself in thinking I have any place Hadnaloy's heart." Straightening her clothing she rubbed her fingertips together. The action caused small traces of violet light to emanate from the friction. I watched it, fascinated, I'd never seen faery magic up close before.

"Hadnaloy has invested much time and magic in me

and does not want to waste it. There is also the fact that I am one of you; she feels that can wield power – that she has leverage."

"Power and leverage over who?" Nathaniel asked.

"You don't know?" Claudette leaned forward, confusion causing a frown to appear. "Surely you know, Lennie?"

I looked between Claudette and Nathaniel, wondering if now really was the time for this tale.

"Rosa and Hadnaloy are rivals. Hadnaloy has been seeking out Rosa and all those affiliated with her, for decades. Having Claudette and Macrucio means she has a full hand to play with."

"She'd use you as pawns?" Nathaniel cried.

"She'd use us for anything if it served a purpose." Claudette replied.

I studied the woman – child, before me. She wasn't much older than I, perhaps nineteen or so. Sophisticated, well-spoken and seemingly the only woman on board a ship of men. How similar we were and how different. Could Claudette be the companion I'd been seeking, or would I be burned? Either way I had to convince her and her companion to let us return to the *Wilted Rose*, with them beside us.

There was no way around it; if the curse was to end, we needed Claudette and Macrucio. As each new heir had been discovered, the dream of breaking the enchantment came closer to reality. The biggest challenge would be the eight of us convincing the Sorceress who'd put the curse in place to set us free. Straightening in my chair, I met Claudette's unusual eyes. She stared at me, no fear or caution lingered there. Only a hope I couldn't fathom.

"Where do your allegiances lie?" I blurted, unable to stop the words tumbling out.

Claudette nodded as she appraised me, one of her long fingers tapped at her full mouth as she searched my face. After a moment she nodded.

"I have always been curious of the *Wilted Rose* and where my history lay upon it. I will join your crew but only as long as we can convince Macrucio. Where he goes I go."

Excitement bubbled within me but I kept my expression neutral. It wouldn't do well to reveal my hand too early.

"He could be of use too," I hedged. "Is there a way?"

"I believe so." Claudette's mouth curved into a mischievous smile,

"You go and do what you need to, whilst..." I stopped mid-sentence, the silence resonating before I stumbled on. "N-Nathaniel and I figure out a way to get back to the *Wilted Rose*."

Claudette leaped off the desk. "I will not be long."

At the click of the door Nathaniel slouched down in his seat. I watched him closely, wondering if he'd noticed my slip. Would he read too much into it? I'd never spoken his name aloud before.

The clarity I'd felt in Claudette's presence was gone, everything had blurred edges now. Was that part of her magic too? The ache had returned along with the pounding in my head. I rolled my shoulders to loosen the kinks but it was no use.

"What do you think? Do you trust her?" I tried hard to sound indifferent, but even I could hear the strain.

"I don't quite know," Nathaniel said as he rested his head against the wall. Within minutes his eyes closed. He looked drained; his swarthy skin held a sallow hue as he pulled in uneven breaths. I wondered if he'd fallen asleep.

"If you had told me a month ago, that I would be amongst cursed pirates and talking figureheads, I would have laughed at you. Yet here I am and I trust you all implicitly," he said.

"That isn't entirely true," I countered. "You were a little hesitant, upon your arrival."

"You caught that?" He asked, opening one eye and then the other. "Well, I feel more comfortable now."

With a wry grin he closed his eyes again, shifting in his seat. His large body took up much of the chaise. Our legs nudged and I swallowed back a yelp. I felt struck each time he touched me. I knew it wasn't repulsion that I felt, but it was something just as powerful.

To cover my reaction, I stood, wandering over to a nearby table, the ornament which sat atop it looked immensely interesting, all of a sudden.

"Lennie," Nathaniel said, grasping for my hand.

Almost snatching it back from him, I turned.

"Yes?"

"Claudette and Macrucio, we need them, don't we?" Nathaniel said, tugging me back to the sofa. "But you feel it will be hard to trust them."

"How do you know that?" I couldn't stop the sharpness in my tone. Despite the ire I felt, I returned to my seat.

Our eyes clashed, as we sat in silence together. The subdued lights, the sweet aroma wafting through the room. The strange chemistry between us. It felt all too intimate. To top it off, the sky blue depths of Nathaniel's eyes held something slow burning and dangerous.

"I feel as if I have known you always," he said, reaching out to caress my cheek. I leaned into his touch, not caring about what it would mean.

"Well, that's done." Claudette appeared in the doorway, her voice bright and cheerful.

In my haste to get away, I fumbled, falling off the chaise with a bump, another bruise to add to my collection.

"Your turn," called the enchantress, pride lighting up her elfin face.

"What did you do with them all?" Nathaniel stood, helping me to my feet.

Claudette's mischievous grin was back in place as she tapped her nose. "Let's just say they are taking a nap."

"What do we do now?" Nathaniel asked, turning to

me for answers.

They stared at me with expectant faces. My mind whirled with a dozen possibilities. Catching sight of Nathaniel's brand an idea formed. In the past, Butch and I used to play games with Caw. It was something we'd happened upon one day. Even in the deepest depth of the ship, if we touched our brands together, we'd summon the bird.

Perhaps, given the circumstances, Caw could come to our aid here and lead the *Wilted Rose* back to us?

"Let me try something," I said, grasping hold of Nathaniel's arm.

Our brands connected, sending waves of heat through me. It spread from the tips of my toes to the top of my head. When the temperature returned to normal, I found the floor beneath me unsteady. That had never occurred when Butch and I'd attempted it.

"What happened?" Claudette exclaimed. The sound of the anchor raising was joined by flapping wings and bird calls, and Claudette's question was answered. Reaching the deck, we found Caw circling above.

"There's something in his beak," I said, as the bird dropped a scroll into the waiting hands of Nathaniel. Scanning the parchment, he read aloud:

"Read the line already written. Once shy, twice as bitten, three as in double but four as in price, but do not worry, there will be ice."

"Is that a riddle?" Claudette said with a frown.

"Rosa Del Mar finds it entertaining to challenge her crew," I said.

"Rosa Del Mar?" Nathaniel queried.

"It translates into '*Wilted Rose.*' She's the figurehead and heart of our ship."

Claudette flipped her hair over her shoulder haughtily. "Ever since I have known Hadnaloy, she has portrayed much bitterness towards the figurehead and the Sorceress who created her."

"They are quite the rivals are they not?" I agreed.

"It appears our leaders are at war, yet we get along so well. Can we perhaps return to our task?" Nathaniel's impatience had both Claudette and myself laughing. Though his glare sent us back to the task at hand.

"Read the lines already written." Nathaniel paused, turning to Claudette "Do you have a place on board which holds books?"

"Yes!" She exclaimed, her confusion evaporating. "Macrucio's study is full of them."

"Could you show us?" Nathaniel asked, gesturing towards the door.

"Of course, follow me," Claudette said leading the way.

We raced below again, passing door after door. No candles were lit and in spite of the darkness, Claudette flung herself through a hidden entrance at the end of the corridor. Following Claudette over the threshold I stilled just inside the room. With a sweep of her hand, Claudette lit every candle revealing a cavernous room.

It was a library. Every available space was crammed with books; they were even strewn across the floor. Nathaniel too stopped beside her, his mouth agape as he took in the splendour.

"This is a place of dreams," he murmured.

"Of many dreams," I said. I wanted to devour every one. To read until there was no more to take in. The few shelves we had back on the *Wilted Rose*, were nothing to this.

"Were we not trying to find something?" Claudette said taking tomes at random and pulling them off the shelves. The muffled thuds of discarded books broke me from my mooning.

"Something in here must relate to the curse, or to us in some way," I said joining Claudette.

The fair haired woman looked mortified. "Like a needle in a haystack?"

"It is bound to be here." Nathaniel said.

His enthusiasm was contagious and I reached for a leather bound edition. Pulling it open at random I scanned the page, nothing of consequence leapt out at me.

"We should put anything we have looked at over here," Nathaniel said, pushing aside a table below a porthole. "Then we know not to look at those again."

"Stupendous idea," Claudette said already placing a book in the allotted spot.

AN HOUR LATER, I was sat against a half filled bookcase, leafing through yet another tome; piles of unread books surrounding me. Nathaniel too was enveloped in stories, though he looked far from disheartened. A smile lit up his face, his tiredness all but gone.

"What if we never find it?" Claudette asked, into the silence.

"We will," I said tossing another volume onto the overflowing discarded pile. It landed at an angle and I sighed, pulling myself off the floor to straighten it. "Rosa knows our strengths; between the three of us we will succeed."

"I wish I felt so confident," Claudette said, as she hitched up her long dress and picked her way through the chaos. "I had better go and check on the sleeping beauties, I would not want Macrucio to see what we have done."

She gave a half-smile before slipping out of the room.

"Nothing," Nathaniel sighed sending a book across the room, his impatience clear. "You are so convinced we will get somewhere, is it all bluster?" He stood too, stretching, before reaching to the top most shelves.

"Certainly not, it's here somewhere; we just have to find what 'it' is," I said.

Claudette sauntered back through the door, humming under her breath, her concern now hidden.

"They are most definitely detained," she said.

The dark humour lacing both her tone and expression made me uneasy, but I didn't dwell on it, we all had our shadows. Besides, a book was heading over Nathaniel's shoulder and in my direction. Something about the cover struck me and I reached up to catch it.

Turning over I brushed my hand over the well-worn tome. The image that had caught my eye, had been a pirate ship, though the cover itself held no title Opening the tattered pages I found a ribbon marking a place. My brows rose as I noted a circled passage:

'For the woman was more beautiful than I, and held such power. The rose and its thorns wound around his fingers, soft as a caress, letting the blood flow...'

Heat pooled in my cheeks, but my embarrassment didn't allow me to miss the folded parchment wedged into the book. Opening it, my heart skittered, scrawling words spelled out:

'To end the curse befalling us all, forgive the one who started it all. To love is to bleed but do take heed. Death is no token remember this.'

"I think this may be 'the lines already written'" I said.

"May I see that?" Nathaniel clambered over the mess, pulling his journal from his pocket.

"Of course," I said turning the parchment so Nathaniel and Claudette could see.

"Do you see it?" He asked eagerly comparing the handwriting of the journal to the parchment.

"Yes, does that mean your father wrote this?" I asked.

"It must." Nathaniel nodded, wonder clear in his face. "Though how did it come to be here?"

"I have no answer," Claudette said to their questioning glances. "I would like to know what it means, however. Could he have copied it from somewhere?"

"I do not know." Nathaniel shook his head, folding up the parchment and stowing it into the journal.

"Perhaps whoever created the poem would like us to forgive and forget," Claudette suggested.

"I don't think that will happen, too much has happened and too much has already been done." I said.

"Maybe we will understand the next clue," Claudette said throwing up her hands in exasperation.

"Three as in double, four as in price," Nathaniel said, returning to our task. "I think it means us, the four heirs."

Claudette and I nodded in agreement.

"What about the ice?" Claudette frowned, reading the final line.

"I just cannot think," Nathaniel said, a frown marring his face.

"Well it has grown colder," I said, feeling the

temperature of the room dip.

"Look!" Claudette cried pointing through the porthole.

No more than a mile ahead, was the *Wilted Rose;* she was docked beside a snow covered island. I couldn't contain my grin, they had found us, we were safe. Home wasn't too far away.

"We had better go. What did you do with Macrucio and the others?" Nathaniel asked, urging us forward.

"I put them in the brig," Claudette replied.

We detoured to the cells and as we arrived at the lowest part of the ship, I pressed a hand to my face to hide my laughter. Claudette had somehow piled the men behind the bars, one on top of the other. She retrieved a large brass key and twisted it in the lock. Nathaniel stepped inside and hoisted the unconscious Macrucio over his shoulder, his breathing laboured. Nathaniel gestured for us to take the lead, and followed us up to the deck.

The *Wilted Rose* bobbed beside us, a few more cracks in the aged ship could be seen, as well as a hasty new patch in one of the sails, our beloved home hadn't exactly left the battle unscathed.

"Is everyone all right?" Butch yelled from the crow's nest.

"We're all well," I called back with a salute, as the rest of the crew gathered near the rail.

"Permission to come aboard, sir?" Nathaniel cried in

the direction of the captain.

"Granted." Came the reply.

"Grab a rope," I said racing forward and taking hold of one.

Behind me, Nathaniel did the same and soon we landed back on the deck of the *Wilted Rose*. Nathaniel lay Macrucio at our feet, in sleep he looked more like the teenager I suspected he was. Boyish and young.

"Who do we have here?" Captain Rourke asked. Sweeping off his feather topped hat, he stepped forward, eyeing the still form.

"Macrucio," I replied.

"You found the son of Roberto?" The captain's eyes widened on the dead weight.

"Do not fret, he is alive."

All heads turned at the clear, pure voice. Claudette landed beside Nathaniel. Her feet making no sound as she stepped closer. She curtseyed in respect, bowing her head to the captain.

"I am Claudette, sir, the lost heir."

The shocked silence that preceded her words stretched on, only to be broken by Ned dropping his pocket watch. The clatter it made startled the group, before the older man picked it up and wandered away, mumbling to himself.

"Sorry to demand something so early in our acquaintance," Claudette said, frowning at the sudden interruption, "but I feel it safest if we contain Macrucio."

Her gaze darted to the sleeping form at her feet.

The captain nodded. "Butch, haul him to the brig."

"Yes, sir," he said, scrambling down the crow's nest.

"Are you sure he's the one for the job?" Claudette asked eyeing the frailness of youngest crewmember.

"I'm sure," Captain Rourke said patting Butch on the back as he darted passed us.

Though painfully thin, Butch pulled the sleeping figure over his shoulder with ease and headed below.

"We all have special talents, dear." Captain Rourke stated, winking at the shocked Claudette and heading after Butch. Nathaniel caught hold of my arm as I made to follow them; pressing his free palm to my cheek, he spoke in a low voice.

"Now that we're home please do not feel we can no longer be at ease with one another," he said.

His face was inches from mine and I instinctively moistened my lips. Nathaniel's gaze caught the action. Tension crackled between us and he moved closer. My heart thudded in time to the forbidden thoughts blooming behind his eyes.

"Are either of you injured?" Davy's question broke the spell and Nathaniel stepped away.

"Nothing to cause alarm," Nathaniel replied, his smile strained.

"Still, I'll go and fetch some ointment for your cuts and bruises." Davy said.

Nathaniel watched Davey leave before turning back to

me.

"Please, do not feel afraid, I wouldn't hurt you for the world."

His expressive eyes were solemn as he joined Davy at the top of the stairs. My own feet were rooted to the spot as I watched them disappear below. From my limited viewpoint I could only hear the slam of the cell door and soon the voices of the crew made their way above deck once more. Rupert had joined them, seeing me, he handed over a damp cloth and a small bottle of pale green ointment from Ned's store.

"This might fix that face of yours," he said with a wink.

"Are you sure you don't want to share?" I replied, eyes widening in faux innocence.

"Fighting talk, little one."

"There's names for people like you," I said, pulling out the bottle's cork and pouring the thick liquid onto the rag.

"Please, my ego's big enough already without more complements to add." Rupert took the cloth, with a purposeful but gentle hand he dabbed the cuts and bruises on my face.

"Perhaps our newest recruit would like a drink?" The captain's voice sounded close by and as he passed, Claudette had hold of his arm.

"Good to have you home, sailor," Rupert said, finishing off his task and stoppering the bottle.

"Glad to be back," I replied.

Davy joined us, his dark eyes inspecting my doctored face. "Are you all right, Lennie?"

"Sure, now that we're back home."

Davy glanced from Nathaniel, who was chatting with Butch, then back to me, but said nothing more. As the silence dragged, Rupert and Davy headed over to the table and to the rest of the crew. I wandered behind them, at a slower pace.

Claudette sat wide-eyed as all around her, men bowed and scraped.

"How about we fetch something warmer for you to wear ma'am?" Butch said, ensuring she was settled in her seat before racing towards his cabin. Rupert and Davy busied themselves pouring a tankard for newest member of the crew. Who knew the hooligans I lived with could be such gentlemen?

Shoving my still-cold hands into my pockets I searched out the rest of my crewmen. Nathaniel had pulled the captain aside; they stood together, deep in conversation. Ned was the only person unoccupied; he sat on the side-lines, watching the commotion.

"Not joining the party?" I asked taking a seat beside him.

Ned scowled at the fussing group. "All this uproar is too much for me."

"What do you mean? You have never complained before," I teased, leaning against his shoulder. He grunted turning towards the ocean, the snowy harbour had long faded from sight and there was no sign of Hadnaloy's ship on the horizon. We sat in companionable silence, watching the ship's progress, though the sound of the excited crew was hard to ignore.

Turning towards the rabble, I watched as Claudette threw her head back, laughing at one of Rupert's jokes as Butch returned with a jacket for her to wear. She pulled it on gratefully and my young friend beamed. My own smile slipped as Nathaniel strolled towards me.

"How are you, after our adventure?" He took a seat at my side, shuffling closer he rested his hand upon me knee. I stared at it, biting my lip as my heartbeat kicked up a notch; it took a moment to find my voice.

"Knowing the eight of us are here, together, is all I've hoped for since I stepped aboard this ship." I sighed. "The sooner this curse is lifted, the better."

The ultimate goal was to help end the bewitchment so I could —No I would not think it, or even hope. I just wanted the freedom of my convictions, without having to fear the repercussions.

"I want to thank you," Nathaniel said, interrupting my wayward thoughts.

"Why? If anything it's I who should be voicing my thanks," I said.

Not looking his way, I pulled the book from Macrucio's study from my pocket. Something had told me to take it and I couldn't refuse the lure of another book.

"No," Nathaniel disagreed, squeezing my knee pulling attention away from the tome.

"You were the one who kept a cool head and remained vigilant during our time aboard that wretched ship."

"It's my job to fight for what's right in this world." I shrugged, tracing the outline of the cover with a fingertip.

"And so you did and shall again," Nathaniel murmured.

"Goodness Ned, you look like you have seen a ghost," Butch exclaimed.

As our crewmate reached us I straightened my leg, moving away from Nathaniel's touch as I too, turned my attention to the older man. He did look strange, his pallor was white and perspiration glistened on his forehead. He didn't reply, but his attention never left the blonde haired female with lilac eyes.

"DEVILS OF THE earth and 'ell all are upon us!" A loud cry sounded from the belly of the ship.

The second Macrucio awoke the entire ship knew it. The screams and crashes coming from below caused anxiety in me that I wasn't used to. I grasped for my sword, anticipating a brawl.

Though Claudette had warned of Macrucio's immense anger, there was no way to prepare for his wrath once he'd awoken. Claudette's lips curled upward as she followed Butch below deck. I pursued her, staying at a safe distance still wary of the newest members of our crew.

Reaching the brig my breath hitched as I caught sight of Nathaniel and Davy who had been guarding Macrucio. They were nursing bleeding lips and bruised knuckles, their wild appearance showed the bars hadn't hindered their prisoner's tirade. Claudette silenced Macrucio with a raised palm; he stared at her, mutinous.

"We are needed here, far more so than Hadnaloy's ship," she explained.

Macrucio lunged through the bars, his bony fingers clawing at the air inches from her face.

'How could you?' He mouthed, her gesture rendering him mute.

"I will return you to sleep if you try to harm any of them." Claudette said. She approached his outstretched hand, taking it in her own. A moment passed before he grazed his finger across her cheek.

My heart squeezed as I witnessed the tender exchange. The curse had to be broken, even if just for those two. Despite Macrucio's darkness, there was more emotion in that one touch than I could ever fathom. It took a long drawn out pause before Macrucio nodded in defeat. A smile lit Claudette's face as she clicked her fingers.

"I will join you... for now," he said, his voice nothing more than a broken murmur. "You there, take me to your captain," he snapped at Nathaniel, his haughty expression not endearing him to anyone.

The captain opened his arms wide as the dark haired stranger emerged.

"Welcome Macrucio, it is an honour to meet you after so long. We could not be happier to have you join us."

"This is not by choice, believe me."

Captain Rourke's nod showed tolerance. "All the same, I hope as a unit we can succeed. Let us visit Rosa and see what she thinks the next course of action should be."

CHAPTER V
GIVEN

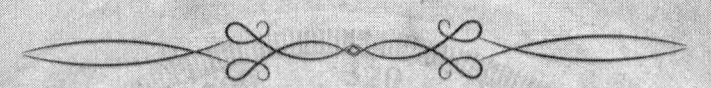

~~~~~~~~~~~~~~~~~~~~

"CAN WE TRUST them?" Butch asked as he scowled at the two newest crew members.

Macrucio and Claudette had settled upon the steps leading to the quarter deck. They sat very side-by-side, their hands clutched between them and their heads close together as they spoke in hushed tones.

I followed Butch's stare, "what choice do we have?" I said.

"I do not like *him*," Nathaniel complained, his narrowed eyes did not waiver from Macrucio.

"Liking him isn't important," Rupert said, leaning against the rail. "We need him, at least until the Sorceress lifts the curse, *if* she lifts it." His mouth twisted, as though the words tasted foul.

"It is the way he looks at Le-at people." Nathaniel stammered staring skyward.

"*She* seems to be genuine enough," Davy said, brushing imaginary creases from his jacket.

"It could all be an elaborate ploy; they were raised by a sea-witch after all." Butch's tone was doubtful.

"I say we do nothing," I said knowing what the reaction would be. As the others made to interrupt, I raised my hand for silence. "That is not to say we don't keep a watchful eye on them, they don't pose a threat."

"Not yet," Rupert muttered.

Despite trying to reassure my friends, I held little trust in Macrucio. Since he'd been released his dark malevolent eyes wandered, they held such intensity I felt sure he had some plot to torture us all. I despised the way his gaze lingered upon me; men had looked at me in such a way in the past, and the returning memories were anything but pleasant.

Yet it was the way he was with Claudette that threw doubt on his true purpose. He was so loving and tender towards her I felt the only reason for his lechery was to make his beloved Claudette, jealous. Returning to the conversation at hand, I glanced around my peers.

"Shall we all agree to remain vigilant, unless provoked?" Captain Rourke, who had remained silent up to that point asked.

"If we must," Rupert groused, pulling a pack of cards from his pocket.

"Then it's settled," the captain said unravelling his map and turning away.

"Come on, let's play a hand," Rupert said leading the way, past the new arrivals and setting himself up at the table.

"So what do you play?" Claudette asked leaving her

perch.

"Anything and everything," Rupert muttered, forcing his glower away from Macrucio to divide the cards.

Claudette gave a wry smile as she settled into a chair. I pressed my lips together; ignoring the dark set of eyes I knew followed my every move. Macrucio was yet another newcomer who made me uncomfortable.

"Where are we off to now, captain?" Butch asked, approaching our leader.

"I am conflicted, for we are in dire need of supplies, especially now we have more mouths to feed," he said.

Wrenching off his hat, the captain picked at the feathers adorning it.

"Why would that be a problem?" Nathaniel asked, flipping his chair and resting his arms across the back.

"I feel we need to introduce our newest crew members to Rosa."

"What's a couple of days more to wait?" Ned said with a shrug. "She's well informed."

"I dare say you're right."

Looking somewhat happier, the captain wandered over to watch us play.

"So we are to return to the Island of Plenty?" Nathaniel took his cards looking hopeful.

"Yes and I say, a sure thing too!" Rupert's grin told everyone all they needed to know.

"Are we ready to play?" Davy asked, his hands hovering over the depleted deck.

The table was far too quiet; there was none of the usual banter. I wondered if it was due to no-one really knowing how to behave around the two people closest to Hadnaloy. The snap of cards or the odd sigh were all that interrupted the silence.

"Caw —there is no use in togetherness if there is no trust —caw," Caw screeched.

I chuckled as Ned's bird swept across the sky, he always knew just what we needed to hear.

"How about we try something different?" I said, laying down my cards.

"Like what?" Rupert asked as he gathered the pack together.

"I have a suggestion, if I may?" Nathaniel said, rolling back his sleeve.

"Go ahead," I said, allowing him to take the lead.

"The brand we wear, how did you discover yours?" Nathaniel said, beaming at us.

My smile slipped as I stared down at my wrist.

"I was a thief and this was my payment," Rupert leaned his chair back on two legs; as he flicked a large gold coin in the air. "My mother left me with a criminal, though she didn't know it at the time. He presented himself as a gentleman and spoke well. My mother was desperate, so parted with both the coin and myself."

The redhead caught the object, turning it over in his hands.

"As I grew, it was apparent numbers were my strong

point. My master put me in charge of all the takings. Anything brought in was given to me to put in our deposit box." He continued to rotate the circle of metal as he spoke.

"Though my job held a high rank I wasn't trusted. Once a week, at least, the master would beat me for entertainment. It was to 'keep me honest' he said, but every time I went to bed bloodied and bruised I vowed I would escape." He swiped his fingertips over the skull which was tooled into the coin.

"One night, whilst the master and the other boys were asleep, I crept to the takings box."

He grinned, looking around at his eager audience.

"There it was, glinting in the moonlight. I knew I wanted this coin since the first moment I'd seen it. I wasn't branded then though, I used a handkerchief to grasp as much loot as I could."

"So you were part of a band of pickpockets?" Claudette said her lilac eyes alight with eagerness as she leaned closer,

Rupert raised his brows as he grinned, all trace of suspicion hidden. "We were the best in the business—"

"—your brand," Nathaniel urged before Rupert could change the subject.

"Well, I raced through the back roads until I reached the edge of town." Rupert continued. "The ocean was mere footsteps away and I had money." He grinned at the memory.

"I planned to stow away on the next ship I saw. As I waited, I untied my treasure and tried to count my fill. It was then my hand fell upon this."

He held out his palm so the newest crew members could take their first real look at Rupert's inheritance.

"The pain was agonizing, I was seventeen and had been battered before but no pain could ever compare to the brand."

"You were a sight, I can tell you," Ned said swigging from his hip flask.

"You would say that old man; you only have one good eye," Rupert said.

His roguish expression grew as Ned hurled the container at him. Rupert caught it mid-flight.

"You are lucky we need you, boy," the older man said, as Rupert twisted the lid and took a sip, wincing as the burn hit his throat.

"This is all so fascinating," Claudette interrupted. "Who is next?"

Her words stalled Ned, he stared at her as though he'd forgotten she existed. His face paled as she turned to look his way.

"I have heard enough stories, you all carry on," The older man grumbled as he strode around the table; snatching his flask out of Rupert's grasp, he wandered below.

"Did I say something wrong?" Claudette asked, puzzled.

"He has always been strange, that one" Rupert muttered, wiping the liquor from his lips.

"Stop it," I snapped, swiping the back of his head. I turned to watch Ned disappear below. *What was going on with him?* I wondered.

"Shall I go next?" Captain Rourke said, his forehead creased, as he watched Ned's descent below.

"Please." Claudette rested her chin on her hands, awaiting his tale.

The captain reached into his pocket and pulled out a worn piece of parchment. Its edges were ragged and a burn mark stained the far right hand corner. The skull, crossbones and rose almost lost in the flaw.

"This may look like a tattered piece of mulch, but it's so much more," Captain Rourke said.

He unrolled it, weighting the corners with a bottle and a tankard. Unlike the maps seen throughout the world, this held no solid drawings. Instead black markings shifted alongside the ships movements.

"What is that?" Macrucio asked, speaking for the first time in days, as he hovered behind the captain. His eyes narrowed at the strange item as it continued to move. It was the first time he'd willingly interacted with the group.

"My father's map shows us where we are in the world, as well as the destination of our next adventure."

Macrucio remained silent, his focus on the piece of paper. Ignoring the man at his side, Captain Rourke turned to Claudette and Nathaniel.

"Did you know I was the only heir not to be taken away from the *Wilted Rose?*"

"How on earth did that happen?" Claudette asked.

"My mother and father were the first to perish, because of the curse." Our leader bowed his head as he rolled the map back up. "In all of the chaos which happened after, I was forgotten."

He turned towards the open sea, as he recalled his childhood. "So not to bother those left on board, I kept out of the way. My favourite place was in the rum store, it was always quiet there. This ship was filled with so much anguish, I needed to escape. Though the pain weighed heavy on my young shoulders, I could not leave this ship, it was in my blood to captain it as my father had done."

"So you were here alone?" Claudette said.

Captain Rourke didn't turn back to the table. "Not long after the brethren and their wives had left or died, Rosa was ripped from the ship. I was then truly alone, that was until Ned arrived. I had already found my father's map, and felt the burn by then. I would have been no older than six or seven."

He continued to speak as he turned further towards the sea. "I'd heard someone boarding, and hid myself in one of the rum barrels. I'll never forget the stench of stale alcohol that filled my nostrils."

He lifted his hand to brush beneath his nose. "Ned discovered my hiding place and tried to explain my fate, but I already knew."

The captain clenched his jaw, the story ending short. Standing he strode across the deck, stilling at the helm, he touched a hand to the wheel.

"I seem to be saying all the wrong things." Claudette looked troubled.

"No, the captain is an old soul. His past is close to his heart. He finds it hard to speak of it at times." Davy assured as he pulled a leather cord from beneath his shirt.

"Should I continue?" He asked. At the surrounding nods he cleared his throat.

"I was naught but a child when I washed ashore. My mother had drowned but somehow I had remained breathing. Though slavery was rife, I managed to escape that path. A lone wanderer found me, curled up beside my mother's body, and urged me to join him. Knowing no different, I followed this aged bearded man with pale skin. Despite his failing eyesight and frail body, he held my future."

Davy's dark eyes stared off as he remembered. "The old man was wise, teaching me the ways of the world and a language only he seemed to know. He carried with him small wooden tablets covered in scratches."

Davy spread out his hands. "Though we spoke, we mainly communicated by these symbols. I'd write them on his skin or rough paper and he'd return the favour. As years went on and we met others, we would send each other messages as others spoke around us." He paused, taking a deep breath before continuing.

"I was seventeen when he died. I never knew his name, or who he really was, but before he took his last breath he gave me this."

Davy clutched the onyx pendant in his palm, the runes carved around the *Wilted Rose* symbol were clear. "He told me this belonged to my mother and he'd kept hold of it, so I'd always have a part of her. I didn't know then that it had been my fathers. I felt the burn as soon as I touched the stone, but I kept myself from succumbing to the pain until I reached the coastline; which my friend had insisted we stopped by."

"Ned came for you, as well as the captain." I recalled and Davy nodded in agreement.

"They did, and you were the first face I saw once the agony had eased."

We shared a fond smile before Butch interrupted the moment.

"My turn," he said, as he untied a green silk scarf from around his neck. "This was my father's, he was a bare knuckle fighter in London. My mother left me there, in that big city, I do not recall my age but I know I was young. I fended for myself and became a street urchin, much like Rupert. Dodging the law and hoping to not be caught by the pickpockets."

He wrapped the scarf around his wrist, tying it with care. "I was found of course, a rag and bone man promised me room and board if I helped with his work. My job would be to fetch and carry his goods; I was cheaper to feed than a horse."

His mouth turned downward as he continued. "Despite being a skinny lad, I was strong. He called me 'Hercules' as I could load and unload his trolley, and pull it along the streets of London without breaking a sweat." Butch puffed out his chest, a cocky grin on his face, all trace of bitterness gone.

"The man I worked for liked to spend weeks at his cottage by the sea. He would take in the sea air and work when he needed to. I never joined him on these trips, that is, until one day he let me tag along on a more difficult job, and I was happy to oblige. Now remember, I had been branded since an infant, but no-one had come for me – not that I knew I was supposed to be taken." he said.

"Once we had arrived at the village, I spotted a ship in the harbour and well, you can guess the rest."

"Everyone has lived such unique lives." Claudette leaned back, her eyes wide in astonishment.

Macrucio crossed his arms. "What about us? Our lives have not just –"

"– We have lived upon the ship or in coves since we were babies," Claudette snapped cutting him off.

"You haven't set foot on dry land?" I blurted. I had been watching them with fascination and I couldn't help but ask.

Claudette shook her head. "I do not recall ever doing so, at least no further than a step or two"

Nathaniel coughed interrupting us and all eyes turned in his direction.

"May I ask how you were branded Lennie?"

His soft request sent shivers up my spine. Both Davy and Rupert tensed in their seats. I glared at them as Butch eyed me with caution. His hand rested on my knee stilling my jogging leg beneath the table. They all knew the story, with great detail. Not that I'd ever said anything. Ned had thought it best they knew.

I suddenly found my fingers very fascinating. I linked them, then separated them. Repeating the action before inspecting the short chipped nails and scarred skin. With a great sigh I spoke.

"My father's sword hung on the wall of my bedroom, I reached for it and I was branded."

"What about you?" Butch was quick to change the subject as he rounded on Nathaniel. I looked up to find Nathaniel still staring at me; his inquisitive eyes were filled with questions.

"I think the big man would like to know a little more from the lady, just as I would." Macrucio's smirk was wide as he slammed his boots on the table, crossing them at the ankles.

"No, I do not need to know any more." Nathaniel shoved Macrucio's boots off their perch. "My own tale is just as short." His accompanying smile looked false, as it joined his serious eyes.

"My uncle and I had both been on the beach the day

you found me. We had been sending flowers across the water in my mother's memory. Once he'd seen the flowers float, he left me alone there, he isn't one for sentimentality."

Butch and I shared a look, so that's where the flowers had come from.

"This journal was buried deep within the sand," Nathaniel said as he held up the worn leather tome he always carried.

"There was the pain and then the ship. I wonder what would have happened, had we never found our inheritance."

Silence settled around the group as we thought about Nathaniel's musing.

"You haven't told us your stories," Rupert said as he turned to the two newest members.

"You both claim never to have stepped foot on dry land, yet you're both branded, would you care to elaborate?"

Macrucio looked bored, but raised his left hand, a large gold ring resided on his third finger. It depicted the curse's symbol. Paste jewels glinted from the eyes of the skull giving it a sinister edge.

"My father was killed right in front of me, after 'e 'ad murdered my mother. 'adnaloy bestowed this ring upon me the day I was brought to her. You could say I was branded from then on." His rolling whiskey toned voice resonated in the stunned silence. Claudette grasped his hand, squeezing it.

"My story is quite unusual," she said, pulling a simple cloth necklace into view. The material was braided and a pendant hung from it. A single golden feather curled into a spiral lay behind the gilded case.

"This feather dropped into my hand at a young age. When I was marked by Hadnaloy, it hurt, but when the curses of eight came to brand me, the pain was so much more."

"Caw," I breathed, eyeing the necklace adorning Claudette's neck.

"Is that the name of the bird which resides here?" Macrucio demanded.

"Yes, he's lived aboard for as long as anyone can remember," Davy said.

"Now we know of our origins, we should all feel better about our journey." The captain's voice rang out across the deck.

"We shall see," Macrucio tugged on Claudette's hand and together they descended the stairs.

"Why is it, that Caw gifted Claudette his feather, but didn't send us after her?" I asked the remaining crew.

"Who knows? Perhaps something in Hadnaloy's power prevented Rosa from sending us, or even detecting her. Caw didn't even mention her or his trip to Hadnaloy's ship." Rupert said.

"It's something to think about though…" Davy said.

"Who says we go and get ready for the Island?" Butch

asked into the contemplative silence that followed.

"That's the best idea I've heard all day." I said as I too stepped away from the table, in search of an escape.

AS THE EXCITEMENT of the night to come enveloped the ship and overpowered the tension; I watched from the side-lines, amused as the crew readied themselves. Davy had at least a dozen hats at his side. Trilbies, bowlers and flat caps, he tried them on one by one, setting them at jaunty angles and positioning his head left and right. Beside him, Butch tried to flatten his hair in the reflection of a tablespoon. Thinking he was the one most in need I joined him.

"Here, let me," I urged, pulling a bone handled comb from my pocket and set about untangling his straw coloured mess.

"Thanks," he said, lifting his makeshift mirror to get a better look at the results.

I chuckled as I tucked the comb away, "Just find a decent barber when we get there."

"Mind giving mine a go?"

My heart skittered at Nathaniel's innocent question. I couldn't run, nor throw a snide remark this time, we'd shared something, we'd returned home victorious together. Plastering on a winning smile, I turned to face him. Trying not to focus on the blueness of his gaze, I took stock of his hair. The tidy style he'd arrived with was now wild and long, skimming his shoulders and falling over one eye. I longed to reach out and brush through the strands.

"Here," I mumbled, pushing the comb at him. I didn't miss his confused expression as I raced away.

THE STARS WERE there to greet us as we docked at the harbour. Lights illuminated the beach, which was already filled. The captain stood upon the quarterdeck, his feather topped hat in his hand as he yelled instructions to the crew.

"All right men, Rupert, Davy, Butch and I will be the first to go tonight, we'll change over tomorrow."

"Could we not all go?" Claudette asked stepping to my side.

I caught Nathaniel moving closer, waiting for the answer. I thought back to a time I asked something similar. Rosa had been the one to respond then. Perhaps her explanation would be the best one...

"Rules are few aboard the *Wilted Rose*," I began. "Aside from the main one. It's our duty to ensure the ship always has a heartbeat." I stared up at the hoisted colours, as I continued: "For no ship is worthy to sail, if it has no one to breathe life into it."

Nathaniel nodded, looking out towards the flickering

lanterns on dry land "So without a heartbeat on board, the *Wilted Rose* could lose it's magic?"

"In simple terms, yes," I replied.

"I understand, thank you, we shall look forward to our turn," Claudette said taking Macrucio's hand and drifting towards the other end of the ship. Nathaniel too strode away, saying nothing as he settled down at the card table.

Not being in the first group never bothered me, I had plenty to be doing. So after waving the boys off, I wandered below to work. Gathering cloths and oil, I set about cleaning the weapons stored inside the armoury. With my mind on the metal blades and the intricate mechanisms of pistols, I didn't have time to think of the man above me, or whatever task he undertook to pass the time. That was what I kept telling myself, as his face kept swimming into my minds-eye.

Hours later, satisfied my chores were done, I took roost upon the rail. From my vantage point I could see the merriment and the party way in full swing. Someone had erected a dance floor on the beach and many were putting it to use. The ladies in attendance wore dresses in the most elegant of fabrics, each one dancing with handsome and chivalrous men. Men like Nathaniel... *now where had that thought come from?*

Thankful he couldn't read my mind, I turned to look at him. He was still sat at the table, staring past me out towards the beach. As I continued to watch, he snapped out of his reverie. Standing, he strode across the deck coming to a stop by the rail. If I'd been a braver woman I would have reached out and brushed aside the hair which fell into his face, covering those vivid eyes.

"It all looks very enjoyable, don't you agree?" He gestured to a young couple who were dancing under the stars.

"If you like that sort of thing," I replied, with a shrug.

"Do you?"

"I don't have many opportunities anymore," I said watching a couple twirl.

"Hmm…" he murmured, sounding thoughtful. "I am sure you don't."

He turned, leaning against the rail as he stared up into the onyx cover of night.

"What about you?" I asked, my skin prickling in awareness. He was mere inches away now. "Aren't you used to those fancy balls and dances?"

"Is that what you think?" His quiet but accusing question had my already pounding heart, quickening.

"I-I had assumed you lived one of those charmed lives, like those people out there." I faltered the words spilling out, had I offended him?

"You could say their lives and mine were once similar," he said his tone thoughtful. He threw me a smile, his expression reassuring that I hadn't caused offence.

"Believe me," he urged. "It does not make me any less of a man. Dances and balls are just frivolous past times, what are they are compared to knowledge and intimacy?"

I blinked. Swallowing a round of butterflies, I reluctantly looked in his direction. The blue of his eyes were darkened by the muted lamps. All the while I chanted in my mind: *'Nathaniel is not Him.'* Hans had once been as sincere as Nathaniel. Would Nathaniel change? I ignored my wayward thoughts and returned to the conversation at hand.

"I suppose," I began. "Yet despite your upbringing, I do not think you any less of a man."

I prayed he didn't read more into my comment than kindness. I couldn't deny I was far too curious about him, he made me feel things I'd long since buried – and never felt worthy to feel.

"Good to know." Nathaniel nodded as he walked away. I merely watched him, waiting for my erratic heartbeat to slow.

IT WAS LATE when I awoke the next morning. My sleep had been plagued by dreams and nightmares, making me more restless than usual. Arriving on deck still yawning, I waved at Rupert, who dealt me into the next card game. On route, I caught sight of Nathaniel leaning over the rail and my tiredness evaporated. A broad smile lit up his face as he talked to a voluptuous young woman with jet black hair, olive skin and almond shaped eyes.

Irked as to why the scene bothered me so much, I

joined the others. It didn't help that the first thing I saw, upon reaching the table, was Macrucio's smug grin.

"*Manana*," he said, devilment dancing in his dark eyes. He hadn't failed to notice my desolate expression. I rolled my eyes choosing to focus on Rupert and his story.

"Did you see the hand I had? Three aces!" Rupert said as he splayed out the deck before flipping the cards over.

Davy slapped the table with a laugh. "They swore you were cheating."

"They just hadn't seen anyone with my skill." Rupert flicked the ace of spades between his fingers before he tossed it skyward.

"Let me guess," I said trying to ignore the low murmur of Nathaniel's voice behind me. "You raced out of there before they could decide otherwise?"

"Too right, I'm not the swordsman among us," Rupert said with a wink.

Though I laughed along, my humour was short lived. My attention wavered, for another feminine laugh sounded behind me. I peeked just once, and instantly wished I hadn't. The doting smile Nathaniel had bestowed upon me, was now beaming at the maiden on the dock. I felt no doubt in whom Nathaniel would be meeting later. I turned back to the others, fighting the sinking feeling clouding my mood. Why did it bother me so much? It shouldn't, we were nothing but crewmates. A small voice inside my head sneered, '*of course you are!*'

The game continued on around me, and though I

smiled and laughed along my fist was clenched tight. I had the most profound urge to bash it against the table or even the Island girl's head.

"Oh damn!"

As Butch caught my frantic whisper, I uncurled my fist. I was jealous. In the most basic, carnal and petty way. I didn't want Nathaniel smiling like that to anyone but me. I ground my teeth... perfect. The fool in me had returned. Just perfect.

It was at that enlightening moment, Nathaniel returned from his *'tête-à-tête.'* He took the seat beside me, grazing my leg with his own. The warmth and my nervousness had me almost jumping out of my seat as I pulled in an audible gasp. With my heartbeat thumping to an erratic rhythm, Butch eyed me one brow raised. Wonderful, I'd been caught.

Trying to look as nonchalant as I could, I scooted my chair back. As it scraped the deck, none to quietly, I shot a sideways glance at Nathaniel. He showed no sign of the touch affecting him; he just nodded to Rupert who dealt him in. Bloody man!

"Got your night planned then?" Rupert's tone was wry but I could tell he was impressed.

"Not at all," Nathaniel said, though he avoided looking at anyone as he spoke.

"Lennie, are you in?" Ruining my composed façade, I jumped at Davy's question.

"I-I had better go and make myself useful," I

stammered, getting to my feet.

"Are you all right?"

Claudette's concerned question was left unanswered as I made my getaway. I headed to the saloon to hide myself in a book or some other distraction. When I arrived I found Captain Rourke behind his desk, his face lined in concentration as he studied his map.

"Sorry to disturb you, sir," I said,

"No you've done no such thing, do as you wish." he said with a wave of his hand.

Tension was etched across his brow as he leaned closer to his task. Not wanting to irritate him by riffling through the bookcases, I headed towards the far end of the room. The saloon had to be my favourite part of the ship. Not just for its endless supply of books, but for the alcove in its far corner. The two walls which flanked the large table were lined with paintings. Art was plentiful below deck, yet despite the many depictions of landscapes and battles, these were most beloved amongst the crew. Each brush stroke told a tale and each subject represented a history. Not only for the vessel itself, but for those who sailed upon it. For they portrayed a cursed man and the woman he had loved. Eight – non-blood – brothers whose story intertwined with the *Wilted Rose*. Perhaps one day, all of our images would be immortalised upon these walls.

Ignoring the chairs, I sat atop the table and stared into the face of my father. It brought me great comfort in being able to see the parents I'd never known. The image looking back was handsome and proud. He had shoulder length fair hair and green eyes, we resembled each other a little, in the cheekbones and brow, and in the stubbornness found in the tilt of our chins. Oh how I wished I'd known him, to learn of his history and to have been a part of his life.

Pushing aside the familiar longing, I turned to my mother's portrait on the opposite wall. Cherie Caron–Roux was immortalised as a respectable and sweet lady. From all personal accounts, she was. It was her former occupation which would contradict those terms. Her dark brown hair, striking beauty and kind brown eyes were warm even in paint. My own mouth, face shape and nose resembled my mother's – though I was a little more worn, scarred, and tanned than my mother. Her friends had often mentioned the uncanny resemblance whilst I was growing up, though I didn't feel as beautiful nor as lady-like as my mother was depicted.

Pain and loss lashed at me as I wiped the dampness from my cheeks. Orphan. The word seemed wrong, yet it was my label. It was all of ours, who sailed upon this cursed ship. Though I never knew my parents I still mourned the loss of a 'real' family unit. Yet my fellow crewmates, as mismatched and strange as they were, had become my family of sorts. Ned was the fatherly figure, always willing to comfort and guide. Captain Rourke, was the eldest brother, stern and formal with a dash of affection.

Davy was the peacemaker. The one who settled all the arguments and was the one with whom I would discuss all manner of philosophy and ethics. Rupert and Butch were the cheeky brothers, who I could rely on for a quick laugh or a game. They kept us all smiling and never let us wallow too long. Claudette and Macrucio hadn't been here long enough for me to slot them into a role yet. Although I was eager to see if Claudette and I could perhaps become friends. Or at the very least allies.

Then there was Nathaniel. The feelings that I felt for him, were becoming less platonic and I didn't want to delve into them just yet. With the thought of the blue eyed man, all my melancholy had lifted. During my quiet reflection, the captain had left. He was never good with my tears.

Shaking off the sadness, I wandered over to the bookshelves. Tracing my fingertips along the spines, I found an old favourite I knew would make me smile. Collapsing upon the pillows at my feet I opened the cover and began to read.

THE CHIMING OF the clock pulled me from my story and back into the real world, I had been lost in the fictional world a lot longer than I'd intended. Pushing the book back onto the shelf I stared down at my tattered attire. If I wanted take in the entertainment on dry land, I would have to freshen up.

The small part of me – the foolish, heartsick, brooding part, wanted to stay on board and wallow. Yet the pirate side, was eager for the taste of good liquor and a fresh game of cards. As I pouted into the silence, the two sides waged war inside my head.

'Come on Lennie, go have fun!'

'Nathaniel will be out there too remember, with that girl. You don't want to embarrass yourself, do you?'

'Forget him! You have just as much right as he to be there. Go! Have a game or two, drink a lot and smoke a little. You deserve to let your hair down!'

The voices argued back and forth, until finally, the pirate side won. I shouldn't change a habit of a lifetime for one man. For that is all he was right? With that thought, I set myself moving towards the door.

Wandering into my cabin, I pulled off my headscarf and shook out my hair. In my distraction I lost my footing and before I could stop myself, I hit the ground, hard. Biting back a curse, I searched for the reason behind my hasty detour.

Littering the floor, were ivory coloured boxes of every size; each one topped by a ribbon. Crossing my legs, my bruised shin forgotten, I grasped for the largest one. Taking great care, I untied the bow and pulled off the lid, simple parchment covered whatever lay inside.

My anticipation grew as I opened the wrapping. A gasp escaped from between my lips as I revealed a cream and scarlet dress. The most refined item of clothing I'd ever seen. My elation turned to wonder as I unfolded it. Standing, I held it against my body. It looked to be just my size. Who would do such a thing? There had to be some mistake...

With keen eyes I looked around the room. My gaze trailed along the small dresser where the wash basin sat, and down to the mountain of books at my bedside. Everything was in its proper place. Not a single item had been moved. As I glanced over my worn blanket, I spotted an envelope lying upon the pillow. Tearing it open I stared down at the card. The stock was textured, thick and obviously very expensive. The handwriting was unusual, curving and looping, but its strokes were strong. This penmanship belonged to a man:

Dearest Lennie,

    Blessed be your night. Eat, drink and be merry.

    Everything in these boxes belongs to you. I could not deny you even the smallest of wishes. Please to do not think me presumptuous, but though you have never spoken them, I could see the longing in your eyes and I want to help you achieve your dreams. Even the smallest ones.

    I hope to see you twirl across the dance floor, a rose amongst many thorns. Though you try to hide it, there is no denying the woman beneath the façade. She is strong, beautiful and someone I would like to be acquainted with. Besides, every girl should be belle of a ball, at least once.

I hope everything meets with your approval and that I have not offended you with my gift.

With much fondness,

My thumb brushed over the final line, the card wasn't signed. I was stunned. The sentiments were so lovely. Albeit flattering and a little formal. Despite the flush I felt, this was dangerous territory. The curse loomed over me, a cloud ready to rain on my sun-filled day.

Turning over the card, I found a simple crest; a fish leapt from a running stream. It was identical to the wax which had sealed the envelope but I didn't recognise it. The people I knew didn't use wax seals.

Returning to the small note, I re-read it carefully. These boxes hadn't been a mistake, they were mine. As I stared down at them all, a conversation I'd had not too long ago came back to me.

"It all looks very enjoyable; don't you agree?" Nathaniel gestured to a young couple who were dancing under the stars.

"If you like that sort of thing," I replied, with a shrug.

"Do you?"

"I don't have many opportunities...anymore" I said watching a couple twirl.

"Hmm..." he murmured, sounding thoughtful. "I am sure you do not..."

Nathaniel's words settled in the silence of my cabin, and I shook myself.

"Foolishness," I muttered,

Nathaniel wouldn't do this — he had organized a *tête-à-tête* with the island woman. There was no way I factored anywhere in his thoughts. This was a mere coincidence, a special gift from an anonymous friend. Whoever they were.

Ignoring all my doubts and questions, I allowed the little girl inside me to squeal with delight. One by one, I lifted the lids of the remaining boxes. Within them I found buckled shoes, a shawl, and countless other accessories for a special night. Puzzled but jubilant, I set about making sure I looked worthy to wear such attire.

No-one was there to question me as I boiled water and hauled my porcelain jug back to my cabin. The sounds of card games, banter and general chatter sounded above me as I rid myself of ship-dust.

Fresh and clean, I scrambled beneath my bed. There amongst the darkness, I found a lacquered vanity case. My hands shook, as I ran my fingertips over the scarred lid. Taking a deep breath I lifted it. The reflection staring back at me was much changed from the one who had once used it daily.

My mismatched eyes were brightened, by the anxiety and excitement burning deep inside me. Was I doing the right thing? Should I just push everything into a corner and pull on my brogues and braces as usual? No. This was something I longed for, I would take this opportunity, after all I might never have it again.

Not wanting to look any more I placed the card over the glass and ignoring the niggling insecurities I found hair pins. Though the face powder and rouge had turned to dust, I got to work, surprised by how easily I slipped into my old routine.

The brush glided through my damp hair, leaving only shine behind. Using the pins, I attempted to replicate the styles I had seen the previous night. Moving my head this way and that, I secured the final one into my hair and nodded in approval, it would do. To complete the look, I removed the card obscuring the mirror. Grasping for my matchbox, I pulled out an unlit bud. Though at any other time I would have struck it against my teeth, I used my side-table. This was a night to be lady-like after all.

I watched the flickering flame dance, before blowing it out. Smoke trailed in the aftermath, sending me back in time. The aroma of too-sweet perfume and stale liquor wafted through the air, and the babble of voices rang in my head along with the sound of a piano. Pushing the lump from my throat, I turned back to the mirror to pencil on a beauty spot.

Now made up I could explore the other boxes. Finding the second largest in the set, I removed the top; with practised movements I lifted the boned corset from its confines. Doing it up, without help, came back quicker than I could have ever imagined. Any negative memories of how I'd learned such skills were squashed before they could fester.

The Lennie in the mirror was some fantasy version that had never existed, a faery-tale, a damned Cinderella. My one wish was that midnight wouldn't strike too soon.

As I admired my shiny buckled boots, a knock sounded at the door. Frowning at the interruption, I gathered my skirts and turned the handle. Filling the doorway was the most handsome gentleman in I'd ever seen. His dark hair was swept off his face, highlighting the brightness of his sky blue eyes. His suit was tailored to perfection, its cut emphasising his broad shoulders and narrow waist. He bowed his head in a respectable fashion and smiled.

"May I request the pleasure of your company this evening, miss?" His formal address threw me for a moment, I couldn't find my voice.

"Uh-you may, kind sir?"

In keeping with the Cinderella theme I curtseyed, albeit unsteadily.

CHAPTER VI
THE CHARMS OF MEN

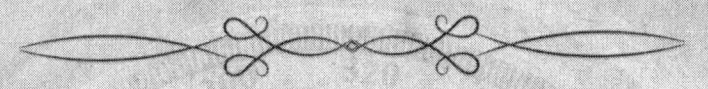

BUTCH'S EYES WIDENED as I stepped onto the deck, "Is that you?"

"Ask me another," I said as I passed my crew mates, my hand in Nathaniel's. Each one was uncharacteristic in their silence. Claudette and Macrucio were nowhere to be seen.

"You're already beautiful my dear, this just enhances it," Ned assured.

His quiet comment bolstered my fragile self-esteem and I grasped for his hand.

"Thank you, so much."

I pressed my lips to his twisted knuckles and his lip trembled. I opened my mouth to speak but the older man shook his head, urging me to follow Nathaniel.

My partner let me go for the shortest of moments, before aiding me over the gangplank. My fingers trembled as he rested my arm in the crook of his. We shared a smile and the tenderness in Nathaniel's gaze had my cheeks flushing. The memory of the note was fresh in my mind.

The Island of Plenty was not only a pirate haunt, noblemen and gentry also patronised the small, sandy plot of land. Due to the trade pirates bought to the island, they were accepted, in moderation. I had never been to the formal dances before and couldn't help but peer over my shoulder in caution, waiting for someone to realise who or what I was.

The ball was already under way as we reached the dance floor. From beneath my lashes I surreptitiously watched the ladies, their movements precise and proper. Delving into my memory, I tried to recall all the dances that had been part of my training, all those years ago.

"Would you like something to drink?"

Nathaniel's question jolted me and I stared up at him, dazed. He cocked his head as he lifted a crystal glass.

"Sorry, yes, I'd love one."

He nodded, filling two with ruby red liquid. Glad I had something to do with my hands, I sipped. Though it didn't have the same kick or burn as the amber liquid aboard the ship, it settled my nerves.

"Would it be too forward for me to say that you look beautiful?" Nathaniel said.

I stared down at my drink as I fought another blush. "Only if it is not too bold of me to say, you cut a handsome figure too?"

I peeked up to find he'd lowered his eyes as colour tinged his cheeks. Recovering, he took my glass.

"Shall we dance?"

Leading me amongst the other couples, he pulled me around and expertly twirled us across the floor. The music swelled around us and I was swept away. The energetic rhythm allowed me to use the skills I had long since buried. I found myself laughing at missteps, all nervousness gone. Once the song was over, we returned to our glasses.

"You are an accomplished dancer," Nathaniel praised, his surprise unhidden by the awe on his face.

"You know your way around the floor too, sir."

"Excuse me, miss; may I have the next dance?"

The intimate bubble Nathaniel and I had created, popped at the stranger's voice. I turned to find a bronze haired young gentleman, waiting expectantly. I floundered for something to say. Having a man of such rank choose me to stand up with, was an honour. I would never have dreamed of such a thing happening. If only he knew… The risk was all too great, and besides, I didn't have the courage or the inclination to stand up with anyone else. Before I could tell him so, Nathaniel spoke.

"I am afraid all of Miss Roux's dances have been allotted this evening, perhaps another time?" His words were polite but firm. The young man nodded, disappointment was etched across his face.

"Certainly, forgive my effrontery?" Giving me one last fleeting look, he bowed and walked away.

"I hope that was not presumptuous of me?" Nathaniel said, as he watched the strangers retreating figure through narrowed eyes.

"Not at all," I reassured him.

After our glass of punch, we took another turn on the floor. The reels and jigs were over and the slower melodies were filling the silence. Our movements were slow and steady as we eased around the floor. Nathaniel was careful not invade my space; his manner was formal and polite. The hand on my back didn't move anywhere inappropriate; but the heat his touch created coursed through me. I was sure he could feel my body trembling. Yet, there in his arms my fears seemed so far away.

More couples joined us as the next song played. As we attempted to circle in time to the music, we were jostled by the other patrons crowding the floor. Nathaniel's gaze was questioning and I answered him with a small nod. At my acquiesce, he pulled me closer and I nestled my head against his heart.

Rather than dancing to the music swirling around us, I kept time to the rhythm in my ear. I had not been so close to a man in four years, and despite the intimacy, I felt little threat. Lifting my gloved hand, I grazed the exposed skin of Nathaniel's nape. The ragged breath he inhaled proved he felt the same way.

"Lennie." The husky tone of his voice, as he said my name, caused the butterflies to return. They fluttered against the walls of my stomach, rife with disquiet.

"Hmm...?" I murmured.

"Lennie was not the name given to you at birth, was

it?"

I stopped swaying as I looked into his face, I found nothing more than curiosity there.

"No, why do you ask?"

The fear I had tucked away, seeped into my consciousness as I pulled back from him. I knew this was all too good to be true. Did he know? Did he expect... something?

"I do not mean to pry," he assured, seeing me tense.

"I would love to call you by your given name. Lennie suits the girl with the sword at her hip. Yet, tonight, the way you hold yourself. You are a lady."

The breath I pulled in took an age to release. The compliment was lovely and I was flattered he saw me that way. Yet I hadn't been called by my birth name since I'd boarded the *Wilted Rose*.

"It's not a name I use any more. I'm just, Lennie."

Grasping hold of his hand I returned to his embrace, trying to literally dance around the subject. Over Nathaniel's shoulder I caught sight of Macrucio and Claudette as they twirled past us. Both had their eyes closed. Macrucio's lips moved in a low whisper against his partner's ear, and Claudette's mouth lifted in response. They weren't conflicted, and my envy was palpable.

"At least give me the first letter, let me try figure it out on my own." Nathaniel urged his tone playful.

I was pulled out of my voyeurism as Nathaniel drew me closer. I laid my head against his chest, smiling to myself. He'd never guess.

"V," I muttered.

"Hmm...V, this will not be easy."

Nathaniel traced a finger across my cheek, making me shiver. I closed my eyes, listening to the strains of the tune playing on the air. As we continued to move, Nathaniel thought aloud. There was no way he could guess, it wasn't a common name for anyone.

"Vera, Veronica, Violet, Virginia, Victoria."

My smile grew wider at each attempt. Opening my eyes, I spied a group of chairs hidden by a large potted tree. Nathaniel caught my idea, spinning me off the floor. We sat, hidden behind the fern.

"Valencia," I whispered, finally giving in. It felt strange to say it again after all these years.

"Valencia," Nathaniel repeated, drawing out the syllables as he nodded. "It suits you."

"Thank you,"

I didn't agree. It suited the girl I used to be. Though said by him, it sounded different, refined even. I looked at our hands, they were laced together on my knee. His large fingers cocooned my own and I wanted nothing more than to take off my glove, to feel the touch of his skin. Shaking myself for even entertaining such a thought, I tried to think of something less dangerous.

"Do you know much about your parents?"

At his question, I shifted in my chair, this was not the subject I wanted to pursue.

"I didn't live with blood relatives, before coming to the *Wilted Rose*."

"I will tell you mine…" he offered, his smile not reaching his eyes.

I hesitated, unsure what to say or how much to tell.

"If you do not wish me to know...?" he said the sincerity in his voice almost made me cave in and reveal all.

"No, it's not that," my reply came too fast. "I just don't know where to start."

"Perhaps you could try at the beginning?" He winked, attempting to relieve my strain. His sweetness pained me. He wouldn't be so sweet if he knew the truth.

I sighed, pausing to pick my words with care. "I was left by my mother in her home country of France. My father had been a musketeer, before he was captured by the curse."

I stalled again, editing. "From what I was told, he stole my mother away from her depraved life and brought her to the ship. Learning of the curse, my mother left me in the care of her old friends. Ned found me and brought me back."

"So you are of French origin? I did detect a flair in your accent. Why did your parents choose to name you Valencia?"

I couldn't help smiling at his question. "I was born at the Spanish port."

"Astonishing." He shook his head in awe, before

barrelling into the next question,

"How old were you when you arrived aboard the ship?"

"Fourteen," I murmured, staring downwards, all traces of humour gone.

"So young."

He tucked a wayward strand of hair behind my ear, the tender touch drawing heat to where his fingers lay.

"I was grown long before then, Nathaniel," I stopped short, annoyed at my runaway mouth. Recovering quickly, I brightened my face with a false smile. "What about you?"

Nathaniel paused for a long moment; I couldn't hold his gaze. As I turned away, he began to speak. "As you already know, I was given to my uncle as an infant."

I nodded, urging him to continue.

"My mother had grown up there after her own parents were lost at sea. She was loved and revered by all, a princess to the local townsfolk. She was to be married to a good match."

Nathaniel looked out at the dancing couples; Macrucio and Claudette were still turning about the floor.

"My mother was said to be something of a romantic; she vowed to marry for love and nothing less would do. When my father, a Romany Gypsy with an art for storytelling, arrived in town, she could not help but follow her heart. Local legend says that he weaved a tale so magical, that it bewitched her to run away with him."

A cloud crossed Nathaniel face. "Most believed my mother to be either dead or at least disgraced. My uncle never gave up though; he has been waiting for her to walk up the beach and into the house for years."

Nathaniel traced the patterns on the back of my glove as he let his words settle.

"When I was left on the doorstep with nothing but a note, it did not unnerve him." Nathaniel continued. "It gave him more drive to want to find her and bring her home. You could say I joined this quest for similar reasons."

He pulled in a shaky breath. "I grew up wondering who my parents were; and if they were alive somewhere. The only proof they existed is right here."

Nathaniel pulled his father, Caleb's journal from an inside pocket. Opening it he revealed a loose piece of parchment nestled between the pages. This one rather well read compared to the note found aboard Macrucio's ship. Nathaniel offered it and I held the delicate item between my fingers like a rare gem.

"Go ahead, read at your leisure," he murmured and I unfolded the page. The parchment was worn and a small tear lined one of the creases. The elegant script was faded but there was no mistaking its sentiment:

My Darling Son,

By the time you read this I will no longer be at

your side. Though I loath to leave you, I must. The reasons for our separation will be explained when we are reunited, which I dearly hope will be soon. I shall miss you so very much whilst I'm gone.

In my absence, I shall leave you in the capable hands of my brother, Henry and his housekeeper, Bess. They took such great care of me when I was without my own parents. Listen to all Uncle Henry has to say, he is a wise man and you will learn much from him. Bess may fuss but she has your best interests at heart, she will be your mother until my return.

My dearest Nathaniel, please know I love you and do not forget me. When I return I will answer all of your questions, I promise.

Forever, my darling son, you will be in my heart.

Your Mother.

Remember; never be ashamed to cry.'

There was no stopping the tears rolling down my cheeks. I hadn't known Maria Davenport, but in reading her letter, it was easy to see how much she had cared for her son. It was plain this boy had not been abandoned, and Maria had been so sure she would come home to him.

"This sounds like your mother adored you," I said wiping the moisture from my face as I handed him back the note.

"Let me —" Nathaniel put away the journal and took out his handkerchief. With much gentleness, he dabbed at my tear stained cheeks.

"Keep it," he urged, holding out the piece of cloth. "A token of our night."

"Thank you."

I folded the fabric and found one corner embroidered with the insignia, NDL. I brushed a thumb over the raised stitching.

"May I ask something?" I said.

"Of course," Nathaniel said. "We are all friends here."

"If your father was so unapproved of, why did your uncle allow you to use his name?"

"A fair question." Nathaniel's eyes lingered upon my fingers as they continued to outline the stitching.

"I was curious about my parents, as most children are. Bess told me many tales of my mother, but could tell me little of my father. She gave me all my mother had offered, that he was handsome and clever." Nathaniel brushed a hand through his hair, his eyes were far away.

"What stuck with me the most was that she'd said he showed her an unfettered kindness, and most of all that his stories held meaning, far beyond entertainment. I felt an affinity for him. I had begun to create my own tales by then. So I approached my uncle to have my name formally changed from Nathaniel Davenport to Nathaniel Davenport -Lee, for the man who was my father."

"Was it as easy as it sounds?"

I was so entranced by his voice; I wanted nothing more than to hear him speak. His full mouth and animated face entranced me as much as his lilting deep timbre.

"My uncle was most upset, he believed my father a devil. I argued – you must remember I was no older than thirteen at this point – that if he was such a creature that I too would be. He could not argue after that, thus N.D.L."

He reached out to touch the handkerchief in my hands. Our fingers grazed one another and I twitched. Nathaniel did not show this affected him as he continued his tale.

"Bess stitched these for me, I felt proud to carry them – to hold my father's name every day."

"Bess sounds like a wonderful woman."

"She is, and the only mother I have ever known."

The silence that followed was companionable. The music floated around the beach and I swayed along with the beautiful strings. My eyes caught Macrucio and Claudette again as they too sat to the side of the dance floor. My heart squeezed as the dark haired man pressed a kiss to the unadorned hand of Claudette.

"Do you have any mementoes from your parents?" Nathaniel asked, breaking my reverie.

Pulling in a breath, I shook my head. "Just my sword, it was my fathers. It's strange; I haven't missed wearing it tonight."

I smiled, touching a hand to my belt-less hip. "Though I lived amongst many of my mother's friends, I've never had anything physical of hers. I'm so thankful that the ship has the portraits."

"They are a great addition," Nathaniel agreed.

With our pasts somewhat revealed, the conversation turned to more average topics. Both of us were avid readers and shared favourite poets and authors. Bit by bit we were getting to know one another. Despite my burgeoning feelings, I could see Nathaniel and I becoming friends. His dark, rich voice captivated me and though the nerves were still there, I didn't feel the need to escape his presence any longer.

"One last dance before the clock strikes midnight?" Nathaniel asked.

A laugh erupted from me; the Cinderella idea I'd conjured while I'd been getting ready, had been at play in his mind too.

"It would be an honour, sir," I said, following his lead.

Being in the protective circle of his arms, my sordid history melted into murky memories. I let my body feel. There was no past or future, there was only the moment. We moved languidly, not paying attention to the rhythm of the music. We had our own, slow and steady, like a heartbeat.

All too soon the dance ended and people began to disperse. Nathaniel sighed as with reluctance, he let me go. I too felt bereft as his warm arms left me, taking with it, the steady beating of his heart. Grasping for my hand, Nathaniel brushed his thumb back and forth over my knuckles. We were silent as we followed behind the other couples leaving the beach.

Not too far ahead, Claudette and Macrucio wandered along the sand, still lost in their own world. I felt a pang of jealousy for their effortlessness with one another. Though both were a little unsteady on their feet. I wondered if it was from too much punch or the fact they weren't used to solid ground.

Nathaniel caught my eye and nodded his head their way. "Would you care to take a stroll?"

"I would," I replied pausing to tug off my gloves and boots.

With the smallest hint of hesitation, I reached for his hand. He took it without question and I hid a sigh. Just as I'd imagined, the touch of my skin to his, was electric. It sent warmth up my arm and across my chest. There wasn't pain, but I did feel unsteady for a moment. Overwhelmed at the current flowing through me, I tried to calm my breathing.

We walked along the waterfront in silence. The moon and dwindling torches lit our way through the sand. The faery-tale world I had stepped into as I'd pulled on my dress earlier in the evening, faded as the noise of the party died away. In the quiet, with only the sound of our breathing filling the empty space, I felt the weight of realisation hit me. It was like a wave had drenched me in ice cold water.

My mind, body and soul were united upon one common emotion. The thought, which would have cheered most young women, chilled me to the core. To even think the word was taboo. I had lost myself in a fantasy world of dances and beautiful dresses; but had come out of it feeling more than I had a right to. My heart pounded in an erratic pulse and I forced myself to remain calm. Being as discrete as I could, I pulled in the sea air and let it out in a long quiet breath. I dared to look at him and a lump lodged in my throat.

Nathaniel stopped beside the water's edge. Bringing me into his arms, he brushed his lips across the sensitive spot at my temple. Burying my face into his chest, I listened to his franticly beating heart as I trembled. Tears fell unchecked down my face. I would die, either way. But I couldn't do that him.

"Valencia, I cannot fathom the feelings I have..."

I pulled back, pressing a finger to his lips. "No, don't even attempt to say anything. Tonight has been magical but now we must go on as though it never happened."

The words hurt as I spoke them, each one a knife wound in my already fragile heart. We had to abide by the rules, there was no other way. His life depended upon it. The confusion and deep seated pain was alight in his eyes. I had no other choice but to hurt him. At least this way, it would only be an emotional hurt.

"This," I said as I gestured between us. "Is all in our heads."

Releasing him, I set off up the beach. The tears continuing to fall. Silent in the sand, I didn't hear him follow me. He grasped my arm; the force sent me spinning towards him.

Our bodies collided and my breath caught as his lips claimed mine. Without letting me recover he deepened the kiss, lifting me off the ground and consuming me whole. I gave into it, reciprocated it. I couldn't get close enough. It was the first time I had ever been kissed like this, and I wanted more.

Wrapping my arms around his neck, my fingers wove into his hair, loosening the ribbon which tied it away. Without preamble, I succumbed to every emotion coursing through me, overriding any thought that told me to stop. As the kiss came to its slow and reluctant conclusion, I kept my eyes closed, knowing if I opened them, it would mean the dream was truly at an end. My feet hit the sand and he pulled away.

"I wanted the end of the night to be just as magical." Nathaniel's voice was hoarse as the pad of his thumb caressed my bottom lip.

"Goodnight, my sweet Valencia, I shall dream of

you."

My eyes remained shut as he pressed a kiss to my palm. Lifting my lids, I could just make out his retreating form as it disappeared into the shadows. My swollen lips still tingled from his touch and my fingertips tentatively traced their outline. Had that really happened?

I'd been kissed before, in my past life. Each time lips had been forced upon mine, I had felt both repulsed and violated. Yet, when Nathaniel had kissed me I'd felt wanton and cherished all at once, feelings I'd never experienced before. My body tingled and all I wanted to do was find him and partake again. Was this what other women felt when they were kissed? I had no other frame of reference. I left the beach in a daze. Stopping every so often to look up at the stars.

There was no-one to meet me as I stepped onto the deck. A single candle burned, lighting a dim path. Wandering down to the living quarters, I passed by the saloon. I could hear my crewmates on the other side of the door, but wanting to prolong the fantasy, I crept by trying hard to not draw attention to myself.

"Do not be fooled by the charms of men." The sinister voice amongst the shadows, sent a chill up my spine.

"What do you know of charm?" I sneered, turning to find a dishevelled Macrucio leaning against the wall. His shirt was open and his trousers unfastened.

"I know enough to feel the pain, of never revealing

my 'earts truth," he said.

"You know nothing of how I feel."

Macrucio shrugged as he stared down at his ring. The eyes of the skull glowed red in the dark.

"Macrucio, come back to bed, my pet." Claudette's call sounded from the half open door a little way down the passage and his eyes flicked behind him.

"I have more insight than you know, my dear. Sweet dreams." With a mocking smile he stalked towards Claudette's room, slamming the door behind him.

I felt shaken as I reached my own sanctuary. My brows knitted as I tried to force Macrucio's words from my mind.

"He knows nothing," I muttered, setting down my shoes and untying my corset. Keeping busy, I methodically undressed, setting things aside neatly and carefully. Tugging the pins from my hair, I climbed into bed.

The varying shades of wood above my head held little in the way of distraction. Snuffing the candle didn't help either, my mind was filled with the forceful yet passionate sensation of Nathaniel's lips upon my own. The masculine scent of his skin and the pounding of our hearts filled me to the brim. I closed my eyes, only to find the image of Nathaniel in the moonlight.

Do not be fooled by the charms of men.' Macrucio's warning haunted me as I turned my face into the pillow.

CHAPTER VII
FOUND

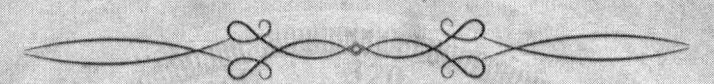

AS THE SUN rose, I lay back to take in the spectrum of colours as they danced across the ceiling. Their vibrancy emulated the feeling of Nathaniel's touch and my heart quickened at the memory. When he'd pulled me close, the world had burst into colour.

Watching the play of light shift and change, I touched a finger to my lips. I could still feel the tenderness of our kiss as if he was right there beside me. A wave of reality hit me, hard. This daydreaming had to stop. Now. I would not to torment myself with illusions and regret, or think of the dampening words Macrucio had forced upon me. I would return to how I was and supress any feelings I thought I had discovered.

Kicking the covers aside I set about picking up each memento of the evening, taking great care to wrap them in parchment and stowing them away. With a heavy heart I closed each box and pushed them beneath the bed.

As I dressed, I scoured the room for things I'd missed. My hand fell upon the white handkerchief. Touching the soft fabric to my cheek, I sighed at the memory.

"Let me...." his soft voice echoed though my imagination. I cupped my cheek, recalling his gentle touch, as he wiped away my tears. I stared down at the stitched initials. The sky blue matched his eyes. I brushed my thumb across it. Ignoring the warmth that spread through me, I stowed the trinket close to my heart.

It was just a dream, I told myself, glaring down at the plain attire, which hung from my body. It was naught but a faint hope, best left alone. This is what my life was to be, there would be no feelings of regret. Setting my thoughts in motion, I picked up my hat and tucked my hair beneath it.

My gaze strayed to the porthole and I frowned through the glass. The new day sparkled like diamonds on the aquamarine water, and the Island of Plenty was now a small speck in the distance. Determined to not let the melancholy affect me, I picked up my sword and headed to the deck.

Butch was stood atop the quarterdeck and I greeted him with a pat on the back. The crease between his brows mirrored mine as he watched the water. I followed his lead as Caw hovered above the fish rippling beneath the surface. Awareness danced up my spine as I felt *him* approach. Using all my will to not react, I focussed on the horizon.

"Any sign of danger?" Nathaniel asked.

"Nothing yet," Butch replied, not picking up on the strain in my demeanour. "I do think we have been lucky so far, having those two aboard you know it won't be long."

Butch jerked his head over to the two newest members of the crew whilst I let myself peek at Nathaniel. His face was drawn, lines of strain pulled his mouth downward, as he nodded to Butch.

Without so much as a glance in my direction, Nathaniel turned and walked away. I swallowed back the hurt, I had vowed there would be no regrets and I wasn't going to break that promise. Though I had selfishly hoped to retain the tentative friendship we'd built before.

"Are you all right?" Butch's question jolted me.

"Fine," I said with a nod.

"You're a little... distracted." He stepped forward and lifted the brim of my hat.

"I'm fine," I repeated through clenched teeth, pulling away from his probing gaze. His eyes narrowed and he shook his head.

"You were nicer before he arrived." Butch's eyes flickered towards Nathaniel. The tall man wasn't paying any attention to us as he joked with Rupert.

"Well..." I didn't have an answer.

"He gets to you," Butch accused. "Did he do something? Was he the one who got you all spruced up?" Butch stepped forward, fists clenched, a muscle working in his cheek.

"No, he didn't–" I paused. "I don't want to talk about this, besides, there's no crime against playing dress-up." I leaned against the rail, not quite seeing the view.

"I have a strong shoulder and a ready ear, I understand why Ned is the person you go to for advice but if you need someone to listen."

"I do know that."

"And dress-up or not, you're a handsome woman, Lennie." He let his sentence hang, his ears reddening.

"Thank you," I murmured, raising up on tiptoe I pressed a kiss to his cheek. As his face flushed to match his ears, I wandered away. He was a good kid.

Across the deck, cards and stories were traded. Nathaniel weaved a tale between the game, and the boys were avid listeners.

"Then what happened?" Rupert asked, picking up from the pile, his eyes not leaving the storyteller.

"Well, the blacksmith–" I didn't wait to hear the rest. Skirting the table I found Macrucio and Claudette sat atop the rail. They stared into each other's eyes as they spoke, every so often, Macrucio would brush his lips across Claudette forehead or cheek. Feeling a twinge of envy, I joined Ned as he worked out the ship's co-ordinates beside the helm. The captain stood close by with a furrowed brow, his compass dial twirling.

"Lennie, if you have a question ask it," he said sharply not looking up.

"Not a question, just a curiosity," I replied.

He motioned for me to continue.

"I'm sure you are aware we have a problem."

Captain Rourke turned to me, his eyes still squinting. "Do you mean Hadnaloy?"

"That and the fact we must introduce Claudette and Macrucio to Rosa."

"I say we get there quick," Rupert said having left the table. He nudged me, a grin lighting up his face. "You never know what those two could be cooking up."

"They do keep to themselves," Butch said from behind me. I turned to find his narrowed gaze lingering on our newest crew-members.

"As you well know, the ship can only go as fast Rosa, or in some cases, the Sorceress wants. If they feel we should return to the cove, they will surely let us know," Ned said. The paleness of his pallor worried me.

"I have a question," Nathaniel interjected as he stepped into our conversation.

My hand gripped my already open collar. Heat flushed my skin as he clasped his hands behind him. He stood mere inches away from me. Pushing out a puff of air, I felt it settle upon my clammy face. Every nerve ending was piqued as I waited for his query.

"Go ahead son," Ned said, stepping between myself and Nathaniel. His intuition right on point, as always.

"I know it is polite for us to introduce people to Rosa, but through your eye-" Nathaniel paused, looking to the older man with an arched brow.

Ned smiled in approval allowing him to continue.

"Well, should your eye not be introduction enough?"

"You catch on quick, Ned hadn't even told you of that skill yet." Rupert winked, throwing an arm around Davy's shoulder as he finally joined the group.

"It's a fair question," Ned replied. "It's true, Rosa can see all I can, perhaps more. Yet she cannot respond with as much speed as she'd like, thus the need to visit her."

Nathaniel looked satisfied with the answer and smiled in fondness at Ned. I stared, none-to-politely either, willing him to bestow the same honour upon me. The smile never came and I turned, biting my lip to stop my emotions from giving me away. I was such a fool.

Rather than punishing either of us, I decided to remain below deck. Though I had cleaned the armoury I had not worked on the main weaponry the ship had to offer. With my filled bucket in hand, I went to work.

The methodical rhythm of dipping the cloth into the water and scrubbing the dark metal helped me lose myself. I didn't think about anything other than my task. I worked hard, not moving until the cannon shone beneath my ministrations. Sweat beaded across my face and down my back. The work cleansed me, allowing my overworked mind to focus.

"Take any more elbow grease to that thing and you'll never want to use it, it'll be far too clean"

Pulling off my bandana, I wiped my face before I turned. Davy was propped against the door frame, watching my progress.

"I needed to think," I explained.

"Well, I can see myself in this one," Davy teased as he climbed up on it.

"Was there something you needed, are you alright?" I asked, throwing my cloth into the dirty water and picking up my discarded hat and jacket.

"I just wanted to see how you are; I didn't see you return home last night after the ball."

"I got home fine. Besides, Butch already checked, nothing happened," I sighed, pulling on my braces and untying my hair, letting it tumble down my back.

"Nathaniel walked you?"

"Yes," my voice cracked, revealing more than I'd wanted. "You know I don't need Nathaniel's protection to walk home, so just ask what you want to know."

I pursed my lips, more at myself than at Davy, he was only looking out for me, but I couldn't help but get annoyed.

"I'm well aware you don't need protection. It's just, after your escape from Macrucio's ship, you seemed closer to him. Now I sense some strain between you."

I bit the inside of my cheek, looking down as Davy continued.

"I know good people, he's one of them."

Davy's words were red hot pokers. They seared my already tender heart. I knew Nathaniel was one of the good people. Truth be told, I missed him. I was foolish to think I could have it both ways. Stupid woman!

Staring through the porthole, I could see twilight

approaching. I felt a pull to be on deck to watch the moon rise. There was nothing more to be done.

"I do believe that he is a good person. In fact, I know he is. I just don't think I am." I pressed my lips together, hiding my face with my hair. I had spoken too much truth and the full extent came spilling out again.

"I don't think I'm good people, Davy. Nor am I good enough for him."

Before Davy could respond, I grasped hold of my bucket and left the room. Tears left trails down my face as I closed the door behind me.

"–AND THAT IS how we play cards gentlemen." Rupert lay down his winning hand and I shook my head as I threw down my own.

"I swear you cheat." Claudette chuckled as she passed over her set.

"It's pure skill." Rupert grinned, scooping up all his matchstick winnings.

"Why do we never play for money?" Macrucio picked up one up, jamming it between his teeth.

"Money is of no use to this ship," Butch said.

"I can see that." Leaving his snide tone ringing in our ears, the entire table watched Macrucio saunter away.

Claudette narrowed her eyes at him, her face was pinched with annoyance. Her entire demeanour changed as Nathaniel approached the table; he proceeded to crouch down beside her and whisper into her ear. I clenched my teeth as they laughed together. In her good humour, Claudette laid her hand upon Nathaniel's arm and I almost cried out in frustration.

Jealousy was an emotion I did not enjoy, an unbecoming feeling, toxic like a poison running through my bloodstream. I had felt it more since Nathaniel had climbed aboard than at any other time in my eighteen years. It was like an apple, ready for the picking – far too close to the forbidden feelings urging me to betray my vow.

As Nathaniel pulled out a seat to continue his conversation, I stood. In my haste my chair clattered to the floor, turning heads.

"Sorry," I muttered. As I righted my seat, my eyes clashed with sky blues ones. It did not last long, for Claudette brushed his arm once more and his attention wavered.

"Ned, send me word when we reach Rosa's," I said, my gaze still lingering upon Nathaniel.

"Of course, child." Ned was sat atop the rail, his forehead creased in a deep frown as Caw flew in large circles in front of him. I watched them a moment before going in search of a story, one that would make me forget my own for a while.

CHAPTER VIII
TEMPEST

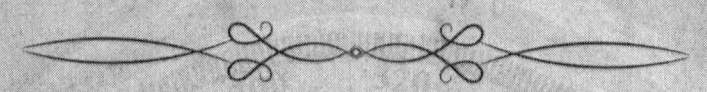

"BACK FROM YOUR adventures I see," Rosa said her jet eyes were alight with our return.

"We have brought the last remaining heirs to you and we're in great need of your advice." The captain swept off his hat and moved aside to reveal the two newest crew members.

"Come forward, son of Roberto and daughter of Edmund, I was convinced we would find you one day."

As Rosa beckoned the two heirs forward, I left Butch's side to support Ned, he shook as though cold. I pulled him to me and rested my head on his arm. He patted my cheek but held nothing in his expression. His eyes stared at the wall, as if seeing something no one else could.

As Claudette and Macrucio stood before the plinth, neither faltered. Their backs were stock straight and their heads were held high and alert. The only indicator of what they were feeling, was their intertwined hands. Macrucio's thumb brushed back and forth over Claudette's fingers in comfort.

"Welcome children, it will take a great deal of time to

integrate back into our family fold." Rosa smiled down at them, her expression warm. "However, to complete the moral mission of your legacy we require your help."

"I am more than willing." Claudette's voice carried across the rock pool, echoing off the cave walls.

"And you, son of Roberto?"

All eyes fell on the dark haired man.

"I shall be honest, I can see you hold a great power and I will not disrespect that." Macrucio dipped his head before continuing. "I am not convinced by what you call your 'moral mission,' yet my life and Claudette's are intertwined, so I have no other choice but to remain here."

He turned to his partner and they shared a long look. "I will bide my time," he said, raising their hands. Pressing a kiss to Claudette's knuckles he turned again to Rosa.

"Under Claudette's word, I will not harm your crew, though I refuse to fight against those who raised and fought alongside me"

"We would not ask that of you, son." Captain Rourke assured.

"No, Brandon is right, all we require is your lineage; the rest is by personal choice. You must remember however, to keep your hearts close, for no good shall come to those who leave them with another."

Rosa nodded her dismissal and the two newest members stepped away. Their heads bowed in quiet conversation once more.

"I shall call upon the Sorceress." Rosa spoke to the group. "We then can move forward on our journey. Remember, I have as much knowledge as you in these matters. Though I am always here to guide you. Remain strong, my children, the wait will soon be over."

With no other news to impart, we made our way back to the ship. As the others around me chattered, I couldn't help but feel a mixture of trepidation and hope. The struggle could soon be at an end for us. As I followed behind the others, I clasped my hands together to stop their shaking. This was what we all had hope for, so why was I terrified?

I looked over my shoulder, intending to speak to Ned, but found no-one there. Hoisting myself up on tip-toes I double checked he wasn't with the group up ahead. As I searched the familiar faces, none of them were my old friend. I did, however, catch Nathaniel's eye.

"What troubles you?" He asked letting the crew pass by him.

We hadn't spoken since the night on the island and with those three words, he'd broken his silence. There was no evidence of either malice or sarcasm in his question, just a look of concern, I must admit a small part of me was overjoyed. The feeling was short lived, however, as Ned's absence immediately returned to my thoughts.

"Ned has not left the cave, I'll only be a minute. Go

on ahead, we'll meet you," I said, heading back towards Rosa's sanctuary.

"I think it would be more prudent for you to return to the ship..." Nathaniel called after me.

"I'll be fine," I urged gesturing him to follow the others.

Nathaniel opened his mouth to argue, his anxiousness unhidden by the crease between his eyes.

"Go, nothing can harm me here," I interrupted.

"If you are sure..." he hedged, taking a step towards me.

"Without a doubt."

Nathaniel watched me for a moment before following the rest of the crew as they turned the corner.

A feeling of triumph filled me, the cursed few were now united, eight heirs together at last, it had nothing to do with Nathaniel's obvious concern. Nor the fact he was finally speaking to me again... no, not at all.

"Ned!"

Rosa's cry sent me running. The walkway now a blur, as my heart pounded in a panicked rhythm. What was wrong? I skidded to a stop as I entered the cove. Ned was crouched into himself, his head in his hands, as tears poured over them and onto the stone floor. Rosa's wooden face was a picture of worry. A frown marred her whorl blemished face as anguish swirled within her eyes. Her body doubled as she reached towards him. I approached them with caution, unsure what I would find.

"Ned, what happened?" I asked kneeling beside him.

"He is merely tired, child." Rosa's flippant excuse didn't match her harrowed expression.

"Aye, she's right." Ned's voice was muffled. "I'm just tired; you young ones seem to forget, I'm older than you are."

"You've never mentioned it before," I said, unsure he spoke the truth, but unwilling to argue with him.

Ned stood, wiping the dampness from his cheeks. His face held lines I had never noticed. For the first time I saw the old man he declared to be.

"I didn't want to worry you, child." He tried to smile but the sadness lingered, turning his expression mournful.

"Do you want to return to the *Wilted Rose*?" I asked, getting to my feet. It was all I could think to suggest as I thread my hand through his.

"Of course." He looked confused by the question. "The ship is my home, my anchor. I hope to never leave."

I nodded, I knew the pull all too well. It was the only true home we'd both had ever known. Perhaps Ned was worried about what would happen, if we were to succeed. We had found all eight heirs now…

Neither of us spoke as we turned to leave.

"Take care." Rosa sounded forlorn as she called after us.

Ned was shaking as we walked back towards the ship. I held onto his arm, aiding him the best I could. He breathing was laboured and we stopped every so often so he could rest. Though I longed to comfort him or even ask if he was alright, I didn't. He looked too far away. My heart ached for him, I just didn't know how to fix what ailed him, nor what pained him so.

Turning the final corner, the ship came into view. Ned's steps picked up a little more speed as we reached our beloved rest stop. Someone had been thoughtful enough to set up the plank and the two of us climbed up and over the rail with ease.

"I think I'll turn in," Ned said, releasing his hand from mine.

I felt bereft without his roughened and gnarled fingers around my own. Not waiting for me to reply, he descended the stairs and was out of sight. I stared down at my empty palm, I wasn't the only one keeping secrets it seemed.

As I scanned the deck, Nathaniel waved; smiling in return I caught Rupert shuffling his cards beside him. The redhead threw a dimpled grin at me as he moved the pack between his fingers. I shook my head at his silent invitation; I didn't feel much like playing.

The warmth in having all of the crew together was gone; Ned's distress had rattled me. What would the future hold? When the curse had been lifted, would I be free? Where would I go? What would I do? My life had purpose aboard the *Wilted Rose*, what did I have once it was taken away? Just as Ned had said, the ship was home.

I was almost out of my teenage years and I knew only one kind of work – although I'd vowed never to return to that life…

The questions tumbled around my mind as I took roost on the top deck. My eyes not taking in the smoothness of the water, but the unfathomable future.

"May I join you?" Claudette asked waking me from my thoughts.

She stood a little way away. Her hands clasped together, a careful smile on her face. She was hesitant, a conflicted set of emotions danced across her face. It was as though she wanted to approach me, but didn't know how.

"Of course," I replied gesturing to the spot beside me. Though we all were cautious of the two newest members of the crew, I couldn't help but like Claudette. She represented what I wished for. Beauty, femininity and could stand up for herself. I admired her and if I was really honest, was a lot more than envious.

"You look troubled," Claudette noted, taking a seat.

"It's too complicated to explain," I said on a sigh,

"You esteem him." Claudette's single utterance was enough to make me turn away from the ocean. Swinging my legs over the rail, I turned to face the deck. The woman's expression was thoughtful as she watched me. Gazing from crewmate to crewmate, I found my target. Tall blue-eyed Nathaniel was hunched over his cards, a grin tugged at his mouth as he lay down a good hand.

"What can I say?" I said wondering how much the other woman knew.

"Believe me, I understand." Claudette's focus moved to the brooding Macrucio, as he leaned against the opposite rail. He didn't look up from a large pewter ring which adorned his finger.

"So you have no attachment to…?" I stopped myself and looked down at my boots. *Stupid Lennie, stupid foolish, Lennie.*

"Well…"

I raised my head again to find something close to mischief, in Claudette's lilac eyes.

"Nathaniel is clever, kind, gentlemen-like and very handsome," she said, checking off each of his virtues on one hand. "He is a perfect catch; however, my affections are settled elsewhere, and I believe his might be too."

"Thank you." I wasn't sure why I said it, but it felt right. She could have him, if she wanted. She was that type of girl. I felt like an idiot, I had no claim on Nathaniel, yet I didn't like the thought of him with anyone else. I was a mess. At least I didn't voice these things out loud. The boys would surely lock me in the brig.

"You have nothing to fear," Claudette assured, pulling me once more from my brooding. "Nathaniel does not see me as anything more than a conversation partner. Besides, you must have seen how he looks at you."

I shook my head, not allowing myself to think on it or

even to dream.

"I hope you get your wish," I said and I meant it.

Despite all my own issues, I'd seen Claudette and Macrucio together. They felt and argued with such passion, there was no denying their chemistry. This curse was merciless, it made us cruel, or in my case absolutely lost.

"I hope we both do," Claudette said, wrapping an arm around me. I reciprocated and we touched our heads together. With any luck, Claudette and I could become great friends. Perhaps I might even let down my wall, just a little, give it time.

Claudette and I sat together in silence, our minds fixed on our own forbidden affections. I felt lighter for talking to her.

"HAVE YOU SEEN Ned?"

I looked up to find Captain Rourke. "Not today," I said.

Since our return from Rosa's cove, Ned had hardly set foot outside of his cabin. Though he'd never been at the centre of things, he'd drawn even further away from the group. Ned was the ships constant anchor, always there to offer advice and a supportive hand. I had relied on him my whole pirate life. I was sure it was more than 'tiredness' which ailed my friend. I just didn't want to push him, to inflict more of the pain I'd witnessed back at the cove.

"I do wonder…" the captain said. "With the ships decent into emptiness, if we are successful, he could be feeling the sting of his inevitable abandonment."

"I had the same thought," I said.

"Really?"

"We wouldn't see him alone though."

"Of course not." The captain's concerned look didn't abate as I made to stand.

"Would you go and see if you can persuade him to join us? Some fresh air might do him some good."

He kept his voice low but I didn't miss Nathaniel's interest from the card table. Seeing that we'd spied him, he tossed down his cards and headed over.

"Of course, I'll do what I can. Any idea where Ned is?" I asked.

"I spotted him toting a pile of books earlier," Nathaniel said.

"I won't be long," I said, with a nod.

Although hiding places were rife aboard the ship, I discovered Ned in his own cabin. He sat in the dark, his candle long since burned out. Both eyes stared unseeing out at the still waters which surrounded us. His fists were clenched upon the arms of his chair, they never moved. I lit a single candle before I sidestepped the mountains of unread books littering the floor. My heart went out to him, he seemed so lost.

"Ned, is it all right for me to come in?"

The older man was startled by my voice, almost tipping himself out of his chair as he heard it. He turned and I could not stop my gasp. His magical eye had grown dull. His good eye was cold and full of remorse.

"Come here, child," he urged.

I did as he asked, sitting at his feet. I took both of his hands in mine, trying to transfer the warmth. His skin was ice cold. Was he unwell?

"What troubles you, my friend? You haven't been yourself," I said.

"No," he agreed. "I have become what I should have been, many years ago."

"You're a good man, Ned, whatever you've done in the past, there is no need to dwell on it."

He returned to staring out of the window. I searched around the room for something to distract him from his sorrow. My eyes fell on an open book on the dresser.

"How about we finish this one?" I suggested, pulling it into my lap.

Ned's smile was more genuine as he nodded. Most of the tomes lining the salon walls Ned had acquired and though it was no rival to Macrucio's immense stash, he was well read. We had shared many stories over the years. Laughing, crying and enjoying the twists and turns in other people's imaginative drama. Lighting another candle, I began to read.

THE FINAL CHAPTER was upon us, as I struck a match to light yet another candle. We had been reading for hours and Ned was quietly half-dosing beside me. As I turned the page, the ship trembled. This was no shudder from our mythical vessel however. This was a knock. The rough sway of the ship woke Ned.

The hairs on the back of my neck stood on end and I pushed the book aside. I stood, just as another nudge caused the ship to rock from side to side. I grasped for the dresser just as a roar sounded above our heads. Before either of us could exclaim, the candles were snuffed out and the room plunged into darkness. I stared upwards as rushed footsteps echoed through the ceiling.

"Stay here," I demanded of Ned, as I headed towards the door.

Wrenching it open, light shone through the cracks in the walls. Unsheathing my sword, I reached for the top drawer of the table just inside the room, it was well known Ned kept a pistol there. The weight of it steeled my focus. Using the dim light, I sprinted towards the chaos. Our crew had converged upon the deck. Macrucio sat atop the rail feigning boredom, whilst the rest of us stood alert.

The water was choppy and wild around us and as we watched for danger a creature emerged from the waves. It was huge. A large disjointed wooden creature, with sails for hair and wild eyes which were narrowed down at us.

From all Rosa had said, this could only be Hadnlaoy. The sea-witch hell bent on destroying Rosa and all she held dear.

Hadnaloy wasn't human; perhaps she had been, once. Now she was made up of the discarded carcasses of the ships she'd destroyed. Each wreck had been pieced together to create a distorted version of a human form. I stared up at the terrifying figure. The pure volume of her screeching caused the ship to quake.

"Defying me will not help your cause,"

I winced at the sharp piercing voice.

"You have no purpose here," Claudette strode forward; she was the only one without an obvious weapon. "I will not let you harm them and Macrucio shall not follow you anymore."

Hadnaloy's grim mouth curved upwards into a sadistic smile.

"Oh no? He is mine, you cannot have him. Or is that your intention?" The creature cocked her head as she glared, "to kill him out of jealousy? He will never be yours little girl. There will always be something between you. Be it me, that ridiculous curse, or some other woman."

Hadnaloy's scarlet eyes rested upon me. Claudette shifted her gaze, doubt was plain on her beautiful face. I wanted to reassure her of Macrucio's affections; but before I could utter a single word, the witch let out a devilish cackle. She found pleasure in the weakness she'd discovered.

Straightening her shoulders Claudette shook the hair from her eyes; her lilac glare focussed on the witch.

"You think less of me because you have no capacity or humanity to care. I do not tolerate evil, thus my dear mistress," She bowed low in a mocking show of respect. "We are at an impasse."

She straightened again, her stance strong. "Be gone or I shall call for the Sorceress and Rosa, I think they would like to see you again."

This time it was Hadnaloy's turn to look uneasy, though her eyes were wild in her disfigured head.

"What power do you have, to command and threaten me? It was I who gave you power, I can easily–"

"–take it away?" Claudette interrupted, dark humour lacing her tone. "You cannot remove your gift. It is too late, I have grown and these powers have grown within me. They are entrenched in my very soul."

Claudette raised her hand and traced a circle with her finger.

"Oh no you don't!" Hadnaloy cried, shooting sparks from her fingers. Claudette hit the floor which sent Macrucio running.

"Mistress, she's hit!"

I raced forward only to have Butch grab one arm, Nathaniel the other. I pulled free as the witch spoke once more.

"Yes my dear Macrucio, see what she's done, she's

turned on me—"

"—Lies!" Claudette screeched. She jumped to her feet, wiping blood from her face and shoving Macrucio away.

Re-drawing a circle in the air, she brushed her hand across it and the shape turned blue.

Claudette muttered incantations under her breath and the circle lifted upwards, growing wider, before surrounding the ship. Gasps sounded from the rest of the crew, for no one but Nathaniel and myself knew of her magic.

The sea-witch roared in frustration as she attempted to break through the protection. She shot her own shower of coloured sparks and yelled curses. It all proved futile however, as the ship was not harmed.

"You will not break through," Claudette said, wiping at the long gash at her face.

"Defy me again, princess," Hadnaloy screeched, "and I will take everything you hold dear. Your threats are as hollow as the feelings Macrucio has for you."

Still furious, Hadnaloy spread her arms, forcing a blast of air forward. Despite Claudette's protective circle, magic couldn't control the sea. The rush of waves threatened to capsize the ship. I couldn't stop gravity as I fell to the deck; my focus remained upon the enraged creature towering above me.

The witch spun like a top, causing a maelstrom. Spouting like a fountain, the centre widened, we'd be done for if the ship got anywhere near to it. Davy and

Rupert yanked on ropes, hissing with the burn which accompanied it. Butch held onto the rail as he kept a close eye on our surroundings, whilst Nathaniel unravelled our co-ordinates. I scrambled to my feet, racing the captain to the helm. We were too late; Hadnaloy had disappeared beneath her own tempest.

As the water battered me from all sides, I glared at the place where the horrifying demon had been.

"You won't succeed, I won't let you," I muttered.

I sheathed my sword and turned my back to the water as it began to calm. The others were dusting themselves off as they caught their breath. Claudette looked shaken but was still standing, her body quivering in frustration. There was no doubt the woman was a good asset to have.

"Are you all right?" I asked, reaching her.

"Nothing a little salve won't handle."

"It will not hold her off for long," Macrucio said in a bored voice.

He lounged against the rail as he ran his fingers through his hair in casual indifference. Though when he looked to Claudette, pain filled his expression.

"I think it would be wise if—"

"—No," Claudette interrupted. "We are staying. At least for now."

Macrucio held open his arms and she stepped into them. She clung to him for a moment before stepping back. Macrucio gripped the hem of his shirt and tugged hard, ripping off a strip. With a tender touch, he cleaned off Claudette's face. I had seen scars on young woman's face before, this must not have been the first time such a thing had happened. I dragged my attention away from the couple and went to check on the others.

"Who knew? She's a witch too," Rupert said, his gaze centred on Claudette.

"She is not a witch," Nathaniel snapped. "She is like Rosa."

"Exactly!" Rupert countered. "A magical creature, more commonly known as a 'witch.'"

"Nathaniel, is right, she is a chosen one." The captain ignored Rupert's mocking as he too stared at the lilac eyed enchantress.

"What is the plan of action until we hear from Rosa?" Davy asked changing the subject.

"I think we should prepare ourselves for the worst." The captain snapped out of his reverie to observe the shining blade in his hand. "We can begin by pulling guard duty. Lennie, take the newcomers below."

The boys parted as Claudette came to stand at my side, Macrucio remained where he was, his gaze on the now still water surrounding us.

"Shall we convene to the saloon?" I said not looking to see if anyone followed behind me. I checked in on Ned, he had returned to watching out of the porthole. The deluge of water nor the sea-witch's arrival had not changed his solemn state. Without disturbing him, I closed the door and continued on my journey.

Entering the saloon I found Claudette and Macrucio by the portraits. My eye however caught Nathaniel, who stood at the bookcases. He looked so at ease as he thumbed through a worn tome.

"Find anything interesting?" I asked stepping to his side and opening my own.

"Much," he said, his eyes travelling from the tip of my boots to the top of my head.

His close appraisal caused my cheeks to warm. I turned away, trying to hide my reaction. My emotions were in free-fall. One moment he ignored me, the next... Trying not to dwell on it, I grasped a book and wandered away

Pulling out a chair at the table, I curled myself into it and turned the page. Yet as Claudette spoke, the book held little comparable interest.

"Macrucio, you share your mother's features." The fair haired beauty stared fascinated by the pictures.

"Well she had to leave me something."

There was a bitterness to Macrucio's tone but Claudette ignored it. She stepped to the next painting; comparing Ferdinand's face to Cherie across the room before turning.

"You look at lot like your mother, Lennie, yet there's evidence of your father's spirit."

I nodded at the assessment. I stared down at the book I held, the page not sinking in.

"What happened to make your eyes that colour?"

I looked up again, startled to find my face inches from Macrucio's. His stare was curious but the two dark abysses bore into me. I bit back a snide retort and chewed on my lip as I leaned my chair back, putting some space between us.

"I don't know." I pulled the words out, one at a time. I didn't like him being so close. Each time he invaded my personal space I felt disgust and repulsion.

"But you have one green, one brown…that is by no means usual."

"I could ask Claudette why hers are lilac," Nathaniel said swinging a chair around and leaning on the back.

I set my own chair back on four legs. I knew Nathaniel meant well, but this wasn't his battle to fight, I didn't need him to 'rescue' me.

"Hence the reason I asked." Condescension coloured Macrucio's tone. "It is the magic which makes Claudette's that fancy colour. Her eyes were green… once."

He turned his head so Claudette was in his view. She returned his gaze and they shared a fond smile. I swallowed hard, forcing myself not to look at Nathaniel.

"Well?" Macrucio rapped on the table and I narrowed my eyes from behind my book.

"Inheritance from my parents," I replied. "Nothing more."

I let the book fall from my hands. The heavy tome landing on Macrucio's fingers. He didn't cry out, or even speak, but his dark eyes glared at me, and I returned it.

We stayed that way for far too long. His breath was warm on my face and I fought the urge to recoil.

"Stop bothering her," Nathaniel's order broke the spell.

Macrucio was the first to look away, and with a smirk I picked my book back up. Macrucio shoved away from the table, the chair scraping across the hardwood floor.

"Fine, but I will find out." His comment held an ominous tone and I could not hide a shiver.

Macrucio joined Claudette at the far end of the table. They spoke hurriedly, in hushed tones and my eyes drifted back over the printed words I held as I tried to ignore the feelings of anxiety Macrucio created. He reminded me too much of the men I'd known in the past. None of those memories were good ones. Ignoring the whispers, I read a passage, and then re-read it, still not grasping its meaning.

"Do you want to tell me what your book is about?"

Nathaniel's voice was soft in my ear and I gasped in surprise. My heart raced for a much different reason than it had done for Macrucio.

"You have not turned the page since you opened it," he noted.

I snapped the book shut, pressing my palms the cover.

"I think I'll go and get some rest," I sighed leaving the others to their own devices; it would be easier to mull things over in my own space.

I wandered down the hall, my mind full. All of my

thoughts merged together. Ned, the curse, Hadnaloy, Macrucio, the past I needed to reveal. I didn't know what to think or how to stop thinking. I was so engrossed in my inner turmoil; I didn't hear footsteps behind me.

Fingers grasped my arm. My first thought was of Macrucio and I spun, my fist raised. A low masculine chuckle sounded and I blinked. Within moments I was in Nathaniel's arms, pressed against the wall. His large frame surrounded me, making my heart skitter and my nerves return. His scent, a mixture of man and ink overwhelmed my senses. What did he want with me? I looked to my boots as I tried to find something coherent to say.

"Valencia," he murmured touching a finger to my chin.

Our eyes met and my breath caught.

"Does he make you uncomfortable?" Nathaniel nodded towards the saloon. His question held doubt. Was he jealous? Did I show something other than disgust when Macrucio got too close?

"What do you think?" I asked, with more nonchalance than I felt. I fought against comparing Nathaniel to Macrucio.

"I know you said we had to 'forget' our night; but I have to tell you, it is all I can think about."

My eyes were instantly drawn to his lips and I moistened my own. Now he had spoken of it, and with him so close, I just needed to taste the forbidden fruit of his lips again. I felt torn, and angry at my weakness.

"I said to treat it like a dream, not to forget it."

My voice came out in a breathless whisper, as he moved closer still. His warm breath on my face sent shivers up and down my body. In the past, whenever a man got this close, I would recoil. I felt no inclination to run in that moment, if anything I wanted him closer still. The thought both lifted and terrified me all at once.

"Either way, I think our tale has just begun. Your eyes hold stories I can only guess at, Lennie, I would like to hear them one day."

Behind his playful tone, Nathaniel held a seriousness, I could feel it; he knew something or at least suspected. Biting my lip I shook my head, I couldn't tell him, he would hate me; and I couldn't see the light and hope wane in his eyes. It wouldn't hurt him, not knowing. I regained my senses, my mind made up.

"I'll see you at guard duty." I said, ducking beneath his arm and making my escape.

"UP AND AT 'em!" Butch barrelled through the door as the sun set. I squeezed my eyes closed, flinging an arm across my face.

"That was not a shift," I complained.

"Would I lie to you?" Butch sniggered as he pulled me to my feet.

"Remind me why I do this again?"

"I think it's because you cannot live without me,"

A laugh burst out of me. "It has to be something better than that."

Butch shrugged. "A man can hope,"

Grasping my jacket and sword from the bedpost, his lips twitched as he handed them over.

"I am off, my beds a-calling, see you at daybreak."

"Sweet dreams," I called, and Butch turned, melancholy passed over his expression as he closed the door behind him.

Feeling bolstered from my banter with Butch, I set myself at the helm. The wood thrummed under my roughened fingers, my mind dull. I woke from my daydreaming as shouting sounded from across the deck.

"What is there for me here?" Macrucio looked enraged as he flung his arms wide.

Claudette was close to tears. "You cannot even do this for me?"

"I would be lying if I said yes, and I made a promise to never lie to you." With his shoulders sagging, he walked away.

Claudette surged forward, tears in her eyes. "You also promised to stay beside me!"

"Let him go," Davy said, wrapping an arm around her. "When he's ready he'll join us."

"I wish I could believe that." She rubbed her hands together, the friction causing her palms to light up. She pressed them to her face before wandering over to the rail.

"What did you just do?" Rupert eyed her with a mixture of curiosity and suspicion.

Claudette raised a quizzical brow. "I warmed my hands."

"Does it hurt?" He pointed down at her palms; they were alight with a burnished gold.

"Not at all, here." She reached out to him and though hesitant at first, he took her hand.

"Goodness," he said pressing it to his own cheek. "I like you, you can stay."

Claudette's laugh echoed across the ship. Biting back a chuckle, I watched Davy take his turn.

"What's so funny?"

My laughter was replaced by a sharp breath as Nathaniel appeared.

"Nothing" I replied as butterflies danced in my stomach. He smiled as he took up his post. It was central to us all and I knew it would be hard to avoid him.

During my time alone I had resolved to distance myself from him, he'd been too close all ready and I didn't want either of us hurt. As I had decided before, it would be best to leave my feelings within dreams.

The time edged on and hours passed by, nothing occurred. The dark sky was void, even the stars were refusing to shine. I worked hard to keep my mind just as clear as the view.

"Cease this nonsense," I breathed as Nathaniel paced

back and forth, agitation clear in his own mutterings and forceful steps. Turning my back on him, I fought to ignore the distraction, his chuntering did not end however, and with a deep sigh I spun back.

"He is rather tense, I feel." Claudette sported a wry smile as she stepped to my side.

"Yes, some of us hide it better than others."

Claudette nodded. "You do very well,"

With a light pat on the arm; she resumed her position further down the ship. Refusing to rise to either distraction, I gripped the rail and kept a weather eye on the surrounding darkness.

When the off duty crew awoke at sunrise, I stepped down from my post. Though the daily chores continued as normal, everyone's attention was on the inevitable battle against Hadnaloy and her underlings. In Ned's absence, Nathaniel helped Davy keep the co-ordinates in check. I had just finished the usual maintenance of the ship's weaponry, when I spied Macrucio and Claudette mere inches apart, their discussion growing heated as the crew worked around them.

"It was wrong of you to leave us out here," Claudette spat.

"I stand by my decision, I told you I would be here for you and nothing else." Macrucio's calm tone had Claudette clenching her hands into fists.

"You are here, my dear Macrucio; but with me? I see no evidence of that." Claudette turned her back on

Macrucio, her shoulders shaking.

"Claudette, you are my sun." Though he spoke in a whisper, his voice travelled. "I cannot fraternise with these people, I just can't. They are the enemy."

She turned back, tears glittering in her lilac eyes. "When will you learn? Hadnaloy has deceived you! You are naught but a tool to her, as much as you like to think otherwise."

Macrucio shook his head, his Adam's apple bobbing as emotion overtook him.

"I do not understand your logic; she is the person who raised us."

"Raised us? She abducted and used us. At least here they have had Rosa and Ned to nurture and teach them."

They stared at each other, their breath coming in sharp spurts as anger and pain thrummed between them.

"Perhaps we can discuss matters in private." Captain Rourke motioned for them to follow and the stillness of the crew ended.

My chores completed, I settled down to read. Despite the heightened tension, I needed something to keep my mind off the conflict. This time, I got lost in the story, the tale spinning images in my mind creating a world all of its own.

"Come play cards."

Butch's yell broke through my absorption; I clenched my teeth bringing the book closer.

"Busy," I muttered, not looking up.

"Come on Lennie, we need another player."

Before I could reply, Rupert had slung me over his shoulder. In the struggle, my book fell from my hands, its binding broken as it lay open on the deck. There was no missing Rupert's look of triumph as he unceremoniously dumped me into a chair.

Without missing a beat, I swiped a hand across his smirking face. The sound of the connection echoed across the sea. Pushing out a breath I sat back down and glared around the table. Davy coughed uncomfortably, Nathaniel scowled as he shuffled his cards and Butch hid his amusement behind a hand.

"My God, Lennie, you made my ears ring," The redhead said, testing his jaw.

I bit the inside of my cheek as I eyed the bright red mark I'd left. I felt a little proud of myself.

"You'll have more than that if you manhandle me again. You are well aware I won't allow any man to force my hand…not anymore." My words were forceful holding a weight I knew Rupert would understand.

"Was that necessary?" Nathaniel asked staring between the two of us.

"We needed an extra player," Rupert said, holding his chin as he swaggered around the table. Before he could return to his seat, Nathaniel thrust out his arm. The force sent the redhead sprawling across the floor, his chair followed after him. Curses spewed from Rupert's mouth as he pushed at the hair in his eyes.

Nathaniel threw down his cards, "You needn't treat Lennie this way," he said, his low voice held a dark edge.

Leaving the rest of us to stare in his wake, he strode below deck. Not caring about the others, I raced after him. Although I was flattered by his gallantry, I had been handling things fine without him.

"I think I've mentioned before that I don't need your help," I called out to Nathaniel's retreating back.

"Lennie, please." He turned, his shoulders sagging.

"No, there's no need, I can handle Rupert." I didn't move, wanting to remain level with him.

"You are more than capable," he agreed. "But why not let me come to your aid for a change?" He gave a half smile, raising himself onto the next step. His closeness made my head swim and I retreated determined to retain my control.

"Because I don't want it, before I came here, my life was void of control, men made my every decision, now I get to choose."

Nathaniel reached up, pushing the hair from my face. "Forgive me?"

Something burned beneath his gaze and as he pulled his hand back, his fingers shook. A small sliver of fear snaked down my back. I nodded, watching as Nathaniel wandered down the hall and knocked on Ned's door.

With the butterflies settling, I decided not to return to the deck. Another book in a quiet spot, sounded like the right idea. Yet, passing by Ned's room, I could hear

Nathaniel, his agitation clear.

Taking a few steps back, I stopped outside the door.

"Hell, this is too damn hard!" Nathaniel pushed out an exasperated sigh. "I cannot say it but the word is on my mind day and night. A man looks at her and I want to crush him." He growled, punching the wall and I bit back a squeak of surprise.

"I know she would hate me for entertaining the idea; but I want to protect her, treat her like a princess and sweep her off her feet."

I smiled at the images he conjured, all the annoyance I'd felt, evaporating.

"Yet all the men here, they do not see her as even female. They treat her as one of them, it is so strange. Do they not see that she is a lady and should be respected? They damn well know how, look at the way they treat Claudette."

His heavy footsteps pounded from beyond the wall as he paced back and forth.

"Though she is a strong woman, I can see she's broken. Something deep inside her is pained and I want to ease it. Ned, you cannot tell me that you do not see it."

I inched closer, spying through the crack in the door. Despite what Nathaniel had said, I was more concerned by what Ned had to say. I knew I could trust him; but Nathaniel wasn't a fool.

"Lennie's a lady," Ned agreed. "And in her life she has been through so much. She has seen things no young eyes should ever have seen; and done things no young person should never have done; but she has survived. I am surprised that she isn't bitter or cold. She would be more than justified at being those things; she just chooses not to be."

Ned stepped forward, leaning into Nathaniel. I had to crane my neck to hear him.

"Lennie's treated as one of us because she wants to be. She's never professed a need for it to be any different and I think she prefers it that way."

I nodded from behind the door.

"She's neither as delicate as you think her, or as strong as the others believe her to be. She is a mixture of the two, plus a dash of her own magic." His smile was fond. "Just let her be herself and she will continue to be honest, the best way she can."

"One thing I must ask of you," Ned said.

"Anything," Nathaniel's reply was instant.

"Please do not say it, or let her, I beg of you. I would hate for either of you to be gone because of some fickle loss of control."

"I understand the rules; they shall not pass my lips. As much as I want to say those three words, I know the consequences, not until the curse is surely broken. Then she will hear it every day of forever."

I leaned against the wall, my hand pressed against my pounding heart. I was wonder-struck. I couldn't even think the three words he avoided; it was too much to risk.

Yet I knew the feelings coursing through me were far from platonic. What were we all to do?

Before either man could find me, I slipped away. My mind whirling and my heart full of things I had no right to be feeling.

CHAPTER IX
DEVIL'S KISS

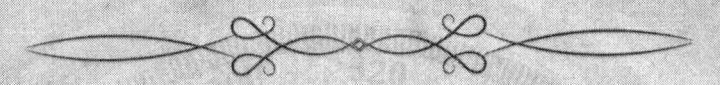

"THIS IS RIDICULOUS." Rupert threw down his sword, the clanging metal grated on my nerves.

"What do you suggest? That we go looking for trouble?" I said.

"No, I just wish that something would happen, all this waiting is far too wearing,"

"It has only been... three weeks." Nathaniel paused, taking in his own realisation.

"Do you see his point?" Davy said pushing back the brim of his hat to stare out at the nothingness, not even the sea-life rippled the water.

"I guess..."

"It is just a ploy." Claudette slumped into a seat, her body vibrating in anger. "She wants us to feel threatened, the more we wait, the weaker she thinks we will get."

"She has a point." Butch pulled out a chair and rested his feet up on the table. His attention centred on the silk scarf wrapped around his wrist.

"What I'm worried about is Rosa; shouldn't we have heard something by now?" I said scanning the sky.

"Well, I guess it would be Ned who'd know," Butch mused.

"He's not well," Nathaniel said, his eyes clashing with mine. "And Caw does not want to leave his side."

"I don't think it's Ned's fault," I snapped as my hackles rose.

"That's what we were saying," the captain assured. "We're in such an impasse it's hard to see where to go next."

"When the captain does not even know the way, it is a sure sign of failure," Macrucio drawled. He swaggered into our group, his lips twisting into a smug smile.

"Just because our moral is at a low doesn't mean we're on the brink of failure." Davy's quiet demeanour transformed from peaceful to ominous through his tone.

Macrucio eyed him with wariness but looked unconvinced. Though the crew were restless and impatient, there was no one more so than Macrucio. The longer he stayed aboard, the surlier he became. He spent his days pacing back and forth, muttering to himself. After nightfall he prowled the shadows, his dark eyes narrowed in belligerence.

I supposed that his ill humour wasn't just drawn from the fact he didn't believe in the cause. Before stepping aboard the *Wilted Rose*, Macrucio had been a captain, now he was just one soul in a network of pirates. He'd fallen so far, in his eyes at least.

As the day dragged on many of the crew wandered

below, either to sleep or find some other entertainment. Butch and I however pulled out our weapons and sparred to pass the time.

"Almost got you there," I teased, as I danced out of reach. Butch stepped forward again, his sword tapping mine. Our faces were flushed with laughter and exertion, as the tussle continued.

Crossing my leg behind me, I shifted the duel. As I turned, the back of my neck prickled with awareness. My unshakable focus seemed to leave me; Butch chuckled as his footwork caused me to topple backwards. Thankfully his quick hands caught me before I could hit the ground.

"Well there's a first for everything," he said, smiling as he set me on my feet.

"Bravo!" Macrucio's applause sounded from across the deck as he drew closer. Butch frowned, not hesitating to push me behind him. I struggled in his grip annoyed at the action. What was his problem?

"How would you like to test my skill, *Bella?*"

I recoiled; the olive skinned man leered at me, making me feel unclean. His eyes scraped across my body. It felt like his hands were all over me. This was nothing like I felt when Nathaniel looked at me. This felt like Macrucio had serious intent. That he could hurt me – and he would.

"We have finished fighting for today," Butch said, his hand tight around his sabre.

"Finished so soon?" Macrucio lifted an eyebrow, his

penetrating eyes never leaving mine. "Come on now, Bruce, the lady has never fought against me, perhaps she could do with a challenge.

"His name is, Butch." I said through clenched teeth. The man knew what he was doing, and disrespecting my friend, had riled me. Just as he'd wanted.

Macrucio's expression spurred me on. No matter how repugnant I found the wretch, he wouldn't see me falter. He had too much Hans in him and I'd never be bettered by such a man again.

"Butch, Bruce, he is naught but a boy, I am a man. Cross swords with me, I might even teach you a thing or two." Macrucio's gazed passed over me once more.

"I very much doubt that," Butch spat, his thin frame blocking me.

"No, I'll spar with him, he might learn something from me." I said. With determined ease I stepped around Butch. Yet as I passed, he grasped my wrist.

"What is my talent?" I asked him before he could argue.

My friend nodded, sighing in defeat. He released me but leaned in close.

"Be careful, this isn't a game," he warned.

"I'm well aware of that." I replied.

Butch offered his sword to Macrucio, the other man shook his head with impatience as he unsheathed his own. It was black. Not just the hilt but the blade. Years of bloodshed had stained the metal.

"Frightened little one?" He mocked, as I stepped back.

"No."

The word slipped out and from our mirrored expression we were both surprised. Inside I shook. This man could kill me; I knew it and he would enjoy doing so. He smiled with malevolence, twisting his hand so his inherited ring glinted. The eyes of the skull glowed like rubies.

"You lie *preciosa*, remember I can always tell," his laughter rang out as he lunged.

I didn't falter and together we matched, step for step. Each swing of a sword was blocked, each step countered. No blade ever made contact with flesh. We twirled, my concentration so focussed there was no room to feel dizzy. All I could see was Macrucio's wicked smirk, one that reminded me of dark rooms and bruises. I wasn't fighting Macrucio now; it was my former life I had to eradicate.

"Macrucio stop!" Claudette ran full pelt, followed by Butch and Nathaniel, I ignored them.

A glint in Macrucio's eye flipped my stomach; before I could stop him he took hold of me and yanked me into his arms. His fingers bit into my skin and as I fought to free myself, he mashed his lips to mine. Frozen, I let it happen; he couldn't hurt me any more than the memories that battered the back of my eyelids. The stench of stale breath, the sensation of coarse hair across my skin and the sloppy way men would use me. Macrucio tasted dark, a mixture of whiskey, anger and evil. He was no different than the men of my past, I was not a person, a woman to be cherished and loved. I was purely a vessel he would use and throw away.

Over the wretch's shoulder I spied Nathaniel, his bright eyes wide, his jaw set. He was breathing fast, and his hands were clenched into fists. Butch had grabbed him, but even with his unusual strength, he was struggling to hold the bigger man back.

"Don't Nate, we have no idea what he's capable of! We want Lennie alive." Butch warned. How own face flushed in anger. The urgency and frustration in Nathaniel's expression caused something to shift within me. How dare Macrucio touch me, in such a way? He had no right!

Anger welled within me, I was not that weak, defenceless little girl anymore and I could remain still no longer. With clawing hands, I grabbed for his hair, his clothes, anything to push him away. He held on fast, clamping down my arms and driving the kiss deeper. I gagged and struggled but he shoved me backwards. My spine connected with the rail and pain shot through me. Nathaniel's cry mixed with my own as Macrucio moved his attack, trailing his lips down my jaw and along my neck. The lewdness he spouted as he continued his ministrations were foul. Before I could scream or cry out again he'd clamped one of his hands across my mouth. My muffled cries amused him, his hot breath across my skin were accompanied by a chuckle.

"Stop!" Claudette repeated, her voice strained.

My eyes pleaded with her, begged to her to stop him. I couldn't fight him off and his lips and hands were becoming more probing. I hated feeling so weak. Claudette didn't look at me. Her body shook as she watched Macrucio. With a clenched jaw, she raised her palms. Pushing them forward she created a rush of air that forced us apart. Macrucio only stumbled at the force, but I was knocked to the ground. My body trembling, I covered my face with my hands.

"Come on, Lennie."

Nathaniel tried to help me to my feet but I shrank away from his touch as Claudette stalked towards Macrucio. With much effort I hauled myself onto my feet by the rail. Ignoring the concerned and pitying looks of Nathaniel and Butch.

"What does this prove?" Claudette exclaimed, her arms flung out in a wild gesture, punctuating her frustration. "She is not the enemy, none of them are."

"If she is the most proficient fighter they have, then Hadnaloy will have no trouble in crushing them." He pointed towards me.

I narrowed my eyes glaring at him. My fingers itched to scrub at my mouth but I wouldn't give him the satisfaction of seeing me affected by his attack. The bastard!

"For a truth seeker, you have a knack for spouting

lies," Nathaniel snarled stepping forward and with clenched fists, stood to his full height. He was a good five inches taller than the wretch.

Macrucio's fingers still pointed upward, the ring he wore no longer glittered. His inherited jewellery spoke the truth, according to what Rosa once told us, and he had been speaking falsehoods. He didn't believe me weak. His expression was stony and mutinous as Claudette spoke to him in whispers; his stare pierced my soul as he let himself be led away.

"Are you all right?" Butch asked, his forehead creased with worry.

"Well, yes," I muttered as I finally swiped my mouth – Macrucio's dark taste still lingered there. I looked up to find Nathaniel's eyes focussed on my bruised lips, I pressed them together, wanting to hide.

"I am glad you are well," he murmured. "Though I'd change that shirt if I were you." Shaking his head, he walked away.

I looked down, my shirt which had once belonged to Butch was torn. I crossed my arms, covering some of the skin on show.

"How about we raid the rum store?" I said as I turned to Butch. He nodded holding out his hand. The thought of touching him repulsed me at first, but this was Butch, the worse he could do was tease me to death. With the minutest of hesitations I took his hand and let him pull me towards a few hours of numbness.

"LENNIE?" MY GLAZED eyes turned to Claudette as I entered the room.

"Shh," I urged, pointing. Butch lay flat out beside me, his drink-laden sleep rendering him unconscious. "I should be strung up, for what I've done." I said, my words slurring.

"Why on earth would you say such a thing?" Claudette asked, closing the door.

"Kiss…" Guilt crept in behind my intoxication. The small sane part knew there was nothing feel guilty for but that part of me was not in force here.

"That is the subject I wanted to discuss, although it seems you are not in the right mind however"

"No, don't leave!"

My indulgence was far too great, my body refused to co-operate. Claudette stepped closer and one incantation later, my self-inflicted fog cleared.

"Thank you," I said, shaking my head.

"I wanted to apologize, for Macrucio," Claudette said.

"Why should you take that responsibility? He's the one at fault." I frowned up at her.

Claudette swallowed hard.

"Ours is a complex attachment. The curse makes it very difficult to show our affection," she paused, swiping away tears. "He likes to test me. Please do not take offence but he has done such things before with many women to gain a reaction from me, this incident is no reflection on his feelings for you."

"So you're not angry?"

"Of course I am, but not with you," she smiled, clutching my hand, "Are you alright? I wish I'd got to you sooner, stopped him, he's…" She stared down, her fair hair covering her face.

"I can't say that it was pleasant, but I have had much worse happen."

"Please, say no more. I shall try to keep him away from you, but I cannot promise anything."

"I'll be fine," I said, "I'm prepared for him now." I began to slur again, and my eyelids felt heavy. Whatever Claudette did, was wearing off.

"I shall leave you to sleep off your ale, my friend," she said.

"Thank you, Claudette I've held such fear. I would hate for you to think ill of me."

"I know, but please, no more fretting, there is no use in being fooled by the charms of men."

CHAPTER X
DECISIONS

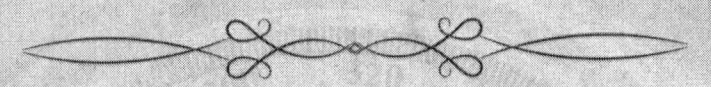

"WE SHOULD RETURN to Rosa," Rupert said as he slammed his tankard down, the amber liquid sloshing over his hand and onto the table.

"Well I think we should wait." Nathaniel turned his expectant gaze on the captain.

"Valid suggestions, both of them." He began. "Yet, Rosa has never steered us wrong before, she will inform us when she is ready."

"What if we die before then?" Macrucio's question hung in the air. He wasn't anyone's favourite person since the kissing incident, so his comment was ignored.

I paid little attention to the conversation, my mind twisted with faded memories and the disturbing dreams I'd had since Macrucio's mouth touched mine. Nathaniel too had become distant, he spent much of his time with Ned. I had avoided the older man's cabin since I'd overheard them talking, but if I was honest I missed their friendship.

Tugging off my hat, I brushed away the creases marring my forehead; the conflict amongst our small crew was too much of a task, even with the worry of what waited for us, somewhere below the water line. I stared unseeing out of the porthole, waiting for something to pull me from the maudlin mood.

"What happened to Caw?" Claudette's voice succeeded. The creature which had flown from Ned's neighbouring cabin, now flapped in agitation, circling the saloon. Passing the porthole, he stilled, his onyx eyes stared with more clarity than the average feathered creature. Screeching, Caw manoeuvred his way through the opening and took flight. I watched his colourful feathers disappear behind the clouds.

"Perhaps being reclusive isn't for him?" Rupert sniggered.

"Ned shouldn't be cooped up like that," Butch stood shaking his head in genuine concern.

"He'll return to us in his own time," Davy said.

"How do we know? He's never been this far away before." Butch clenched his fist as worry marked his face.

"I do not know him at all well, but from what I have seen, he is not a foolish man. I say we should leave him to work through whatever ails him, and support him when necessary." Claudette stared around her, awaiting a response.

"Here, here," Nathaniel agreed, leaving the table to settle by the bookcases.

Caw's sudden departure could only mean one thing, Rosa needed to communicate.

THE WATER WAS calm, the skies clear. As I leaned against the rail a breeze lifted my hair from my face and brushed over my skin, easing the strain. I opened my eyes in time to see Caw emerge through the clouds. His impressive multi-coloured wings reminded me of a rainbow. As he flew closer, it was plain he clutched a scroll within his talons.

"Caw brings a message, caw."

Heads turned as the he circled the skies. Captain Rourke stood, joining me. He caught the scroll as the bird flew past and Ned appeared on the deck, the first time in a week. Caw settled himself upon the older man's shoulder, swaying as he came to sit at the card table.

"What does it say, Captain?" Claudette asked as she approached.

'Dear All

I am troubled to hear Hadnaley has made her presence known. Though I am unsurprised to find she is less than happy with Macrucio and Claudette's decision. We each have to be on our guard and cautious, so the ship does not fall foul of her terror. By now the crew of her fleet are well aware of the newest members of our own; I hope they will show mercy in the face of their old friends.'

Macrucio scoffed as the captain continued.

'The real reason for my writing, is that I have been in contact with the Sorceress. She is pleased each of the heirs has been returned to what she calls, their 'most rightful place.' She has bid me to instruct you in the following: Please do as I ask immediately; gather at the saloon table, once there, await further instruction.'

As Captain Rourke uttered the final sentence, the crew hurried to the saloon. Anticipation was plain on every face that surrounded me as we waited. I sat mute staring into space, though when I had spared a look at Nathaniel; his expression was of pure calm. This would be the first time I had interacted with the creature responsible for the curse. It both frightened and thrilled me all at once.

Minutes stretched out and no-one spoke. A single foot tapped out a disjointed rhythm and all eyes were drawn to the culprit. Macrucio linked and unlinked his hands whilst a muscle worked in his jaw. He fought hard to contain whatever demons lingered within him and an ominous look dimmed his eyes.

"Heirs to the Eight Brothers of *Rosa Del Mar*, you are once again united."

The voice echoing through the room was clear and strong, as though its owner was right there with them; yet only nine bodies remained.

"I do not fool myself in imagining your effort to

reunite has anything to do with my yearning for the *Wilted Rose* to always have a heartbeat, you have your own. You wish for freedom. Absolute freedom." She paused.

"You long for companionship, emotional attachment," she spat the words as though they tasted foul. "I can understand such needs, though I know too the outcome of losing yourself to trivial things such as heartbreak. The aftermath of such a blow is branded onto my heart as deep as those you wear."

I stared at my sleeve, not needing to pull it back; I knew the pain of both ills.

"I could easily hand over your wish, bid you adieu and watch my hard work fail with every broken heart. There is also the welfare of my ship to consider. I do not want it deserted again. Thus I am conflicted in my choice."

The tension mounted with each word and the silence dragged on. I held my breath, my fingers crossed beneath the table.

"I need more time to deliberate over your request. I shall reveal my answer within four and twenty days. Keep your hearts close my crew, for no good shall come to those who leave them with another."

The chandelier hanging above us flickered, signalling her departure. The silence that followed was eerie. Shock and disappointment tinged the atmosphere, as the Sorceress's words settled. I had a strong inkling that she wasn't deliberating. We were nothing but toys, to do with as she wished. Her similarity to Hadnaloy left a bitter taste in my mouth. I felt fooled. All of our effort could have been for naught.

Annoyance, anger and hurt had my hands curling into fists. As I stewed, the silence was shattered by a toppled chair. I snapped my head up in time to see Macrucio race to the door. In his haste, he wrenched it from its hinges and threw it aside.

The crew followed, concerned at what he might do. The lamps were dim, yet we were able to see Macrucio as he turned on us. He looked deranged; his hands were yanking at his hair from the roots.

Mumbling in Spanish, he stumbled around in circles. Nathaniel and Davy came from behind, grasping his arms and steering him from danger. He succumbed, falling to his knees in despair. I searched for Claudette, she was stood frozen her lilac gaze trained on Macrucio. Where he knelt caused my heart to drop. Beneath him was the blood red stain, the same one which had given the ship its infamous reputation.

"You promised!" Macrucio's angry cry was strangled as though it was extracted from him unwillingly. "You promised, when we came here, all would be well, that we would be free from restraint. Hadnaloy was right, you were lying."

Macrucio buried his head in his hands, a muffled howl came from deep in his chest and Nathaniel and Davy stepped back.

"Say it Claudette, say it and let my suffering end."

"I will not." She shook her head, her body trembling, her hands clenched at her sides.

"We cannot live through this together. We have been inseparable since childhood and I have wanted to say the words so many times. The Sorceress has no intention of changing her mind." Macrucio accused, echoing my earlier thought.

"She has no desire of releasing us. I do not want to be in a world that does not have you in it. I cannot do it but you can." He tugged at his hair again.

"You can release me, tell me how you truly feel, in that heart of yours, and you will go on... and I will die, knowing."

"Macrucio, please don't make me do this." Tears fell down Claudette's cheek as she pleaded.

Macrucio's mood shifted again, his eyes held a coldness which matched his mocking smile. He got to his feet, steadier now.

"I knew it. I have always known you were weak. You have hidden your weakness behind the power Hadnaloy bestowed upon you. Behind the smoke and flash, you are nothing but a whimpering harpy!"

He spat out his words, each one a slap. Claudette's head snapped back as if he had struck her. Her elfin face was pale as she watched him carefully.

"No magic can finish this." Macrucio continued. "You promised to stay with me forever; yet you stand there able to end this differently and unwilling to do so. Tell me the truth and I will spend the afterlife happy and content in the knowledge you feel the same as I do."

Claudette scrubbed her hands across her cheeks; her lilac eyes were hollow as she stared at him.

"What about your promise? If I do this, you will not stay with me."

"This world does not need me. I am of little importance, a mere bump in your journey. You, *mi corazón*, you are here for a reason."

The coldness in his eyes softened, as Claudette approached him. Each step she took looked like torture, as though the weight of the task dragged her in all directions. I wanted to pull her back, gag her even. Yet my feet were stuck, shock rooting me to the floor. Claudette's journey ended and she pulled Macrucio close. She rested her head against his chest as he stroked her temple.

"Say it." His plea carried through the silence. "Tell me,"

The words cracked as he buried his face in her hair. My legs shook as Claudette pressed her lips to his, their arms winding around each other as they locked eyes. Tears streamed down Claudette's cheeks as she mouthed the phrase she had been forbidden to utter.

"You can do better than that." Macrucio's tone held a harsh edge as he urged her to speak.

There was a long pause. I felt Nathaniel move to my

side but I didn't dare look away from the tragedy about to unfold.

"*Te amo*," Claudette's voice shook and Macrucio fell.

A pained cry ripped from her, as her knees gave way. She sprawled over him, her body convulsing in agony and grief. My gaze was pulled to the dead man. His eyes were closed as though asleep. In death he had lost all of his malice, he looked like a small boy, lost. Guilt welled inside me as I stared as his still form. A small part of me was relieved, he could no longer touch me.

"No!" Claudette's cried through her sobs and all thoughts of me, were forgotten. "My love, awaken, please, my darling!" Claudette begged.

She brushed the hair from his face and wiped the tears still glistening. As she continued to sob, she lifted his hand. Pressing a kiss to it, she removed the ring he'd inherited, placing it on the third finger of her left hand.

"I will go on my love; I will go on as you asked of me. With your name as my own you too, will hold a place in history."

It was awful. The sight of a man so tortured, lying dead upon the deck. It was enough to send me into my own spiral of sorrow, yet a question would not abate. Why did he die so fast? All of our parents lived long enough to marry, bear and even hide their children. Was Claudette's magic to blame? Was her power enough to annihilate the man she felt so much for?

My mind was made up, the Sorceress was no better

than Hadnaloy, she may have other methods, but her cruelty held the same power. The faery-witch was a heart collector, someone who stole the beating, emotion filled organs for her own amusement, and I knew I had to end it before someone else succumbed to the curse.

CHAPTER XI
LOST INNOCENCE

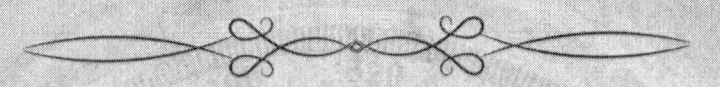

CLAUDETTE'S BODY SHOOK as she screamed into my shoulder. I stroked my hand down her hair and across her back. I didn't speak, or throw around words of comfort. They were all empty and meaningless. Around us the men stood waiting, their hats doffed, heads bowed.

"Come on Lennie," Nathaniel said touching my shoulder.

I stared up at him, unsure of what to say.

"Lennie, let her go, we need to get her to bed, it's not healthy being out here." Nathaniel urged. I knew they really wanted to move Macrucio but Claudette was still clinging to him.

"Claudette, come on," I urged.

The devastated girl said nothing, but her cries grew louder.

"Come on dear, let's get you to bed," Captain Rourke had knelt beside us. Prising my friend from my arms.

"No," she sobbed, as her fingers slid from Macrucio's. Butch met them as Captain Rourke helped her stand. With an ease of a giant, he lifted her into his arms, cradling her like a child, and descended the stairs.

I remained on my knees beside the body. He looked to be sleeping there. Barely hours before he'd attacked me and almost violated my body. I'd hated him, I'd feared him and now, looking at his lifeless form... I pitied him. All he wanted was to hear Claudette say the words and now we all would pay. Claudette especially.

"Walk with me?" Nathaniel asked helping me to my feet.

We walked in silence, both of us lost in what had just happened.

"Dead... just like that," Nathaniel breathed. "Yes." I nodded, trying to avoid the darkness threatening to overwhelm me. My thoughts drifted to Claudette and my heart broke for her. What would she do?

Nathaniel led us to an empty room, the one he shared with Butch. One side, I guessed was his, was strewn with books and papers. With gentleness, he sat upon the bed and pulled me into his arms.

As he rocked me back and forth I tried hard to not think about the dead man and his love, somewhere aboard the ship. The horror of what had just happened hit me and I began to sob. Tears flowed unchecked down my cheeks and I nestled my head against Nathaniel's fast beating heart. An incident, as tragic and disturbing as the one we'd just witnessed flickered through my memory:

It was late, almost three, my last client had gone and I was finally alone. I had already stripped the bed but his odour lingered as I curled up on the mattress. The self-loathing I'd come to rely upon surrounded me, the numbness was more of a comfort than the alternative. The sounds of others padding around the Châteaux, filled my semi- consciousness as I tried to forget the night's events.

As I was about to enter the black hole of a dreamless sleep, the door creaked, signalling a visitor. 'Please don't be another client,' I thought as I uncurled myself. It was Hans; his large frame filled the doorway, blocking the light from the hall. He looked wild, dangerous and drunk, a half empty bottle dangled from one hand.

"Valencia," he growled, stumbling towards me.

Sensing this was not one of our heart-to-hearts; I sat up and shifted backwards. My body slammed into the metal bed frame, hard. Hans was strong and somewhat agile, even when intoxicated. He leapt forward grabbing me with ease, the bruise came fast and I gasped.

Hans didn't acknowledge my discomfort as he wrenched me towards him. Our bodies colliding. In our closeness, I could smell the stale alcohol and cheap perfume that always clung to him.

"Mon Oncle, vous me fait mal!" I cried desperate for him to awaken from his drunken stupor.

"Hurting you, am I?" He gripped me tighter, before throwing me back on the bed. His sky blue eyes narrowed in frustration.

My last ray of hope died within me, my Uncle's intention was all too clear as he wrenched off his braces.

"Oncle," I pleaded "Je taime, ma pas comme ca!"

Tears drenched my face as he advanced on me, the bottle in his hand falling to the floor staining the bare wood. Blind panic raced

INHERITED ✺ 231

through me as I looked for a shield, anything to stave him off. I hoped my cries were loud enough for one of the girls to hear.

I grasped behind me, searching for something to aid my cause. My fingers grazed my father's sword; the distinctive hilt seemed to jump from the wall into my very hand. Before I could blink, I screamed. What was that noise? Was that me? My body was spattered in crimson, as I fell from the bed, onto Hans' lifeless body…what had I done?'

The waking nightmare ended and my face was drenched in tears. Swiping them away I stared around me. I was still in Nathaniel's arms, his eyes filled with concern as he murmured to me.

"You are all right, Lennie, everything is over." Seeing I was alert, he paused, his hand grazing my face, "Are you well?"

"It was a nightmare, a disturbing daydream that is all," I said attempting to brush it off and failing miserably as my tears continued to fall. His wretched blue eyes, they were far too familiar.

"You gave me quite a scare," Nathaniel said.

As the memories tried to resurface, I pulled in calming breaths. Nathaniel's soft voice had me focussing on him, I stared at his mouth, rather than his eyes, not wanting to compare them to the ones in my memory.

"Who is Hans?" he asked.

At Nathaniel's question, I tried to exhale but found nothing there. The walls were closing in on me as I fought to breathe, I had to escape. Stepping out of Nathaniel's arms I began to see black spots; they clouded my vision, making me sway.

"Lennie," Nathaniel murmured, confusion etched upon his face as he reached out and steadied me. I shook my head without answering. Stepping out of his arms once more, I walked through the door, closing it behind me.

The corridor was deserted and for that I was thankful. My need to escape had me falling through the saloon door. To my relief the room was deserted. With my heart pounding, mind whirling and my entire body tense, I curled up in the corner of the room. Enfolding my hands over my head, I broke. Tears fell with unabashed sorrow and I let the darkness take me.

"WHAT DO YOU mean 'she's distressed'?" Ned's voice reverberated through my aching head.

"She seemed to fall into a stupor after it happened. She kept repeating a name." Nathaniel sounded strained, his voice shook as he spoke.

"What was it?" Ned demanded.

"Hans."

The door creaked further, and I uncurled myself. Ned knelt before me, his face haggard and drawn.

"Child…"

"Ned, I didn't mean to disturb you," I mumbled into his shirt.

He pulled me close, resting his cheek on the top of my head. "Come on little one, I know this brings back all kinds of memories but the boys are fretting,"

Looking over Ned's shoulder, I found Butch and Nathaniel hovering in the doorway, their foreheads creased in concern.

"How's Claudette?" I swiped at my face as Ned's turned greyer still. He let me go but kept hold of my hand.

"From what I hear, she wanted to be alone."

"I understand." I could recall my own experience. When I'd reached the ship, I locked myself away. Too afraid of what I had done and what others would do to me.

Ned's rough finger brushing back and forth across my knuckles, brought me back to the present. I watched his actions for a moment before I pressed my face into his shoulder.

"I don't want to lose his trust or friendship," I began. "But I have to tell him, don't I?"

"Yes, my girl, if he feels as you do, it will not matter."

He pressed a kiss to my forehead, sealing his blessing and gently setting me upright. I trusted my old friend above all the others and knew his advice and approval would be right to follow.

"Come on, Butch," Ned said turning to the younger

man. "Let us leave Lennie and Nathaniel to talk."

Butch nodded letting Ned pass by him. The young blonde's intense gaze then focussed on me. He stepped further into the room, crouching as Ned had, so we were at eye level.

"Before I go, I just have to ask, you are well, aren't you? You haven't riled the curse too, have you?"

"No, those words haven't been spoken, not by me at least," I replied.

Relief flooded his face and he squeezed my hand, turning he raced through the door. I didn't miss the glare he sent to Nathaniel before closing it behind him.

"Sit with me?" I asked.

I stood and Nathaniel joined me at the table. He hadn't spoken at all but without prompt he took my hand and brushed his thumb over my knuckles, just as Ned as done. His hands too were rough, but not as gnarled. I covered his fingers with my free hand. Looking right into his eyes I moistened my lips. *Here goes nothing...*

"I should've told you this a long time ago. I was too afraid before; worried you would reject me for what I once was."

"Why would I reject you?" Nathaniel said, shaking his head. Confusion causing another frown.

"You'll see," I murmured, pushing out a breath I started my tale.

"As I've mentioned, I was born in Spain; though I grew up in France. What I didn't tell you is that my mother was raised in the *'Quart de Plaisir,'* a fancy name for the underworld. It was a place where the glamorous and the rich could mingle with the depraved and poor. It was no different from their everyday lives. They had people catering to their everyday needs; why not have slaves for their pleasure too?"

I realised how bitter I sounded and shook my head, continuing with what I hoped, was a more detached tone.

"My mother was one of the many women who worked and lived in a large house in the centre of the district. Most people simply called it the 'châteaux.' The owner was Hans; he oversaw the business, took care of the girls and managed the clientele."

Nathaniel's hand jerked as I said the name.

"My mother, it was said, shone like a diamond."

I gestured over Nathaniel's shoulder and he turned. It was a portrait of a beautiful woman. Long blonde hair, porcelain skin and ruby red lips. Nathaniel brushed his fingers across the back of my hand, urging me to continue.

"None of it mattered when my father, Ferdinand, arrived. He was handsome, well-built and dashing. He rode with his fellow Musketeers, defending towns and villages in rural France. It was after such a battle my father came to the seaside village where my mother lived. The locals informed the men of a place where those in uniform would be welcomed."

Ferdinand followed his comrades to the 'Quart de Plaisir.' The Châteaux of disrepute blazed temptingly from across the main plaza. With tentative steps he approached it, unsure what he would find there. Stopping beside his friends, he spotted a woman upon the porch steps, her nose buried deep in a book, an odd sight among the surrounding men and their partners. Reaching her side, Ferdinand doffed his hat and cleared his throat.

"What, pray tell, do you read?"

"A mere novel, kind sir," she replied closing the book, to look up at him. Her green eyes held a plea and though Ferdinand didn't know what she needed, he felt a great urge to protect her.

"You look cold," he said pulling off his jacket and wrapping it around the woman's under-dressed form. As she opened her mouth to thank him a voice sounded.

"It's fifty francs to spend your time."

Ferdinand looked up to find a tall, blue eyed man. He wore an elaborate brocade waistcoat weighed down with gold. In one hand he held an open bottle and in the other, a lit cigarillo.

"Hans, he—" the woman began.

"—No, it's alright." Fumbling with his pocket book, Ferdinand handed over the money.

"Is there a place we could talk?" He asked, taking the woman's hand.

Blinking in surprise, she nodded, leading him through the house. Reaching an empty room, she locked the door behind them. They spoke for hours, revealing their pasts and their hopes for the future. The young woman, Cherie, had been borne to the life she now lived. Hans had always held a soft spot for her and treated her like a pet. Yet despite her special treatment, she loathed the occupation. She dreamed of a modest house, with a husband and children to complete a respectful life. He in turn wished for a place to come home to, his life was filled with danger and violence, but he wished for peace.

Ferdinand spent fifty francs each night of his leave, just so he could talk with Cherie. He became enthralled and wished for her hand. Hans felt threatened by the young rugged Musketeer, Cherie brought in the most revenue and he could tell she had distanced herself. Accusing Ferdinand of not paying one night, Hans and the young man wound up brawling in the square.

Adapt at all elements of battle, Hans grasped a sword from another patron. Ferdinand however wasn't armed. Though usually unnoticed, the sculpture in the squares centre held a sword. The face of the pirate holding it seemed to call to Ferdinand. The maiden with him resembled Cherie, this fact settled him.

The elaborate handle of the sword glinted in Ferdinand's hand. He ignored the burning sensation taking over his arm as he continued to fight. The duel was well matched; both were good swordsmen. Yet with their fading verve, Ferdinand's youth came into play. Managing to nick Hans across the face and using some expert footwork, he got the Château's owner to the floor. Hans, his ego bruised, forbade Ferdinand to enter the 'Quart de Plaisir' ever again. Cherie was inconsolable as her love was led away…

"He was rescued by the *Wilted Rose*, as he lay fraught and beaten on the beach. Yet when he was able, he returned for Cherie and they eloped. Once married, they returned to the ship and it wasn't long before I was born…" I stared at Nathaniel for a second, weighing my words before continuing.

"When my mother learned of the curse, she talked to the other women on the ship; no one believed it, not until…"

"Until…?" Nathaniel said, urging me to continue.

"Captain Rourke's mother, Kathleen, she was the first one to perish. Then one after the other, heirs and their wives began to go missing. Some moved their children to safer places. My mother bundled me up and took me away. I was left at the Châteaux. She knew, despite the debauched lifestyle she had once led, the women there would look after me."

"Do you know what happened to your mother?" Nathaniel reached across the table and brushed his fingers down my cheek. I leaned into his touch before answering him.

"From the stories I was told, she tried to get back to the ship and my father. I can only guess she managed to do both, before dying. I've never been told how her life ended. My father, it's said, went mad with grief and passed away soon after."

"This still does not answer my question," Nathaniel said softly. "Why would I reject you for your mothers past?"

"Because her past and mine are one and the same." I stared down at our intertwined hands, I felt as scarred as the table they rested upon. I knew the inevitable was on the horizon.

"You mean..." Nathaniel began, realisation draining the once shining blue of his eyes. I nodded as solemnness overtook me.

"I need to understand," he insisted.

"You truthfully wish to know?" I wanted to give him a chance to walk away, I wasn't sure I could stop once I started.

"Please," he pressed, "your mother must have thought she was right, to leave you there." Something close to anger burned deep within his expression, but he repressed it well.

"She did," I agreed. "The ladies always assured me my mother would return and she would take me away, to live some wonderful existence."

I spread my hand, as though creating a new world.

"Even when things got worse. I clung onto the hope. Not so much that she herself would come for me; but that someone would. The fighter within me just didn't want to remain feeling weak."

"Yet your mother did not return."

Nathaniel's words were soft as he brushed the hair away from my face. I knew he was waiting for me to fill in the gaps in the story. Though I feared doing so, afraid it would harm my connection with him. I gazed into his bright blue eyes and found strength there, a willingness to take all the information and listen. With a small sigh I continued my tale.

"Where is Victoria?"

Uncle Hans had wrenched open the door of Clara's boudoir. Though he was dressed for the night's proceedings, his face was already flushed and his eyes were glazed. I sat reading fairy-tales upon Clara's bed. At Uncle Hans's entrance I had scrambled back towards the wall, making myself as small as I could. I had always been afraid of my beloved uncle when he was drunk.

"You gave her the night off, Mon Chéri." Clara used a soothing tone as she tried to placate her master. It didn't work. Uncle Hans' jaw was clenched and stress caused his entire body to shake.

"I have got two important customers downstairs and no Victoria, what am I to do?"

In his annoyance, his gaze landed on me. My eyes were wide as I cowered in the corner. He was not averse to slap or kick out at me when he was in this mood, I still had a tender swelling under my hair, from the last time.

"Ah ha!" he exclaimed stalking across the room. He grabbed my arm yanking me from the bed.

"Get her ready, I want her downstairs in half an hour."

I whimpered in his bruising grasp.

Clara took a step towards us, her expression pleading, "She's just a child Hans, Cherie's child."

"I wouldn't care if she was the Princess of Sheba, I want her ready."

He flung me at Clara. "Do not make me ask again."

His voice was low, but no less threatening. His eyes resembled oceans, which threatened to drown anyone who stood in their way.

Clara waited until Hans had slammed the door, before urging me to the dressing table.

"Come now; let us play dress-up."

I had been through the same make-up routine before, though the last time I'd primped in front of the mirror, dolled up in rouge and lipstick, it had all been for fun. This time it felt wrong. I refused to look at my own reflection; the game had become far too sinister.

Clara painted my lips and styled my hair. The older woman's hands trembled as she dabbed on powder and sprayed perfume. The corset and floating skirt were both far too big for my childish frame. Yet Clara's shawl hid the flaws, creating a womanly shape.

"Do not cry, Ma Chérie," Clara's own voice cracked as she brushed the tears from my painted face. "I'll stick close beside you tonight. Just pretend you are a princess in one of those books you love."

The smile she bestowed upon me was false. Too much sweetness lifted her lips and too much sadness clouded her eyes. She opened the door and beckoned me through it. Struggling to play along, I trembled as I took slow and tortuous steps towards the main staircase. I'd never been allowed into the public parts of the house after the sun had set. The lamps flickered, throwing dim light across the crowded space below me. As I descended the stairs, music floated up and the light became clearer revealing a sea of men.

I stalled in my descent; there were at least three men to each woman. All of them were dressed in tailored suits and smelled of strong cologne. Clara urged me on as others turned to look. The *females in the crowd stilled in shock, their mouths gaping as they saw me. To them I was the child they helped to raise, the little girl they read to at night before they began their evening's work. No-one expected to see me on those stairs.*

I spotted Uncle Hans; he stood a head above the rest of the crowd. His hair covered his face as he spoke to two exceptionally well-dressed gentlemen. As I reached the bottom step, his blue eyes clashed with my mismatched ones. Something close to regret flickered within his, but it was gone long before I could tell. Replacing any doubt was his snake like smile. He gestured me forward and I stepped into hell.

"This, my good men, is my protégée." He pulled me close and I struggled not to recoil. "She can sing, dance, play piano and is well read."

Uncle Hans grinned proudly, rocking on his heels.

"Scrawny one though." The man, who stood closest circled me. His gaze was speculative, as though he examined cattle rather than a girl.

"She makes up for it in spirit." Uncle Hans assured.

I tried to calm my breathing. I may have been young but I was no fool. I'd lived in the Châteaux long enough to know what went on when the lamps were lit.

It wasn't that which affected me so much, though that in itself was terrifying, it was Uncle Hans' betrayal. He was the only father figure I'd ever known. I'd trusted him to love and protect me; yet here he was, displaying me like a piece of meat ready to be sold to the highest bidder. Was I worth so little to him, or was it that he had planned on this all along? Perhaps this was the reason for all of his attentiveness, all of his kindness and teaching was to prepare me for a life of strange men and wrinkled sheets. The thought made me sick to my stomach.

"I will take her." the second man's voice was high and clipped.

His ratty face held little softness and his long nose stuck up, as though something foul smelling just wafted past. With much flamboyance he flipped open his pocket book and pulled out a large amount of currency.

"A discount is in order, do you not think? Her mind is not why I am here, after all." His guffaw turned heads and sent shivers up my spine.

Nathaniel had tensed so much, that my hand had become cramped within his. I flexed it and he loosened his grip, an apologetic look flickered across his face before the tension returned.

"Are you sure you want me to continue?" I asked.

Despite his obvious discomfort, he nodded.

"Well…"

My eyes widened as the ratty man wrapped his fingers around my arm. Clara's expression was anxious but she was helpless under Hans' restraint. All I could do was let the man drag me through the crowd and down to the guest rooms.

A candle set in a pink tinged lamp sent a ruby glow across the ceiling. The smell of roses overpowered me as I pulled in a steadying breath. In my peripheral, I saw the man move. I turned to find him stepping out of his shoes and yanking off his braces… before I could protest the world went black.

THE FIRST THOUGHT I had upon awakening, was how cold I felt, the second, the all-consuming pain which filled my entire body. Something close to despair rocked me to my core, rendering me mute. The dim light bouncing off the walls shone with feebleness upon the bedside table. A pile of crisp fresh notes lay there. Payment for services rendered. I turned away from them and pulled the covers over my head, all the while praying for death or anything which would allow me to escape.

"She's a baby, Hans, how could you?"

Raised voices from beyond the door startled me awake once more.

"You weren't here. I needed someone."

"Blame me, Hans, lie away your guilt. I want nothing more than to snatch that precious child and leave this hell, to take her away from all this. The only thing stopping me is the guarantee of a hearty meal and a roof over her head."

The door swung wide and light poured through the opening. I buried myself further into the blankets. I heard Victoria gasp as she took in the aftermath of the night. The older woman strode to the bed; pulling me to her she marched upstairs, not looking back. I merely clung to my favourite mother figure, too lost to cry out or even thank her.

Returning to her suite, Victoria bathed and dressed my bruised and ruined body. As she brushed the knots from my hair, she *comforted me with words of solace and understanding, before tucking me into bed.*

I curled beneath the covers. Tears fell hard and fast as I willed myself to sleep. Life would never be the same…

"So," I sighed, brushing away my tears. Nathaniel turned towards me, his face too was damp.

"No wonder you avoided me when I first arrived."

"I was scared," I agreed. "Your eyes are the exact same colour as my uncle's – as Hans'" I paused with a shake of my head. "There are no traces of him within you, despite my initial fear, I knew that. Your eyes hold only kindness. They express all you mean to say without having to speak the words." I squeezed his hand and a small smile lifted my lips.

"I also know you would never use your stature to intimidate or hurt me."

Nathaniel nodded, a tenderness replacing the torn expression on his face.

"How long did this go on?" he asked.

"Almost two years. Victoria and Clara were always there to dry my tears and hear my woes; it was not the perfect childhood by any means, but there was no choice. What Hans wanted he got. He would not have been easy had we argued or refused – though I did attempt at times. I was always beaten down," I said.

"How did you escape such a life?" Nathaniel resumed caressing the back of my hand. The gesture proved comforting.

"Ned appeared. I just knew, from the moment he held out his hand, I could trust him. He arrived just in time and I left."

I half-smiled at the memory. "When I first stepped aboard this ship, I hid from the captain; I didn't know who to trust besides Ned. There was Rosa of course but she overwhelmed me with her beautiful sadness."

Wistfulness filled my expression as I recalled my early days.

"By the time Butch, Rupert and Davy arrived, I'd become comfortable, more open. They were like brothers and I fell into step with them. They taught me to play cards and hold my liquor; all the while I bettered my skill as a swords-woman. They took me in as one of their own and I never demanded to be treated any different. I didn't feel so threatened by them; they gave me little reason to feel that way."

"Until I arrived?" Nathaniel said.

I pressed the back of Nathaniel's hand to my cheek.

"I guess I cannot always tell, what made those cogs whirr?" I teased.

He smiled cupping my face with both hands.

"I am thinking," he began "that the woman who I hold right now, is the most intriguing, brave and beautiful soul imaginable. I could not hope for a better person to allow me into their life."

He pressed a kiss to my forehead. The touch of his

lips against my skin lightened my heavy heart a little. He hadn't run away, that was a good sign.

"Thank you." My voice broke on the simple phrase and renewed tears spilled over in my relief. I had laid my soul bare and he hadn't shied away. He knew my darkest secrets and that was enough. There was no judgement nor resentment, just friendship and that was what I had hoped for, at the very least.

CHAPTER XII
TRUTHFUL AWAKENINGS

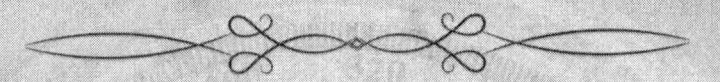

THE SOFT LIGHT of the setting sun was all that illuminated the room. It threw strange shadows across the unused bed. The table beside it held a forgotten candle, burnt out and useless. A single chair rocked back and forth in a solemn rhythm, the creaks of the wood echoing in the silence. The creator of the noise stared unseeing through the porthole as the sun fell behind the horizon awaiting the morning.

"Claudette?" I said.

My voice sounded loud in the quiet room. The chair stopped rocking as its owner turned. I couldn't hold back my gasp, Claudette's once magically colourful eyes were now a dull black. The two abysses had nothing left.

"I cannot stand to see the sun, the new day used to mean hope," she intoned.

"I wanted to tell you I've been where you are now; but that would be a lie." I murmured, moving further into the room. I perched on the bed clasping my hands together.

"My victim—" I stumbled over the word. "—Was a man

I regarded as family, an uncle of sorts. It's not the same as your soul-mate."

"But he died." it wasn't a question.

"Yes,"

I touched the sword at my hip. "I was so frightened by the power the curse held over me. I asked Rosa to put an enchantment upon my weapon. Only those I mean to harm can be damaged by it now. I could never carry it with me otherwise."

Claudette reached out and we touched hands. I tried not to show any reaction to the cold temperature of her skin.

"Thank you," Claudette said, her words were full of emotion but her eyes remained flat. "I can see from your example the pain will ease."

"It'll never leave you," I corrected. "You'll just get stronger as the day's pass. I'm here for you, we all are. We'll get you through this."

I squeezed Claudette's hand before releasing it.

"There are moments when I think I will be fine. Then I recall that he will never again grace my doorway, never talk to me of our future, to even defy me against my truth and light."

Claudette stared down at the oversized ring on her hand. The skulls gemstone eyes were as jet as her own. I nodded, swallowing back a lump threatening to form.

"We're here, you're never alone in this, remember that," I said squeezing her hand once more to ensure she heard me.

Claudette nodded, as her eyes strayed out to sea.

"I won't let you grieve alone," I said, leaning over to press a kiss to the top of her head.

"Thank you." came her shaky reply.

"I'm just a call away, don't forget," I said pulling away and leaving her in peace.

I shut the door behind me. Pushing out a breath, I leaned against it. Despite my conviction, I knew Claudette wouldn't be fixed in an instant. Four years later and I still felt broken.

"How is she?"

I turned to find Ned. He hovered in his own doorway across the hall.

"She knows we're here for her," I replied.

The older man looked grey again and before I could say more he closed the door, wiping his eyes as he went. I watched him go, worried for the both of them. The moral on the ship was dropping rapidly, we had to find an answer soon.

As the day continued, my thoughts did not wander far from Ned. I was so unsure of the change in him, though I had narrowed it down to Claudette and Macrucio's arrival. Leaning against the rail, I tried to link the two occurrences, what did they have in common?

"May I ask you something?" Nathaniel asked, coming to stand at my side.

"Of course," I replied.

"How did Ned come to be here? I understand why the eight of us are." He gestured between us. "Where does Ned fit in?"

With my lip between my teeth, my gaze wandered over to the lone older man, reading behind us. Caw was sat atop his shoulder, his head bowed, following his companions finger as he traced the words.

I replied to Nathaniel with a question of my own. "Do you ever wonder about Rosa?"

"Of course, I have read much about her in my father's journal, but there are still things left unanswered."

"Why she's no longer part of the ship?"

Nathaniel nodded. "Amongst other things."

"Rosa and Ned have both spoken of the time leading up to her departure and his arrival. It does not make for joyful listening," I warned.

"I never believed it would."

I leaned back against the rail, my eyes trained on the space where a figurehead should have sat. Nathaniel stood close by, waiting for me to begin.

…Soon all Eight Brothers and their spouses were feared dead. The Wilted Rose *set sail again, holding neither captain nor crew. The lack of heart aboard the ship made the sailing hard and slow. The Sorceress returned to the ship during this 'wilderness' period and was aghast at Rosa's lack of discipline. In a fit of rage, the Sorceress banished the wooden woman from the ship. Rosa was sent to an abandoned cove in the centre of the ocean.*

Whilst in her prison, Rosa was visited by an injured man. He pleaded for his health in exchange for labour or price. Rosa did not question him; but fashioned a wooden eye. Her payment for her kindness was simple, watch over the Wilted Rose.

Though still banished, Rosa could now oversee the ship through the eye she'd made. The Sorceress rewarded such ingenuity by allowing Rosa's power to influence the ship once more, though she was not granted permission to return.

The next task for Rosa and her lone crewman was to locate the heir of each brother and return them to the ship. Thus the crew would be reunited. The injured man boarded the ship, ready to serve. Searching and familiarising himself with the layout, a small noise alerted him to the fact he wasn't alone. Following the sound, he found a child. The young boy was hunkered down in a rum barrel below deck. He was in fact Brandon Rourke, the former captain's child. Rosa had of course known of the child's whereabouts, they'd communicated in a fashion and she'd provided for him. Ned's presence, however, would ensure he wasn't reared wild.

With Ned's knowledge and Brandon's tenacity and leadership skills, the two of them manned the ship. With indirect help from Rosa, the years progressed with them finding four more heirs.

"Goodness," Nathaniel breathed.

"Ned told me the story, years ago, he was the man Rosa found. She fixed him up and sent him here. No one knows of his life before this, not me, not even the captain; and Ned half-raised him."

"A great amount of mystery then?" Nathaniel too had

turned to look at the oldest member of the crew.

"I think it's more of a tragedy," I mused, I had a few theories when it came to our Ned. "He has always held such compassion and willingness to help others. I think he uses that to make up for something, something terrible."

"Could it be repentance?"

"Perhaps…"

THE DREAM SHIFTED from lush green meadows covered in wild flowers, to cells of a dark, damp prison. The contrast almost awoke me right there, if not for the echoing cries that tugged at me.

"Oh, no!" The wailing voice brought tears to my own eyes, I had to help them. They were in pain, so much anguish. Yet I was locked away. My hands clamped around the ice cold bars and I shook them with all my might, there was no way out.

"Wait!" I yelled, as I kicked, yanked and clawed at the metal.

The cries ripped through me. I had to help them; they weren't going to make it. My gut instinct told me that soon it would be too late.

I awoke with a start pushing the tangled hair off my face and I stared around me. The sobbing, though quieter, had lingered. In the stillness, the noise carried through the cracks in the ship's walls. Rushing, barefoot from my bed, I grasped for my sword before following the sound. The urge to comfort the person was as intense as it had been in my dream, yet I knew being unarmed would be a sure fire way of getting myself killed.

At first I thought it could be Claudette. Stopping outside her room, I peered in. My friend was sleeping in her rocking chair. Silent tears tracked down her face. Touching the woman's hand, I found it again cold. Grasping the blankets from the bed, I covered her sleeping form and shut the door.

Reaching the saloon, I paused. The crying was louder now. Easing myself through the half-open entryway, I stepped into the room. Taking my time I looked for the source. My eyes widened as I found it. Ned was sat beneath the portraits, his head in his hands. His body shaking as another sob ripped through him.

"Oh my goodness, what's wrong?" I exclaimed discarding my sword and sinking to my knees. Pulling him to me, I rocked him back and forth.

"My wife, my baby…"

His words were muffled but I understood, staring around me as I stroked his face. What had upset him? We were sat beneath a portrait of Rosaline the stunning wife of Edmund, the one brother without a history.

Across the room another painting depicted mysterious man. The cursed pirate had possessed sandy coloured hair and brown eyes. He'd been the resourceful one; the one who could get out of scrapes almost unscathed. My attention returned to the man in my arms. My fingers brushed through his tousled hair; the grey had sandy streaks threaded through it.

Ned's crying had just about ceased, though a few watery hiccups jostled us. His face turned up to me, as my mind circled around a hundred, 'what ifs'.

"You know, don't you?" His expression was both relieved and frightened.

"I don't want you hurt," I murmured. "Your secret's safe with me, Edmund."

It wasn't until I spoke his true name, that everything slotted into place. Claudette wouldn't be alone any more. Her father was alive and so close. The reasoning behind Ned's behaviour started to make sense too. The silences, the frailty, it had all to do with seeing his daughter for the first time in over twenty years.

"I have never understood this, how I came to be the last one." Shaking his head he lifted his arm, in the dim candlelight the outline of the brand was there for me to see.

"How did I not notice?"

"I keep it hidden," he said, wiping his face. I continued to rock him as we sat together in silence.

"It doesn't make any sense," I said.

"No, it doesn't," he agreed. "But all I can tell you is what I know."

Sniffing back another tear he gazed off into his past, his voice shaking to begin with:

When the realisation of the curse hovered over the ship, Edmund had urged his pregnant wife to leave, even rowing her to shore himself. He felt guilty for sending her away; but he needed to know they would be safe.

After the ship's demise, he returned to the place he had left his small family. He found no sign of them. He searched for years, there was no trace. As he moved from one seaside town to another, he asked the locals if they had noticed a mother and young child. At one such place, someone mentioned they had seen a woman fitting Rosaline's description. Though the townsfolk spoke of dark clouds which had stolen the woman and child away. Edmund knew all too well the power that Hadnaloy held and he was convinced that it was she who was the culprit.

Insane with rage, he raced to the water's edge, cursing the demonic witch and urging her to fight him. None of his threats or demands were ever answered. Failing his attempt at revenge, he attempted methods of suicide. Sure that if Hadnaloy had taken his family, they would most certainly be dead. In dying, he could join them and together they could live in paradise.

Each attempt at death; be it poison or hanging, was in vain. He was rescued each time. His last try was to weigh himself down with stones and wade out to sea. As he lay back, staring at the moon, he thought with deep longing of his wife and child. The weight soon pulled him under and he felt consciousness leave him.

"Awaken," a smooth voice demanded.

Edmund retched as someone kicked him in the gut. Water spouted from his mouth and a sharp throbbing pain clawed at his face. He pressed his hand to his right eye and pulled in a ragged breath. Where there had once been clear vision, pure emptiness remained.

"Wh-What have you done?"

"Be thankful it was not your neck."

Edmund stared into the face of Hadnaloy, the sea-witch, her lips twisted into an evil smile. Edmund's blood ran cold, his prayers would finally be answered, and he would die.

"Somehow, for some reason, she let me go. One minute I was to be executed, the next I had washed up at Rosa's cove." Ned shook his head, still confused.

"What happened when you got there?" I asked.

"Well…"

Edmund stumbled through the catacombs. A sure and steady voice guided him; he was in no shape to help himself. Before he was freed, Hadnaloy had dealt the final blow. She had relished in telling him in great detail, that his wife and child had been murdered.

Edmund was somewhat aware of his destination. He hoped Rosa would take pity on him and maybe grant him his wish. He reached her, soaked to the skin and covered in blood. She allowed him a small time to wallow in his sorrow, before she made her decision.

Edmund would return to the Wilted Rose *under the guise of 'Ned'. He was to complete a quest; his mission was to round as many heirs as he could find, to secure the curse's demise.*

The newly dubbed 'Ned,' remained wary of the task, yet it

would allow him to think of something more than his grief. It gave him a purpose.

The most significant change would be his new eye. Using a single petal from the wooden rose she held, the figurehead fashioned a small orb. This was no ordinary peep-hole however; it would be Rosa's view aboard the ship and a vital link to the figurehead herself.

Arriving aboard, Ned re-introduced himself to the home he'd once known. Upon further investigation he picked up clothes and weapons, as well as his loyal pet, Caw. Hunting through the hold, Ned found another essential, a crew mate. Young, Brandon Rourke, the son of the ship's former captain, had hidden himself away. He'd lived alone on the ship's meagre resources, and his own inherited map, waiting for someone to find him. Together they used their tools to search for the remaining heirs.

Ned drifted off in my arms, he had been through so much and all alone, he'd survived, but at what cost? I watched the flutter of his eyelashes; his face was less tormented in sleep.

CHAPTER XIII
HIDDEN MESSAGE

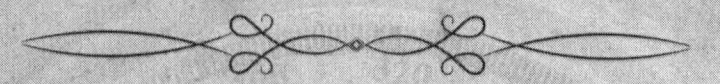

CARDS WERE FLUNG and expletives growled as the boys became embroiled in their game. Throwing down my own failed hand, I left the table. The way the group was carrying on, I wouldn't be missed. Wandering below I passed by Ned's open door, I smiled as I saw he rocked back and forth with a book in his hands. The colour had returned to his cheeks and his magical eye sparkled as he took in the prose.

"Did I not teach you anything? It's rude to stare," he said not looking up from the page.

"Just passing through," I countered.

It cheered me to hear his responding laugh as I wandered by the door.

Strolling onward, I headed into the saloon. It was empty, just as I liked it. The musty aroma of unread stories filled my nose urging me to begin a new one. Though trailing my fingertips along the spines, I found nothing but used tales. Lighting a few candles, I dragged a chair closer to the bookshelves and grasped for the first book within my reach.

"Tales of flight perhaps?"

The question caught me off guard, and the chair beneath me wobbled. With more ungainliness than grace, I toppled off the chair. The book I'd chosen hit the floor a second before I did.

"Ouch," I muttered, dusting down my britches, checking the heels of my hands for scrapes.

"I am the cause of many an injury for you," Nathaniel said as he aided me to my feet. I rolled my eyes, ignoring the tingle of my skin as he touched it.

"It would help if you didn't sneak up on people."

Nathaniel chuckled at my exasperated tone. He stooped to collect the fallen book. A frown appearing as he read the cover.

"What is it?" I asked as he turned the tome my way. It held the symbol of the *Wilted Rose*, along with an inscription; which read *'Para ganar una respuesta que uno sólo debe mirar dentro'* – 'to gain an answer, look within.'

"I think we should give this an audience," I said.

"Lead the way," he said gesturing towards the open door.

The brightness of the midday sun had me blinking as I stepped back onto the deck. Ned had moved from his room but still had his head bowed over a book, the rest were still entangled in their game. I wasn't sure how to explain what we'd found, but stepped forward to try anyway. Before I could speak, however, Caw rose from Ned's shoulder, screeching. He swooped with such speed and I yelped in shock. His long talons snatched the book, leaving scratches on my skin. The bird circled above us, his anxiety plain.

"Caw!" The captain bellowed and the bird stilled, dropping the item into the captain's hands. Now calmer, the bird took up residence on our leader's shoulder.

"Where did you find this?" The captain's tone was both awed and coarse.

I took another step forward, my wounds seeping blood. "I found it amongst the bookshelves."

The captain lifted a shaking hand and opened the cover. Where pages should have been, a lacquered box sat. Its lid was covered in multi-coloured gemstones; they shone like a prism in the sunlight.

"I haven't seen this since I was a child." Captain Rourke spoke almost to himself. "It was how I contacted Rosa after she'd been banished. It was my one lifeline to the outside world."

He placed the book on the table and pulled out the long, thin box. Lifting the delicate lid, He revealed a scroll. The parchment was as stained and ragged as the map he always carried.

"So Caw wasn't the only way to communicate then?" Rupert eyed the bird.

"No, son." Ned came to stand beside me. Pulling a handkerchief from his pocket he wrapped it around my bleeding hand.

"Caw didn't arrive until Ned did." the captain's eyes

hadn't left the parchment.

"Shall I?" The older man asked, reaching for the box.

Something shifted in the atmosphere as Ned's hand touched the lacquered wood. The ship came to a stop, the sails dropped and waves ceased our movement. Ned unravelled the scroll, mouthing the words as he read.

"What does it say?" Davy blurted before ducking his head in sheepishness.

"Nothing of importance." Ned did not meet my curious look. He took his time rolling the scroll before placing it back inside the box.

"May I?" The captain reached for it.

"Of course, but the message isn't for you," Ned said cryptically.

"Who then?" Nathaniel asked.

Captain Rourke read the scroll with a frown. "Lennie, I think you should take a look."

"Me?" I asked, what did I have to do with some old message toting contraption?

With a swirling stomach, I took hold of the offered note. My heart pounded in anticipation, but the parchment revealed nothing. I turned it over, still nothing. Confused, I turned to Ned.

"Just wait, child," he advised.

I returned to the scroll and the butterflies resumed their dance. A lone phrase was now scrawled across the page...

'It is up to the fighter to battle for the treasure of truth~

Sorceress

"Anything you want to share?" Rupert said.

As I stared at the words, I wondered what I should do. Placing the scroll back in the box, I stared at the expectant faces gazing back at me.

"I've no clue as to what it means," I said.

"Can you share it?" Butch asked.

"I don't know."

Ned stepped to my side. "I say we leave her be and whatever she's been told will be revealed in due course."

"Thank you," I said, taking a seat at the card table. Nathaniel joined me, mirroring my solemn stare and contemplative silence. Despite my mind being full of 'whys' and 'how's', I hadn't missed the ship's sudden stillness. During the reading of the scroll the anchor had dropped. Could it be that the ship waited for my moment of clarity?

"You look troubled, can you not share anything?" Butch asked, crouching beside me.

"Treasure," I said.

"This ship is not used to pillage though"

"No, but there are all kinds of treasure."

I looked up at Butch, the cogs whirring inside my head. If there was treasure to be found there was only one way we were going to find it.

"That's it!" I exclaimed racing to the captain. "I need the map, sir!"

He handed it over without question and I laid it out,

staring at the shifting shapes I waited for them to still. Soon a cross bloomed from ink stains.

"Look!" Nathaniel grasped for the scroll I held. The script read something new.

'Where there is a cross roads treasure awaits ~Sorceress'

"This cross marks whatever the Sorceress wants us to find."

The crew stared at me, their eyes wide.

"How did you do that?" Davy gasped.

"I don't know. This must be what the Sorceress wants us to find… whatever 'this' is."

The anchor had risen at my revelation and the ship had begun to sail again. I had been right!

"Come on girl." The captain left the table, his low voice carried as he stroked the ship's helm.

"This is our own journey, no magic will help us with this one, boy." Ned said as the ship continued on at a steady pace. "We will have to keep a weather eye."

"Well you have that covered," Rupert said with a wink, nudging the first mate.

As the others plotted of what they'd do with their presumed buried plunder; Nathaniel and I congregated in Claudette's cabin. After filling our friend in, the three of us sat contemplating the strange occurrence.

"What I would like to know, is why Lennie was chosen to spearhead the mission?" Nathaniel said

"You do know each of our fathers had a skill that enforced the power of the curse?" I informed them.

"Is that true?" Nathaniel asked, leaning towards me, always ready for another story.

"Of course, though my father's skill was swordsmanship, not geographical prowess."

I moved aside the blanket covering the porthole. I stared through it, perplexed, the sun had been covered by darkening clouds, it wouldn't be long before it rained.

"Maybe the Sorceress wishes to test you?" Claudette suggested.

"I don't think it will be gold."

Heads turned as Ned appeared in the doorway.

"There's no such need for it, it has to be figurative treasure."

"Could it be punishment?" Nathaniel whispered.

His question had me staring right at him. Guilt filled his eyes and my stomach dropped

I had thought of it too, though my own stemmed more from thinking ill of the Sorceress, rather than my burgeoning feelings.

"Due north, I think we're here," Butch's cry from above muted any response, of which I was very thankful.

"Let us see what awaits us," Claudette whispered.

Surprise stilled me for a moment, before I took hold of Claudette's offered hand; the enchantress hadn't left her room in weeks. Nathaniel and I shared a hopeful look as we followed her lead. Ned following close behind us.

CHAPTER XIV
TREASURE CHEST

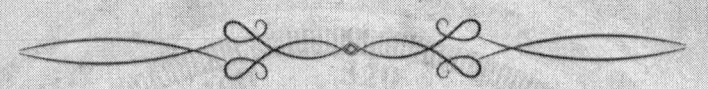

"SHOULDN'T WE SLEEP on it? Perhaps go back and wait for daylight?" Butch's attempts to sound casual fooled no-one as we scrambled up the beach.

"What use is it to turn around now?" Rupert asked, wiping his forehead.

"I say we start digging." Davy thrust his torch into the sand and trudged towards the trees. Caw followed, swooping overhead and out of sight.

"We could, but do we really know what is out here?" Nathaniel questioned as he too set down his lit baton.

"Nathaniel has a point," Captain Rourke said squinting down at his map, holding it near the flame.

In the dim light I spied an object hanging from Butch's belt, he grinned catching on.

"Here," he said placing his compass in my palm.

The dial faced upwards, swirling in erratic patterns before settling. Walking away from the group, I centred myself and worked on instinct. With steady steps I followed the needle to a part of the beach hidden by sand dunes.

When the dial stilled, I sat bowing my head, I focussed on the sound of the waves and the breeze blowing through the palm trees.

"I pray this is what you truly want." the distorted voice seemed to rise from the sand itself.

I opened my eyes to find the crew had created a circle around me. They all searched for the source of the ominous speech, finding no-one.

"It is what we want," I replied as the others nodded in agreement.

The ground trembled beneath us and I stood on shaky legs. One step, then two, I launched myself towards Nathaniel. Turning in his arms, my mouth formed a perfect 'o' as an ornate chest appeared.

"What could it mean?" Claudette asked; her piqued curiosity causing her eyes to return to their unusual shade of lilac.

"Lennie, you called it, perhaps you should be the one who opens it," Nathaniel said, though I had to peel his hands from my waist.

Stepping back into the circle I knelt before the chest. Carvings covered the entire wooden surface and intertwined as though telling a story. Although I studied it with care, I could find no clear indication to where it began or ended. Even the metal holding it together was intricate; as if the builder had sewn the pieces together. It's detailing was delicate and accomplished. The lock wasn't where you'd expect it either. Instead of a keyhole, a faint outline of the *Wilted Rose*'s symbol gazed up from a small square plaque. I raised my arm and pushing back my sleeve, I placed my wrist upon its twin. Though it hadn't seemed difficult before, breathing grew easier. Even my head felt less cluttered. All the stress and tension had melted away.

Warmth radiated from the metal and through the cracks in the wood light began to spill. As it brightened, it reminded me of dawn. A moment passed before the chest opened. I shielded my face as the light poured; behind my arm I saw stars. As it dimmed, I edged closer, peering inside.

"My goodness," I breathed, plucking a small parchment note from the box.

'Dearest Valencia,

It pains me to leave you in a place you will loath as much as I did, but I know the girls at the Châteaux will look after you, until I can return. My word as your mother, I will not stay away forever.

Be proud of whom you are my daughter; for there is naught greater than the love a woman can hold. You are my greatest achievement and my most beloved treasure.

I leave my love with you,
Ta Mere'

Tears threatened to fall as I read the note. I had never known the woman who'd borne me. In nineteen years, all I had learned of my mother's past came from second hand information. Yet in my mind, the wonderful yet flawed woman, could be some fictional character in a novel I had read. This note proved Cherie had existed and that she'd cared for me.

"*Mere,*" the French term for mother fell from my lips as I dove my hand back into the depths of the chest. Another ragged piece of parchment lay at the bottom. With eager hands I turned it over and my breath caught.

'There is no worse trial than trust. To not trust those who are responsible is to drown. There is need, hope, adoration and hate-where do you set your allegiance?'

The strange note was written in the same cursive as the message which got us to the beach. I looked over my shoulder, though I saw my crew-mates I felt something else linger, somewhere beyond them, but not too far away.

A shiver ran through me as I returned to the letters. What had caused this to happen and why now? Before I could ask myself any more questions, the lid snapped shut. Silence echoed around the island as I returned to the outer circle.

"Here let me" Nathaniel said grasping my hand.

"Does anyone else wish to try?" I asked, as I folded my legs beneath me.

"What do we expect?" It was Rupert's turn to look anxious.

"I'm not sure; I received a letter from my past and something more cryptic."

"May I?" Ned asked as he reached out for the two pieces of parchment.

Staring at the letter from Cherie; a fond smile lit up his scarred face. Yet picking up the second his forehead furrowed.

"Please, Ned, do tell us what's going on," Rupert's frustration was clear through his facetious tone.

"I don't know, son, what concerns me most is what this means."

"Should we proceed? what do you suggest?" Rupert's question came more serious now as Ned's expression sobered the group.

"I don't see the harm in hearing the truth," the words felt like a stone in my stomach but I gave a shaky smile as Nathaniel stood.

"Go ahead," the captain urged and the tallest member of the crew stepped forward.

Kneeling in the sand Nathaniel mimicked my actions. Resting his wrist upon the metal, he was granted access to the chest. His breath hitched as he pulled out a single scrap of parchment and mumbled the quote scrawled across it.

'Those who dwell on their heart lead lost and worrisome lives, let us live through nothing but thought and structure. Frail emotion and trivial tales hold nothing but hurt and pain.'

"This is no one's truth," Nathaniel murmured. "This is just cruelty against what I myself believe."

"If it's true to one, it doesn't make it true to all," Ned called out to him.

The older man's wisdom eased the worry in Nathaniel's eyes. Scrunching the page in his hand, he returned to the circle.

"What worries you son?" Ned asked.

Though the worry had eased, there was a pensive look on Nathaniel's face.

"Lennie received a letter from her mother, I had hoped." He paused. "I had thought my mother, or even my father would have left me something. Even the smallest of letters."

Ned sighed. "Perhaps your journal is letter enough? That is filled with your father's notes, thoughts and findings."

Nathaniel reached into his pocket, the well-worn journal flopped open in his palm.

"I guess…" he murmured. "I suppose I was selfish to wish for my mother's thoughts and ideals."

"There is much to learn, my boy. You'll know of your mother soon, keep reading that journal, she's sure to shine through somewhere." The older man gave Nathaniel an encouraging smile.

Nathaniel gave a stilted nod and closed the journal.

"Thank you," he said.

"Let's carry this on shall we?" Ned replied. Staring around the circle, his good eye trailed to our redheaded crew mate.

"Go on, Red, take a turn."

With a nod, Rupert traded places with Nathaniel. His hands shook as he claimed his own gifts. The crew watched with interest as Rupert lost himself in his own letter. His eyes reddened and he cleared his throat.

"Damned sand," His muttered thickly as he brushed the back of his hand across his eyes. His damp fingers reached back into the chest revealing one more.

'Numbers are facts, they are stable and bold. Leave all your mischief to those who are less able. Become both sides of a single coin.'

The captain took his turn next, the group laughed as he read aloud, the letter from his father. The former captain's flamboyant yet steadfast information left everyone warm and hopeful. The second item stalled the captain however.

'Leaders are left to chance, do not be the one who gets caught out, devils rise amongst the ranks, beware of mutinies and trust those closest to defy you.'

"Another sentiment which goes against the recipient's beliefs," Ned's confusion caused more doubt to simmer within my conscience.

Butch looked uneasy as he sank to his knees. He hesitated, holding his wrist over the metal before touching it to his skin. Light flooded his face as the chest opened and with bated breath he stared at his own personal treasure.

"You can do this Butch," I called.

Plunging his arm inside, he retrieved the pair of notes. A smile lit up his face as he held up his treasure.

"Wonderful," he said, leaving the chest and settling beside me.

"It truly is," I agreed, squeezing his arm.

"What about your second one?"

'There is naught more dishonest than dishonesty to yourself. Be true, there is more to life than infatuation; use your strength to overcome it.'

"Does that mean something to you?" I asked.

"It makes sense," Butch said, avoiding my gaze. Which was odd, Butch was usually more than willing to share anything with me.

Davy took his turn, striding across the space, as the chest slammed shut again. Before he found his letter, he set about drawing runes in the sand around himself. Settling in front of the vessel, Davy drew one more symbol in the air and rolled up his sleeves.

Davy's first treasure was a piece of paper covered in

symbols. The code would have taken me a long while to decipher, but Davy's eyes quickly filled with tears, as he folded the page and traced yet another symbol there. Claudette and I shared a look and soon the fair haired enchantress went to comfort him. On her journey she picked up a wayward shell, turning it over in her hands. As she reached Davy, the item has transformed into a gilt frame. Opening the back, she urged him to place his treasure within it. Flipping the frame over, she lay it in the sand. The message was now safe and easy to view.

"Thank you, my dear," he murmured. Touching her cheek, he drew another character with his fingertips. Nodding in understanding Claudette returned to her place in the circle.

Turning back to the chest, Davy pulled out his last gift. Though there were yet more runes, the emotion Davy showed with the first was no longer apparent.

'Deciphering truth is much your task; the gift you possess is noble and grand. Never forget the truth can hide amongst the characters, you have to look harder than most to find it.'

Claudette was the last to step forward. Her excitement was palpable as she retrieved a single sheet of paper.

'The truth is closer than you think; loneliness is not yours. Your punishment is over. Macrucio is in paradise...of this I am sure.'

"What about my personal letter?" Claudette asked.

My eyes flickered to Ned but left him just as quick.

"Did my mother not care? Did my father not want me to know of his hopes, or his dreams for me?" Claudette's voice was constricted, her deep lilac eyes which had returned, shone black once more.

"I was not given one either" Nathaniel began but Ned silenced him with a raised palm.

"Child, please come here."

Claudette went to him, taking his offered hand.

"Listen to me," the older man commanded.

Each word carried weight. Everyone stilled awaiting his wisdom.

"Your father loves you; believe me, despite there being nothing to prove it in that shiny box. You do have something of his you know?"

"I do?" Claudette looked up at him, curious.

"You inherited his resourcefulness. Each of the heirs have been handed down a skill. Edmund possessed the knack of keeping himself, his ship and his loved ones out of danger, the best he could at least."

I fidgeted in the sand, trying hard not to look too eager, would Ned reveal himself?

"Despite being captured, I'm sure he searched for you and your mother for years."

"Thank you," Claudette murmured, burying her head into Ned's chest. He stilled for a second before patting her back in comfort.

Dawn broke as we turned back towards the ship, Ned and Claudette leading the way, their heads bowed in deep conversation. Rupert frowned, watching them.

"They've become close, all of a sudden. What do you think it means?"

"Ned must have his reasons," I said, hoping the older man would do the right thing.

CHAPTER XV
FIRST MEETING

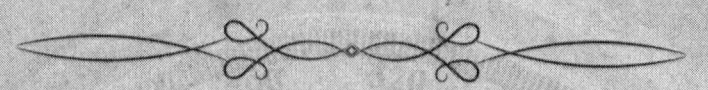

"**I THOUGHT YOU** were playing," Rupert groaned, as I shifted a card from one side of my hand to another. I squinted and pursed my lips, trying anything to prolong the torment of my crew mates.

"If you don't stop, I'll come over there and—" Butch trailed off looking somewhere over my head.

I felt Nathaniel's presence, even before he laid his hands on the back of my chair.

"You were saying?" There was humour laced in Nathaniel's tone.

"Just that Lennie needs to get a move on…"

The blonde looked disgruntled as he glared at his cards. I found the whole thing too funny to be annoyed at being 'rescued' yet again. Butch was our 'Hercules in disguise,' and for Nathaniel to intimidate him, I couldn't help but chuckle.

Rupert's lips twisted into a smirk. "I wouldn't say much more, my friend, I still have the bruises from the last time."

"Caw, where are you?" Claudette's call had us turning

from the banter. She stood atop the stairs looking skyward.

"Where is he?" she asked.

"Last I saw of him was on the island, perhaps he is on a mission from Rosa?" I replied.

Claudette nodded as she twirled an envelope between her fingers.

"He'll be back soon; he always finds his way home." Captain Rourke assured wandering over from the helm.

THREE DAYS CAME and went without any sign of the multi-coloured animal. Although he had been absent for long periods in the past, the ship was full now.

As we dug into our hearty lunch, bantering and fighting over the last of the ale, the sound of fluttering wings and bird calls overpowered any trivial bickering. Our meal all but forgotten, the eight of us piled onto the deck. Caw was sat upon the rail, a roll of parchment attached to his leg. Captain Rourke was the first to step from the group.

"Welcome back," he said, attempting to release the scroll.

Before he could untie the cord, the bird flew out of reach. Landing near Ned he ruffled his feathers, his knowing eyes glinting. Ned smiled his confidence apparent. The bird and the older man had a connection.

One we could only guess at. Yet as Ned reached out, Caw spread his wings and set off again. He headed straight in my direction, landing on my shoulder, proceeding to squawk in my ear.

"Perhaps the message is for you?" Butch grinned as I wrenched away from the noise. Caw thrust out his clawed foot and I untied the parchment. My fingers fumbled as I unravelled it.

> *Valencia,*
>
> *You are privy to many secrets and are all too reckless with your affections. Thus you have yet to prove yourself. I have chosen a task for you. Despite the resilience you possess, you have yet to show what a broken curse has to offer. The Wilted Rose will dock soon; meet me beyond the trees.*

The well-formed words were identical to those left to each heir within the chest. The small but clear cursive, spoke volumes. I was in trouble, big trouble.

"What does it say?" Nathaniel asked.

His concern almost tipped me over the edge. Shaking my head I rolled up the scroll and brushed passed the group.

Climbing the rail, I stared out at the rippling water beneath the ship. It coasted just enough to jostle me as I awaited my punishment. For that is what the letter had hinted at. Although the others hovered close by, they didn't question me. I was thankful for that, as I wouldn't know how to explain anyway.

"What is wrong with her?" Claudette sounded troubled, I tried to block it out but the conversation just would not abate.

"We're not at liberty to pry," Davy said.

I stilled as he drew the rune for comfort upon my back. His soft touch could not ease the tension and feeling of dread, I remained stock straight on my perch.

"I'm sure she'll tell us when she's ready, Lennie's not one to be pushed."

Ned's words were heeded and no more was spoken about it, at least within my earshot.

The water surrounding us seemed to go on for miles with no sign of land. The ship felt slower, as though it was drawing towards its destination reluctantly. Or was that just me? I felt as adrift as the ship itself – what would become of me? Would I be prosecuted for my own truth?

The sun had set by the time Butch called out "land ahoy," though we wouldn't reach it for a few more hours yet. My mind had been turning over what could be in store once we got there. What torture would I have to endure? What or who was I about to encounter on the mysterious plot of land? Would the Sorceress have some other mythical creature to enforce her rules? Had I agitated the curse? Would my theory of something just as cruel as Hadnaloy come to fruition?

My questions continued until the early hours of the

morning. There had been no movement from the other inhabitants of the ship for hours. I surmised they had all fallen into a dreamless sleep, their thoughts easy and light. I dismissed my bitter thoughts away to play amongst the ever increasing questions.

The anchor slammed into the ocean floor, toppling me backwards. Getting to my feet I tried hard to swallow the butterflies. My face felt too warm, feverish even. Pressing my hand to it, I frowned. My skin was frozen. Annoyed, I yanked off my hat throwing it to the floor, my hair falling loose around my shoulders. Adjusting the sword at my hip, I wrapped my coat around myself and headed for the rope ladder.

"Valencia."

I stilled as Nathaniel stepped from the shadows, the hat I'd discarded in his hands.

"Please stay."

The two words pierced my heart; they screamed 'don't leave me.' I closed the gap between us reaching up to press our foreheads together. He wrapped his arms around me, pulling me closer still.

"I will return, I promise," I said, wishing I had the nerve to press my lips to his. It could be the last time. There was too much risk though, I'd already been called up on my 'reckless affections.'

Nathaniel's eyes were filled with concern as I stepped from his embrace. His mouth half open, ready to call me back to him. Committing his handsome face to memory,

I descended the ladder. All the while hoping my promise wouldn't be broken.

Jumping from the ship I landed in the shallows. The breeze swirled around me, lifting my hair as I shivered. Nathaniel's warmth ebbed away as I pulled my coat closer around me. Using the moonlight as a guide, I made my way up the beach to the forest beyond.

Despite the inky blackness of the trees, a strange blue light shone like a beacon urging me forward. There was no concept of time, for I'd felt it slip away. It could have taken minutes or even hours to reach the clearing.

A stream was the one obstacle in my path. Beyond it was a small span of treeless earth. Wary, I crossed the bridge, the silence disturbed only by the stream flowing beneath me. Reaching the other side, I found the source of the unusual light. Across the clearing a fire of shining blue flames, crackled. Surrounding it, large fallen logs awaited visitors. Twigs had been arranged in the space between the blue flames and the logs, though not as learned as Davy, I recognised the crude shapes as runes.

Unsure of what to do next I perched on the nearest make-shift bench and watched the strange flames flicker. The questions which plagued my journey had evaporated on the trek, and my mind held nothing but curiosity for the fire, and how it was created. I was so lost in the mystery I didn't realise I was no longer alone in the clearing until a voice spoke.

"You have grown strong and worthwhile, daughter of

Ferdinand."

Pulling in a gasp I turned. The creature which stood before me was no bigger than a child, yet I would have sworn she was a wood nymph. With pointed ears, translucent skin and a halo of woodland flowers in her silvery hair, the small woman held a strange presence. Besides the creature's obvious beauty, I couldn't draw my gaze away from her magnificent opaque wings. They fluttered in the breeze like the leaves above us.

So this was the mighty and powerful Sorceress, the magical being who could bring a grown man to his knees. This was the one creature with the means to end the lives of me and my crew mates.

"You look puzzled, child," the Sorceress said as she came forward. Reaching out her pale hand, she pressed the palm to my forehead. Despite the coldness of my skin, I felt warmth spread through me. Fear wasn't a factor, I was sure I should feel scared, yet my most overriding feelings were of wonder.

"You mentioned in your letter, you have a task for me," I said, finding my voice.

The Sorceress broke contact and although my skin tingled, the heat faded almost instantly.

With a shake of her head, she appraised me, her eyes travelling from my hair to my feet and back again. "I am unsettled by your heart. It feels fatal yearnings."

She shook her head in disapproval, "You are a fighter though; it is in your nature to defy those you feel have wronged you."

She turned away, twisting and untwisting her fingers as her brow furrowed.

"I understand you and your crewmates wish for companionship, I too have felt the urge, though I do know the heartbreak that comes with it. I only wish to prevent you all from experiencing such a pain."

It was as though I wasn't there, she circled the fire, spouting thoughts at random, before stopping before me once more. Her once jet eyes now held a circle of blue light.

"You need to bring your crewmates here," she said. "We shall meet after the moon crosses the sky and I will reveal my decision."

"Why? What will that do?" I knew my snarky tone sounded rude, but she had terrified me with her letter and the questions it had blossomed. Now I was to be her messenger? I touched my forehead, it still tingled from her touch.

She turned narrowed eyes on me. I held her gaze, never straying. I wanted to stand, to tower over her, but I knew I could only push so hard. She held the key to all our futures after all.

"Your challenge will not be getting them to me. That, my dear, will be easy," The Sorceress said. "Your hardest task will be to pick up the pieces of honesty that will be scattered once they get here."

"What does that mean?" I sputtered, unsure if

'scattered pieces of honesty' was a good thing.

The Sorceress again placed her hand upon my forehead; warmth pooled there before travelling throughout my body. Closing my eyes, I revelled in the feeling of power welling inside me. Was she forcing me with some kind of influence. I tried to pull away but her warm hand did not waiver.

Then, all too soon it was gone.

The breeze hit me. The sensation felt like I'd been doused with an overzealous wave. The earthy smell of the forest had been replaced by the fragrance of the sea. Opening my eyes, I found the *Wilted Rose* docked just as I'd left it in the shallows. The jarring change unsettled me for a moment. The sun was high in the cloudless sky and I was unsure as to how long I'd been within the trees.

Pulling myself from the sand I brushed down my clothes. I still felt the weight of worry that oppressed my entire being, but something else lingered amongst the pressure. As I tried to recall my interaction with the faery Sorceress, the conversation came back to me in riddles. With nothing but confusion as my companion I trudged back to the ship. My mind was again full of questions, none of which, I could answer myself.

As my foot touched the deck, the group converged upon me, all talking at once. Nathaniel grasped me around the waist and sat me down, as Butch shoved a full tankard of amber liquid into my hand. I sipped at it, finding the burn of the whiskey held nothing in comparison to the Sorceress' power.

"Where have you been?" Ned demanded, his face was pale as he rested a hand on my shoulder and looked deep into my face.

"S-she wants to meet us... a-all of us," I stammered my eyes darting at the faces which surrounded me.

"Who?" Rupert asked, rubbing at his eyes. They were bloodshot and his lip was split. Had something happened whilst I'd been away?

"The Sorceress, she wants me to bring you all to her forest," I said, catching sight of injuries on Butch, Davy and even Nathaniel's faces.

"What do you mean, the Sorceress?" Davey spluttered, his drink toppling from his hand as he stared at me.

"The Sorceress?" The captain barked, moving closer, "What were you thinking? You should have taken one of us."

I looked to our leader, his flushed cheeks and panicked eyes held mine. I shook my head, as I attempted to explain,

"She asked me to go alone," I told him.

As they bombarded me with more questions I covered a yawn. Tiredness sapped my energy as I tried to answer them all. My body ached with unknown weariness and my head drooped onto Nathaniel's shoulder.

"Boys, Lennie looks unwell."

Nathaniel's gentle statement came just as my weighted

lids forced my eyes closed. Someone took the tankard from my hand and strong arms surround me, not long after, dreams were all I knew.

CHAPTER XVI
CURSED AGAIN

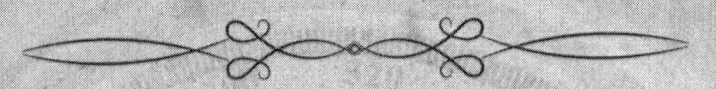

THE STRANGE DIMNESS of the cabin sent chills through me. My blankets did little to keep out the deep seated cold. The candle on my table had burned low, casting shadows. I'd slept the day away and twilight now faded into darkness beyond the porthole. Had the forest and its blue fire, all been a figment of my dreams? No, I wouldn't be that lucky, this was real.

Taking in my surroundings, I could see I'd somehow made it back to my own room. My jacket was folded at the end of the bed, my belt and boots sat on the floor beside me, nothing seemed too out of place.

A large yawn overtook me and I stretched out my cramped limbs. That was when I saw the figure in the shadows. My heart leapt and my fingers grasped for my sword. I could hear my heartbeat pounding in my ears as I squinted through the half-light. A large body overflowed a rocking chair in the corner of my room. Lanky legs were stretched out and crossed at the ankles, whilst hands were clasped over a flat stomach.

They were hands I recognised. Long fingers, callouses

and ink stains. A large ring glinted in the dwindling candlelight. It was Nathaniel. He'd stayed with me, maybe even watched over me. I couldn't pull my gaze away; I felt stirrings of appreciation as I looked into his peaceful face. He was a good man. One that had no business with the likes of me, but beside me he stayed.

In sleep, Nathaniel's big frame seemed less intimidating. All his tension, pomposity and rough edges were smoothed out. I tried to swallow back a sigh. Brushing a hand over my face, my eyes swept over his form. His unbuttoned shirt revealed a tanned chest and a hint of hair which peaked from beneath the fabric. I pressed my lips together, the urge to kiss the exposed skin was running rampant within me.

No, I couldn't even entertain such a thought; it would just be another 'reckless act.' I stepped back. If I wanted to convince the Sorceress the curse was worth ending, I had to stop my wayward thoughts, lest they become more than that.

I turned away, slightly irked at my own self-preservation. Any other reckless young person wouldn't have waited. Though most people my age hadn't seen, done or experienced half of what I had either. This was the right decision, at least for now.

Despite my brush with the all-powerful Sorceress I still felt bitter. Why was I singled out, weren't the others reckless and all too free with their truths too? As I tripped over my new questions in silence; something close to pain pricked along my wrist. Pushing up my sleeve, I found my brand burned clearer than ever. Staring at the crimson rose, the once faded colour, had taken on a blood stained hue and if I wasn't mistaken, more leaves had bloomed around the crossbones...I pressed a palm over the skin and heat radiated from it.

"Valen–" Nathaniel trailed off as he shifted in his sleep, a small smile played upon his lips. Startled by his voice, I stared at him. Was he about to say my name? Was he dreaming of me?

Climbing from my bed, I tiptoed towards the rocking chair, waiting for him to speak again. Much to my chagrin, his soft snores revealed nothing more than his contentment. I caught sight of his journal on the low table beside him a discarded quill and ink well sat close by. I had the almightiest urge to pick up the tome and discover Nathaniel's inner life, but I resisted, instead I returned my attention to the sleeping man. After a few more moments of watching him, I began to feel silly, what if he woke up? How would I explain the fact I was ogling him without seeming strange? Shaking myself at my foolishness, I slipped from the room and onto the deck.

The sun peaked through clouds as the ship stayed anchored in the shallows of the mysterious island. In daylight, the forest looked just as foreboding, even without the ethereal illuminations. No sun filtered through the dark trees, no birds swooped around them. It was far too quiet.

I clambered onto the rail, letting my legs swing back and forth to the rhythm of the questions which filled my mind. What had the Sorceress meant? What truth would I have to clean up?

"How are you?" Claudette's question broke through my incessant, whirling mind.

"Fine," I lied. "What about you, how are you feeling?"

Jumping from the rail I followed Claudette to the card table. She still looked strained, her tired eyes were a deep purple now. Lines had formed around her mouth and her skin, which was already pale, looked sickly. Before we reached the chairs, she turned.

"You came face to face with the Sorceress." Claudette began, ignoring my question. "She has marked you."

"Marked me? What do you mean?" I squeaked.

With a firm hand, Claudette steered me back to the rail, her finger pointed at the clear water below us. The waves were steady but there was no easy way to see my reflection.

"Allow me," Claudette said, waving a hand in front of her. As she finished the action, section of the water became still. I pulled in a gasp as I spotted it. Upon my forehead, peeking out from beneath my hair, was the shape of a wilting rose. Just as the skull was branded upon my wrist, this image was seared onto my face.

"What on earth is it?" I cried pushing aside my fringe.

"The captain asked Ned to find out for you,"

Claudette said. "We did think about sending Caw, but we used this instead—"

From her pocket, she pulled the jewelled box and the scroll within.

"Rosa replied to us with this" she said. Unravelling the parchment, the enchantress began to read:

'The Sorceress has informed me of what she has done, and much like Hadnaloy did with Claudette and Macrucio, the Sorceress has claimed Lennie as her own. Lennie is now tied to the faery queen, heart, body and soul, just as I am.'

Claudette expression turned grave as she continued to read. "The curse will be stronger within her, more so than any of her comrades."

"Damn!" I cussed. The urge to stamp my feet was great but I withheld it. "I am more of a fool than I thought."

"Oh Lennie, please don't fret, it will all work out for the best." Claudette consoled.

"What do you think about all this?" I asked her,

"I can sense the power within you. Though you have no magic yet, Rosa too holds the same brand upon her forehead – it must link in some way."

Claudette handed me the scroll to read for myself, and pulled a handkerchief from her pocket. Running it through her fingers for a moment, she made it disappear entirely with one swift shake of a hand. The action held me captive, would I one day be magical? Did I even want to be? Or was this new brand some sick form of control? Either way, I wasn't going to sit back and let the Sorceress possess me. This was my life and I was going to have it for my own.

"She called me a fighter," I muttered, my fists clenching at my sides. "And fight is what I'll do. She may possess my lineage but my future is my own."

ONE HOUR PAST sunset, the ethereal light of the fire illuminated the forest once more. It would soon be time for the crew to venture towards it. Despite the eagerness of the others, I felt like I was about to be dragged back into the trees kicking and screaming.

The boys had driven me mad with questions and guesses of what they were to expect from this expedition, and to escape I holed myself up in the saloon to read. I kept my mind adrift upon some magical isle, the characters a mixture of the fantastical and ordinary. It soothed me, made me less angry. I was so entwined with the story that when the lamps gutted, throwing the entire room into darkness, I growled.

"This is not funny boys," I yelled.

There was no laughter, nor the sound of scrambling feet to right their joke.

"Rupert, please, this has gone on long enough."

No one responded and gloom fell around me like a suffocating mass. I stepped away from the bookcase, the silence eerie.

"Lennie are you in here?" Nathaniel called through the abyss.

"Yes," I whispered, caution edged my reply.

I could hear Nathaniel stumbling in the dark and after a few moments his hand found mine.

"This doesn't feel right, what happened?" I murmured.

"There is only one way to find out."

Taking our time, we stepped through the dark, hearing nothing but the creak of the ship. What could have cause every candle to douse at once? As we edged towards the stairs I felt glad for the weight of the sword at my hip and the warmth of Nathaniel's hand. Whatever we were about to encounter, those two things gave me courage.

We reached the bottom of the stairs which led to the deck, water lapping against the ship but soon a new sound appeared.

"Come and play little sea worms, come see what I have for you. You will not be disappointed my dears."

My insides turned to ice and I gripped tightly to Nathaniel's hand. That voice meant only one thing. Hadnaloy. She sounded deranged. Although her sanity was already questionable, the witch was usually controlled. That was all gone now.

"What? No takers?" She cried.

The stillness off the water was long gone, waves crashed and the ship shook.

"I just want to talk with you all," she said her tone all too sweet.

To Nathaniel's left, the glint of a gun signalled the arrival of someone below with us – Ned.

"What do you want Hadnaloy?" Claudette's voice rang out clear and true above our heads.

"Oh, my sweet girl, how does it feel?" Hadnaloy's retort was laced with sarcasm.

"What do you want?" Claudette repeated.

"Macrucio." Hadnaloy dragged out the name, pain tugged at the edges. "You killed him. You. Not these weak heirs, not the curse but you."

"He begged for it!" I screamed.

Nathaniel's protests went unheard as I stormed out to face the sea witch, my sword drawn.

"It was not Claudette's fault; he goaded her, pleaded with her. If anyone's at fault, it's you." I thrust a finger towards the witch, "You held such power over him."

My body shook with suppressed anger and my breathing came out fast. Claudette didn't need this witch causing her to spiral again. Her lies would not bode well for any of us.

Hadnaloy's eyes pulsated red as she glared, willing me to cower. I refused to comply.

"You dare throw blame at me?" The witch shrieked "You are nothing but a weak, despicable, cursed wench?"

"I may well be those things but I know the truth too."

My jaw clenched as my anger grew. The names were nothing I hadn't heard before. She was merely irking me.

"The truth, coming from a woman taught to use men for money? You would not know truth."

Hadnaloy reached out and moved my hair aside, revealing the new brand. I batted her twig like finger away.

"Well, well, well. *Rosa del Mar* the second." The sea witch's lips twisted into a mocking smile. "Let us hope her sticky end does not repeat itself." She sounded anything but sincere.

"If it does, I intend to complete what she started." I threatened.

"What would that be?"

"To end you."

She laughed, a rolling belly laugh that had my blood boiling. Her malevolent eyes flickered over my shoulder, to where Nathaniel and God knows who else now hovered.

"Leave them out of this, this has naught to do with them," Claudette demanded, her voice strained.

The sea-witch's face twisted into a harsh grin. "Do you not think it amusing, the only two people defending this 'great' ship are women? Where are those brave knights to rescue these damsels in distress?"

Hadnaloy cackled as the waves whipped around her. She clicked her fingers and the instant the noise ended, the atmosphere tensed. Through the darkness, the yells of my crewmates filled the air. Someone grabbled me from behind and I struggled in their hold. Beside me Claudette's captor got a swift spark of something in the face. Dusting herself off she balefully stared down at the writhing form at her feet.

Looking up at me, she mouthed, *"Keep still."*

Though I loathed to have this stranger's arms around me, I remained unmoving. My position was too vulnerable, I was the closest to the ship's edge and thus closest to Hadnaloy. I trusted Claudette, I could see that she would have my back. She knew Hadnaloy better than any of us and knew just how to play this dicey situation. I hoped.

It was times such as this, I wished I was adept at a bow and arrow. I had a clear shot of the witch from where I stood. I couldn't help but think, perhaps I should've followed Ned's lead and carried a pistol.

"You will not get away with this," Nathaniel threatened as around us the sound of sword play and flying fists grew louder. Nathaniel's gruff protest distracted the witch and I locked eyes with Claudette. She gave an almost invisible nod and lifted her hand. My captor crumpled behind me. His arm was still at my neck as his legs gave way, I went down with him.

As we hit the floor, I scrambled for my sword which had dropped in the tussle. We were surrounded. As well as Hadnaloy towering over us, each man was deep in battle with an underling. Where was the Sorceress? Her forest was mere footsteps away, was this not her rival too?

"Macrucio was not the be-all-end-all," Rupert taunted through the melee.

My heart sank as Rupert's voice carried over the chaos. His captor threw him to the floor but he kept on fighting back.

"Ah, the son of Charles, the one of value," Hadnaloy scoffed. "Bring him to me."

Rupert was flung between Claudette and I, before being shoved to his knees in a demeaning bow. A cloth was pushed into his mouth and bound.

"That'll keep you quiet," one of the brutes grouched.

I brandished my sword at the fiends waiting for their next move.

"Despite your best efforts, your women have already said the same thing. I knew my protégée; he was a man after my own heart." Her gaze seemed far away, there was even a trace of fondness in her expression.

"He would have been great, a legend, if I had not been so mistaken in my choices."

She returned to the present, glaring at Claudette. Beside us Rupert continued to struggle. His muffled insults shattered the silence as he yelled from behind his gag. I fended off a few of the underling's keeping an eye on my friend.

"Enough!" Hadnaloy snapped, turning her unyielding eyes on the redhead.

Rupert didn't stop, his captor ripped off his gag and Rupert bared his teeth.

Hadnaloy's mouth twisted. "Nothing left to say?"

"I have plenty," he muttered, yanking his arms out of his captors hold. He stood, brushing himself off.

"As you said, I understand value. You hold none."

Thrusting his hand in his pocket he pulled out his father's inheritance. The gold coin glinted in his palm punctuating his words.

"Is that right?" Hadnaloy mocked.

She raised her hand, sweeping the coin into her waiting grasp with little effort. Rupert clenched his teeth, grasping after it.

"You dare touch my father's prize?"

Rupert's green eyes spat fire and he raced forward. His boldness turned my stomach as the witch scoffed.

"Prize my dear boy? This has bought you nothing but pain."

The sea-witch flicked the coin high into the air and caught it with ease. As she moved the glittering object between her fingers, the skull pattern was no longer a dull gold; but blood red. Her lips moved inaudibly as she shifted the coin back and forth. Rupert clenched his teeth again his eyes never leaving her.

Hadnaloy's smile was sly, as she pressed the coin to her lips. Finished with her torment, she threw it at Rupert who caught it in both hands, his eyes glazed over, as he stared down at his inheritance. What had she done?

"I am not finished," Hadnaloy warned, turning back to Claudette. "You will pay for Macrucio's death. You dragged him here against his will and I will never forgive that."

Her fingers clicked one more time and she and her men disappeared beneath the water. In an instant, the lamps were re-lit, revealing the roughed up crew. I turned a triumphant smile on Claudette but found my friend curled up on the floor. Her whole body writhed in pain as she clutched her arm to her chest.

"What happened?" I cried as I reached her side. The others gathered around us.

"Burning fires of hell!" Claudette's scream ripped through me like a knife.

"Have I not suffered enough at her hand?" she cried as her body convulsed.

"Let me see child," Ned urged.

The older man's touch seemed to calm her. He pulled back her sleeve to reveal Hadnaloy's brand. The skin at her wrist was a bloody mess, as though someone had taken a blade to it.

"Let's get this cleaned," he said.

Together Ned and Claudette headed below deck. I sheathed my sword as I watched them go. Concern for my friend and anger for what had happened swelled within me, as I tried to fathom the evil Hadnaloy had yet again inflicted.

"You were brilliant," Butch said pulling me close;

looking into his face I found a cut across his cheek.

"Claudette and Rupert did the same," I said using my sleeve to dab at the blood. "I just don't know where I got my guts from."

Wincing Butch brushed off my fussing. "You inherited it from your father; he was a fighter, just like mine. Perhaps meeting the Sorceress honed that gift?"

"There is no need to worry about lineage," Nathaniel's said. His concerned expression was centred upon Butch's hand at my waist.

"Oh?" I said stepping out of Butch's arms, a strange feeling close to guilt clawed at me.

"You are strong even without that."

Nathaniel's sincere words were overshadowed by Butch, as he wrapped his arm around my shoulder; his smug expression was not missed by either myself or Nathaniel.

"Anyway," Butch said too close to my ear. "The Sorceress has increased it tenfold, I'm sure."

"The Sorceress," I exclaimed, disentangling herself and rushing to the rail. The blue light still burned amongst the forest. "We had better go."

"Lennie!"

I stilled, Davy's cry held pure fear in a single word. As I turned I found out why. Rupert's empty eyes were blazing as he ran towards me, his sword was held aloft like a dagger.

"Rupert?" I gasped, my hand instinctively grasping for

my own weapon.

He never reached me. Nathaniel sprang from my side, grappling Rupert to the floor.

"Are you all right?" Butch asked. He wrapped me in his arms as Davy and Nathaniel wrestled Rupert into submission. Though I was shielded I didn't miss the sound of bone on bone.

"Stop," I cried, pushing Butch away and yanking at Nathaniel's shirt.

"Leave him, he doesn't know what he's doing."

Beneath the two men, Rupert lay bloody and spent, Nathaniel and Davy both were breathing heavily and the discarded sword lay inches away.

"I demand an explanation!" The captain roared. His face was flushed as he watched the proceedings.

"Rupert turned on Lennie," Butch said, his eyes wide.

I skirted around the group and knelt before Rupert.

"I do not think it wise" Nathaniel protested.

I lifted my hand, cutting off his warning. Turning back to Rupert, I placed my palms on either side of his battered face. Shuffling closer I looked deep into his much changed eyes.

"Rupert, this is not your doing, this is Hadnaloy. If you're still the man I know, fight!"

Rupert said nothing, his dull eyes held no trace of mischief or friendship. Anger boiled within me as I let him go.

"I think we need to keep a watch on our friend," I

said, solemnness clouding my tone.

"I agree," Davy said. He still grasped Rupert's arm, though the redhead was beyond struggling.

"I don't like the idea, but he's dangerous," Davy continued.

The two were usually in sync, two sides to the same coin. He looked lost as he stared down at his possessed ally.

"I think Hadnaloy has meddled with something deep inside him and Lennie seems to be the target," he said.

"She's going after us, one by one," Nathaniel said.

The captain pushed back his hat and rubbed a hand across his forehead, "That looks to be the case, doesn't it?"

"What should we do?" Butch asked.

"Perhaps we should tie his hands, then we should get going," the captain said pulling a line of rope from his belt.

CHAPTER XVII
TAINTED

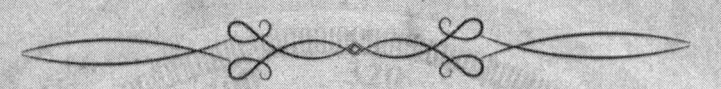

THE ANTICIPATION OF seeing the Sorceress was no more, Rupert and Hadnaloy had seen to that. We were subdued as we made our way towards the forest. My breath caught hold of the chill in the night air, sending smoke-like wisps to dance amongst the moonlight. It created an ever misting fog as I wandered. It kept me focussed on the now, rather on what was about to happen.

The sand left our footsteps mute, though as we reached the forest even the slightest crunch or stumble stalled our progress. We all were nervous, I could tell by the darting eyes and jerky movements of my comrades. I was more than eager to be back aboard the *Wilted Rose*. It felt wrong to leave it after what had just transpired.

My palms were slick from nerves, apprehension and adrenaline coursed through me, thrumming in time to the rhythm of my heart. What more could we encounter? Would Rupert try to attack again? Shaking off the thought, I led them through the cluster of trees, not slowing down as I strode over the wooden bridge. I paused just short of the cyan fire, waiting for the others to catch up.

"Davy," I murmured as they gathered around me. "I think these are runes."

I pointed to the twigs which still lay in their strange formations. His brooding features held thoughtfulness as he glanced past my finger.

"I think you're right," he said with a nod. Still staring he plunged his hand beneath his shirt and pulled out the pendant he'd inherited from his father. Taking slow and careful steps around the blue fire, he brushed his thumb back and forth over the stone.

"Can you decipher them?" Nathaniel's lilting voice rumbled through the trees. A creature swept across the clearing, its wings fluttering in surprise at the interruption.

"They represent each of us. Look at this one." Davy knelt at the head of the circle. The twigs beside him formed a zigzag.

"This is the rune for 'sun'. I believe this is meant for the captain. People follow the sun."

Davy's calm aura doused my fears, my anxiety paled with the sweep of his hand.

"This one," he continued, pointing to the next symbol.

"This has to be for Butch. It represents 'Oak', which to me, means strength."

The two men shared an understanding smile. Davy

stepped once more, pausing in front of a simple cross.

"X marks the spot," he chuckled. "This is clearly my rune, it means gift."

He traced the symbol on his palm before moving on. He paused, crouching to get a closer look at the next group of sticks. He glanced up at Rupert in annoyance. His friend looked distracted as he stared unseeing through the trees. We had removed all of Rupert's weapons so his unadorned belt looked naked beside everyone else. Since meeting aboard the ship, Davy and Rupert had been inseparable it was so sad to see them so out of touch with each other. Davy's usual calm had been replaced with straight, tense shoulders and a permanent scowl. It didn't suit him.

"Rupert's depicts wealth," Davy muttered.

I didn't miss the baleful glare he bestowed upon his friend before continuing.

"These look similar," Claudette said, stepping into the circle.

"You're right," he agreed all trace of tension ebbing away as he replied. "This rune means mouth and as our storyteller, I believe this rune is for Nathaniel."

"Mouth?" Nathaniel frowned as he stared at the twigs. Biting his lip he pulled out his journal and pencil, before scrawling something across the page.

"Lennie, this one's yours," Davy called and I stepped from the group to meet him. Staring down at the mismatched twigs, I felt connected to the strange cross shape with diamond accents. Mine, this represented me. What on earth was it?

"What does it mean?" I said aloud.

"Spear." Came Davy's reply.

I nodded, content with my allotted symbol. I couldn't fault that.

"This one has to be yours Claudette," Davy said stepping around me, to stand beside the rune.

"It means 'game.' Resourcefulness culminates in a game, am I right?"

"Like cat and mouse." Ned spoke as Claudette and Davy nodded.

"Is this one Ned's?" Claudette asked. She was stood next to the final rune. It reminded me of a church spire.

Davy shook his head. "This is the symbol for serpent."

His tone spoke volumes as he wrapped his hand in Claudette's. Realisation hit, as her eyes darkened and she shivered in the warm glow of the cobalt fire.

"This was for Macrucio," she whispered, Davy didn't answer but kissed the back of her hand.

"What about Ned?" The captain asked, a frown marring his forehead as he spoke.

"No need to worry, son, I am well catered for."

Oblivious to the stares of his crewmates, he strode around the circle, stopping on the other side of Macrucio's rune. His symbol was gauged in the dirt, no evidence of twigs remained.

We stood in silence, letting all that Davy had discovered settle. I tried hard not to worry about the next step. I hated not knowing what I had led my brethren into or how it all would end. Had I doomed us all to further misery and harm?

"Anyone hungry?" Butch swung a canvas bag from his shoulder and delved inside.

"When did you do that?" I asked, taking the apple he offered.

"Before everything turned foul, I'd packed a few provisions for our journey."

His boyish smile was infectious and soon we all were digging into, bread, cheese and ale. As the evening drew on, we settled into a more casual atmosphere, trading stories and jokes to pass the time.

Nathaniel, Davy, Butch and Ned had huddled together in a game of cards once the stories dried up, whilst the captain stood watch over the comatose Rupert. Wanting to keep busy, I set about gathering up the empty bottles we'd left around the fire.

"We have about a handful left," Claudette murmured, handing me another.

"Well, then should we not return to the ship for more?" Butch called as the game disbanded.

"We have had plenty" The captain's tone was curt as he stared down at his map. As Ned took a seat beside our leader he glared at the redhead. Rupert had not spoken or even acknowledged what he had done since leaving the ship. I wished the others wouldn't blame him; it wasn't Rupert but Hadnaloy who had run at me with that blade. Rupert and I may niggle and banter but he never would have tried that in his right mind. I knew that.

"What on earth are you up to?" Claudette's question to Nathaniel, awoke me from my brooding. Nathaniel was busying himself collecting long pieces of wood.

"Just something I read," he said, continuing his work.

I moved closer to the journal, lying open on the log. A rough sketch of a tented structure took up half a page and beneath it a set of clear instructions.

"I thought we might be here a while," he said. Picking up a branch he kicked aside the debris.

"My father called it a 'bender tent.'"

With force he pushed the branch into the dirt, bending it over into a semi-circle; he repeated the action further forward before tying a central one with a weed stem.

"What now?" Butch asked, following Nathaniel's lead.

Contemplative, Nathaniel's bright eyes scoured the darkness.

"We need something like tarp, even moss or leaves would do."

"Where oh where would we find such a thing as moss?"

Everyone turned. Rupert's sarcasm held a hardened note but at least he sounded somewhat familiar. All eyes were on him as he snatched one of the remaining full bottles in his tied hands and tramped off into the trees. Davy raced after him, annoyance plain on his face. The captain shook his head, stowing away the parchment he set about aiding Ned in building two more tents.

"Should we go after them?" Nathaniel asked, as Claudette and I finished our bases. I shrugged, delving my hands into the moss close by. The dampness of the foliage chilled me but I worked fast, patting it over places that were tied. Butch and Nathaniel found larger leaves from surrounding trees, piecing them together to form a shelter.

"This looks splendid!" Claudette said her elfin face spattered with mud as she covered the remaining holes. I hadn't seen her so happy in days. The transformation was stunning.

"I think so," Nathaniel agreed. "I just hope the rain holds off, I am not so sure how steadfast they will be."

"Rupert and Davy, they'll need a place to sleep," Butch said. He stared over my head, the way they'd walked.

"It couldn't hurt, I suppose," I agreed, grasping hold of a few pliable sticks.

An hour or so later with all the tents completed, Rupert and Davy had still not returned.

"I wouldn't worry yourselves," Ned said. "Rupert has been on these tangents before, besides he needs to think about what he did."

"Yes, Ned, but this is the forest," Butch said, worry lining his face.

"He won't come to much harm. Davy is with him." Claudette sounded sure but I couldn't be so confident, Rupert seemed very different since our run-in with the sea-witch. Something had changed within him and not for the better.

Night drew on and the others drifted off to asleep, protected by their make-shift tents and warmed by the fire. I sat in the opening of my own. Butch had provided books as well as cards in his sack and I sat reading, a tome in one hand and a tankard of amber liquid in the other. Turning pages, I smiled at the tale weaving through my mind like a flicker-book. I didn't look up as something crashed through the undergrowth.

"If you have arrived to cause havoc I'd rather you return from where you came from." I droned, reading on the final line of the page before looking up at them.

Rupert held a broken bottle in one bandaged untied hand and a cigarillo dangled from his lips. His cheeks were rosy in the firelight and his eyes were wild in his head, swirling around the camp. Beside him, Davy stared exasperated at his friend, dried blood covered his lip. What trouble had they gotten themselves into?

"He's still much altered, but more like himself now." Disapproval coloured Davy's quiet tone.

"I can see that." I said. The stench of stale alcohol had me wincing, as I pushed long dormant memories away. "Throw him in there, he can sleep it off."

I pointed to the tent opposite as Davy wrenched the

unlit smoke from his friend's mouth and shoved him forward. The redhead dropped the remains of the bottle, grasping the last full container, which sat by the fire, he pulled out the stopper with his teeth.

"No!" Rupert pouted as Davy made to take it.

"Fine, on your sore head be it," he muttered and I hid a smile behind my book. I turned the page as Davy and Rupert settled in for the night.

"Who on earth...?" Nathaniel's sleep heavy voice had my stomach flip-flopping.

"Go back to sleep, it's only Rupert," I said.

"Ah so he has returned."

Nathaniel sat up, shifting to the mouth of the tent. His hair was dishevelled falling over his hooded eyes. He crossed his legs, turning a sleepy smile in my direction. He was shirtless his tanned skin glowing in the blue tinged firelight. I looked away, was he trying to drive me mad?

"What is your book about?" He asked.

"Nothing of consequence," I said, folding down the corner and stowing it beneath my rugged pallet.

"No, let me see," he urged. His grin grew wider as he leaned over me, grasping for it. I pulled in a sharp breath as his fingers grazed first my own hand and then my thigh. His eyes clashed with mine as he pulled the book towards him. I moistened my lips as he paused, his breath fanning warmth across my face. He moved closer and my breath caught.

I closed my eyes, would he kiss me?

"One day," he murmured. Pressing his forehead to mine before rocking back onto his knees.

The moment over, his smile was teasing once again as he read the book's title.

"Ah… no wonder you did not wish me to see. The brave swords-woman has not been reading of action and war, but of romance."

His mocking tone reddened my already flushed cheeks and I looked away. His touch jolted me as he turned my head to face him.

"There is no shame in a little romance."

His face was inches from mine again and I willed my heart to slow down. He brushed my lips with the pad of his thumb, the warmth of our body's surrounded me and the aroma of the forest mingled with his unique scent.

"Oi, get your own tent,"

Rupert's drunken slur broke the magic and Nathaniel let me go, handing back the book and melting into the darkness of his sleeping quarters.

Fighting to calm my breathing, I touched the spot where his fingers had been, my eyes trained on the tent to my left.

"Goodnight," I murmured as a stiff breeze shook the trees. Pulling my jacket around me, I lay my head down, knowing if I did sleep, it would be riddled with dreams.

RAIN BATTERED THE forest, sending leaves crashing in on the crew. I couldn't contain my laughter as the groans coming from Rupert's tent frightened the birds. I turned onto my side, ignoring the dampness. The rolling belly-laugh felt good, it had been such a long time.

"Such a nice sound, hearing you laugh."

Nathaniel's deep voice startled me into silence and I stared wide eyed.

"I did not mean for you to stop," he said, a frown causing his brows to meet. He reached out a hand, aiding me to stand.

"Thank you," I murmured, as he let me go, his absence was replaced by a tingle.

"Grubs up men," The captain called. He dished up the meal, handing out crusts of bread and broth.

"I don't pity you, it was all self-inflicted," Butch mumbled around his spoon, as Rupert pushed his food away in disgust. Had some of the spell worn off? Or was it lying dormant? I was unsure as I tucked into my own breakfast.

"Leave me be, you rat," Rupert groused, his skin taking on a greenish hue.

"Drink this, it will make you feel better." Claudette handed him a small container, smoke rose from the top in an aqua colour. The smell was sickly sweet and Rupert wrinkled his nose.

"What is this?" He demanded.

"A tonic for what ails you."

"What if it's a potion of poison?" His petulant tone held little trust.

Claudette shrugged her shoulders, untroubled. "You will just have to find out."

She offered it up again and he snatched it begrudgingly.

"I feel he may be bewitched," Claudette murmured as she took a seat beside me.

"I thought so, how can you tell?"

"Though I do not know him well, I am sure his belligerence is far from normal, his glassy eyes and then there is the attack on you."

I nodded. "Yes I felt the same, Hadnaloy has done something, hasn't she?"

"Yes, I have seen this trait in her work before."

"Should we tell the others?"

"I think it will be revealed soon enough," Claudette sighed.

Nodding, I eyed Rupert, with each sip of the mysterious beverage, his grimace grew more pronounced.

"What did you give him just now?"

"A cure, at least for his sore head as well as something to 'tame the beast,' so to speak."

She winked in mischief.

Sunlight spread throughout the forest, casting green light throughout the clearing. The soft sounds of the sea and stream close by kept the soundtrack of our waiting.

With the dawn, there was no arrival of the Sorceress.

"Should we take a look further afield now we can see?" Butch asked, as we cleaned away our breakfast.

"I don't think there is any harm. Shall we agree on one more night before we return to the *Wilted Rose*?" The captain said unravelling his map, the compass needles were still at his side.

"Would it be wise to leave the ship so long?" I said wringing my hands, my foot resting on the bridge.

"The ship will be fine," Ned said, taking my arm and steering me back to camp. "Caw is ready to warn us of any trouble, he's the heartbeat on board for now and besides, we're in heart of where the ship was created. We are in fine shape here."

"So we wait?" Rupert's impatience held less sting, now his cup was dry.

"That's all we can do." Davy spoke softly, his fingertips tracing a rune at his feet.

"Perhaps our resident bard could pull out a sorry tale?" Captain Rourke's lips twitched as he turned to Nathaniel.

"I'm sure I could find something," Nathaniel replied with a smile.

"You're in for a treat," Butch whispered as I stared at Nathaniel.

"I knew of your heritage but I've never heard your work," I said.

"It pays to stay in my presence, don't you know?"

Nathaniel winked; turning back to the crew he began to weave his tale...

AS THE AFTERNOON sky drained of its colour making way for the evening ahead, the eight of us settled down to await our host. No one spoke and the silence grew. My mind wandered, as the blue flames danced before me.

"Welcome to my humble home, I've seen you've made yourselves comfortable." A bell-like voice said into the silence.

We were pulled from our reverie as the creature stepped into view. Just as I remembered, the Sorceress was the image of a woodland faery. Petite and delicate, her unusual irises commanded power and no-one could look away.

The Sorceress folded her feet beneath her as she sat beside the fire. Her eyes were cast downward as her dainty fingers carved patterns into the mud, the whole scene made me nervous. I longed to reach out and link my fingers with Nathaniel's but was fearful of what the Sorceress' reaction might be. Instead I folded my hands together and studied the circle.

My gaze flickered to Rupert; he looked drawn as he stared beyond the group and out into the trees. His fist was circled around his father's coin. The skin on the back of his hand was taught and shook with tension.

As I glanced from person to person, my heart resumed its heavy thudding rhythm. Had I led my crew mates into a trap? After a few moments of silence, the Sorceress lifted her soiled hand towards the fire. The flames flickered faster, casting a strange glow across her already luminous skin. Her attention never left the fire but when she spoke her voice was clear and true:

> *"Seven heirs plus one,*
> *The deed is done,*
> *Echoes of old and new*
> *Mark each of the chosen few*
> *Death to one great heir,*
> *From loves cruel glare,*
> *Starves the soul of feeling*
> *And prevents us from healing*
> *Let us join together.*
> *Old and new forever,*
> *Eight of you*
> *Mismatched crew*
> *Form a tryst anew"*

The flames rose, threatening to burn the forest to cinders. Before they could cause any damage, the Sorceress pressed her palms together and bowed her head. The fire rained down as she mouthed in silence.

The blaze never touched the eight of us but swept around the circle. My eyes widened as the flames brushed past me, emitting a heat that did not burn. I had only seen a circle of light such as that once before; Claudette had conjured it for our protection.

The Sorceress looked up and the blue light faded. In its place, a circle of sparkles flowed like a current around us. With purpose, the Sorceress strode around the fire. She lifted her clean palm and placed it upon my forehead. The warmth pooled over my heart and spread through my body like a bloodstream. I tightened my fists as both of my brands burned.

"Valencia has become my vessel. She holds the blossoming feelings you all like to call love."

Her tone held mocking as she spoke to the circle. I couldn't fathom what my own expression revealed; my feelings were merely mustard seeds yet to grow. What would the crew think of me now? I fought not to turn as both Butch and Nathaniel, let out audible gasps.

"You have asked to be freed from the curse, passed down from your fathers." The Sorceress continued. "Yet you all fail to be honest, not only with each other but with yourselves." Her words were low but no less commanding.

My breath locked in my chest as the Sorceress lifted her hand. An icy chill surrounded me, replacing the warmth. This didn't trouble the Sorceress, as one by one she touched my fellow crewmen, on the shoulder, the arm, never in the same place and never for long. The last in her journey was Ned. He sat staring at his feet, his hands clasped as though in prayer. He shook at the Sorceress' touch.

"There is a frightful amount of deception within this crew. I am in disbelief that so much can be hidden, whilst in such close proximity."

She hadn't taken her hand from Ned. He eyed her warily, his expression pleading.

"Claudette," the Sorceress called, ignoring him. "There is a whisper in the wind you were bequeathed very little in the Chest of Forgotten Treasures, is that right?"

"Yes, your grace, though Nathaniel gained very little too." Claudette ducked her head in respect before continuing, "Although my father has given me so much already,"

Claudette echoed Ned's words of comfort. She smiled as she held her damaged arm close to her body. The pain was etched by the strain in her face.

"Oh is that a fact?" The Sorceress straightened. "What if I was to tell you—"

No! What was she doing? Claudette couldn't find out like this.

"Please!" I cut in, getting to my feet. Just like with Hadnaloy, my courage left no room for fear. The Sorceress ignored the interruption but I continued on, regardless of the implications.

"Haven't you hurt us enough?" I demanded.

"Hurt you?" The Sorceress spun, she could no longer

disregard my outburst and her strange eyes narrowed.

"You have been ripped from your debauched lives, given a place to live, food to eat and companions to enjoy life with. Where pray tell, is the pain? I see no hurt."

"Enough." Ned straightened his shoulders brushing past the Sorceress, he approached Claudette. As he walked, I could almost see the man he had once been. He stood straighter, a smile lit up his face. If you took away his scars and grey hair, he almost looked his rightful age.

He did not hesitate in taking Claudette's uninjured hand as he reached her.

"Please forgive me for what I am about to tell you," he paused, weighing his words. "I am your–"

"–You are my father."

They spoke in unison and my heart swelled.

"You knew?" Ned asked.

"Not in the beginning; but I always felt we were connected."

Her smile lit her face and even from where I sat, I could see the unique colour return to Claudette's eyes.

"Papa," she murmured wrapping her arms around him.

The Sorceress watched them curiously, her expression had softened.

"Touching, the love of a child and their parent. It is the purest form of love. I cannot tamper with it."

"Does that mean that if Claudette was to say she loved Ned, neither would perish?"

Rupert succumbed to tears as he spoke, moisture ran down his pale freckled face and he failed to wipe them away. All of us had turned to look at him, that was the most lucid he'd been since Hadnaloy had appeared.

"You are correct," the Sorceress replied. "A blood bond is not something you can break. Bonds of the heart however" The Sorceress paused, stepping towards him. She looked contemplative as she stared at his red ringed eyes.

"Something is amiss with your aura, son of Charles." She said standing in front of him, her gaze barely level with his.

"I noticed it before but it is stronger now." She pressed her lips together as she cocked her head to one side.

"Give me your hands," she commanded.

Without hesitation he held them up to her. His coin faced upwards from his right palm. The eyes of the skull still glowed; the red mixed with the blue of the flames cast a strange mauve tinge.

"Tainted," the Sorceress hissed, her delicate wings fluttered in agitation.

A wild look came over her as she turned. Hovering inches above the ground, she grasped the lapels of Ned's jacket wrenching him away from his daughter. She brought their faces within inches of each other; her wide dark eyes stared straight into his.

"Rosa, I know you can hear me, she has blighted us

with her evil." The Sorceress' voice bordered on hysterical.

Caw burst through the trees, confirming Rosa's acknowledgement, before soaring skyward. Letting go of Ned, the Sorceress turned to the captain.

"To Rosa's cove my dear and we shall convene this meeting there. Keep everyone on their guard." She glanced at Rupert. "I am afraid he will have to be detained."

The captain nodded before gesturing to Nathaniel and Butch. The two men did as they were bid, flanking Rupert. He stared up at them, his expression resigned.

The Sorceress presented her palms to the fire again, the sparkling circle returned to its original blue. She raised it high and swept it back to its home. Seeing this as an official dismissal, the captain stood.

"Come on men," the captain said as he led the way, rushing over the bridge and through the trees.

Nathaniel was quiet as he walked beside me, one arm restraining Rupert. Disappointment clouded his face as we walked up the beach. I lagged a little further behind, my mind muddled with so many thoughts. Would Rupert return to us? What did our future hold? Would the curse ever end?

So distracted, I missed my footing and the sand came up to greet me. Before I could hit the ground, however, Nathaniel's arm shot out. As his skin touched mine, pain ripped through me. Beyond my own scream, I could hear

Nathaniel's deep howl of agony. There was no choice but to fall, I curled on the sand and allowed myself come apart.

Burning, stabbing, biting, all forms of pain attacked my being and gnawed at my mind. Images of my past, present and future anguish filled me up as they danced across my lids. Nothing could stop them.

Someone picked me up rocking me back and forth and whispering gentle nothings. I couldn't stand it, I writhed within the hold.

"Leave me," I gasped. The pain was torturous.

"You'll be fine." the captain's voice was close enough for me to fathom that it was he who carried me. Claudette too was close by, muttering incantations I couldn't understand. Her cool fingers touched my face and the strange words she chanted caused the pain to ebb. I sighed as only a dull ache remained. *Thank goodness*, I thought as my lungs allowed me to breathe again.

Reaching the ship, the captain placed me on the deck, I lay back looking skyward, though I saw little of it. The others gathered around me, concern plain on their drawn faces and furrowed brows. Nathaniel and Davy left to put Rupert in the brig. I caught sight of Nathaniel and he too, seemed to be recovering from the pain. His vivid eyes were tear filled and the strain around them told me everything. This was no coincidence.

I turned away from the group their eyes bore into me and I was in no mood to talk. What had happened? Did this reaction have something to do with the Sorceress and the new connection which was now between us?

Though the silence resonated throughout the ship, I laid waiting. My mind still held echoes of the pain filled delusions. Death, hurt, pain. The thought caused tremors to pass through me. Nathaniel hadn't returned to the deck and I was sure he'd felt the pain too. It had to be linked in some way.

"Lennie, can I talk to you?" Butch asked as he knelt beside me.

I sighed but rolled over to face him. Everyone else had dispersed and for that I was thankful.

"Yes?" I winced as I coughed the hoarseness away.

"You should rest; let me help you to your room." Butch made to lift me.

"No!" I yelped recoiling from him.

"What's wrong?" Butch exclaimed. His eyes held hurt as he backed away.

"I don't want to hurt you," I murmured.

Pushing myself onto my knees proved a challenge as my weary limbs fumbled on the slippery surface. As I got to my feet I swayed, biting the inside of my cheek as I clutched the rail.

"I don't think you will," Butch muttered but stopped as I threw him a dark look.

He swallowed hard before be pulled something from his pocket.

"Here, I think you should see this." Butch handed me

a folded sheet of parchment. I looked at it in confusion.

"It's something Nathaniel dropped," Butch said walking away.

I watched him leave before I turned in the opposite direction. He'd grown so sullen since Nathaniel's arrival, he used to be such a cheeky lad. Pushing my concern aside as I reached my cabin, I lit a candle and I put my weary body to bed. Curling up in the blankets, I unfolded the parchment. Reading it with care, I felt the tears as they fell down my cheeks. They weren't from the lingering pain, however. The simple verse Nathaniel had written was so pain filled and honest. I wasn't the only one undertaking 'reckless behaviour' Nathaniel had laid his heart out on a paper. No wonder I wasn't the only one to be punished.

"Oh Nathaniel," I whimpered.

I folded the note and placed it with the handkerchief, close to my heart. As much as I knew it was wrong of me to keep hold of it. I couldn't pass it back. Not only had the lyrical verse touched me, how would I explain my having it? No, I would keep it, perhaps I would have a chance to slip it back into his journal.

Wiping away the evidence of my tears, I blew out the candle and laid my head down. Nathaniel's writing echoed in my mind, along with the memories of the pain I'd felt when he had touched me. Would that pain always be?

Despite these distractions, I fell into a restless sleep. My dreams were filled with the same disturbing images and pain filled words, they were my only companions until I awoke to the sound of the anchor.

The cove shone like a beacon in the ever present darkness.

"Where's Lennie?" I heard Butch say as I dawdled at the bottom of the stairs.

"She'll be along, I'm sure," Ned replied as he spotted me climbing the deck. He gave a half-smile before ushering the crew onward.

I waited until the everyone had left the ship. Once I knew it was safe, I descended the rope ladder alone. I sighed as I found Claudette waiting for me. Neither of us spoke as we followed the men into the cove. The companionable silence was just what I needed, and despite my initial irritation I was thankful for Claudette's quiet strength.

Rosa was joined on her plinth by the Sorceress. The faery's small frame was curled upon the stone. She used a flat metal object to carve the rock surrounding her. Atop her tool was the sign of the *Wilted Rose*. The concentration creased her porcelain skin making her look more human somehow.

"You took an age in getting here." The Sorceress didn't look up through her disapproving welcome.

"I told you mistress," Rosa said patiently "Lennie fell prey to your power."

Her expression held such empathy as she stared down at me.

"Nevertheless." The Sorceress' gesture was dismissive. "We are in trouble. Rupert, son of Charles, has been bewitched by our enemy."

I turned, Nathaniel and Butch flanked the redhead, his expression solemn as he watched the magical being.

"How did this happen?" The Sorceress glared at them. Her whole body vibrated in anger as she made to stand.

"Hadnaloy attacked us; he took Rupert's c-coin." Davy faltered.

"We have to destroy it. The piece of her embedded within Claudette is no longer, I can sense that." The Sorceress mused aloud.

My gaze turned to my enchanted friend. A large raw welt had appeared where Hadnaloy's mark had once been.

Close by, Rupert chewed on his lip and jogged his foot, shaking his head.

"There's no warrant for your panic," he said. "I'm harmless."

"Rupert," Rosa's voice was soft, a pleading note that echoed off the walls of the cavern. "Please let us destroy all curses which befall us. You almost hurt your fellow crewmate, we don't want that to happen again, do we?"

Rupert opened his mouth to argue more but something flickered in his eyes as they locked with Rosa's. The wooden woman nodded and the redhead sighed, Butch and Nathaniel took a step back as he pulled the coin from his pocket. With one flip of his thumb, it took off. The light caught each facet as it arched over the small pool below the plinth. Without ceremony it landed at the Sorceress' feet.

"Tainted," she hissed, holding her metal tool like a weapon.

Clenching her teeth, she stabbed at the offensive object. It did nothing but push the coin onto a boulder that rested in the water.

I felt my limbs awaken, as if they were being pulled by puppet strings. A voice inside my head said, *'end this'*. My body returned to its own control as I wended my way through the boulders and benches. Momentum had me walking towards the plinth, stopping just beside Rupert.

"Yes, child?" Rosa didn't look surprised to see me standing there. Was it her voice? Or was it the Sorceress' that had brought me there? Whoever it was, I knew why they'd got me to my feet.

"I wish to try," I appealed, unsure why I needed to but something nudged me to continue.

"Go ahead," Rosa agreed, her hands spread wide.

"Wait." The Sorceress' command stalled me. "You felt deeper pain then the depths of hades, did you not?"

"Yes," I said my tone curt.

"Do you understand why such a thing should happen?"

"The object of my affection, aided me." My monotone delivery and contemptuous gaze spoke volumes.

Fire laced anger bubbled through my bloodstream. As

it reached boiling point, I wrenched the sword from my belt. I wielded it over my head before slamming the blade into the coin. The chime of metal on metal crashed in my ears. A loud ungodly scream echoed from the depths of nowhere. My chest pounded as I stared down at the now halved coin. Sheathing my weapon, I bent to pick up the pieces. They felt warm to the touch but the distorted halves of the symbol were no longer a cursed red.

"I apologise for the damage," I said.

Without pausing, I tossed Rupert the pieces and left the cove without a backwards glance.

Tears fell unchecked as I walked back through the tunnel and out towards the *Wilted Rose*. Rupert's pain was over, but mine was nowhere near past.

"Lennie!" I turned as Rupert raced to catch up.

"Yes?" I said brushing aside the tears.

"For whatever I did, I'm sorry," he said.

"There's no need, I knew it wasn't you."

"Len, I almost killed you." He took a step closer. The spark had returned to his eyes and his cheeks were flushed once more.

"But you didn't," I stated. "Now stop being so sincere, it's not normal!"

"Piss off!" He scoffed, shoving me away with a wink.

"That's my boy," I murmured as he raced back to the crew.

MY TEETH CHATTERED as I pulled my shaking fingers beneath my sleeves. The blanket I'd added to the pile that littered the bed did nothing to ease the stinging cold. No matter what I did, I just couldn't get warm. As much as I wanted to call out, I couldn't risk it, the fear of hurting someone else had me biting the sheet to stop the scream. The cotton touched my tongue making me retch.

Since returning from the cove, my body had been going through extremes, from scalding heat to freezing cold and every other temperature in between. Frustration propelled me out of bed. Taking the best part of the blankets with me, I shuffled out the door.

Low burning lights guided me onward and the sounds of sleeping patrons had me carefully passing each door. Something within me was saying goodbye to each person beyond the wooden entrance.

Reaching the deck, rain splattered the sails as they filled and emptied with each gust. I stood transfixed for a moment watching them. The rhythm it created kept time with my throbbing heart. The pain still lingered, tingling the blood in my veins and giving me a constant headache behind one eye.

The wind whipped my hair around my face as I leaned over the rail. I was so tired of fighting for an unobtainable dream. No matter what hoops we jumped through or how low we bowed and scraped, we were all still cursed. The Sorceress wasn't going to change that, she had her own sick game and we were merely the pawns. No matter if we ended the curse wouldn't we all die anyway? What was the point in it all? Curses, heartbreak, friendship, it all ended in pain. Same ending different journey.

My thoughts darkened as they tumbled around in my muddled brain. Death couldn't be any more painful than what I'd already been through. It would be like falling asleep, wouldn't it? Like drifting off to a dreamless abyss where faery Sorceress' couldn't curse you, where my body would never be used again. It sounded like paradise. It sounded grand.

Making my own decision on these matters meant that my death would be on my own terms. There would be no outside influence besides the fact I was now a 'vessel.' The Sorceress had chosen me just as she had chosen Rosa. I knew, deep in my soul, I couldn't compare to the wooden woman, and would not compete even if I had the energy to. All the fight and feeling I had once possessed was gone. I was tired, too bone weary to even muster up any spirit. The fear I usually ignored was front and centre. My fight had been demolished and that is what scared me the most. Death didn't frighten me; it was a means to an end.

Dropping my blankets, I reached inside my nightclothes and pulled out Nathaniel's handkerchief. His scent still lingered upon the fabric and floated in the air around me. I pulled in the aroma and drew my final piece of courage from it. That was all I needed, one small piece. Unfolding the gift, I retrieved the note Butch had handed me. I didn't need to open it to know what it said. The shivers took hold again and I stowed away the two priceless objects I would keep though they had no use in the place I was going. I focussed myself and soon my body stopped convulsing. I was still and I was ready.

I climbed aboard the rail, my bare feet wobbling only a moment before I righted myself. The damp breeze whipped around me, threatening to throw me off balance, but I wouldn't allow it. If I failed at this, then I truly was a failure.

Closing my eyes, I pulled in the sea air and let my words whisper on the wind:

"Take my soul, take my heart. Store it away, rip it apart. All that glitters barely passes for gold. Here I go, to places untold."

Pulling in one last breath I stepped off the rail, spreading my arms out like wings. The rush that coursed through me was intense. Like flying, falling, sinking and euphoria all at once. Yet my anguish refused to let me experience any joy in the feeling. Tears mixed with the rain as Nathaniel, Ned, Butch, Rupert, Davy, Claudette, the Captain and even the women who raised me, flashed before my eyes. A small modicum of regret tugged at me but it was long gone before I was catapulted into the ice cold water I craved. Darkness consumed me as I was dragged below and I begged for freedom no more.

CHAPTER XVIII
PERMISSIONS

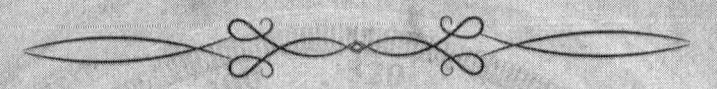

WAS THIS DEATH? Or was this merely purgatory? All I knew for sure was that I didn't feel cold any more.

"Death is only for the honoured."

The voice was recognisable as it invaded my subconscious.

"You are an unworthy and selfish girl," the person scolded. "How dare you?"

I'd failed, I knew I wasn't dead. The voice belonged to the Sorceress and I would have been free of the magical creature had I perished. I opened my eyes and my vision was clear, only the coarseness of my throat and the tiredness of my body gave proof of my jump into the depths.

"I needed to think," I croaked. I wasn't aboard the ship I was on land, the scent of earth and nature surrounded me. I turned back to the Sorceress, determined to explain.

"I'm naught but your slave, you have bewitched me; it was all I knew to free myself."

"I am here to help you," the Sorceress argued,

"despite your obvious compulsion to harm yourself. Do I want the curse broken? No. It is up to you and your crew mates to show me otherwise. I am not convinced thus far."

She spun, soaring through the trees with a flutter of her striking wings.

I frowned; I wasn't in the forest clearing as I'd first thought. I was nestled in the grass of a large meadow. I lay upon the warm natural mattress, surrounded by wild roses and foxgloves. Their sweet scents overpowered any other and I drew them in again and again. Satisfied I felt well, I attempted to sit; the world revolved for a moment before it settled. Reaching out a hand, I touched a dew stained petal.

"This is her meadow."

I stilled. I was sure I had imagined the all too familiar voice but there he was. His bright blue eyes saying far more than his words ever could. His iris's held pain and anger and my shame increased tenfold. How foolish I was to think it wouldn't matter to him. Or how his reaction would mean so much to me.

"Nathaniel."

His name fell from my lips and I fought the urge to run into his arms or beg forgiveness at his feet. The memories of the last time he'd touched me were fresh in my mind and I would be damned if I hurt him further.

"What is this place?" I asked, attempting to stand.

"It is part of the Sorceress' forest," Nathaniel replied.

"When we had rescued you, she brought us all back here."

"The entire crew came back?" My mind whirled with a hundred different thoughts and questions.

"We didn't even hear you." Nathaniel swallowed hard, stepping forward; his face was filled with the anguish he could no longer hide. "Why did you do it, Lennie? Did you not know how much I–"

"–Of course I did," I interrupted. "I just couldn't bear it any more. I feel pain, even now with you here, my heart throbs."

I pushed out a ragged breath, my palm resting over the erratic heartbeat at my chest. "I'm so sorry I wasn't strong enough"

Nathaniel edged closer; he was mere inches away now.

"I have something of yours, we found it in the water." He said.

Nathaniel pulled from his pocket, his handkerchief. It was neatly folded, though dampness had seeped into the fabric. The wrinkled paper which accompanied it looked ruined.

"Should I ask where you found that?" He said as I brought both items to my chest.

"Are you angry?"

"No, I'm glad you carry a part of me with you. It's just that I write so many things, I wished you would have found something more fitting. A sonnet perhaps…"

"I would like to read them," I said. "If you let me."

Nathaniel nodded, opening his arms, beckoning me forward.

"I want to, I just–" I hesitated.

"Come here," he urged.

I couldn't resist his request and swallowing back my trepidation, I fell into his arms. Tears filled my eyes but I wasn't crying from pain. Warmth that came from feeling, rather than magic, filled me up and made me whole again. How could I have been so wrong? There was so much I would have lost had my plan worked. This time, failure was something I was glad for.

"Please do not ever think that I could live in a world, without you in it."

Nathaniel pressed a kiss to the top of my head. He paused and I stared up at him. A seed of an idea bloomed in his eyes alongside his smile.

"I want to take you home," he said.

I pulled back, a frown creasing my forehead.

"Home, you mean where you were raised?"

He nodded his elation lighting up his face. "I want you to meet my Uncle and Bess."

"Are you sure I would be welcome?" My nervousness piqued as his excitement grew. This felt very wrong, I couldn't be among his people, I would be run out of town or worse.

"Uncle Henry will adore you," he assured, spying my wariness.

I wasn't convinced. I knew that Nathaniel and I shared

something special and that in any normal circumstance I would meet his family. My background and breeding were miles apart from his and this definitely wasn't a normal situation. Yet his eagerness prevented me from even uttering my fears.

Though stunned by the idea, I allowed Nathaniel to lead me through the maze of trees and into the more familiar clearing. I could see the strain and even anger in the expressions of my crew mates as we reached them. They all looked up as I approached them.

"I want to apologise to you all—" I began.

"—Please sit," Captain Rourke interrupted.

I did as he bid, perching on a log. Nathaniel sat beside me, wrapping his hand in my own.

"I don't know how to explain," I said, tears pooling in my eyes. I dashed them away, I had no right to cry, I had let my fellow crewmates down.

"There's no need," Butch said as he crouched before me, grasping my free hand tightly.

"There is!" I argued. "I felt there like nothing was left for me here, that I wanted to die on my own terms. I was wrong."

I pulled in a breath before releasing it slowly. The effort was painful.

"I have a family here. You're all part of me and I would have harmed you more if I had succeeded. I promise you all that I will never try that again."

"Glad to hear it," Rupert said, nudging Butch out of

the way to grasp me in a bear hug.

"Here, here," Davy said raising his tankard.

"I just hope my stupidity has not weakened our chances of eradicating the curse."

"One mistake does not a failure make." Nathaniel rhymed, causing smiles throughout the group.

"Do you think I could talk with you a moment?" Ned asked.

Nathaniel shared a smile with the older man and with a brush of his lips to the back of my hand he let go.

My heart contracted at the sight of Ned's weathered face; I could see what my frivolous actions had done. Swallowing back my mounting regrets I clutched Ned's hand in both of mine.

"Wait," Claudette cried stopped us on our journey. She flung her arms around me gripping hard, before pulling back.

"If you try that again I shall see to it you are hexed most brutally in the next life!" She scolded. "Forgive my frankness but I regard you as a sister, losing you would kill me, never forget that." Claudette's eyes stared deep into mine.

"I have promised. I'll not break my word," I vowed.

"I am so glad to hear it, please proceed Papa," Claudette said, her smile returning as she swept away.

"My daughter gets her dramatics from her mother, I'm sure." Ned chuckled as he led them through the trees.

"Pray tell, to where do we journey?" I quirked a

mocking brow as Ned led us further into the trees.

"You will see soon enough child."

Though I still felt weak from my foray into the ocean, the walk didn't tire me. Ned kept the pace slow, staying quiet so we both could listen to the sounds of the forest. Woodland creatures scurried around our feet, while birds rustled the leaves above us. Caw followed close by, soaring amongst the branches, stopping here and there to converse with the other inhabitants of the forest.

Ned came to a stop in a large clump of trees. Though it was still day, the sun scarcely made its mark through the dense leaves. The light that did manage to escape sent green tinged shafts across the undergrowth and anyone within it. Pulling a knife from his belt, Ned rested a hand against the trunk, without warning he began to carve at the wood. I watched, perplexed as he continued to hack at the tree, collecting the small pieces of bark into his hand.

"What has my home done to offend you?"

I yelped in surprise, as from a knot in the trunk, a small creature flew. Her hair was spiked up from within her crooked flower halo and her dress was patched and frayed.

"Thought that would wake you up, how are you, my dear Tatters?"

"Only you would remember that nickname."

The small faery crossed her arms as she hovered in mid-air. One wing drooped causing her to hover at an angle. I would have laughed had it not been for the creature's dark expression.

"I just wanted to introduce you to someone, meet Lennie."

I tried not to look too excited. I had read about faeries and met the Sorceress but she had yet to be introduced to any more winged forest dwellers. Though the Sorceress was small, she was nowhere near as tiny as Tatters. This creature could sit comfortably on my hand and still have room.

"Pleasure to meet the lady," Tatters said disdain dripping from each syllable.

Ned chuckled. "Tatters was much like you and I, Lennie. She's had times where she felt she had no purpose and was full of pain. She saw the light and now would you look at her."

"I'm the epitome of happiness and light." The faery rolled her eyes and turned away, flashing her patched up wings.

"But you have survived."

"I sure have. Now stop hacking at my tree and go back to that God forsaken ship."

"As you wish Tatters."

The faery flitted back into her home leaving me and Ned alone. He smiled to himself as he munched on the bark he'd cut.

"You wanted to teach me something," I guessed.

"Correct," he said, offering me a portion of his find. I

took it and nibbled.

"Is eating this really any good for you?" I asked letting the unique substance slide down my throat.

"It has not killed me yet, has it?" He chuckled before turning serious again.

"Though she is grumpy and perhaps a smidgen bitter, Tatters was a faery on the brink of destruction. She and the Sorceress were not on the best of terms and Tatters nearly defected to the dark side, her mistakes were large."

"What happened?"

Ned paused, weighing his reply. "Tatters saw the light and found something in the Sorceress that she knew was different. I don't know the entire story but when I have visited I always make a trip to her tree. She reminds me of myself. No pain is enough to die for, Lennie remember that."

"I know that now," I finished the bark in my hand and turned to leave.

"Did you notice how sweet that was?" Ned asked.

"Like fruit." I agreed touching the exposed sap of the tree and tasting it.

"Tatters magic is such, that even the Sorceress is envious. Remember we all have gifts child."

"Thank you," I said, taking the older man's hand.

"I can tell that something else troubles you," Ned said as we wandered back towards the clearing.

"Nathaniel wants me to meet his family."

"Most would be elated." Ned stopped and I took a

few more steps before turning to face him

"You, child, are more than worthy." He reached out and touched a hand to my cheek.

"Please, Ned, you know they will to hate me. I'm no prize for a man of Nathaniel's rank. Besides we are still cursed. Would it be the wisest decision?"

"Whatever you decide will be right, child."

I nodded hoping he spoke the truth. Grasping his hand, we continued on.

The two of us emerged from the trees as the rest of the crew were beginning their evening meal. Ned joined the others, grabbing a plate and digging in. I shook my head at Claudette who offered up a dish. instead I wandered over to Nathaniel. He'd set up a quill and ink on the bridge and laboured over a letter. Balled up pieces of parchment were littered around him and some even floated on the water below.

The horror of my jump that haunted his features had evaporated, and a wide smile now lit up his face. I couldn't deny, I liked the change in him. He signed his name with a flourish, his eyes sparkling as he found mine.

"I cannot wait for his reply," he said. Standing, he pressed a kiss to my forehead before going in search for Caw.

"Mind if I join you?" Butch asked coming to sit beside me.

"Sure," I replied. We both swung our legs back and forth as we sat in silence. Butch's boots brushed the stream below us, causing ripples.

"I wish I knew what to say to you," he said finally breaking the quiet.

"I've been chastised enough, Butch."

"I just – I don't know what you were thinking." He ran hand through his already dishevelled hair.

"It seemed logical at the time," I said, leaning forward to make faced into the water.

"Now it doesn't?"

"Now it doesn't," I agreed.

"Well, don't let it happen again, we need you, Lennie – I need you." He nudged my shoulder and we returned to our silence.

"LENNIE," NATHANIEL CALLED as he raced through the trees.

It had been less than an hour since he'd left the clearing but I knew what was coming. I shared a knowing look with Ned before I turned to meet Nathaniel half way. As I walked, what felt like large knots, tightened in my stomach. I pressed a fist to my abdomen trying to calm the sensation.

"Yes?"

"Listen to this." Nathaniel's face was flushed, as he opened the envelope and read with gusto.

Dearest Nathaniel,

I am so relieved to hear you are safe; I have been most concerned by your disappearance. Now that I have heard from you, I would be overjoyed to see you and in such good health.

In response to your letter, you and your friend would be most welcome to return for as long as you wish. I appreciate your continued search for your mother. I just wish it was not from so far away.

Stay safe and return soon, my dear boy.

Your Uncle,

Sir Henry Davenport, Esq.

Nathaniel's excitement was clear as he finished, his bright eyes said it all. There was no eagerness in me to leave, and the guilt I felt in that hurt. Foreboding clouded my conscience, I knew this trip could not end well. No matter how well I kept my p's and q's.

"We'll have to be granted permission," I warned, hoping this would deter him.

"The Sorceress will let us."

The conviction Nathaniel expressed stalled my next excuse. I sighed as I followed him through the trees.

Since arriving on her lands, we had not seen much of the Sorceress, nor any of her loyal subjects. We had no idea where she resided; did she live in a knot like Tatters, or perhaps a faery palace? Nathaniel and I looked in all manner of locations. Rock pools, flowers beds. It was close to dusk when we stumbled upon a clump of trees nestled deep within the forest.

A small blue fire lit the Sorceress' face, illuminating

her unfocussed eyes. She acknowledged nothing but the flames. We approached with care, our steps soft on the moss covered ground. I steadied my breathing, the only sound amongst the dimness. The fear built within me and I forced it away, focussing on the Sorceress.

Could this attempted trip anger the wood nymph? Our relationship was already fragile. I was still unsure of my feelings towards the all-powerful creature; could this be just the thing to tip it over the edge?

"You are here to request permission," the Sorceress said without preamble. "Though I see trials ahead of you, I must let you go."

She sounded resigned. "I see defeat, pain and almost death. You will attempt to ease those negative contributions, you will succeed."

She blinked as she sat up and moved her focus to us. "Be gone, before I change my mind."

CHAPTER XIX
OLD FRIENDS &
NEW ACQUAINTANCES

"SO ENGLAND IS our next destination, agreed?" Captain Rourke slapped his hand on the table, signalling the finality of his statement.

"Here, here!" The group chorused.

I remained quiet, though no one but Claudette noticed. Her unusual eyes narrowed in my direction as my crewmates cheered and chattered around us. As the men filed out of the saloon, Claudette closed the door behind them. I watched her pick her way around the table, her hands brushing the frames of the portraits which flanked it. Stopping at the chair beside me, she settled herself into it.

"I thought you were fond of Nathaniel?" She said.

Above us, the sound of a card game filtered through the ceiling. The scraping of chair legs and inaudible ruckus punctuated the quiet below.

"I don't deny my affection for him," I said picking at the many flaws in the wooden table.

"And yet...?"

"Yet, I'm not a woman gentlemen take home. You

don't know much of my past Claudette, I'm not proud of what I once was," I said. My gaze strayed to the portrait of my mother, what would she have done?

"Does your past dictate the woman you are now?" Claudette asked. She grasped my arm, forcing our eyes to meet.

"Yes, I'm wary, suspicious and as much as it irks me to admit it, I feel weakened by it."

Claudette shook her head. "You my dear, are strong. Your past has given you lessons from which you have learned. You are well read and speak with such eloquence, what is it about you that they will hate? That you are a pirate? What is Nathaniel, a knight?"

Her question stalled my argument, I had not thought of that. Yes, here aboard the *Wilted Rose*, Nathaniel was a fellow pirate, my equal. But back in England he was a nobleman's nephew and of higher rank and class.

"This is not reality Claudette; we're in our own world here. We have different rules and etiquette," I said with a shake of my head,

"Think what you will, but that man adores you. The fact that he wants his family to meet you is a sure sign that he wants to have you in his life, beyond the curse."

The light of hope Claudette had conjured glowed bright within me, but I extinguished it almost instantly – it would do no good. With a sigh I reached into my jacket, pulling out the handkerchief.

"We don't even know if the curse will be lifted yet,

I'm not the Sorceress' most favourite person if you recall."

I ran the material through my fingers before tracing over the embroidered insignia.

"You wanted nothing more than to leave this earth before; at that moment you felt there was no way forward, am I right?"

Claudette's words were low and soft; they were hard for me to ignore. They were all true, at that time. I stared at the memento in my hands as Claudette continued her diatribe.

"This is a future, something to live for. What harm will it do meeting the people who shaped the man we see today?"

"It sounds simple when you say it like that."

"That is because it is," Claudette wandered to a porthole. She swiped her hand over the condensation clouding the window leaving a mere trail of distorted glass.

"As much as I'm protesting, I know I have to go. I couldn't break Nathaniel's heart like that."

Claudette turned back, something close to pity clouding her expression.

"I know you are scared, Lennie, these people are naught without their propriety, rank and honour. Yet Nathaniel himself is not a pure bred man, nor are many of the aristocracy, as much they profess to be."

"How did you get to be so smart?" I teased.

"Macrucio was not the only one who used to read." She winked, wandering through the door and leaving me alone with my thoughts.

So there it was, I would be journeying to England, in reluctance and fear but with my head held high. At least I could say I was broadening my horizons.

"ARE YOU READY for tomorrow?"

I turned to find Nathaniel leaning against the door frame of my cabin. He looked contented and calm, something I'd been feigning immeasurably since our return to the ship.

"Almost," I replied, folding my jacket and laying it on the end of my bed.

"Do you miss your home town?" Nathaniel asked, stepping over the threshold. "I know you have uncomfortable memories, but do you miss the place?"

I slumped onto my mattress bringing my knees up to my chest. "I don't think about it much."

Nathaniel sat beside me wrapping an arm around me. He stayed quiet, waiting for me to continue.

"I certainly miss Clara and Victoria and wonder what their lives are like now." I said.

"Do you miss the language?"

"French?" I said through a chuckle.

Nathaniel had taken a lock of my hair between his

fingers and was playing with it. I watched fascinated for a moment before I replied.

"Sometimes, though there are many chances to use my knowledge in French, Spanish and English; our opportunities to travel are wide, you know?"

"Oh I think I noticed," he teased nudging me.

"Why the questions?"

"Home," he said. "I adore my uncle and Bess but in being away from them, I have discovered myself without all the notoriety, expectation and pomp of Nathaniel Davenport-Lee. I like this Nathaniel."

"Well I don't find him too bad either," I said grinning up at him.

"Land ahoy!"

Our locked eyes blinked as Butch's call signalled our arrival.

"Well this is it." Nathaniel leapt up, visibly anxious to leave.

"Yes," I breathed. "Dear God, let me live through this." I muttered to myself, slinging my duffle bag over my shoulder.

Reaching the deck, I was greeted by the entire crew.

"We shall see what the night life has to offer and will meet up with you soon." The captain was the first to wish us good luck.

Ned pulled me close. He didn't speak, but the fear already building within me was clear in the older man's grey eyes.

"Take care," Butch mumbled as I let the older man go.

"Butch," I called, catching hold of his arm.

"Take care," he repeated, clearer this time as I let him go.

"I will."

Butch nodded, his hand hovered close to my face but didn't touch. He swallowed hard, shaking his head before dropping his arm.

"I know you have the same fighting spirit as I do. Go get 'em!" He flashed a boyish grin that didn't meet his eyes, before joining the others.

Claudette was the last to say goodbye. Pulling me into an embrace she whispered low.

"Do not accentuate your flaws but do not deny them either." With that said, she pulled away.

Nathaniel and I bid them farewell stepping onto the harbour. The dock was laden with people, yet I felt no anxiety in being surrounded – I'd been raised amongst crowds. Nathaniel took hold of my hand, guiding me onto the loading area. Carriages lined the gravel, dropping off and collecting patrons. As the two of us headed further into the throng, a dark horse-drawn town carriage pulled up beside us.

"Master Nathaniel?" the driver said.

"Blanchard?" Nathaniel double took the man who had just dismounted.

He was a nondescript gentleman dressed in a clean and smart uniform. A simple crest of a stream with fish leaping was sewn over his heart. The man, Blanchard, smiled before shaking Nathaniel's hand.

"We have been awaiting your return, Sir."

"You are here for us?" Nathaniel asked, raising a brow.

"Certainly."

I held tight to Nathaniel as he helped me into the carriage. I sat as demurely as I could. Crossing my legs and attempting to stare wistfully from the window. My clothes let me down though, they were nothing like the other ladies which sat in the vehicles surrounding us.

I pulled off my hat, letting my hair flow over my shoulders, hiding my face. Nathaniel joined me and with a slight jerk, we were off. Nathaniel remained silent beside me, not awkward, not troubled, just taking in his old life as it passed him by or so I guessed. A small smile played on his lips so I knew he wasn't worried. At least one of us wasn't.

I couldn't fathom what my reception would be at the Davenport estate. I wasn't a person of rank or good standing. Yet I was the woman Nathaniel cared for, would that count for something? All of Claudette's well-meaning wisdom held little amongst the feelings of inadequacy threatening to overwhelm me on the journey.

The carriage wound its way through the town and away from the harbour. I grasped Nathaniel's hand as I stared out at the passing scenery. Fearful of what was to come and what I might have to endure.

"I promise you will find the house very

accommodating," Nathaniel murmured, pushing a stray lock of hair from my face.

I smiled through my nerves, wondering if 'house' meant same thing in my estimation as it did in his. The carriage rolled its way through another small street, people gaping at us as we passed. Nathaniel was still recognisable, despite the obvious changes he'd gone through, over the past year. His hair a tad longer, his tan a little darker, his chin covered in stubble, but the same blue eyes stared back at them. The driver slowed the horses as we entered a pair of wrought iron gates.

Stable hands rushed to and fro, tending to the many vehicles which lined the drive. Blanchard eased our horses to a stop before jumping off to help tether them.

"Does my uncle have guests?" Nathaniel asked, leaning out the window.

"Yes Master Nathaniel," the driver said bowing his head. "He has a ball every year at this time."

"Of course," Nathaniel replied frowning at the bustling scene.

I squeezed his hand as I surveyed the main house. My stomach lurched as I looked up, and kept on looking. It rose for miles. I had never seen a place so grand in scale. Light emanated from every window. Even though the night surrounded it, the building – I wouldn't call it a house again – was a sight to behold.

Nathaniel left the carriage first, aiding me as I stepped onto the gravel. I wobbled on the stones grasping hold of his arm. He looked down at me with a winning smile. I wondered if he held any nerves at all. He looked calm enough, though his gaze was wary as he took in the surroundings.

"Should I inform your uncle of your arrival?" Blanchard asked.

"Please," Nathaniel said, as he led me up the wide stone steps towards the entrance. The doorman's eyes widened as he bowed us through.

There was so much to take in, the foyer was grand with dark oppressive panelled walls. A staircase stood against one wall, winding upward to where a wide bay window showed the sun setting. People were everywhere, their clothes elegant and their discussions muted, no one paid attention to us. Music billowed from a room further along the corridor and the sounds of lively dancing echoed off the walls.

I couldn't stop looking at a painting which hung above the door at the end of the passage. The woman staring from the frame was dressed in a formal gown, her painted half-smile held many secrets. Her bright blue eyes were so piercing; they could only belong to one person. Maria Davenport, Nathaniel's mother.

Trailing my gaze to the opening beneath it, I spied an older woman with greying hair. Her pale uniform was crisp and unsoiled. As she walked over the threshold she muttered to herself, worriedly wringing her hands in her pristine white apron.

"Evening, Bess."

Her head shot up and she stilled at Nathaniel's voice. Wrenching her hands from the fabric, she pressed them to her mouth.

"Nate, is that you?"

"Of course it is, I have not changed that much surely?" He let go of me to wrap the woman in a fond embrace.

"Oh, my dear boy, how I have missed you."

Nathaniel wiped tears from her face as she spoke.

"I kept telling your uncle you would be back one of these days and here you are. Come and warm yourself before you greet him," she urged as she started back down the corridor.

"Bess before we do that, allow me to introduce you to someone very dear to me." He pulled me closer, his arm circling my waist.

"This is Valencia Roux." he said.

Bess gaped, her wide eyes staring from Nathaniel to me and back again. Tears spilled down her cheeks for a second time. *Oh no*, I thought, *it's happening already. I'm so glad I hadn't unpacked anything.*

To my surprise, the housekeeper smiled. "My dear girl, come to me."

She stepped forward and pulled me into her arms. The embrace spoke volumes. Of all the things I thought I would encounter, acceptance from Nathaniel's cherished motherly figure wasn't one of them. I too had to brush away tears as I stepped back.

"Come through, my children, warm yourselves," she said, beckoning us to follow.

Bess led us to a small drawing room. The warmth of the fire seeped into my bones, banishing the chill from the draft riddled hallway and soothed the tension I'd built. A shelf by the window held a small collection of books and as I held my palms towards the flames, I studied the titles. I couldn't stop my smugness; I'd read them all.

Turning away from the heat I found Nathaniel pacing. A year and one day aboard the *Wilted Rose* had made him restless on dry land. I felt the itch too but restrained myself by merely tapping a rhythm out on the handle of my sword.

"Nathaniel!"

A rotund man in a well cut suit stood at the door. Red faced and jolly, his eyes held something dark that I couldn't quite trust. They looked out of place amongst his cheery features, the tension returned and I wrapped my arms around myself, an unconscious gesture but one of protection.

"Uncle," Nathaniel acknowledged, stopping mid-pace to shake the man's hand.

"You cannot believe the relief and rapture I feel knowing you are home and are safe," Sir Henry said.

"I am here for only a short while," Nathaniel explained, stressing the word 'short'. "I wished to introduce you to Valencia and to show her where I was raised."

"Valencia?" Sir Henry questioned, his gaze meeting mine; the trademark Davenport blue was dull in his face.

Instead of shrinking from his stare, I matched it, watching as contempt changed the blue of the nobleman's eyes, to grey. He looked me up and down, a leer forming on in his face. I felt naked under his stare and I didn't like it. Finishing his task, Sir Henry pressed his lips together.

"Well," Sir Henry said as he coughed uncomfortably. "As you can see, we are in the throes of a party. Perhaps you and your... *friend*" he emphasised the word, the turn of phrase sounded condescending to my ear. "would like to freshen up?"

"Yes." Nathaniel nodded frowning at his uncle, the inflection hadn't been missed. "Are you there Bess?" Nathaniel said turning towards the housekeeper who hovered discreetly by the door.

"Yes Nate dear," she replied, stepping over the threshold.

"Please show Lennie to the lavender suite, there should be something for her to wear in storage, if she so wishes."

He looked to me, his expression tender and reassuring. I nodded my assent, ignoring the curious smile on his uncle's face. Of course I'd dress as Nathaniel wished me to. I had to feign some decorum didn't I?

"Very good, my dear boy," Bess replied.

I followed the older woman out to the foyer. Taking the stairs, I scanned each painting that lined the walls. I stilled as I found a portrait that could have only been Nathaniel. He looked young and brash, no more than fifteen. His suit was painted in a regal colour setting off his tanned skin and sky blue eyes.

"Handsome devil was he not?" Bess chuckled. "Or should I say, is he not?"

I fought the urge to blush as I trailed after the housekeeper. One flight of stairs and a never ending corridor later, Bess opened one of the many doors lining the route. She stepped aside so I could enter.

"Best room in the house," Bess said, nudging me into the suite.

I had never bore witness to such an elegant place. Simple in decoration, the white walls and furniture brightened up the room and made it feel open. Lavender bedding, flowers and accents added just enough to the décor to make it feminine and light.

"Make yourself comfortable, dear, I will be only gone a moment."

I smiled gratefully as Bess slipped out the door. I went to stand beside the windows – at least there I couldn't ruin anything. This side of the suite overlooked the stables and the fields beyond it. The working boys and footmen who had been relieved of their duties, lounged against hay bales smoking and shooting the breeze.

Just as she'd promised, Bess was back within minutes.

I turned at the click of the handle, the housekeeper stood with a cream dress over one arm and shoes dangling from her fingers. She stepped further into the room, laying them out on the bed.

"Do you need my help, miss?" Bess' tone was kind as I floundered.

"I think I might, ma'am," I replied finding my voice.

"Ma'am would be for someone else, I am merely Bess."

"Well, Bess I'm no 'miss' either, I'm just Lennie." I held out my hand and Bess shook it without hesitation.

"Let us make you the belle of the ball," Bess said as she set to work.

THAT SURELY WASN'T me, looking back from the glass. I couldn't stop staring. Although I'd spent many nights in front of the mirror, before I'd been cursed there was no resemblance between the woman in the reflection I saw now, to the one I'd once known. My skin was flushed by nature, rather than powder or rouge and my mismatched eyes were bright with nerves and excitement. I caught Bess smiling behind me and returned it with shyness. Looking away from the reflection, I smoothed imaginary creases in the beautiful dress that draped my figure.

The fit was too good, like it had been tailored just for me. The cut made me sit straighter with my head held higher. I felt regal and refined – nothing like the girl in britches and braces.

"That dress was kept for Miss Kitty, but you wear it so much better than she ever would. I couldn't have dreamed a more beautiful partner for my dear Nate." Bess sighed, laying a hand on my shoulder. I could think of nothing to say in response so I remained silent as I patted the older woman's arm in gratitude. Who was 'Miss Kitty' though?'

After the housekeeper had departed, I continued to stare into the mirror, rearranging my hair to cover the mark on my forehead. Bess hadn't mentioned it, but I'd seen her hesitate when she'd combed my fringe. I brushed the hair aside, hiding the blot on my face.

Though I somewhat looked the part, inside I was the same girl with a low rank and murky past. Turning away from my image, I stood. My heart thudded wildly and I placed my hand to my chest, feeling the erratic pulse against my palm. Inhaling slowly, I released the breath; the soft wisp of air seemed to echo around the sophisticated room.

He cares for me though, I thought as doubts trickled into my concentration. Knowing I'd do nothing but fret if I stayed on my own I straightened my shoulders, lifted my head and put one foot in front of the other. Nodding to myself I stepped purposefully out onto the landing.

As I hovered there, unsure of where I should go and trying to remember all I could about etiquette and tact, footsteps sounded nearby. Nathaniel rounded the corner and I was awestruck. Though I'd always found him handsome, that was nothing compared to the sight walking towards me. Tall and confident, his suit was a replica of the one he wore upon our first meeting, even down to the shiny buckled boots. His long hair was tied back away from his face. It highlighted his tanned skin and emphasised his trademark eyes. I couldn't pull away.

"My goodness, Valencia, you look…"

Nathaniel stilled a few steps in front of me. Taking my hands in his, he pressed his lips to my knuckles. I smiled, ducking my head in bashfulness.

"Thank you, you look wonderful too," I mumbled my face flushed.

"I cannot help but wish we could walk in there dressed as we arrived," Nathaniel whispered as he tucked my hand into the crook of his arm. Smiling, he steered me towards the grand staircase.

"You do?" I asked, as I concentrated on not falling down the elaborate steps.

"Of course…"

The rest of his explanation was interrupted as we approached the door to the ballroom. A man-servant cleared his throat, before calling just above the crowd noise.

"Mr Nathaniel Davenport-Lee and Ms Valencia Roux."

The entire room stilled, the silence resonated

throughout the party. Nathaniel looked oblivious as he walked us further into the gathering. I had the fleeting wish for my sword, wearing it had always brought me courage and with the many eyes that gazed at me I could have done with at least a modicum of it.

"Please do not stop your merriment on my account, continue in these wonderful festivities and I will explain my absence in due course."

Nathaniel's words placated them, at least for now, and the ball resumed. The scrutiny of the crowd made me more conscious of my low standing. I didn't hold myself as straight as they did, nor was I as delicate and soft. I avoided the prying eyes and the gossiping whispers and followed Nathaniel to the punch bowl. His smile held encouragement as he handed me the crystal glass. I sipped at it as Nathaniel turned to speak to a gentleman sporting a monocle.

"So, you met Nathaniel at sea?" I feminine voice asked.

I looked up to find a young lady in a chic gown, her hair and build were similar to my own, there was even a small resemblance in her face. Her expression held wariness but she seemed harmless enough.

"Yes, I did," I replied with a nod.

"Where are my manners?" the girl said, aghast. "I am Katherine Gouldon-Charles."

"Lennie, I mean, Valencia Roux." I returned shaking the offered hand.

"Charmed." Katherine smiled and I couldn't help but return it. There was something inherently likable about her. I couldn't quite place it.

"Oh, Kitty, how are you?" Nathaniel grasped the woman with familiarity and leaned down to press a kiss to her pale cheek.

"Splendid my dear, thank you."

The woman's face pinked at his touch and my smile slipped. Perhaps she wasn't so likable after all.

"You look well, Nathaniel; we all were so worried we had lost you," Kitty said, looking up at him through her long lashes.

"I have only returned for a short time." He repeated the phrase he'd used earlier. Though his expression was fond, the seriousness in his eyes were sure.

"Oh you are to leave so soon?" Kitty's brow furrowed.

"I wished to introduce Valencia to my old life before beginning a new one."

"Is that so? It all sounds like a true adventure." She gave me a speculative look, the corners of my mouth turning upward.

"Well, we must circulate," Nathaniel said breezily, as he guided me away.

"Nice meeting you, Valencia," Kitty called after us.

"Yes and you," I replied.

"Do not forget us, Nathaniel dear, we would hate for you to leave without a proper catch up."

"I would never forget you, Kitty," he said, a softness

in his tone as he pulled us into the throng.

"My apologies," he murmured, as he eased me around the edge of the dancers.

"Old friend?" I guessed, fighting the jealous monster raging within me. Nathaniel's jaw tightened as he scanned the room.

"Kitty...Katherine is the woman my Uncle chose for me to marry," he explained, as my heart sunk.

I'd thought as much, the woman was Nathaniel's perfect match in every way. Staid, wealthy and beautiful. His hand brushed down my arm as I continued to fret.

"We never felt affection for one another; Kitty's desires hanker for someone a little different than myself."

Nathaniel's eyes sparkled as he nodded towards a group of people. Katherine had joined a young gentleman in regimentals, her hand resting on his arm as she laughed.

"Her family doesn't approve?" I asked my smile a lot more genuine now.

"Francis is poor; he has no standing or property. He is an acquaintance of my family through the local trade." Nathaniel said.

"Really?" I watched the soldier carefully; did I look as nervous as he did?

"Would you like to dance?" Nathaniel's question broke through my reverie.

"What a perfect idea."

I lost myself in the music. Though we couldn't dance

as close as we had on the island, Nathaniel's touch set currents running through me. His size demanded space and as the guests gave us a wide berth, I felt both protected and cherished in his affections.

We gazed at each other, my attention focussed solely on him. The music flowed from the band into my bloodstream and filtered through my feet. Nathaniel bowed to me as the song ended and led the way to the edge of the room. Tapping my foot along to the next song, I watched the couples as Nathaniel spoke to yet more acquaintances.

"May I take the next dance?"

I stilled as the soldier Nathaniel had pointed out earlier, held out his hand to me.

"Dear Frankie, how the devil are you?" Nathaniel thrust his own out, shaking it with enthusiasm.

"Very well, I'm so glad to see that you have arrived home safely."

Francis visibly relaxed with the handshake and I could tell the officer felt more at ease with Nathaniel than anyone else —besides Katherine. His smile was more genuine and his demeanour less rigid. I couldn't help but like him too.

"Of course," Nathaniel replied.

"Would it be impertinent to ask again?" Francis raised his eyebrows in my direction. I looked to Nathaniel; his expression held ambivalence. Well if he wasn't greatly opposed, then I would take a turn. I was eager to speak with the soldier.

"It would be an honour," I said, wrapping a hand around the soldier's offered arm.

"Take care of her," Nathaniel demanded. His bright gaze never leaving me.

"You have my word." Francis promised, his grey eyes more serious than the situation warranted.

The music began again and we took a turn around the dance floor. I hunted for something to break our silence but couldn't think of anything suitable.

"Thank you for accepting my request." Francis glanced at me before resuming his original stare, somewhere over my head.

"It's a pleasure, sir."

We continued to dance in silence for a few more bars until I could no longer hold in my curiosity.

"We're in the same situation aren't we?" I said, hoping it would open a more elaborate conversation.

"Ms Roux, I'm not sure I follow," Francis replied. This time his attention remained focussed on me.

"We both vie for the affections of people well above our station." I said.

A muscle worked in the officer's cheek. His faux smile held little humour as he twirled me around.

"Does it get better?" I asked facing him again.

"I cannot tell you," he sighed.

His eyes scanned the fellow dancers, Nathaniel stood just beyond them, his eyes never leaving the dance floor as Katherine spoke animatedly at his side. When Frances spoke again his words were hushed and brisk.

"The secrecy makes me feel even lower than my rank. Kitty and I cannot show our affections as we would wish." He sighed staring with longing at his beloved.

"I truly understand," I said.

"I believe you do."

"Now, enough of this formality," I said. "Do you play poker?"

My partner blinked but countered my smile, nodding as he spun me on the floor. "We have a wager most nights."

"Glad to hear it, if I can escape for a few hours, may I join you?" I twirled, returning to face him. "Where do you play?"

"The officers mess, the local tavern, even in the kitchens here."

"I don't know how long I shall be here, but I'll try and come play a hand."

"I'll look forward to it."

The tune ended and Francis bowed, "It was a pleasure to dance with you ma'am."

"The pleasure is all mine," I replied with a curtsey.

After all the formalities had been done with, I edged my way through the couples alone, only to find Nathaniel waiting for me, his eyes alight at my return.

"You seemed to enjoy that." He greeted, handing me another glass of punch.

"I like Francis, he's an amiable man," I agreed finding my partner across the room. He raised his glass in my direction and I lifted mine in return. An almost inaudible grunt had me turning to find Nathaniel scowling.

"Do I detect something green in your tone, Mr Lee?" I teased, sipping at the glass, enjoying the feeling.

"Valencia, any man who looks at you, is a man I envy."

His tone was light, yet the sincerity leapt from his eyes. He brushed a finger across my cheek; the tender touch put truth to his words.

"I feel a parallel with Francis." I said.

"Our situation is different." Nathaniel dismissed.

"How so Nathaniel? Look at us."

"We are equal Valencia, please remember that. Are we not but cursed pirates after all?"

His words hit me with their truth and I wasn't sure how to reply to them.

CHAPTER XX
TRUTH HURTS

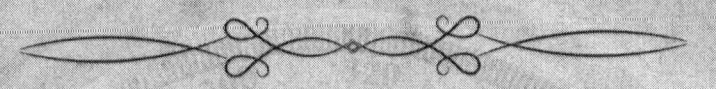

"BRAVO," KATHERINE CALLED, applauding as the ball flew into the trees.

Nathaniel raced after it as Francis made runs back and forth. Cricket wasn't something I knew a lot about, yet Sir Henry had insisted the 'young people' who had remained at the estate, should all join in.

Sat amongst the many refined young ladies in their elegant outfits, I didn't feel too out of place. Bess had found me a comfortable but fine dress fit for the occasion. All the young men had stripped down to their shirts and braces. I couldn't help but admire their style, my own set tucked away in my room wouldn't have been out of place... well as long as I wasn't the one wearing them.

"The militia has made you soft," Nathaniel chided as he returned to the game, twirling the ball in his hands.

"The sea has made you quicker," Francis retorted, slapping him on the back.

"Now, now boys, let us get this game going," Sir Henry cried. He sat upon a blanket, a large and opulent picnic spread out beside him.

"I am finished, Uncle," Nathaniel replied tossing the ball at Francis while he mopped his brow. "Forgive me everyone, I wish to show Valencia more of the grounds before we leave."

"Nathaniel, your friends have all stayed to spend the day, let us not be rude." Sir Henry clenched his jaw. I could see the gentleman's burning disapproval of his nephew's new found attitude.

"We must be going, sir, truly." Another soldier spoke. "We officers would be happy to escort the ladies to their carriages."

An idea bloomed in Sir Henry's eyes. "Well could you not take my dear nephew with you, and his guest of course."

Nathaniel spun around, his cheeks reddening, "We have not been invited, uncle, I must insist on my original plan."

"Thank you, Sir Henry," Katherine interrupted. "It is true, Parson's has just reminded me, that we are needed at another luncheon, not many hours from now."

Her gaze flickered to Nathaniel, who mouthed his thanks.

"Very well," Sir Henry grouched, as he poured more wine, throwing the empty bottle down much harder than necessary.

"Valencia," Katherine murmured as I made to stand. "It was lovely to meet you, please take good care of my dear friend."

"I'll do my best," I promised. I looked over my shoulder to Francis, who stood with the other men. Claudette's words echoed in my ears as I saw his gaze catch Katherine's.

"Please find a way to be together, *everyone* deserves some happiness. Don't let propriety deny you of something special, I begged.

"You are a wonderful soul, thank you." Katherine praised. "Take care," she urged, gathering her parasol and skirts and patting my arm, before rushing after Francis.

My mind was full with how difficult truth and affection was, as Sir Henry and his young companions made their way back to the house without me.

"Want to practice with me?" Nathaniel asked pulling his braces back onto his shoulders.

"I'm not much for cricket," I replied.

Nathaniel laughed as he thrust a bat out in front of him, duelling with an imaginary opponent. With a quirked brow he stepped around me, brushing against me. Excitement joined the waves of feeling thrumming through my body. Though I'd felt inadequate amongst Nathaniel's friends, a scuffle with blades would not leave me lacking.

"Sounds like fun, I should change though," I said, trying hard to contain my eagerness.

"I would like to learn from a professional, meet me in the courtyard?"

His smile was warm as pressed his cheek against mine, his arms coming around me to pull me into a swift embrace.

"Of course," I breathed, as he pulled away.

"The courtyard, ten minutes," he bid, turning away to tidy up the remnants of the game.

"Right," I said, hitching up my unfamiliar skirts and racing towards the house.

PULLING MY HAIR from the collar of my jacket and folding it into a braid, I raced down the entrance steps. Now I was back in my britches, braces and boots I felt the weight lift. There was less expectation somehow. I was just plain Lennie again. I couldn't contain my mirth; what if some of Sir Henry's high class friends stopped by? What would they think? At that moment I didn't much care. I felt comfortable and little else mattered.

Taking the stairs two at a time, my sword tapping at my thigh with each step, I scanned the large entranceway, Nathaniel hadn't told me where to find the courtyard. Reaching the foyer, I found it deserted; no-one milled around to dust the ornate items that were displayed there. Hovering on the bottom step I waited, hoping to catch someone as they passed.

"Having trouble dear?" Bess strode across the marble floor, her hands once again in her apron.

"Nathaniel asked me to meet him in the courtyard; would you be kind enough to tell me the way?"

The corners of Bess' eyes creased as she smiled. "My dear girl it is easy, turn right from this door, once you find the iron gate and roses, you will have found Nate."

"Thank you," I said,

"Enjoy yourselves," Bess called after me.

I could have sworn I'd caught a twinkle in the older woman's eyes as she turned to walk the way she'd come.

Dragging open the large oak door, I paused at the front step, the long sprawling driveway seemed to go on for miles. A few men worked further down the steep path but the stillness and quiet of the space chilled me. This wouldn't be a place for children to play, no wonder Nathaniel spent his life amongst books.

Following Bess's simple directions, I turned right and headed through the opening at the side of the house. Just as the housekeeper had described after the iron gate, roses cascaded from the courtyard walls, I leaned closer pulling in their sweet scent. Despite the feeling of not belonging, I had to admit the estate was beautiful, if not a little overwhelming.

Leaving the flowers, I walked under the stone archway. Nathaniel stood with his back to me his hands in his pockets as he stared skyward. I couldn't help but take in the form of his body and the tan of his skin. Every preconception I'd had was now torn to shreds.

Knowing him more now, I likened him to a slow

burning fire. He warmed beneath the surface, never scorching but always there. Though his underlying temper, something I'd seen only glimpses of, resembled that of a storm with all the lightning and thunder that came with it. He was also tender and sweet to a fault, something I'd never thought I would experience with such a man as Nathaniel. I felt my heart swell as I edged further into the courtyard and loathed to disturb him.

Instead of interrupting his quiet reflection, I surveyed the space. This wouldn't be my largest arena. Yet a duel did not rely upon where it took place, only the skill and cunning of those wielding the swords.

I pulled off my jacket and tossed it aside, along with my hat and without preamble yanked off my braces, letting them hang from my hips. I was steadily rolling up my sleeves as Nathaniel spoke.

"Ready?" Nathaniel asked as he spun, unsheathing his weapon.

I nodded doing the same. It felt good to hold a sword again, it seemed like an age since I'd felt its weight.

Bowing in courteousness we started to duel. He stepped, I stepped. Together we lunged forward, neither of us touching the other. The duel became a dance, our movements in sync. The echoing clash of weapons formed the rhythm. Move after sweeping move, the courtyard became a ballroom.

Though I was the far more experienced fighter, I lacked the formality Nathaniel's taught skills held. My eyes never left his and I didn't need to pre-empt his next move, my instincts already knew. Our fight had no agenda to hurt or win, which was my usual goal; this battle was a vehicle to show admiration and affection. As we continued to circle one another, a mischievous smile crept across Nathaniel's face and before I knew it, I was tangled with him on the floor. Our swords discarded and our laughter unstoppable. The spell our dance had weaved was ended by the sound of applause.

"Well done, bravo! That is the best I have seen," Sir Henry boomed as he came towards us. "What on earth is this creature?" he asked as he raised his hands towards me as I retrieved my discarded sword.

"She is a marvel," Nathaniel agreed.

"Would you do me the honour of a bout? All in jest of course," Sir Henry asked.

I eyed the gentleman, his once amused smile now held the quality of a shark, one that had just spotted its prey. I stopped myself from raising my sword prematurely; though my instincts wished otherwise. With as much subtly as I could, I covered one hand over the other forcing my weapon to remain facing the ground.

"Of course." False politeness coloured my tone.

The feelings I'd experienced just before my skirmish with Macrucio resurfaced with the acceptance of the challenge.

"Nathaniel, why not go and visit Bess? I'm sure she will have a treat of some kind, waiting for you in the kitchens," Sir Henry said his eyes never left mine, as he spoke to his nephew.

"Uncle, I do not think…"

"It'll be fine," I interrupted. "I promise."

I hoped my voice didn't belay my underlying tension.

"As you wish," Nathaniel said.

He looked uncertain but doing as he was told, walked through the archway and out of sight.

I returned to my defensive stance, as Sir Henry picked up Nathaniel's discarded sword.

"You are a talented woman, Valencia," he said weighing the weapon in his hand. Satisfied, he shifted to the left.

"Thank you, Sir," I said with a shift to the right. I remained focussed, despite my opponent's obvious attempt at distraction. What was he playing at? Though I'd only just made his acquaintance, I knew enough to believe that his words were an insult, rather than a compliment.

"So well spoken for a harlot," Sir Henry spat.

This time I faltered and the sound of blades scraping together, pierced the air.

"Oh yes, I am well aware of your history."

He continued to step and I followed him.

"I have had the fortunate experience of frequenting your little home town."

I swallowed the bile that had risen, *this couldn't be happening…*

"You were one of my patrons." It wasn't a question.

Sir Henry's triumphant smile told me the answer.

"Do you think I would let my nephew fall for a filthy guttersnipe?" he snarled.

The insult felt like a slap and he used my shock against me. Despite his age and size, he pounced faster than I could imagine. I could do nothing as I was slammed to the floor, the air gushed from my lungs leaving me winded, my sword flew from my hand. My head colliding with the cobbled floor didn't help either.

"You're no better," I spat, my head throbbing. His body crushed me but I was determined not to give into his intimidation or his weight.

"I am a well-respected man," he sniffed, as though it settled the matter.

"A man who frequents houses of disrepute and preys upon young girls? If that is well respected, then I want no part of it."

Henry gaped at me, his dull eyes wide. In his stunned state, he didn't fight me as I pushed at him with all my strength. He dropped to his knees as I dusted down my clothes.

"I feel a great deal for your nephew, he's fully aware of my past and accepts it. Show me a person who has never sinned and I'll show you a liar."

I glared as I stood over him, "We all have skeletons, Henry Davenport." I flipped my wrist to reveal the symbol of the *Wilted Rose*. "Some more than others."

I picked up my sword and without another look at the wheezing man, walked away. I knew I'd won that small battle but it didn't matter now, the war had begun.

I stalked back to the house in a daze, stopping beside a bush to empty my stomach, my body shuddering with disgust. Wiping my mouth, I dragged myself into the opulent mansion. Doors and corridors melded into one and before long I had become lost in the maze of rooms. The wood panelled hall I stood in held no resemblance to the pale papered ones leading to the Lavender room.

Taking a few more steps I turned a corner and pulled in a breath. Despite my woe I had found the one place I needed, a library. Stepping down into the overflowing room, I sighed in awe. Stories were lined floor to ceiling, more impressive than even Macrucio's collection. Books were everywhere. The smell of leather binding and parchment filled my nostrils and had me wandering the shelves. Out of all the pomposity and regal manners nothing compared to the lavish book cavern. I could only imagine Nathaniel's life amongst the walls of literature.

Though the ugly truth of Sir Henry still plagued my thoughts, surrounded by stories I felt less anxious. My hands drifted along the spines of classics and before long I had pulled one from its confines and curled up amongst the bookcases. I'd barely made it through the first page before my own questions overpowered my thoughts.

My mind and body were both sickened. How could fate deal me such a hand? What would Nathaniel think?

Clutching the book to my stomach, I let the pain wash over me, and succumbed to the misery.

"Valencia, are you in here?"

Nathaniel's voice broke through my sorrow and me scrambling to my feet. Wiping my face, I returned the tome and peered around the bookcase. Nathaniel leaned against another, his arms crossed over his chest. Weariness clouded his face as he rested.

Stepping from my hidey-hole I linked my hands together, staring anywhere but at him.

"Sorry, I needed…"

"If in doubt, read." Nathaniel nodded reaching for a tome, flicking through it, he smiled, "Whenever I felt lonely or saddened I came here, this was my sanctuary and these," he held up the book, "were my playmates."

Finally looking at me, he paused.

"I knew it, come with me," he said disposing of the book and gripping my hand. Leading me through a series of passages and hidden doors, I rushed to keep up with his long strides. Neither of us spoke as we turned onto a familiar corridor. We met no one as Nathaniel opened the door to the Lavender room. Closing it behind us he urged me to sit. I sunk onto the soft mattress; my eyes heavy.

"My goodness, you look ill, I knew I should have never left the two of you." He brushed the hair off my face and sat down beside me. I couldn't speak; I stared up at him, waiting for the moment he would run away screaming. He must know, he must know all I did now, why wasn't he recoiling?

"I spoke with my uncle," he said and I pulled in a sharp breath. "Or I should say, argued." Nathaniel chuckled as he wrapped me in his arms. "He told me that—"

"—I didn't know, please believe me!" I pleaded tears fell without abandon. "I would never have recognised him. Those men were nothing but mere shadows in the night. Phantoms whose job it was to torment and torture me."

"Please do not cry." Nathaniel's plea was as tender as his touch. His fingers caught my tears, brushing them away. "Naught but the curse can halt my affection."

"Nathaniel…" I murmured relief and gratitude constricting my voice once more.

I buried my face in his chest, feeding from his warmth as he spoke words of comfort into my hair. Once my tears had dried, we lay together, against the pillows. Nathaniel held me close and I listened to the steady thud of his heart. I had never just laid beside a man before and never had I been treated with such delicacy. Each moment with Nathaniel was something new to experience and learn.

"What you need to understand is that my uncle has had an incredible but pain filled life." Nathaniel's voice held a gentle rhythm that kept time with his heartbeat. "He had lost his wife, child, siblings and sister to the sea. One by one his family has been ripped away from him."

Nathaniel sighed and I raised my head. He stared off into some other realm, his fingertips traced random patterns on my skin.

"It has taken me a long time to realise that his jovial manner was just a façade. Under all his pomp and smiles is a bitter old man."

Nathaniel's vibrant eyes were filled with sadness. "I am not sure what his plan is but he will not let us leave easily, not now."

Untangling myself from Nathaniel, I stood by the window. Below people went about their tasks, oblivious to the turmoil within the grand house.

"Do you truly wish to leave?" I pressed my palm to the cold glass. The numbness would help when he admitted he would rather stay. It was mere moments before his arms wrapped around me once more, his chin resting on my shoulder. I wanted to throw him off, demand he return to the ship and stay with me forever. But I didn't, I leaned into him, breathing in his unique scent of ink and man.

"Whilst aboard the *Wilted Rose* I did miss certain things," he said, pressing his lips to my neck. "For instance, I missed Bess, but being here now, amongst my old life, I feel trapped."

I turned to look at him, his face held nothing but truth.

"I hope to leave here with you, safe and healthy. To find a place we can be free."

"That's all I hope for too," I said, reaching up to caress his cheek. We shared a smile before returning to the shelter of each other's arms.

CHAPTER XXI
KITCHEN DUTY

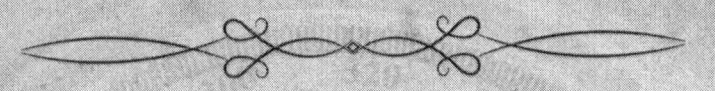

"UNCLE, HOW CAN you accuse her of such a thing? There is just no way that is true," Nathaniel insisted.

"So why has the most priceless of my cigar cases gone missing? There is no one else it can be," Sir Henry countered.

"I know it to be a lie." Nathaniel vowed.

"You do?" Sir Henry sounded unconvinced. "So you know of her whereabouts after sunset?"

"Yes, Valencia and I were talking most of the night."

"You were in her room?" Sir Henry was outraged. "I knew she would make you as sinful as she."

"Uncle." Nathaniel stepped forward, towering over the older man. "I am indebted to you for your kindness, for taking me in and raising me. Yet you prevent me from becoming my own man and deciding things for myself, I need to become who I was meant to be."

"I will not lose more of my blood, especially not to a vagabond harlot who fraternises with witchcraft and the sea."

I ground my teeth together. Nathaniel and his uncle

had been arguing all morning. It had all erupted when we'd tried to leave. The two of us had been at the gates when one of the chamber maids had flown across the gravel. Between her breathless wheezes, the maid had urged us to return to the house, as Sir Henry had 'urgent business' he had to discuss with us. Nathaniel's kind nature had him turning around and trudging back up the driveway. I heard his resigned sigh as I'd followed after him.

Not able to take any more of their fighting, I left my perch on the stairs and wandered through the house. The elegant furnishings and paintings which had intrigued me hours before, now made me feel unwelcome. Each picture held mocking half smiles and still disapproving eyes. Not wanting to lose myself has I had done before; I decided to visit a place I knew. Reaching the courtyard, I settled on stone steps attached to a wooden door.

The sound of women singing and running water led me to assume it was the kitchen entrance. Listening to the pining lyrics of whoever worked behind the door, I picked at the hem of my coat.

There had to be another way to ease the conflict I had caused between Nathaniel and his uncle, or failing that, a way to escape the stone prison we found ourselves in.

"Valencia?" I looked up startled, to find Bess.

"Sorry, am I in your way?" I apologised as I made to stand.

"Goodness no, my dear, I just wanted to make sure

you were well."

"As well as could be expected," I sighed, returning to the step. Bess shook her apron, smoothing it out before settling beside me.

"I can see you both want to leave. No matter how much I'd love you both to stay, you need to live own your lives in the way you want. Sir Henry doesn't see that I'm afraid." Bess unlatched a brooch from her blouse. It was shaped like a bow, the yellow gold and gemstones mimicked the flow of the ribbon it resembled. Though aged, it was beautiful despite its flaws. I didn't want to question how a housekeeper, no matter how beloved, got her hands on such a trinket. Bess smiled fondly as she held it up for me to see.

"It's lovely," I said.

Bess turned the item in her hands, the light bounced off the facets making it sparkle. The older woman looked thoughtful as she stared at the wonder in her hands.

"Maria gave this to me the night she and Caleb eloped. I felt it signified that no matter how far she went or how long she was gone, she would always be tied to this place, to the people here who loved her." Bess smiled remembering. "She told me she loved Caleb and nothing in the world would stop her from leaving with him. I was sad to see her go, wonderful girl she was; but just like you and Nate she knew her own mind and heart."

"Do you think she regretted it?" I asked.

Bess shook her head. "No, her life was just as it was

supposed to be. Both Sir Henry and Nathaniel believe she is still out there somewhere."

"What do you think?"

"I want to believe too, but I fear she has perished." Bess stopped, a smile playing across her lips. "Do you know, my girl, you remind me of her?"

"I do?" I frowned unsure of Bess' intention.

"Yes, in her spirit, her fire and her determination. You are a perfect woman for my Nate. You are smart and strong and not scared to speak to him as his equal; most women cower beside a man of such rank."

"I have so much feeling," I said pressing a palm to my chest.

"You cannot say it child?"

I smiled back at the woman without humour, "and you say I'm not scared."

"Here," Bess pressed the brooch into my palm, wrapping my fingers around it.

"I couldn't–" I protested.

"You can and you will, child," Bess interrupted. "This now ties you here, to me, to Nathaniel and his mother."

"I don't know what to say, Bess, thank you," I watched the stones sparkle as they caught the light.

"How about we take a trip to the kitchen?" Bess suggested, as she pulled out a handkerchief and dabbed at her eyes.

"I wouldn't want to be an inconvenience..." I said as the older woman shook her head.

"Nonsense," Bess said, grasping up her skirts and making for the door. I tucked the brooch into an inside pocket, before following.

The cook, maids and other servants were busy preparing the evening meal. They all acknowledged Bess' arrival with a casual nod but their mouths stood agape as I stepped in behind her through the door.

"Ladies this is Valencia, Master Nathaniel's companion. She is to be treated as such."

"Yes, Miss Bess," they chorused but as I sat at the table, their eyes followed.

"Can I help?" I asked, as a maid no older than myself, shelled peas close by.

"Err…" The girl didn't look up as her face flushed.

"Let me." I insisted pulling off my jacket and rolling up my sleeves. After washing my hands, I returned to find the girl still hadn't moved. I plucked a pod from the bowl and with practised movements, I shelled it.

"You know how?" The girl's blush melded into a new one, as she watched my deft hands.

"Sure, I'm not a princess; do you see any other visitor dressed this way?" I said, pointing to my rough-hewn attire. I smiled at the young woman, a glint of comradery in my eye.

"I guess not…"

The afternoon sped by as the curious stares became tentative questions, and then easy conversation. By the time the sun had set we were all settled around the table, behind us pots simmered, awaiting the call from the power upstairs.

"So once you have left here, where will you go?" A round faced maid asked.

"I don't rightly know," I said, shuffling a deck of cards. "I'll step back onto the ship and follow where it leads."

The maid sighed, "Sounds awfully romantic."

"It does?" I asked, quirking a brow. Being on the inside, it did not match to the sweeping love stories I'd read about for as long as I could remember. It was strange to think about what people assumed my life was like, not knowing themselves how I truly lived.

"Yes, of course," the maid said, leaning closer, her gaze off on some imaginary boat. "Setting sail, doing whatever you please… freedom."

"Is it not the same for you?" I asked my expression confused as I took in the faces around the table. These women seemed free of propriety, at least below stairs.

The chief cook scoffed, "Do be serious darlin', we have to live, breathe and eat for the master and his needs. We 'ave one 'our off on a Sunday when we need to be in church, then we 'ave to be back 'ere to make 'is roast." She cackled, before standing to stir something.

"That's all well and good, my dear," Bess said. "But there's more to life than freedom."

I brushed a hand over the brand on my wrist, nodding. I had to agree.

"Well ladies, I see you have found fresh meat." Nathaniel's grin created blushes as he swaggered into the kitchen. I glanced up from my cards, to see the strain behind his smile.

"Come with me?" He murmured and I made to stand.

"Leaving in the middle of a game?" The cook tutted in mock disapproval.

"Next time," I promised, taking Nathaniel's hand. At my touch the tension in his body eased. I turned to Bess and pressed a kiss to the housekeeper's cheek.

"Thank you, you've made me feel most welcome."

"It was a pleasure dear, remember what I said." Bess' eyes grew soft as she took in the two of us.

"Don't forget your jacket miss."

The girl who had been shelling peas did not meet my eyes as she handed over the item.

"Thank you," I said, as the maid scurried away.

Following Nathaniel out the door, I slung the jacket across my shoulder, pushing my arms through the sleeves. I frowned, something weighed it down. Feeling inside I found the brooch Bess had given me but it was what in the outside pocket which had me incensed. My hand touched cold metal and I pulled it free. I gasped; there in my palm was a gold cigar case with an enamel lid. It was dotted with jewels and filled to the brim with smokes.

"That bastard!" I growled.

"What is it?" Nathaniel asked.

"No wonder the maid looked fraught."

Spinning on my heel I stormed back down the corridor, passing the kitchen.

"What has happened?" Bess's question and Nathaniel's answer went ignored as I slammed my way into Sir Henry's study. The rogue was sat behind his mahogany desk, his mouth surrounding an unlit cigar.

"Knocking is the usual form of entry if I recall, or did they not teach that to you in your school of disgrace?" He sneered, flicking a match and lighting his smoke.

My chest heaved as I fought to retain my composure. My hands balled into fists at my sides and the sharp edges of the box dug deep into my skin.

"Lennie," Nathaniel was breathless as he reached the doorway.

I stepped forward, my whole body trembling in anger.

"I may be a lot of things, *Sir* but a thief isn't one of them," I spat, slamming the expensive item on the desk.

"See, son," the wretch said, his eyes staring over my head, at Nathaniel. "She had it all along."

Sir Henry blew a smoke ring as he grinned, smug in the thought of his triumph.

"As I said," Nathaniel stepped over the threshold, his hand touched my shoulder. "Lennie was with me all night. How she came to possess your property, I have no idea. If I find out however, who trespassed upon my visitor's privacy, I shall not be responsible for my actions."

My thoughts went to the young maid and I turned to

go. Fear slithered down my spine as I saw Nathaniel's vivid eyes. They focussed on his uncle, and despite his cool and clipped tone, were wild and filled with fire.

"You should do well to remember your place, boy." Sir Henry stood. "You are merely my ward and an illegitimate one at that."

"I would be more than happy to leave, *dear* uncle, though from our previous discussion I recall you 'forbidding' me to do so."

"I am right in demanding you remain, you owe me boy. You hold the name of Davenport and I own you," Sir Henry growled, biting through the cigar. The lit end fell to the desk, singeing the wood.

"You do talk some nonsense, uncle," Nathaniel scoffed, high colour flooding his cheeks as his anger grew. "One day there will be nothing left here but dust, overgrown weeds and long lost memories. I shall be long gone from this place and if I so choose it, without the name of Davenport!"

Taking hold of my hand he pulled me from the room, letting the door slam behind us.

Maids scurried as Nathaniel led me through the quiet halls. Reaching a drawing room, he shut the door before folding me into his arms. I reciprocated, not knowing what he needed but wanting to help him. I brushed my hands up and down his back, hoping it would sooth him. Had it really been two days since we'd walked through the door? It felt like weeks.

"Thank you," I murmured into his shirt.

The steady thud of his heart reassured me as my own anger died down.

"For what?" Nathaniel asked, pressing a kiss to my forehead.

"For believing that I didn't take that cigar case."

"I know you, Valencia and I know that poor maid had no choice in the matter."

"So she won't be punished?" I pulled back, searching his face, he'd looked so angry before.

Nathaniel shook his head. "It was an empty threat; Sir Henry has a lot to answer for." He shook his head, tugging me to the window.

"We are surrounded," he whispered. Beyond the glass, militia stood every few yards. There would be no means of escape through the boundary walls.

"It is the same all the way around the house. He called them last night, one of the maids let slip as we were leaving. I thought we'd get away before it came to this."

I squeezed his hands as I scanned the guards; from where we stood, I couldn't make out their faces. Was Francis among them? Sir Henry was using his power and influence to keep us here. Surely there were more important thing for the militia to do than keep us lock inside a gilded caged.

"If only we could get a message to the crew." I thought aloud.

"It would not work" Nathaniel sounded defeated as

he slumped to the floor. "My uncle is incensed, we pushed him too far, I fear." Nathaniel's head was in his hands, his guilt plain.

"What do we do now?" I asked, kneeling beside him. Wrapping my arms around him, I pressed my lips to his cheek, trying to bolster him.

"We wait. It is all we have."

CHAPTER XXII
HANGING

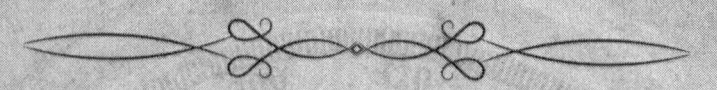

"**STOP GRINDING YOUR** teeth the noise drives me to distraction!" I griped, my fingers drumming on the window pane.

"Like that noise?" Nathaniel groused.

He pounded the table in the same tempo as my fingertips. I bit back a sharp reply and crossed my arms. I turned my back on him, striding over to the bookcases.

"Damn it to hades!" Nathaniel muttered.

I felt the heat flood into my face and my hackles begin to rise as Nathaniel growled at something through the window. The militia were still stood waiting, though their ranks were less than structured. Boredom had led to the line of men smoking and trying to peer at Nathaniel and me like me were caged animals. It did not help my annoyance. Where was their discipline?

"We should focus on something productive," I said, hopping onto the polished table in the centre of the room, turning my back on a few leering officers.

"You are right," Nathaniel agreed, stepping from the window. "Come here."

I went to him, thinking he was going to hold me, but I gasped as he tightly grasped my arm. Without ceremony he shoved up my jacket sleeve to expose my brand. Though his grip was tight, I caught on, staying still whilst he repeated the action on his own shirt. With much more gentleness he clasped hold of my forearm so our brands touched.

"It worked back on Macrucio's ship," Nathaniel said, as we remained stood together.

"We tried, but we were at sea then," I said letting go.

There had been no heat, no arrival of our fellow crew men. We would have to escape on our own. As he tidied up his shirt, Nathaniel paced. Distracted, he wrenched open a drawer, it was filled with used papers and spare quills; pulling out a sharpened tool he turned it over in his hands.

"Looking for something?" Curious, I followed him as he opened another.

"I am not quite sure yet, look in those over there." He pointed to another bureau in the corner.

Wrenching open drawers and cupboards, I continued to search for anything of use. Finding only quills and ink, I continued to hunt. Nathaniel strode across the room; pulling a picture from the wall, he struck it across his knee and the carved wooden frame splintered.

"What on earth, are you up to?" I cried racing over to him, my eyes wide.

"Getting us out of here." He knelt to retrieve a sheet

of parchment from the remnants.

"How?"

"This is a map if the entire estate, uncle Henry had it drawn up a few years ago." Dipping a quill, Nathaniel scanned the paper.

"We are here." he daubed a cross where he pointed.

"Which means we're in the centre," I said.

"Well, we do have guards all around here," Nathaniel made dots to represent the militia.

"If we could find a way to bypass them, then we would be home free."

"There could be a way," Nathaniel ran his finger from where they were, along the maze of corridors and out through the kitchen courtyard. "The fence panel is loose here; it leads straight out to the beach."

"Is that the place we found you?" I asked.

"Yes."

"A lot has changed since then," I said as my mind cast back to that first day and the soggy flower that had turned my world upside-down.

"For all of us," he agreed, wrapping his arms around me, all trace of annoyance gone.

"Let us plan our escape," I whispered, gripping his hand.

"The trouble will be getting to the fence without being detected."

"Do you think a distraction would help?" I raised an eyebrow, a coy smile on my face.

"You have an idea?"

Nathaniel's expression was wary but I refused to explain. Walking back to the window I stared out at the militia, the faded sunlight made them mere shadows. Their brass buckles that seemed so handsome in the candlelit ballroom now looked sinister in the glow of the lamps.

"How about we play a game of cat and mouse with these toy soldiers?" I shrugged off my jacket as I spoke and headed for the door.

"Lennie—"

Nathaniel was interrupted as I was thrown to the floor, three cloaked strangers filling the doorway. Nathaniel had me on my feet and behind him as the men stepped over the threshold.

"We have a warrant to arrest this wench," the smaller of the men said.

"On what grounds?" Nathaniel demanded.

"Many, son, now step aside, we have no quarrel with you."

The stranger pulled off his hood. His cap and badge informed them he was the town's beadle.

"You take her, you take me too." Nathaniel stood firm, glaring at the intruders.

"This is no business of yours, stand aside." The beadle spoke as if reprimanding a child. Nodding to the two burly men flanking him, they stepped forward.

Despite Nathaniel's size he was no match for them;

they held him down as the Beadle yanked me through the door. I struggled, biting, kicking wrestling my captor but his grip was too strong, I couldn't loosen his hold. I was dragged down the entrance steps and into a waiting carriage. There I was shackled and the horses were urged on at a fast pace.

My last sight of Nathaniel was of him kneeling in the doorway, his lip bloody and his bright eyes filled with anger and worry.

THE RAIN CARRIED through the bars disturbing the candles and leaving the shadows to dance upon the ceiling. Waves crashed against the walls as the storm swelled, it would be a tempestuous night. I turned away from it, resting against my straw pallet; it stank of its previous occupant. Would I leave my own mark here?

Thoughts tumbled around my head, now I had been incarcerated would their lives go back the way they were? Would Nathaniel marry Katherine? Would the curse never be broken? Would Rosa ever return to the *Wilted Rose*?

I reached out to the wall, the stone was cold to the touch and part of it fell away in my hand. Rolling onto my stomach, I lifted the debris and pressed it to the remaining wall. Trailing dust, I spelt out my heart:

I WILL NOT WRITE MY NAME UPON THIS STONE, FOR I

AM NAUGHT. ALL I WISH IS TO COMFORT THOSE WHO COME AFTER ME. DO NOT FORGET TO LISTEN TO YOUR HEART, EVEN WHEN IT SPEAKS IN FORBIDDEN TONGUES. ONLY THEN WILL TRUTH BE HEARD.'

"Wench."

I refused to respond to the guard's call as I finished my note.

"You will hang, *wench*. Sir Henry is well respected in this town." His laugh held little humour, as he dragged my sword across the bars.

Not perturbed, he waved my father's blade with menace and kicked out at the cell. He bit back a curse as he stubbed his toe. Despite my troubled thoughts, I could hardly swallow the laughter bubbling within me.

"I would not be smirking, Missy," The guard growled — his ego bruised as well as his toe.

I turned away from him, I didn't need my final few hours to be full of antagonistic threats and name calling. For I knew they were going to kill me, it was inevitable.

I lay back down, turning towards the wall. This was all wrong. All my thoughts of death had gone, I wanted to live. I had promised and now my promises would be broken. All thanks to a landed gentry man with little thought for the boy he raised.

The guards came for me as the storm ended before dawn. My heart hammered in my chest and the tiredness that I'd been fighting thrummed through my body in the form of adrenaline. It caused my hands to shake and I clenched them to stop the trembles. I didn't struggle as they clamped my wrists in chains and dragged me out to the town square. I would do this with dignity, and if there was a chance to escape, I'd take it – cowardly or not.

The gallows were built high, a stage for those wishing to watch death up close. The noose swung back and forth awaiting a user casting shadows across the cobbles. The creaking sound of rope moving against wood sent ominous chills through me as I was pulled along. *Hello, dear Grim Reaper, who knew you took the form of rope...?*

The jeering officer raced ahead of me. Taking a sandbag, he wrapped the noose around it, tugging it tight with a flourish. He flashed a sadistic smile pulling the leaver with glee. The sandbag crashed through the trapdoor, leaving no misconceptions that the job wouldn't be well and truly done.

To prevent my escape, they chained me to a large work horse. I stroked its silken coat as I murmured meaningless nothings in its ear. The animal's warmth gave some comfort, even if it was temporary as it nuzzled me. The innocent tenderness brought tears to my eyes. I brushed its topknot aside to reveal kind eyes.

"I wish you didn't have to see this," I whispered, running my hand over its long nose. It licked my hand as I continued. "No creature should see such things. This just isn't right."

The guards hovered, their hard eyes sharp, as a crowd

gathered in the square. I even spied young children with their mothers. *Who would bring their child to the reality of death and with such willingness?* I thought, as a small voice whispered in my ear: 'someone who would watch an innocent woman hung…'

The seconds ticked by far too slow, so much so I was sure the town clock had been tampered with. It should have been an hour glass, each grain counting the moments before I died. It didn't matter; my heart thudded far too hard, like a bright shining target, showing all and sundry how alive I was at that moment.

The clouds were clearing as the sun rose. Burnished pinks lit the sky sending rays of light across my weary features. The first signs of dawn usually filled me with a feeling of renewed hope – a new day, a fresh start. This morning, I felt as though dawn ended the day. I would never see another.

Again they came for me, men wearing black with severe expressions. They unlocked my bounds, saying nothing. The horse whinnied, as though it understood what was about to happen. Its head dipped as I was pulled through the crowed.

"Whore!" A man shouted, as others jeered.

"Harlot," a woman cried as she hurled rotten fruit. It slammed into my face, dripping mildewed juice into my eyes and hair. Shaking it off, I turned to the woman, my stinging eyes alight with anger. At that moment the last thing Claudette said to me pounded in my ears. *Do not accentuate your flaws but do not deny them either.'*

"I'm not perfect, I cannot deny that!" I cried ignoring the crowd as they scoffed and spat around me. "But look at yourselves, are you so faultless that you'd watch an innocent woman hung and feel no guilt? I'm a person, flesh and blood the same as every one of you, doesn't that count for something?"

No one answered my plea but the jeering stopped. My captors pulled me towards the gallows. They paused once more before the towering instrument.

"Get up," a guard growled, not attempting to be gentle as he pushed me forward. I crashed into the stairs scraping my knees, the stumble causing me to bite my tongue. Regaining my balance, I counted each step as I took them, there were ten – ten steps to death.

My captors yanked me over the trapdoor and secured the noose around my neck. Silence resonated as I let them do their work. I focussed on small things. The sound of my breathing, how limited the breaths were. The town clock ticking down the time until dawn. The feel of the rope, as it passed over my skin. How rough it was as it curled around my neck. I stared into one guard's eyes, their hazel colour was muted and he stilled as he caught my gaze. Letting go of the binds he crossed himself, bowing his head.

"May God have mercy on your soul."

"What's your name?" I asked, not caring for the others which surrounded me. The man looked up once more.

"Lawrence, ma'am."

Another guard grunted in warning, but he did not steer himself away.

I nodded. "Thank you for your blessing, for I know you think I deserve this, I'll go to the hereafter, holding that blessing close."

"This is my duty, miss, I follow orders. The verdict is not up to me."

He crossed himself again, kissing his fingers as he turned away.

"God go with you, Lawrence." I murmured.

Lawrence's actions touched something deep inside me. I had never felt the need to pray before, of course there had been times a prayer would have been comforting, but I'd never done the deed, never felt worthy. Right then however, I felt that now was a good a time as any. I closed my eyes and spoke to the one person I thought might listen. It couldn't hurt anyway.

"Dear God, I'm a sinner, I admit it. Yet I've heard that we're all your children. I also heard tell that forgiveness is divine. If my sin is to express my heartfelt feelings, then send me to hell this instant. Amen."

Opening my eyes I scanned the crowd. People of every creed and class had come to see my end, including girls of my former profession. They looked at me with pity for getting caught and with fear that they too would have the same fate.

As I took in the faces of those who would be the last

to see me alive, I found Francis. Smart and straight in his brass buttons and red jacket, his expression forlorn as he stared up at me. I tried to smile at him but it felt wrong. More like a grimace or an apology.

"Take my mistakes and make them right," I mouthed.

He nodded and with a hand at his heart he turned away.

Resolving my destiny, I glanced towards the horizon. If I looked far enough, I could see the ocean. It was strange; I'd felt the lowest despair and had wanted to die not too long ago. A lot had happened in the time between then and now, even if it had only been days. I would be breaking the promise I'd given to my crew mates. It pained me to admit defeat.

A ruddy faced man came to stand at my side. He looked official and grand in a purple sash which covered his red coat. A black hat was set at a jaunty angle upon his head. His grey eyes were serious and held little sympathy as he cleared his throat and held up a scroll of parchment.

"We are here today, to persecute a worthy criminal. So worthy she has been given no trial. I hear by grant Valencia Roux guilty of prostitution, piracy, kidnapping, thievery…"

The list went on and on, things I had never heard of, let alone committed, were being thrown at me. It had all been the fabrication of Sir Henry.

Sure enough, the man himself appeared from the

shadows, as the final note was read. There was not one ounce of his nephew within his face and for that I was thankful. Just as I had an inescapable past, Nathaniel had someone cruel and bitter within his.

"We hereby sentence you to death by hanging."

I felt my scalding anger reach boiling point, as Henry grinned in my direction, his expression boasted triumph.

Closing my eyes, I waited for my final breath. I filled my mind with Nathaniel. The handsomeness of his face, the gentleness of his touch and the way his voice sent me on journeys. Journeys I would never see in this lifetime.

"I wish there had been a time for us," I breathed, bowing my head I awaited the end. The floor beneath me disappeared and I fell into oblivion.

CHAPTER XXIII
LIFTED

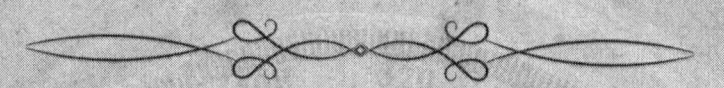

WAS THIS HEAVEN or hell? I had been in this purgatorial state once before. This couldn't be death; my imagination wasn't that creative. I was surrounded by the smell of Him. The aroma of ink and man filled my senses, I was in his arms and home again. The sound of splashing forced my eyes open. I had been right; Nathaniel was the one who carried me. He raced alongside the rest of the crew, as they crossed swords and fists on their way to the ship.

"Nothing can hurt you now, I have got you," Nathaniel assured as he leaped up a ramp and onto the deck.

"Go!" The captain's cry caused the ship to shudder before taking off northwards.

From my perch in Nathaniel's arms, I saw the guards and bystanders at the water's edge, breathless and defeated. A strange glittering smoke dispersed around us and Claudette smiled in victory.

"I thought I was dead for sure," I gasped, as Nathaniel settled into a chair, letting my body rest in his lap. The skin on my neck felt raw and my throat ragged.

"Caw managed to find me," Nathaniel pulled me closer. "He allowed me to send a message to the others."

"He found you?" I gaped.

"Yes after you left I touched my brand to my journal, it brought Caw to me."

"Goodness," I shook my head. I should have thought of that.

"Then I was able to send a message to our crew—"

"—We stormed the barricades," Butch's grin was infectious but his eyes still held concern.

"The guards put up a good fight but they were no match for us," Nathaniel pressed a kiss to my forehead and I leaned closer. "I am just so glad we got to you in time."

"Claudette slowed your fall and Nathaniel bolted through the crowd, before you…" Rupert pressed his lips together, rubbing his nape.

"We wondered what had happened to the two of you, it didn't feel right." Davy's calming voice soothed me.

"Where's Ned?" I asked realising the older man wasn't contributing to the tale.

"Now do not fret," Claudette said, patting my arm. "Papa has a special mission from the Sorceress. I have not seen him since we reached England."

"Have we left him back there?" I struggled against Nathaniel's hold, we couldn't abandon Ned!

"No," the captain said. "We are headed towards him

actually."

By the time we greeted open water, I felt a lot more like myself. In my free hand I held a half full tankard. I sipped at the amber liquid and groaned as a realisation dawned on me.

"My sword," I whined, my face scrunched up as I stared at my bare hip. That damn guard had it the last time I'd seen it. How in the hell was I going to get it back?

"Here." Butch unbuckled a second belt from around his waist and handed it over. "One of the guards had it. He didn't take too kindly to my request, or my right hook, for that matter." Butch winked, as I pulled the leather through the belt buckle.

"My goodness, what would I do without you?" I exclaimed, grasping his hand and kissing it with enthusiasm.

"Let's go find Ned, eh?" He mumbled ducking his head, his ears growing pink as he pulled his hand away. I smiled as he turned and scurried up to the crow's nest.

The ship crossed a large stretch of ocean before the Island of Plenty came into view. Shouts and whoops of jubilation rang throughout the ship. Some of the crew were ready to relax. Butch, Davy and Rupert raced to the rail, their boots touching the wood almost in unison

"Boys." The captains call stalled their descent, "Caw's message said we had to find Ned first."

"Of course," Rupert agreed and they turned away

from the shining lights illuminating the beach.

When the seven of us had strapped on packs of weapons and food, we headed onto the beach. I eyed the dance floor atop the sand, nostalgia nestling in my heart.

"Memories are there for us to remember time we have lost and what is to come." Nathaniel's voice, low in my ear sent shivers through me, he cupped my cheek and pressed a kiss to my forehead. It had become a tender habit that made me feel cherished.

"I will never forget that night," I breathed.

"May it forever be a dream," he intoned.

My guilt returned as he paraphrased my request from that night.

"Or use it as a tool for the future," I suggested, looking up at him.

He didn't break eye-contact, as he nodded,

"Sounds like a noble plan."

"Come on you two," Rupert yelled.

As Nathaniel and I joined them, Captain Rourke pulled a scroll from his coat and began to read:

> *"No X marks the spot where Edmund stays*
> *Ruin your fortunes and end up in graves*
> *Three of you will resume good honest lives*
> *Four of you will win beautiful wives*
> *Capture the cloud and banish the night*
> *What you seek belongs on the right.*
> *Gold waits where Ned rests*

The place of bullion and treasure chests"

"Could it mean he's in the tavern, isn't that called 'The Dead Man's Chest'?" Davy offered as we murmured our agreement.

"What does the map say, Captain?" Rupert asked.

Captain Rourke unravelled his map, grabbing rocks to ensure it stayed open. We all gathered closer as the ink moved.

"*No X marks the spot.* This will not be easy," Claudette mumbled.

"Does the second line mean if we fail to find Ned, we perish?"

"Let us go with Davy's thought," I said, as if Nathaniel hadn't spoken. "Even if it's right off track, perhaps someone has seen him."

I couldn't take my eyes off the foreboding red 'X' which had appeared on the weathered parchment.

"As I live and breathe," the bartender cried.

I smirked at the reaction to the crew's appearance. The locals of the tavern turned and eyed us before yelling over one another. Rupert and Butch were pulled into a card game whilst Davy settled beside a bearded man with a handful of marked stones.

The captain and Claudette headed towards a group of men around Ned's age. They gathered around the fair haired lady as she spoke in hushed tones.

"Lennie, it has been far too long, cards or gin?" A

group of adolescents called over as I made my way to the bar.

"Have you boys seen Ned?" Well aware of Nathaniel's stare I wandered towards their table.

"Nope, not seen him since you all were here last." The lad at the head of the table chewed on a toothpick, eyeing Nathaniel.

"Well if you do…"

"Come on, Len, we could do with another player." A smaller lad with fluff covering his top lip waved a deck of cards my way,

"Another time boys" I promised. I turned to find Nathaniel scowling behind me at the toothpick kid.

"Friends of yours?" He asked his tone firm, his eyes still on the boy.

"You could say that," I said with a smirk. Skirting around him I strode to the bar. The aged, toothless bartender grinned as I reached him.

"Oh, my girl, I had wondered when you would come and see me again."

Despite my urgency to find Ned, I smiled. "Kenny, I'm not here for my health."

"'Course not, what's your poison?"

"Poison?" Nathaniel's exclaimed from behind me.

"Another cursed one? That ship of yours must be mighty full," The old man said, nodding to the Nathaniel.

"Ken this is Nathaniel, one of the newcomers," I introduced.

"Welcome to the Dead Man's Chest, Son." Ken reached out his hand and Nathaniel shook it, his blue eyes suspicious.

"I...?"

My tone was weary. "Please, this is important, have you seen Ned?"

"Not since you were last docked here."

"Perfect," I muttered, "Thank you anyway."

"Please if you see him, give him this," Nathaniel said. He placed his journal on the bar; scrawling a note he ripped the page out and passed it to the bartender.

"'Course." Ken stowed it away in his shirt pocket.

Nathaniel nodded and grabbed my hand. He pulled me through the crowds to the rest of the crew. The six of them had converged at a corner table. They were huddled together, deep in discussion.

"Any luck?" I interrupted.

"Nothing," Claudette looked concerned. "I thought he'd be back by now, or at least easy to find."

"We'll find him," I said, determined to keep everyone's spirits up, including my own. There was no use in fretting just yet.

"Rosa would know, surely?" Rupert blurted.

As we left the tavern, the captain unrolled the map once more.

"What is this place?" Davy pointed to the red 'X' which had caught my attention earlier.

"It is Shignolds corner, it is said to be where a

hundred and one slain pirates now rest." The captain glanced at me, we'd both been told the story by Rosa before the boys had arrived.

We took our time; each step carried weight as we turned right passed the tavern. The memorial was closed off by a circle of ship wrecks. Passing by the rotting wooden carcasses, we found ourselves in a small area filled with aged pirate memorabilia. Chests that had once been filled with treasure, weapons and compasses of every shape and style were all displayed upon the sand. Stepping amongst the long forgotten items we came across an iron gate. The captain pulled it open with ease and in silence the group gathered just inside.

Calmness settled throughout the group; it felt right with what lay in front of us – a hundred and one graves, each showing a different unique marker. It wasn't until I'd witnessed this amount of death first hand, that I realised hearing the story and experiencing the reality were two very different things.

My gaze moved up and down the aisles, taking in each of the heart-breaking tombstones. Some markers depicted personal quotes, favourite objects, or things of interest. Whilst others showed a simple number, word or phrase. Upon reaching the last grave, my breath caught.

A single bronze rose bloomed out of the ground. At the foot of the grave sat a small figure with long silver hair, plaited to one side, her back held delicate but drooping wings. The creature was curled into itself, rocking like a pendulum; her dark eyes stared far off somewhere we couldn't see.

"Many, many moons ago I had a beloved." Her voice was soft in the silence, no one dared to interrupt her.

"He was named Gaspard and we loved each other most ardently. We were to be married by the snow fall. When Gaspard professed his affection, he swore to me he would love me for all eternity. He never knew what it meant, for he was a mere human and I had already been bestowed the faery's gift. I could not die."

From the tips of her wilting wings to the bareness of her feet, the Sorceress was unrecognisable. Her pain etched face continued to stare at the stone, her eyes the colour of jet ink.

"I was naught but a girl then, powerful in my magic but inexperienced. My name was Ravenzara and I lived in the forest amongst the faery-folk. He stole me away from those who had stolen me first. We absconded and he bought me to his ship. He vowed we would marry."

She still hadn't raised her head; but tears glistened like diamonds upon her elfin face.

"As our love bloomed, my powers too grew in strength. All I wanted was for us to settle down, to live like those I had seen strolling through my forest. Yet he was a pirate, a traveller of the sea. He could not remain upon dry land for long. He yearned for open water and the freedom it gave him.

"Though I missed my forest, I vowed to follow

Gaspard anywhere."

A small smile played across her face, as she remembered. "However, those on dry land thought pirates were thieves and vagabonds, but we were neither. Gaspard and I were part of a crew that fought against the fiends who caused harm, evil and corruption. They caught up with us though and they struck us down. My magic meant little to the ocean and our ship sank."

She bit her lip, her eyes glazed. "I managed to escape but my beloved and our comrades were killed. Gaspard never did fulfil his promises to me."

Her breathing laboured, as her sobs overwhelmed her.

"So enraged by what I perceived as his betrayal, I stole a child from the nearest town – a navy officer's daughter. Even as an infant she was intelligent and serious. She was perfect for what I had planned. I gave her what the faery-folk gave me, the gift of magic."

The Sorceress waved her hand, creating a small wisp of smoke; it dissipated almost as soon as it hit the air.

"I then channelled my hurt and anger into building a boat, a strong and noble vessel, suitable for a quest. Setting sail I left my heart buried in the sand." The Sorceress sighed; pain had carved faint lines on her porcelain skin.

"I see now what I acted upon in anger was the wrong choice. Gaspard did not leave me of his own free will, I that know now. He would have kept his promise had he lived. I am also aware of the foolishness and arrogance of my own youth. I should have given him the gift of immortality too. I can see, by all you have battled through, it would be a mistake to prolong your fear and suffering."

She stood, her small frame looked frail, her grand power no longer fuelling her presence.

"Ned is safe; he is hard at work, preparing Rosa for her return to the *Wilted Rose*."

Hope bloomed within me as I gripped Nathaniel's arm.

"Come," the Sorceress said beckoning us forward. With quiet camaraderie we gathered before her.

She stepped forward, laying her cold hands upon Butch's branded wrist. In a low but audible voice she uttered seven words. '*Ser libre Rosas marchitas, amary ser armido*' which translated to: 'be free Wilted Roses, love and be loved.'

When it came to my turn, the Sorceress' fingers curled around my own wrist and I closed my eyes. The Sorceress spoke and I felt something close to shackles lift from my pounding heart. Opening my eyes, I stared at the brand on my wrist; more leaves were threaded between the wilted petals dotted up my arm.

"Thank you," I whispered.

"Live long, love filled lives, I beg of you."

The Sorceress' unusual eyes held depth as she made contact with each crew member. "I have but one request before you set off for your new journey."

"Anything," the captain said offering himself to the faery-queen.

"Destroy Hadnaloy; she is the final thorn in the *Wilted Rose's* side."

"Thank you Sorceress, we will fulfil your request without argument," Captain Rourke vowed, his eyes glittered as he bowed in respect to her.

"Well my crew, take heed, she will be waiting for you, *bon voyage*, to you all." She blew a kiss towards us; a puff of pink smoke flowed from her palms, creating a blissful euphoria.

The mood was buoyant as we made our way back to the ship, everyone spoke at once. Nathaniel and I trailed behind the rest, fighting our smiles and not quite knowing what to say. Casting shy glances at him, catching him doing the same. I chuckled, grasping hold of his hand and cradling it to my chest.

"Lennie." Nathaniel stopped to let the others walk further ahead.

"Yes?" I took hold of his free hand, awaiting his reply.

"I love you," Nathaniel said, each word clear, precise, and true.

My tears fell unabashed as my heart doubled its beat. It sounded like music, like wine, and treasure. I couldn't speak for a moment, the emotion overcoming me. Nathaniel disentangled a hand to brush aside my tears.

Finally finding my voice, I stared into his bright, adoration filled eyes and said, "As I love you."

Our bodies collided and we were consumed by each other. A culmination of all we had withheld, flooded into those three little words and that earth shattering kiss. My heart thudded in my ears as I lost myself in Nathaniel.

"Look here fellows, Lennie's gone and got herself a man!" One of the boys from the tavern called from the door. I stilled in Nathaniel's arms a moment, before I succumbed to giggles.

"I suppose we do need air after all," Nathaniel whispered, pressing his lips to mine once more.

"The others will wonder where we got to," I said releasing the hold on his hair.

"Yes, they might," he said pulling away with reluctance.

Hand in hand we raced back to our floating home, our breathless laughter and stolen kisses slowing our progress. Reaching the beach, we found the crew assembled before the *Wilted Rose*. Ned stood atop the bough. His pride was founded, as Rosa was situated in her rightful place, at the head of the ship.

"I want to thank you my children," she announced, beginning her speech as Nathaniel and I joined the group. "I am elated you proved to the Sorceress that above all else there is truth. The curse is lifted and you all are free. My gratitude holds no bounds."

She beamed at them all, her fond gaze resembling a proud mother. As she reached Claudette, her smiled slipped.

"My dear, amongst our triumphs we have failed you."

The enchanting fair haired woman shook her head, "Though Macrucio is no longer here, I am not without love. I regard my comrades as siblings and I have a father whom I adore."

She smiled up at Ned, her concern all but gone.

The captain stepped forward, "Though we are all relieved and overjoyed, the Sorceress has given us one last quest."

Rosa pressed her lips into a firm line. "Hadnaloy." She spat the name, not needing to say any more.

CHAPTER XXIV
SITTING DUCKS

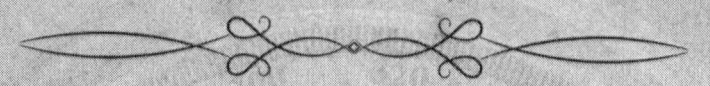

SNOWFLAKES TUMBLED AROUND me, I flung my head back, spinning amongst them. Joy bubbled from deep within and I let out a laugh. The fervent feeling of youth which erupted from me lightened my mood and energised me. I felt so good. I hadn't had this feeling since I was a small child. I could take on the world at that moment, holding nothing but a smile and kind word.

"Enjoying yourself?" Nathaniel stepped into the flurry, the whiteness landing in his hair and sticking to his lashes. I stopped revolving, my smile growing as he neared.

"Did you ever realise we're naught but children?" I said

I cupped my red cheeks as my breath floated around me in a cloud.

"We are?" he replied pushing his hands into the pockets of his jacket. His nose going pink in the cold.

"I know nothing of your age," but I'm not yet twenty."

I raised an eyebrow before I twirled once more.

"Well yes," he said stepping closer, his large frame shadowing me as the snow continued to fall. "I have just turned twenty, thus my childhood is now gone."

Grasping my icy hands, he pulled me to him. His skin was warm as he brushed his rough cheek across mine.

"Yes, no longer are you permitted to whimsy. Poor ancient Nathaniel," I teased.

"Wise too." Mischief danced in his cerulean eyes and I turned my attention to our joined hands.

"Very modest," I said.

Nuzzling into his chest, the steady thrum of his heart cheered me like a familiar song. Nathaniel's tender hands played with my hair as we stood amongst the wintry showers.

"I imagine you have not had much chance to play my love; you do as you wish." Pressing a kiss to my temple he pulled off his coat, wrapping it around my frame.

"Don't catch cold," he murmured wandering back the way he'd come.

Nathaniel's warmth wrapped around me, a mixture of ink and pure male filled my nostrils as I threaded my hands through the sleeves. Enveloped in the jacket, I resumed my whirling, though with Nathaniel's assumption the game had lost its glow a little.

When I was a child and the snow had ground the *Quart de Plaisir* to a halt, Victoria and Clara would play outside with me. They would build snowmen and pull me along in a sleigh built by the patrons.

Yet the moment I had begun to work for Hans, the luxury of playtime was no more. Along with the other ladies of disrepute, I was expected to clean the Châteaux and sew more costumes for when we re-opened. Hans was at his most surly, having nothing more to do than drink and yell insults at his staff and if I was particularly lucky, take a hand or poker to me.

The painful memories jolted me. A phantom pain ran up my leg and across my back. The flakes were thicker now and beginning to settle upon the deck. The surrounding water held a haunting stillness and the air smelled clean and crisp. I leaned against the rail, staring out at the wintery scene.

"Penny for them." Butch stepped beside me, sweeping off his hat to dust off the snow. The redundant action was enough for my lips to twitch in amusement.

"They're not worth that," I replied.

"Lennie." He spoke my name in warning.

"I think too much."

"Yes, you do," Butch agreed.

"What do you suggest?" I asked, gazing out at the frozen landscape.

"Nothing, I have no experience in what ails you." His tone held traces of resentment.

"You know what afflictions I suffer?" I nudged him, a playful grin on my face.

He jammed his hat on his head; his eyes held devilment mixed with a little mystery.

"In my limited knowledge of the opposite sex, it could mean one of one of four things."

"Only four? You do have a limited knowledge."

I grunted as Butch jabbed me in the ribs.

"Do you want to hear my theory? I've plenty of things more pressing to do."

"Do go on." I mocked and with a low bow I gestured for him to continue.

He sent me a withering look before counting off his ideas on his fingers. "The four I believe are: Men, their past, their heart and their futures."

He didn't look my way once he'd finished, choosing to stare off into the middle distance.

"I'm impressed, but can I ask you a question?" I said.

"Only one? He teased, earning him a taste of his own wrath. As I prodded his stomach, he groaned aloud.

"Can I speak?"

"Carry on," he said, clutching at his torso.

"Men and the heart, I thought they were the same thing."

"You would think so." he said.

"You don't?"

"For matters of the heart, fine things can happen…for matters of men, well anything is possible."

"We already have a resident bard, his name is Nathaniel," I said, hating at how obnoxious I sounded.

"Where do you think I landed such a line?" He winked, his cheeky grin showed little remorse.

"You read his work?" I exclaimed in jealousy.

"We do share a cabin, dearest Lennie."

I batted him away as he tapped my nose.

"That would be private."

Though Nathaniel had offered to show his writing, I had never had the pleasure.

"Not so private when he leaves his writing scattered all over the place," Butch groused.

I had no answer; I turned from him, my hand gripping the chilled rail. The ocean seemed more vast – would we complete our task?

"Do you think we'll find her?" My shift in mood and subject felt sudden even to me.

"Hadnaloy?" He asked and I nodded.

"If you ask me, I think Hadnaloy knows what we're doing, she will make this as difficult as she can." Butch surmised.

"She's not the only one who can play games though."

"No she's not."

The snow drove the crew below deck for much of the day, yet as night fell the flakes dissipated leaving just the cold. My mind couldn't settle; no book or conversation could kill the restlessness I felt.

It was far too quiet; the silence ate at me, gnawing on my conscience. The vague sounds of my sleeping crewmates and the water lapping against the boat couldn't stop the overwhelming sense of nothing. Tossing my unread book to one side, I wrenched off my bedding and padded out the door.

Reaching the deck, I spied a lone candle through the mist; like a beacon I followed it. The source of light sat atop the card table, it spilled across Nathaniel and the parchment he wrote upon. Words covered page after page and ink stained his fingers. Watching him work, my anxiety faded. Seeing the stories unfold before me, gave a comfort I only found whilst reading.

Not wanting to interrupt him, I turned, leaving him to his prose.

"Lennie…"

I spun, tripping on the blanket I'd wrapped around myself. Nathaniel's eyes were alight and sparkling with creativity and the cold.

"Sorry I didn't mean to disturb you," I mumbled, staring down at my bare feet.

"Nonsense my love, come and sit beside me."

I did as he urged, his arm came around me and he pulled me closer. As he kissed my cheek, I picked up a discarded quill and ran it through my fingers.

"Writing, I see," I rolled my eyes as my cheeks coloured. Despite our new found closeness, he still made me nervous. I felt such a dolt, of course he was writing, stupid girl!

"The pen is mightier than the sword, or so they say," He said grinning at the foolish cliché he imparted. He pushed the hair from my face and I stared up at him.

"Well if that's so," I said finally pulling myself from

his hypnotic gaze. "What do you write? Is it some epic tragedy which will have us all in tears?"

"I hope not," he said leafing through the journal. "I have been reading through my father's entries and felt the urge to document my own history.

"I think it's a grand idea, you showing future generations how we lived, just as your father did."

"Maybe," Nathaniel said, laying down his quill and reaching for my hand. He brushed his lips over my knuckles, paying particular care to linger over the third finger of my left hand. My heart fluttered in my chest but we both remained in companionable silence.

DESPITE THE CURSE being eradicated, we as a crew remained focussed on our quest. Though no-one wanted to go 'Hadnaloy hunting,' we knew we had a large debt to repay to the Sorceress. Our gratitude was immense and the fear that the Sorceress could take away our new-found freedom kept us alert.

Sailing aimlessly, or as Butch called it, 'without purpose,' took a toll on the now joyous crew. Rosa's closeness gave us new things to learn though; and any time I spent away from Nathaniel was sat on the rail beside the wooden woman.

The snow had passed and the ship eased through warmer waters. In the dim glow of a candle I cleaned my sword, only Rosa's soft singing broke the silence.

"Rosa." I sheathed the blade as I spoke.

"Yes my child." The figurehead stopped mid-song and turned her head.

"Something has been circling my mind…" I continued.

"Well ask me dear, I would hate for you to be distracted." A smirk lifted the side of Rosa's mouth.

"How did Hadnaloy come to be such a rival?" I leaned further over the rail, wanting to see Rosa's face.

"She is not a rival as such," Rosa disagreed. "More like a person willing to risk everything, to get revenge."

"Revenge, what have you done?"

Rosa smiled at my confusion. She lifted a hand and used her finger to write in the air. The letters sparkled in the darkened sky. 'H.A.D.N.A.L.O.Y' Rosa brushed her wooden rose across them and they re-arranged to form a new word. YOLANDAH.

"Did I ever tell you of the first couple aboard the *Wilted Rose*, once it had been cursed?"

"The tale of the woman bewitched?" I gasped, my eyes were wide as I took in the floating letters.

"Yes," Rosa nodded as she stared up at the stars; they twinkled in the ebony backdrop of night. "This tale may seem pitiful and somewhat shallow but that is who Hadnaloy was and always will be."

"Will you refresh my memory?" I asked.

"Of course,"

After Rosa had become the figurehead of the ship, it progressed as well as it could, yet when a doting couple were pulled aboard, the infamous nature Rosa had originated was solidified. Colt and Yolandah arrived soaked to the skin but very much in love. Both were young, attractive and — as most in their position do — felt the entire world was on their side. Rosa could see the culmination of the besotted couple and cursed ship would not end well, and urged them to remain aloof and distant whilst aboard the Wilted Rose. They ignored her of course, believing the talking figurehead was a side-effect of their ordeal.

Yet as Yolandah slept below, Colt returned to the deck, curious to know the history of the ship. The dark stained section of wood and the talking figurehead both held the most interest to him.

Rosa revealed her tragic tale- that she had held someone close to her heart but that love was doomed. The proof was the dark stain where her beloved Dominico had been slain. Though intrigued by Rosa's cautionary tale the, young man failed to see the connection between the story and his adoration for Yolandah.

Every night onward Colt would return to Rosa, to listen to her stories and to slake his thirst for curiosity. Yet Yolandah was a shallow woman, more in love with herself than her partner. She felt flattered that someone such as Colt — a man of importance, had chosen her over all the others. Though every night, he slunk away from her bed to fraternize with the 'devil creature.'

One week into their stay, the couple had retired to their cabin. With only moonlight to bother them, they indulged in each other's company before falling to sleep. Colt waited for the soft snores of his *love to ease into a rhythm before he took his usual journey to the deck.*

The click of the door was Yolandah's signal and she opened her eyes — jealousy and fury pulsed through her body like blood. Agitated and restless she raced from her bed, knocking a vase of Roses — a flower Rosa kept aboard the ship to remind her of her Dominico. Yolandah grasped at the fallen blooms, blood seeping from her palm as the thorns snagged her skin. Still livid she raced to the deck, seeing only red as she spied her trophy and the creature locked in a fervent discussion.

"Did we wake you, my love?" Colt asked.

It would be his final question as Yolandah lost all sense. Soon fresh blood stained the deck and a single rose floated to meet the still chest of a kind man.

"Now neither of us can have him."

"You have no heart," Rosa cried, her anguish was pure as she glared at the fiendish woman; the beauty shown on the outside concealed the ugly and gnarled being within.

"What use is any heart?" Yolandah was smug as she flipped her hair.

Rosa's anger outweighed her rational mind and she raised the wooden rose she held. Flicking her wrist Yolandah transformed. Screams of anger and fear echoed around the ship as her body withered, her smooth youthful skin began to wrinkle and pale before her eyes.

"Now what you represent reflects the evil you hold inside. Go from here and learn to find the beauty within."

"You shall pay for what you have done here," the crone spat.

Before she could say any more, Rosa had swept her floral sceptre a second time and the woman was gone.

Finishing her tale, the figurehead stared at her reflection in the water below.

"Years went by and I heard nothing more from Yolandah. I perhaps was arrogant in my belief that I had destroyed her." Rosa shook her head.

"More years passed and I started to hear of an evil sea-witch and her terrible power. I heard she was clever and she was successful in her bouts." The figurehead's lips pulled downwards and regret laced her tone.

"Within all this, her soul had been lost. The Sorceress became angry; this being I had punished had left her mark all over our territory and not in a positive way. The Sorceress tried to find her, to stop all she had become, yet somehow she evaded our leader."

"If you transformed her into a crone, why now does she look so huge? Was it her power which had caused her growth?" I asked.

"Her ambition was to usurp me, to become what I am. From the information I have managed to gather she has used all the wrecks of the ships she has destroyed to create armour. It is a façade to intimidate, in becoming that creature; she now held two of my traits."

"What of the magic?"

"She befriended someone." Rosa paused weighing her words. "A creature powerful enough to transfer their abilities. The creature knew what they had done but it was far too late."

"They were tricked by her?"

Rosa shook her head. "No, nothing like that. The creature felt cheated, even hurt and retaliated by willingly gifting their power, a power almost as great as the Sorceress'"

"Retaliated against you and the Sorceress?"

Rosa turned away and I knew I'd asked the wrong question.

"If I have offended you...?"

Rosa's lips were pursed but replied, "to answer your question, yes."

I remained quiet, not wanting to cause more strain. Things were beginning to make sense now. To slot together, like a well formed puzzle. The more Rosa spoke of Yolandah, the more Hadnaloy seemed less frightening, at least in some ways. She was a fake, a once shallow person who had become a smokescreen.

THE OCEAN BLED into blackness as the *Wilted Rose* ventured forward. Never in the five or so years I had been aboard the ship, had I wanted Hadnaloy to appear. Now, it was all I desired. The debt had to be repaid, I didn't want to return to the loveless state we had all spent too long in.

"Nothing like a scary stretch of water to brighten the journey, is there?" Butch whispered, trying to diffuse the tension.

I shot him a smile but my focus had no room for humour.

"Captain, would you permit me a folly?" Claudette's request interrupted the silence and had us turning from our posts.

"What do you have in mind?"

"As Hadnaloy's heir, I had a signal to summon her. She may guess I would attempt it, but it is worth a try."

"Go ahead," he acquiesced.

Claudette flushed as she noticed her audience but stepped to the rail. She lay out her left palm, tapping it with her right forefinger, whilst her thumb touched the scarred former brand at her wrist. Sparks flew from the centre of her hand towards the sky. All eyes watched the horizon but as minutes passed there was no sign of response.

"What now?" Rupert asked, his eyes still trained on the view far out to sea.

Claudette's expression was thoughtful. "I have done all I can."

"It's all we can ask for, my girl," Ned said, pressing a doting kiss to her forehead.

The long tense silence returned as they waited. Nothing stirred.

"Perhaps since Hadnaloy removed your mark, you've

lost that link." Davy patted her shoulder in commiseration.

"She knows we're here," the captain murmured from the helm.

Rosa nodded, "She will bide her time, she is not fool enough to come at us with full force. She wants the uneasiness to create vulnerability. Thus we are an easy target for her to take."

From the apprehensive faces of my crewmates, the sea-witch's plan could well be working.

The silence filled up the ship driving me mad. I had taken to reciting poetry under my breath to stave off the ominous feeling the quiet brought. A little way off, Claudette made violet flames dance across her palm. Her failed attempts to call her former mistress seemed to irk her and the annoyance was plain in her frown.

"You are troubled." Nathaniel did not attempt to touch me as he spoke.

"Have you ever heard of the term 'sitting duck'?" I turned away, though I yearned to be enveloped in his arms.

"Of course, is that how you feel?" He kept his voice low, leaning closer.

I nodded in reply and began to pace.

"I've been aboard this ship five years," I said, continuing back and forth. "I've never felt unsafe, never, but now…"

"Do you wish to leave?" His eyes darted to the crew,

no-one paid any attention to us.

I shook my head, my hand on my sword. "Land calls to me, the anonymity of towns and villages, we could all hide, but no. We owe the Sorceress." I stopped, staring out at the dusky twilight, nothing reflected, not even the moon.

"I wish something would happen, even if we sailed away, this waiting is torture." Nathaniel lessened the gap between us, gathering me in his arms.

"I know, my love," he said as he pressed a kiss to my hair.

"Nate, we need your advice," Ned called.

I stepped back at Ned's request. Swiping at my eyes I gestured for him to join the older man.

"Do not feel guilty in speaking of those things, everyone feels the same, you are the brave one to reveal it." Nathaniel said.

He watched me and I pasted on a smile. "Go, Ned needs you."

I pushed at him and with reluctance he left my side. I rested against the rail, my focus on the strange stillness of the water. There appeared to be nothing there. Not one creature, magical or otherwise. It was such a strange night, there was no breeze and the air was neither cold nor warm. Yet I shivered at the unusualness of it all. Pulling my jacket around me, I tried to recall the poem I'd recited earlier.

As I mouthed the fragmented verses there was a

disturbance in the water. my eyes held the spot, waiting. Sure enough something moved beneath the depths. It was the first sign of life I'd seen since we'd dropped anchor. Could it be Hadnaloy or one of her underlings? My hand clasped the hilt of my sword as I took a step back from the rail. I wouldn't shout for the others yet, I could take on whatever it was.

The ripples were growing as I waited, my body tense and ready for the fight. My anticipation increased as an object broke through the surface. I edged closer, my curiosity overruling any caution.

The item was gold, angular and aged. Was it a weapon? my heart raced as the object emerged to its full potential. I lifted my heels off the ground, eager to get a better look. All my expectation was in vain as it revealed itself — A picture frame, worn, battered and old. Darn, I was spoiling for a fight!

I didn't shift my attention though despite the disappointing display. Could this have been a trap? The painting within the frame was hard to see in the moonlight, yet its features did seem familiar. Aware it wasn't my most intelligent idea, I grasped a lantern, shining the light over the water, I gasped as discovered who was painted there.

"Maria Davenport?" I observed. What was a picture of Nathaniel's mother doing in the water?

Dropping the lamp, I grasped the rail. "Butch, come here!"

Clambering over the side, I heard the sound of running footsteps.

"What on earth?" Butch growled his breathing heavy.

"The picture," I replied, clinging to the boat with one hand, as I swung the other towards the frame.

"Damn," I muttered, as it floated out of my reach.

"Lennie, leave it," Nathaniel's voice made me pause. I turned to see him climb over too.

"No, stay there," I shouted as I swung my arm again. "It won't take long, your mothers portrait is not too far off."

I was determined to get it for him. Something inside me demanded I succeed. I may not be able to return his mother to him, but Nathaniel was damn well getting this portrait!

"Leave it," Nathaniel pleaded again.

I ignored him, throwing out my arm as the frame floated towards me.

"Yes!" I cried in triumph, as I yanked the frame in my direction. Gripping it close I began to climb back up the ship. As I turned, a sinister laugh sounded somewhere in the depths below.

"Lennie?" Nathaniel's eyes were wide as my fingers lost their grip on the rope ladder. Both he and Butch reached out for me as I scrabbled to find purchase.

"No, we won't let you fall," he yelled.

I had lost all form of speech as my fingertips brushed Nathaniel's, with one last fleeting look, I sunk deep beneath the jet ocean.

CHAPTER XXV
POTION

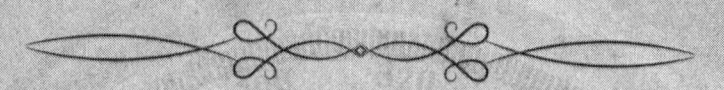

THE WATER COVERED my head and panic rose within me. As water filled my lungs I felt the edges of my consciousness fading. Barely a moment before I succumbed to the sea, I was hauled through a cave opening and the water ended. The shadow which had hold of me allowed me to pause. The water spewed from my mouth, my throat raw. Before I could properly gauge my surrounding or even recover I was dragged again.

Screaming wasn't an option, as I was pulled through tunnel after underwater tunnel. I couldn't even focus on what passed me by. Flashes of colour and strange smells attacked my senses as my arm felt as though it was being ripped from its socket. Whatever steered me was strong; my hand was clamped in a vice like grip which didn't feel human. It was claw-like and dug painfully into my wrist. I was sure it was drawing blood. Why on earth had I begun this stupid escapade in the first place?

My stomach tumbled as I wondered if the journey would ever end. My thoughts were finally answered as I was let go. The jolting stop sent me airborne and I flailed helplessly, my heart in my throat as I flew through the air. It was far too late to cry out as I landed, my body colliding with a wall. The crack my head made upon impact should have rendered me unconscious, yet I saw nothing but stars and black spots. Blinking them back I pressed a shaky hand to the back of my head as the darkness swelled. Brilliant, my day could have been so much worse...

Dripping wet and in pain, I tried to focus. I had landed in what looked to be a corridor. At either end, thick wooden doors held large metal locks. Memories of my time in the English prison swam into my mind and I felt the walls closing in. The ominous half-light which surrounded me gave little comfort.

It took time but my breathing eased and the pain coursing through my head ebbed away, leaving a dull ache. No one had appeared and now a little more lucid, I looked around. Gauging my surroundings, I found myself very much alone. The corridor held an encapsulating silence that even the water surrounding it did not dare disturb. My sharp breaths came quick and fast as I stared at the adornments lining the damp stone walls.

As with the cove where Rosa resided, every inch of stone was carved or displayed some form of art, although these were crude and rough, less meaningful in some ways. On unsteady feet I stumbled up the narrow passage to take a closer look. The most detailed creation was a tapestry situated close to the furthest door, the delicate work looked so lifelike. The face which stared back at me looked like Maria Davenport, but somehow it wasn't. Instead of the family's trademark sky blue, the eyes of the portrait were a murky green. As I stared into the face, a sense of foreboding surrounded me.

"What do we have here?" A voice muttered.

The nape of my neck prickled, the hair standing on end as the owner of voice approached. I remained still, feeling a very easy prey.

The voice continued. "My face was such a trophy. I could steal the heart of any man. Steal it, crush it, manipulate it…"

I spun, catching myself from falling by grasping the wall. Standing before me, wasn't the twelve-foot monster I'd been expecting. Instead an aged hag with a distorted face, looked up from a contorted frame. The crooked eyes were a vibrant blood red.

"She took my beauty and stole my dazzling life, all because I allowed jealousy to get the better of me. I can never return to the person I once was but that weakness will never plague me again."

I clasped my hands in front of me, taking in the strange looking creature. Just as Rosa claimed, the large demon who had scared so many was little more than a façade. Behind it was this fragile, crooked witch. Though I wasn't fool enough to disrespect her power – like the Sorceress – Hadnaloy was not all she appeared.

Rosa's story came back to me; this creature once was Colt's love, who valued her looks far more than her man. Beneath even this costume, the 'all powerful' Hadnaloy was just Yolandah, a jealous, bitter woman and nothing more.

"I refuse to pity you," I said the courage building within me. "You have done so many terrible things, hurt many people. All I feel is sadness, for the good you could have achieved."

I looked at the haggard woman square in the face. "Your heart is as withered as the rest of you."

Anger flickered in Hadnaloy's strange eyes as she measured my insult. When she replied her voice was low and dangerous.

"You my girl, are insufferable and all too free with your truth." She turned her back on me. Which I had to admit was a gutsy move.

"I cannot deal with you now," Hadnaloy remarked.

Clicking her fingers, a man-servant appeared. Tall and muddy eyed, he bundled me through the nearest opening.

As I was thrust over the threshold, I stumbled. The door slammed hard behind me leaving the sound ringing in my ears as I fell to the stone floor. My spinning head twirled in confusion. One moment I'd been exploring the carvings, the next I'd been accosted by the true Hadnaloy. Now... I wasn't quite sure where I was.

The smell hit me first as I dusted myself off – rotting fish – the very same stench I'd found aboard Macrucio's ship. Pushing the memory out of my mind, I focussed on my surroundings. It didn't help matters, my stomach rolled at what greeted me. The shelf lined walls were filled with jars, each containing various unrecognisable floating objects and congealed liquids. Beneath them sat an empty cauldron over an unlit fire. Tools I didn't recognise littered a table beside it.

One item looked like a knife, though the blade was a jade green colour and held jagged edges. Another was a wooden amulet, with a carving resembling Hadnaloy's crest — a ships wheel with two crossed swords. Other more macabre items littered the table, each covered in what looked like blood and entrails, the sight made me so nauseous I had to look away. I didn't want to know what they were all used for. What darkness was created here nor who was doing the creating.

Turning to look at anything aside from that menacing part of the room, I came face to face with a bookshelf. Scanning the spines, I plucked one at random, it's velvet cover weighed heavy in my hands. Turning the pages, each one tipped in black, my eyes grew wide and my heart pounded.

Crude sketches of wounds, dissected animals, mutations and black magic seeped out of the paper like evil. There were spells and curses scrawled onto page after page, darker than anything I'd ever seen or read about before.

Placing the book back onto the shelf, I gazed at the

many volumes in confusion, why did someone as powerful as Hadnaloy need potions when with a click of her fingers she could cause death?

Stepping back from the bookcase I tripped, knocking over an easel. A spell book thumped to the floor, scattering a single sheet of parchment. Righting everything, I crouched to pick up the loose sheet my breath catching.

The page was flawed; ragged edges patterned one side, as though it had been ripped from its original home. The penmanship was familiar, masculine and rugged. My stomach clenched as I placed its origin. The script held a close resemblance to the early entries in Nathaniel's journal. Swallowing the heavy sense of foreboding, I read the ink stained parchment.

There was talk of many potions, but Rosa detailed only one in relation to Hadnaloy. If she were to gain this, Rosa has told us, we could all be doomed. For gaining beauty opened her to more followers, shallow one's who would follow her face, even if her purpose was evil.

The Potion of Beauty Everlasting

Ingredients:

One pearl from a clam rained by blood

Three purple daisy petals grown from love

One piece of mountain rock, burned by the sun

Milk from a palm nut, blessed by the sea

Thorns from eight roses, wilted by harm

Oil from the bark of a wood nymph's tree

Life-blood from a person whose beauty you envy

Once every ingredient has been obtained, unite them under a silver moon and recite the following incantation:

Join these together, by dark of night

Take one sip and all will be right

Beauty will be returned to a haggard face

Power will come with renewed grace.

How foolish to have written it down, even saying if Hadnaloy got hold of it, we'd be done for! Each of the ingredients had been crossed out, with one exception: *'Oil from the bark of a Wood Nymph's tree.'* I knew why, the only wood nymphs known to Hadnaloy would be the Sorceress and perhaps Tatters. They would never allow Hadnaloy and her underlings to enter the forest let alone perform dark magic amongst their beloved trees.

If the sea-witch did manage to get the final ingredient, her power would surpass Rosa and the Sorceress, then they would all be at the mercy of the darkest of evil. With her renewed beauty she could gain more followers – just as the journal entry had said.

My mind raced, there had to be a chance to right this. Folding the page into my pocket; I glanced around the room. My eyes ventured with much reluctance to the disturbing jar filled area and I caught sight of a cage hidden amongst the strange ingredients. It wasn't large but the metal was ornate. Butterflies decorated the aged bars. I stepped closer, within its confines stood a phial. The image projected what Hadnaloy could one day be. Evil encased in beauty. The liquid within the glass sparkled in a strange mauve colour; the same hue of Claudette's eyes.

"It will be locked, of course," I muttered, climbing upon a stool and grasping the cage with both hands. My breath stilled as I stood frozen in position. Turning towards the door, I waited for it to crash open, to be toppled from my perch and captured further. Seconds ticked by with nothing to break the silence.

Letting out a pent up breath, I yanked at the opening again. As I predicted, it wouldn't budge. I knew I had to destroy the contents; it would give Hadnaloy more power and make her even harder to conquer. I had to win; there was no way I could return to my silent-hearted ways. To be cursed again would be a fate worse than death.

Jamming my fists into the pockets of my jacket, I stared around the room. My fingers grazed my sword and a flash of inspiration struck. Unsheathing the blade with a flourish, I swiped at the cage. The clang echoed around the room and I stilled. In my excitement, I'd forgotten I was at the mercy of a powerful sea-witch. I again, awaited the inevitable, I couldn't be lucky twice in one day...

The silence surrounding me was eerie, not even the sound of the witch's underlings littered the air. No one came; but I wasn't going to be so frivolous again. Third time might not be so very lucky. I'd been so sure my sword would work. Shaking my head, I rolled up my sleeves. My brand stared back at me, its toothy grin, mocking. As I glared at it, another errant thought blossomed... but would it work? I could only try. I was running out of options.

Willing to try absolutely anything, I pressed the brand on my wrist to its twin embossed on my sword. Pulling it away, the skull's eyes glowed red. Torn between my fears and not wanting whatever I had created to fade, I lifted the weapon and swiped it towards the bars. With ease the blade cut through the metal and fell to the floor with a crash. I grasped the unharmed phial stowing it with the handkerchief and broach.

Racing to the door, I slammed the handle of my sword against the lock. It split in two and I pushed through the opening.

"This was all too easy," I muttered, rushing over the threshold. My thoughts came back to haunt me, as water trickled from the ceiling and under the opposite door. As I pondered on a way to escape the corridor, the leak went from a stream to an ocean, its current fast and frenzied as it caught me. I tried to fight my way through the gulf but the surprise capture had weakened me. With what little strength I had left I forged forward, heading towards the locked door I'd arrived through.

Battered by the ever increasing water level, I wrestled with the door. My sword, feet and fists smashed helplessly and soon it crashed open, sending me upward with the flow. The increasing current moved me on and I rose to the surface, sputtering and gagging.

"Help!" I cried, sinking beneath water, my tired body losing momentum. The inky blackness made it impossible to see. Kicking my weary legs, I propelled myself above the waterline.

Though my sagging energy slowed me down, I managed to get above sea-level. With my breathing becoming more regular, I floated across the water and I reached into my sodden clothes, relieved to find everything accounted for.

Taking my time I pushed onward finding no sign of land or sea traffic. With my panic rising once more I tried to think of something other than my predicament. Each ingredient that had been crossed in the recipe seemed simple to acquire, at least for a witch. Though there was one which had bothered me since I'd read it: 'Life blood from a person whose beauty you envy.'

As I continued to swim in circles, my mind tumbled over many ideas. One which I tried hard to push away kept coming back. Biting my lip as tears formed in my eyes – Maria's picture wasn't floating in the ocean without reason.

"Lennie!" Turning I saw a figure gaining on me in a row boat. He was blonde and slight and I'd know that boyish face anywhere.

"Butch," I sobbed, flailing my tired limbs. With as much effort as I could I attempted to meet him.

"I will be right there, stay where you are," he called. Reaching my side, he plunged his hands into the depths, yanking me out, his inherited strength making the task easy.

"We have been searching all manner of places for you," he said as he wrapped his arm around me, brushing the dampness from my clothing.

"Never mind that." I dismissed wrenching out of his hold. "I need to...I want Nathaniel...potion...Hadnaloy." I panted and gasped. My ordeal mixed with panic, left me incoherent.

He frowned. "What on earth are you on about?"

"Nathaniel's mother, she was down there. Hadnaloy

had captured her."

My tears fell without pride, my body convulsing with fear, panic and cold.

"Don't worry about a thing." Butch slung an arm around me again and pulled back his sleeve.

Well aware of his intention I did the same. Connecting our brands brought a tingle of heat before the *Wilted Rose* appeared in the water, stopping beside us.

"We need help down here." There was a hysterical edge to Butch's cry.

Nathaniel was the first to slide down the rope ladder. He landed in the row boat, pulling off his jacket and wrapping it around me, his arms followed but I squirmed in panic. I was so happy to see him, but I had to tell him my theory.

"Nathaniel, your mother," I gasped.

"Lennie, you are delirious," he said as he tried to warm me.

I shook my head, growling in frustration. No one was listening. Grasping his face in both of my hands, I stared deeply into his eye as I spoke. The words were slow and precise, despite my obvious fear and pounding heart.

"Your mother was down there."

"What?"

"She was there, I know it." The sobs ripped through me again and I let him go. "But she's gone, she's gone now."

"My mother?" Nathaniel eyed the jet water with an

unusual expression. He let me go and looked ready to jump in himself.

"Nathaniel, don't try it, we cannot afford to lose you," Butch said echoing my own thoughts. The younger man put a restraining hand on his shoulder.

"Mother." Nathaniel knelt over the side of the boat reaching out, his fingertips skimming the surface.

"We have to get Lennie on board," Butch said.

Nathaniel snapped out of his angst. "of course," he said. Let's get you dry."

With Butch's help, Nathaniel aided me over the rail.

"What in God's name happened?" Ned raged as he and Claudette rushed to help. Landing on deck, my legs promptly gave way. Without missing a beat, Nathaniel scooped me up, cradling me like a child; he sat at the card table.

"Just take your time," he said, though his expression still looked pained as he pressed his lips to my forehead.

"I was dragged to Hadnaloy's lair," I stated. There was no point in 'frilling' it up

"You get all the fun," Rupert muttered, his eyes danced with humour.

Butch nudged the redhead in the ribs as he thrust a tankard of amber liquid at me. I guzzled it, my throat burning as it hit my stomach.

"Easy," Nathaniel warned wrenching it from my mouth. "You have to be lucid."

I nodded as I wiped the alcohol from my mouth.

"I was stupid," I sighed, remembering. "I spoke out of turn and was thrown into a room. It was strange, there were jars everywhere."

"You were in the potions room?" Claudette said in disbelief.

"You know of this place?" I tried to sit straighter but in Nathaniel's strong hold I merely shifted a little.

Nathaniel righted me on his lap, noticing my plight, but refused to let me go.

"Yes, I was allowed in once, it was not a comfortable place. Macrucio would spend hours there. Devouring the books, mixing concoctions..." Claudette trailed off as everyone stared at her. "What has this got to do with you?" She asked, turning to me.

"Well..." I scrambled around in my pockets, pulling out the phial and the damp parchment. "I found this."

I handed the torn page to Nathaniel, his expression changed from curious to angry as he read.

"She stole it," he said through clenched teeth.

"It looks that way," I agreed.

"What is written there?" The captain stepped forward and Nathaniel handed it to him.

"I believe a magical concoction to get Hadnaloy her beauty back and in turn more power" I explained, returning to the tankard, sipping slower.

"I can't believe she managed to get hold of such a thing!" Rosa's shock was plain.

The crew converged around our figurehead. I held

onto the back of a chair, my legs still unsteady.

"What should we do with it?" I asked.

"We smash it of course." Nathaniel's tone was still hard, his hands clenching into fists.

"Calm yourself," Rosa demanded. Nathaniel shoved his hands in his pockets and went to lean against the rail.

"Lennie, how far gone is this?" Rosa asked.

I pulled my gaze from Nathaniel, his jaw muscled worked back and forth and I knew what I was about to say would anger him further.

"It's almost complete, there's one ingredient missing."

"Whose lifeblood did they use?" Davy asked, reading from the parchment.

"If what Lennie says is true, then it was my mother's." Nathaniel's voice cracked and I went to him. Taking his hand, I pressed it over my heart.

"She will never finish this." There was no doubt in my statement. I would see it was so.

"The last ingredient needed, is oil from a tree in the Sorceress' forest, which will be nigh on impossible for her to get."

"I wouldn't be so bold in my convictions," Rosa said with a darkened tone.

"What do you suggest?" The captain asked.

Rupert and Butch finished reading over Davy's shoulder. Their expressions were expectant as the three of them came to stand beside me and Nathaniel.

"I think Nathaniel was right. We should dispose of it;

we just need to do it in the correct way."

The eight of us congregated around the card table. Each one glaring at the phial waiting for the moment Rosa allowed us destroy it. I still couldn't understand how something so beautiful could harm us so much. The colour sparkled in the twilight like a beacon of evil.

"It's strange..." Rupert mused, ending the silence. His hands reached out but did not touch the glass. "I sense this to be something of importance, yet, its owner does not give it a lot of value. It shows just how far Hadna–"

"–Rosa, how long do we have to wait before we end this?" Nathaniel's question crossed Rupert's ideas, his impatience apparent. I grasped hold of the hand he was about to lift, squeezing it in warning.

"Your fury will not help," Rosa replied. "I need to think carefully. I am not used to this form of magic. Potions and black magic are no use to me. My power is derived from the woodland creatures that hide within the trees and flowers. Theirs is a pure and defined art."

Rosa lifted the sceptre she carried, "Witchcraft has no place in my world. Hadnaloy's magic is a mystery to me, there are some similarities but her power has been contaminated in some way. I do not want it to continue."

She turned so she could see us, her deep solemn eyes scanning the table.

"If we were to pour away the liquid, we could pollute the oceans on which we sail. If we smash the phial, the poisoned glass could do more than cut us. If I was to make it evaporate, the rain that comes after could kill us all."

Nathaniel bowed his head, his discontentment plain.

"Rosa, I know Hadnaloy, she will not suffer this gladly. She will come after us, it is best we do not have this in our possession when she does," Claudette said. With purpose she strode across the deck and touched the wooden woman's arm.

"Please let us do this with speed," the enchantress pleaded.

"You are right my dear but we must consult with the Sorceress."

THE FOREST NEVER failed to overwhelm me. Even in the sunlight, it loomed dark and ominous. The blue flames of the Sorceress' fire were nowhere in sight as we edged up the beach. My palms were slick as I carried the phial and its recipe. I knew the Sorceress would have the answer, yet we hadn't fulfilled our promise. Hadnaloy still lived. Though I had spoken my truth to the crew, the Sorceress' bitterness was deep rooted. Would she be disappointed? Would we?

"Back so soon?" the faery leader said.

She rose from the forest floor taking hold of the captain's hands, and kissed him on both cheeks before beaming at us all. The change in her demeanour was both strange and lovely all at once. I didn't relax my all too wary position afraid she'd turn at any moment.

"We have some mixed news for you, your grace." Claudette curtseyed, her cheeks flushed.

"Mixed? What has happened?"

I stepped forward, stumbling over what to say I thrust the objects forward. "I–I managed to acquire these from Hadnaloy's lair."

"Hadnaloy's lair, you say? You mean you were captured and managed to escape?" The fae-queen rocked back and forth on her heels, shock registering on her face.

"Yes Ma'am," I replied.

"You are a fighter." The Sorceress fluttered around me, her eyes filled with curiosity and pride.

"What is this?" She asked, stopping before my outstretched hands.

The captain stepped forward, his hat in his hands. "It is a potion, one that could end us all."

His reply was greeted by silence.

"We require help, though you have given us so much all ready."

The Sorceress urged him to continue with the twirl of a hand, but it was Davy who spoke instead.

"We need assistance in destroying it, we don't know how."

"Very well." the Sorceress nodded. Reaching out her hands with caution, she took the bottle and parchment from me. Turning away, she floated through the trees. We all followed at a hurried pace, arriving as she held the recipe towards the flickering blue flame. It caught in an instant and was no more.

Without ceremony she held up the phial, turning it in her hand, she watched the mauve liquid as it sloshed behind the glass. Her lips moved so fast and her voice was so low that no-one could make out her words. With firm hands she held it over the warm the blue flames. A small puff of lavender smoke erupted from the centre and the Sorceress nodded. As she closed her fingers around the stem it disappeared in a cloud of dust, the remnants fell into the flames like glitter

"Finished," she said brushing herself off.

"Thank you Sorceress. Again." The captain flourished his hat, as he bowed.

"We seem to be racking up quite a debt to you ma'am," Nathaniel said. The worry clouding his face with a frown was ever present in my heart.

"All I want is what I have asked for, Hadnaloy – gone."

CHAPTER XXVI
RESOLUTION

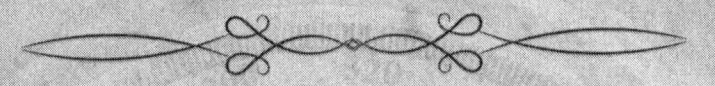

UPON OUR RETURN to the ship I took roost atop the rail. The soft undulation of the ship helped calm my restless mind. So much had happened since the day that flower floated into my life bringing the boy with the cerulean eyes. I would have done many things differently, but the feelings I felt and the results, I would never have changed.

"No matter how much the sea has freed me; it has trapped me just as much." I said as Ned rested beside me, his hands dangling and his scarred face weary.

"That is has, my girl," he said. "You did well. Not many leave Hadnaloy's presence in one piece. Let alone escape her lair and with something valuable." His face was lit up with pride.

"You did it," I countered.

"I did."

"Did you feel so disenchanted afterwards?" I twisted so I could see his face clearly.

"What an odd question," he said pausing to think over his reply. "I felt cheated, at least to begin with, now I don't know."

"I feel nothing, I'm numb."

I touched the spot over my heart. Though I hadn't lied, all too much had happened for my heart to give anymore. My love was still strong for Nathaniel, just too much was at stake now I'd given my heart away, not only for me. It was like the curse all over again, just on a smaller scale.

Ned took hold of my hands, forcing me to look at him and breaking me from my theorising.

"Good things will come to you child, especially now you have done this." Patting my cheek, he walked away.

"I'm not so sure," I murmured after him.

Ever since Ned had rescued me from the *Quart De Plaisir*, he had been something of a father figure. I loved him as if I were his daughter, and yet somewhere in the deepest darkest crevices of my being, I resented him. How could it be that he was spared whilst the others all had perished?

I pushed the selfish thought out of my mind. It was wrong to think such a thing, evil even. I was lucky to have Ned be the parent I'd never known. Some people didn't even have that.

Deciding a change of scenery might draw me out of my maudlin mood, I wandered below. Though I didn't have the inclination to read, I knew the saloon would be a place I could find some peace. I wasn't expecting to find Nathaniel there. His large body resting against the bookcase. The soft rise and fall of his chest told me he was sleeping, an open book rested in his hands.

My heart skipped as I stared into his handsome face. Tension strained him, even in sleep. I wasn't the only one who suffered from melancholy. Nathaniel's original decision to join us had centred upon the search for his mother. Not wanting to add to his pain, I backed out, closing the door behind me.

"Please stay." Nathaniel's voice stalled me mid-step. His tone was soft, broken.

Without pausing, I turned the handle again. Crouching at his side, I held him to me. He broke, burying his face in my neck; his hot tears drenched my skin. I couldn't believe a man of such scale and strength could hold so much hurt.

"It will be fine," I whispered, as I stroked his face. Not quite knowing what his pain stemmed from I could only guess.

"I thought I would see her again, we could have been a family," he sobbed.

I ran my fingers through his hair, hoping to bring some comfort as I said, "I believe she tried her best to get back to you. Why else would she be anywhere near Hadnaloy? Your mother wanted the same things you did."

"I hoped she would meet you," he whispered, raising his head. His bright eyes were pained.

I pressed my lips to his, trying to transfer some of his pain to myself. I'd take all his hurt, every ounce he held, if he would smile again. Had he felt this way when I revealed my past?

"I've not experienced what you have," I said. "I always knew my mother and father were not coming back for me, even when the ladies at the Châteaux told me they would. Deep down I knew."

I sighed, as Nathaniel played with my hair.

"What I do know is that family aren't those who have borne you, or even raised you. They're those who choose to accept you, for every flaw."

"You mean us?" Nathaniel asked.

"Yes this crew, you, me, we're a family. No matter what came before." I pulled Nathaniel closer, as he tugged a book from the shelf behind us.

"Shall we lose ourselves in someone else's lives for a while?" His smile wobbled, he was trying hard.

I nodded and with gentleness which belayed their size Nathaniel's hands opened the leather binding.

The story he told sounded familiar. Glancing at the cover, my breath it was the book from Macrucio's study!

"Something wrong?" He asked.

"I recognise the story that's all." I hid my sadness behind a smile. He turned his attention to the pages, his deep lilting voice wound with vibrancy through the tale.

I was overcome; the story told of loss, longing and tragedy. It was as though someone had taken all of our lives and put it down on paper. My tears spilled over and I let myself break too. My woe was stalled by my name being called from above.

"Lennie!"

Claudette's call sounded strange. Nathaniel snapped the book closed as we stood. Wiping away our tears, I tried to work out what was wrong in Claudette's tone. Racing to the deck I skidded to a stop. I rocked back on my heels, as the anchor hit the seabed. Nathaniel steadied himself, grasping my shoulders as he almost collided with me.

To most the nondescript shoreline, the houses abutting it looked harmless, and they probably were – but I would recognise them anywhere. It was what lay beyond the tumbled down village that turned my skin cold and caused my blood to boil.

"Turn around," I demanded. I clenched my jaw as I stared at our harbour.

"The Sorceress must have wanted us here," Captain Rourke said, resting a hand on my shoulder.

"I don't care, turn back the way we came." I spun, my focus on my escape.

"The captain is right child."

Rosa's response went ignored as I stalked towards the stairs.

"Lennie..."

Nathaniel's voice made me stop. I was shaking but I lifted my gaze to meet his.

"Yes?" My reply was curt, all traces of compassion gone. I was in no mood to play games or dwell on poetic fancy.

"Sometimes you have to go home," he said.

He stepped forward to brush my cheek but I pulled away. I felt thirteen again when the thought of a man even attempting to touch me, had me recoiling.

"I'm already home," I growled, backing away and with shake of my head, I raced below.

I returned to my cabin. Yanking open a drawer I pulled out a thick blanket. With quick hands I covered all of my portholes. I didn't want to see the past; it already ate away at me.

"Lennie." Ned banged on the door. "Get up there, the Sorceress must want you to resolve something, even Rosa believes this to be true."

"I resolved enough the last time," I yelled and kicked out at the door, the force left cracks in the wood.

Behind it Ned growled.

"Leave me be," I pleaded slumping to the floor.

The fading footsteps of the older man allowed me to exhale. I thumped my fist against the floor and the satisfying crunch of bone against wood had me bouncing up on the balls of my bruised feet. Pent up anger pulsed through my bloodstream and I couldn't remain still. My hands itched to hit more than just inanimate objects. I wanted to strike out at the world for what it had done to me.

My knuckles throbbed in pain and I collapsed onto the floor again. My feet tapped out an impatient rhythm as I flexed my injured hand. Bile, anger and pain festered in my mind as the memories flooded back. I glanced around the small cabin. This was home, not the Châteaux where I was raised. That was a place where I was beaten, abused and forced. That was no home. That was a prison.

I caught sight of the worn lacquered box beneath my bed and crawling towards it, I pulled it from the shadows. My fingers brushed across the scarred lid, Clara had given it to me: *"Have this* Chérie, *you're a lady now."*

I had been ten and the only treasures I'd owned were trinkets of dried flowers, used perfume bottles and broken jewels; but I had cherished that box as much any chest filled with gold and silver.

As my life took a turn, it became the place to keep my powder and pins. There was nowhere I would go without such a treasure chest now. This was a reminder of a time when I had felt both loved and worthless. It had made me grow. Would the girls who worked there now have such a prize? Were there still working girls? Was there even a Châteaux left?

It took much soul searching before I returned to the deck. My anger and fear were deciding factors, yet my curiosity was what spurred me onward. Were Victoria or Clara still there? Now they were free of Hans' what had become of them and the Châteaux?

Despite this urge to know, I felt like I was in chains being pulled through fire as I took a slow walk back.

"To find forgiveness within yourself, you must first

seek those in your past who need to forgive you. The future will then be clearer than any rock pool..." Rosa's words resonated in the silence as I walked passed my crewmates.

"Let us be done with this," I muttered, vaulting the rail.

"Valencia" Nathaniel called. "Whilst I am here, no-one will hurt you."

I glanced up at him, "You cannot save me from ghosts."

Dusk was on the horizon leaving the main village quiet and deserted. The only sound came from our group as we wandered between the cobbled streets. What awaited us, if nothing had changed, was the opposite. Loud and bright with no thoughts of sleep. The dividing stream loomed ahead and I sucked in a breath. We had arrived in at the gates of my own personal hell.

A young girl was sat upon the bridge. She looked clean and neat, no sign of destitution claimed her attire. A hint of rouge lit her cheeks and a beauty spot was dotted above her lip. She stared at the water, not noticing our approach.

"Are you well? Do you need help?" I asked in my native tongue.

The girl yelped, leaping to her feet. Her wide eyes stared at us as she backed away.

"Please, please do not hurt me," she pleaded in broken English.

"We're not here to hurt you, we were looking for Clara or Victoria." I said, stepping forward carefully.

"Victoria? I work for Victoria!" She scuttled further backwards, her arms over her head in protection. "Please leave me alone, I promise I won't tell anyone."

"What about? What is there to tell?" Nathaniel edged around me, a frown creasing his forehead.

"You're all pirates aren't you?" She slackened her arms though her face still showed fear.

"After a fashion, I suppose," I agreed.

"They're forbidden here in the *'Quart de Plaisir.'*"

The young girl pointed at the board nailed beneath the entrance sign. It read: *'aucun pirates admis, car ils seront suspendus'*—no pirates admitted for they shall be hung.

Even those not fluent in my native tongue, could not miss the crudely made noose, swinging below the warning

"Should we continue?" Rupert asked.

"I don't want to, but I do want to see who put that ruling in place." I glanced towards sign. "Hans is no longer here, Victoria and Clara were always good to me. There must be some reason for the ship to bring us to this God forsaken place."

"I shall run and tell Victoria of your arrival," the girl said, dashing across the bridge.

"She's probably going to tell the men-folk and we'll be killed before we even set foot inside," Rupert muttered.

"Always the man with the silver lining eh, Red?" Nathaniel quipped, slapping Rupert on the back.

"Shall we go?" Claudette said her lilac eyes on me.

"Yes," I said. My hand rested on the hilt of my sword as we approached. My heart pounded as I set a foot upon the creaking wood. I'd sworn almost five years before, that I would never cross the bridge again. Yet here I was, breaking my vow.

Ned stood at my side. He of all people knew how much it would take for me to return. With him beside me I stood a little straighter.

"Any thought on where to take us?" He asked his wooden eye glinting. At least we'd have Rosa with us too.

"The main square," I said and my footfalls never faltered as I charged forward.

Not much had changed as we headed through the hustle and bustle of the district. The rich meandered amongst the street performers, throwing change into rugged hats and instrument cases. A few of the locals eyed me as we passed by and I pulled my hat lower, not wanting to be recognised quite yet. I faced forward, determined to reach my destination.

Relinquishing Ned's arm, I marched on ahead my speed picking up. I hoped the others were at my heels and I turned to check. As I did, someone grabbed my arm dragging me from the path and into a side street. My name cried out from beyond the crowd but I couldn't answer, my mouth was covered and I was bundled into a doorway, pinned between my captor and the exit.

"Thought you'd swan back in here and take over eh?"

I blinked into the half-light. I didn't recognise the man's face.

"Sorry sir, I'm unsure how I have offended you." I mumbled into his palm. My mind whirling, what options did I have?

"Oh I know who you are Valencia," he said, drawing out my name like it was filth. "My sister, Bettina, she lived with you. Worked alongside you. Was Hans' pride and joy."

He let go of my mouth and whipped out a knife. As he cleaned out his nails with the tip, he pushed his knee into my thigh so I couldn't move. I watched him carefully as I wracked my brain for Bettina. My minds-eye conjured a shockingly thin girl, about eighteen, with pale grey eyes and yellow gold hair. Yes, I remembered her.

"Your sister, is she still here?"

"Yes," he said. "She still works for Victoria, though it's all gone above board now, unfortunately."

He came closer and his eyes filled with lust. I clenched my teeth and brought my knee to his centre. He went down with a groan and I raced back into the street.

It was bedlam, and not the good kind. I wrenched out my sword as Butch raced by pursued by a fire breather. Across from me, Ned and the captain fought men of varied sizes and shapes. Claudette had found room atop a statue's plinth and was shooting sparks from her fingertips, aiding Butch with a water hex.

I couldn't see Rupert, Davy or Nathaniel, but I lifted up my sword and went to work. Patrons and artists alike were battling with us and despite our meagre crew, we were holding our own.

"Lennie!"

I turned from besting a juggler, to find Rupert, bloody but bright eyed.

"You're hurt," I cried.

"'Tis nothing," he dismissed, striking at an approaching opponent.

"Where are the others?"

"That girl collard Davy and Nate, they're bringing reinforcements."

"What?" I cried.

A suited man with yellowing teeth dove between Rupert and me. I brandished my sword but I failed to catch him. He leapt around me, giggling like a child and I roared.

"Ah kitty wants to play," he taunted pulling a small dagger from his belt and letting it fly. I jumped too slow and as I readied myself for a counter attack the blade embedded itself in my side.

The pain hit my very core and I cried out, blood pounded in my ears but I refused to fall. With another roar I ran at him, my sword impaling him in his centre and we went down together. Sound grew muffled and the world blurred. I felt nothing but the pain and the steady beat of my heart.

A FAMILIAR SCENT of honeysuckle and spices from far off lands was the first thing I noticed. The second was the bed I lay upon. It was soft. Downy pillows were beneath my head, the best cottons and silks were surrounding me.

"No!" I screamed, sitting up and gasping at the pain in my side.

"Now, now, baby girl, you're safe."

Pushing my hair from my eyes, I came face to face with one of my childhood mentors.

"Victoria," I cried wrapping the woman in a warm embrace.

"Careful," she urged, not hiding her chuckle. "You've had stitches my dear, you were very lucky."

"Everyone else?" I asked.

"A little battered but nothing a stiff drink and a good game of cards couldn't handle."

I returned Victoria's smile with a relieved one of my own.

"He's a little dedicated though," Victoria said, nodding across the room.

I gingerly turned to find Nathaniel just as I had a few months earlier. Taking up a rocking chair, fast asleep.

"He hasn't left your side, he's read to you, brushed your hair, he truly loves you, my dear, I am so glad you found peace," Victoria said her eyes were filled with tears.

"How long have I been asleep?"

"Almost four days, no-one knows you're here, well except for Tia. She said you'd met upon your arrival."

"Yes," I said, recalling the young distressed teenager.

"Lay back down, my dear," Victoria urged, plumping my pillows. "I shall be back with water and maybe a spot to eat."

She stared down at me with a fond smile, her hand brushed across my cheek.

"I never imagined you would return" she said wrapping me in her arms. "My goodness Valencia, I just cannot believe how much you've grown."

As she held me, I pulled in her scent and revelled in the good memories it conjured.

"I shall be right back," she repeated, kissing my forehead and leaving the room.

With the snap of the door, Nathaniel sprang awake. Disoriented he blearily stared around as I had done. Spying me awake, he leapt from the chair and was beside my bed in an instant.

"I was so worried," he said, pressing kisses to my fingers. "I thought that bastard had killed you."

"It will take more than a wretch with bad teeth to take me down," I said.

"I have never been so frightened. You have almost

been taken from me so many times…"

"We live a dangerous life, my love." I brushed a hand down his roughened cheek.

"You don't know what it means to hear you call me that," he said, leaning into my touch.

Before we could say more, the door swung open admitting Victoria, carrying a tray. Following behind her, was the rest of the crew. Just as Victoria said, they all were nursing battle wounds but nothing more than busted lips and black eyes.

"Looks like I got all the fun again…" I said as Rupert clambered onto the foot of the bed and stretched out.

"Yep, always said that," he deadpanned, shoving his hands behind his head.

"Now," Victoria interrupted. "Drink this, darling girl and then you can tell me what brought you here."

She handed me a glass before taking a seat beside my bed. I sipped at the water, watching my crewmen find their own seats.

"I was sent here." I began. "We think whoever it was, feels I need to resolve something."

Ned and the captain nodded at my explanation. Victoria gazed at them before tipping my glass in the direction of my mouth. I smiled around the glass, she used to do that when I was a child.

"You have nothing to resolve," Victoria assured. "Hans' ghost haunts us all."

I caught her watching out of the window, her eyes

were wary and she was wringing her hands. She turned back to me, her teeth pressed into her bottom lip.

"It's so wonderful to see you, my dear," she smiled before returning to her worried stare; "but it's not safe for you to be here. The girls who believed Hans had cared for them, have sworn revenge upon you and the pirates who helped your escape. They almost caught you. If some of my more loyal patrons had not managed to distract them, the wretch's would have strung you up there and then."

I couldn't hide my trembling hands. "What about you, what are your thoughts?"

"I think we are well rid of him," Victoria spoke with blunt honesty; there was no remorse in her words. "He hurt every one of us, most of all you. I'm adamant you wouldn't have killed him willingly, no matter how much he deserved it."

"I didn't." tears spilled over as relief flooded through me. "Thank you."

I embraced the older woman, overwhelmed at being thought of as innocent.

Rosa's advice came back to me. *"To find forgiveness within yourself, you must first seek those in your past who need to forgive you. The future will then be clearer than any rock pool..."*

I understood now. Victoria's forgiveness – or rather acceptance, felt freeing, just as the lifting of the curse had.

"We will have to find a hiding place for you all; the

ban on pirates is indelible. You'll be hung if you're found. We can't keep you here much longer, no matter how much I'd love for you to stay." Victoria said, ever the practical lady.

"Who put the new law into place? Pirates were the best clientele, after the rich." I asked with a grimace at my own recollections.

"Those few, who felt Hans was theirs alone, were able to gain a following, the people of the village were confused at what happened. They felt Hans was no different from them. Those who decided this were worried for themselves. What if their women turned on them? Pirates, no matter how good, couldn't be trusted in their eyes." Victoria shook her head as though the idea was foolish. I swallowed back a retort. It wasn't Victoria's opinion after all.

"I wonder what we need to do here, what the Sorceress wanted us to do?" Rupert said, breaking the silence.

"Maybe she wanted us to stop the hate." Claudette's notion hung in the air.

In her hand she held a flask. She crossed the room with it, the familiar rotten aroma permeated the metal and I knew it was one of her potions.

"Try this, it'll speed up the healing process and if we are up for another battle at least you'll have some strength."

Setting down the empty water glass, I unscrewed the

container and chugged down its contents. It was warm and muddy and I almost brought it back up. Wiping my mouth I handed back her flask.

Victoria's eyes widened. "Your colour is almost back to normal already."

"Check her wound," Claudette said.

Victoria approached me with trepidation, her fumbling hands finally lifted the sheet and my night shirt. We both gasped as she lifted the bandage. Though my skin was puckered and red, there was no blood or sign of infection amongst the stitches.

"That was a mess less than an hour ago," the older woman cried.

"Claudette is special," I said, winking at my friend.

"She surely is," Victoria replied in wonder.

Gathering herself as the sound of men drifted through the window. She turned to the group.

"There will be no exceptions made for any of you, this law is solid. Besides, you are the reason they made this ruling and I don't say that to offend."

"None taken," Ned said, his hand clasped around his daughters.

"Valencia?" Victoria stood by the closed door; questions were etched on her beautiful face. "You are barely healed, what do you think?"

"Let them come."

The cheer rang out from the seven other pirates and I felt comforted to know I wouldn't be alone. Though I wanted to meet my foes head on, I was injured. Despite Claudette's tonic I would have to be careful. I didn't have the element of surprise either, I was sure half the town knew I'd been stabbed.

"Victoria!"

The room froze. Someone hammered on the door, rattling the windows in their urgency.

"They have sent for the *mousquetaires*, the ship your friends arrived in is about to be surrounded. The laundry reported the blood stained sheets!"

"Damn, I knew we should have burned them," Victoria lamented.

"*Merci*, Tia! Do anything you can to prolong their arrival at the beach and do it with speed." Victoria's tone was firm as she handed out her orders.

"Of course," the voice replied. I peeked through the lace curtains, just as the girl I'd met on the bridge, raced back up to the Châteaux.

"Let us show them who and what we truly are," The captain said.

"Let Victoria and I help Lennie change before we do any showing hmmm?" Claudette said ushering the men from them room. Nathaniel attempted to argue but Claudette fixed her unusual eyes on him and pointed at the door. With one swift peck on the cheek he followed the others.

"Smitten," Claudette tutted.

"I'll go a fetch a jug and a wash cloth," Victoria said,

shutting the door behind her.

Raising her hand, Claudette lit the rest of the candles in the room. Taking my time, I got out of bed and turned to straighten the pillows when my eyes were drawn to the painting above my bed.

The image had my heart skittering and my throat closing. Before I could drop to the floor, Claudette grasped my shoulders, steadying my balance.

"Lennie?" The auburn haired woman stared wide-eyed at me, my own gaze centred upon the painting which hung above the headboard. It was a portrait of a man. His long curling hair lay across his shoulders and his eyes stared out, a bright vivid blue.

"Hans," I gasped sinking to my knees, my body convulsing in shudders.

"Nathaniel!" Claudette cried as my unmoving stare remained upon the painting. I soon felt arms surround me, lifting me off the ground.

"What happened?"

"Is she all right?" Victoria's voice broke me from my stupor.

"Oh dear God." Victoria pressed a hand to her mouth. "Valencia I beg your forgiveness, I never use this room, I had forgotten."

My gaze flickered between the false blue eyes and Nathaniel's very real ones. As he held me, my love's mouth was set in a firm line.

"I should have cleared this place." Victoria said. "We

were all too concerned with all the blood you were losing."

"Do you need kindling madam?" Nathaniel asked, setting me on my feet.

"Kindling, what for?" I asked in confusion as Victoria gave him a knowing smile.

"I think that would be perfect," Victoria said as Nathaniel pulled the large portrait from the wall. With swift movements the frame and painting was in pieces.

"You have a skill for destroying art," I teased, my humour shaky but returning.

"Yes, it comes in useful; excuse me a moment," he said stepping from the room. We could hear the fire crack and hiss as the tinder caught light.

"You have a good man there, my dear," Victoria murmured.

"Well we like him," Claudette said, a coy smile flitting across her face.

I grinned as I stepped toward the headboard. Where the painting had hung, was an un-papered piece of wall. Reaching out I touched the loose brick in the centre of the square.

"Have you seen this?" I asked Victoria.

"Never," Victoria replied.

With nimble fingers, I worked the brick loose, pulling it from the wall. Within the hole was a small metal tin. I yanked it free, causing it to rattle as I set it between the three of us, on the bed.

"Hans had many secrets," Victoria murmured.

"Should we open it?" I asked, running a hand over the scratched metal.

Claudette's hand hovered over the box, nodding she sat back. "You will not find danger in there"

"At least physical anyway," I muttered, pulling at the lid, it was stuck fast. Grasping my belt which hung from the bed, I used the tip of a dagger to turn the lock. With a snap the lid opened, revealing a hotchpotch of items.

Lifting a ragged piece of parchment, I unfolded it. A charcoal sketch revealed a woman with delicate features and long flowing hair.

"Your mother," Victoria's expression was far away.

"*Ma Mère?*" I repeated.

"*Oui.* Hans always held her in the highest regard." Victoria moved aside more drawings to reveal a pair of small hair clips covered in simple stones.

"These things belonged to your mother too."

"Why do you think he kept these things, could he have loved her?"

The thought repulsed me in a way but there was something close to truth in my question, I could feel it in my memories. Like the way Hans would look at me, or even mistakenly call me Cherie. He was always uncharacteristically kind in those moments.

"I believe Hans loved your mother as much as he could love anyone, your father stole her away, at least that is how he felt."

"Is everyone dressed in there?"

The captain's call jolted us and I piled the items back into the box.

"Almost," Claudette replied, helping me on with my trousers and shirt.

"They won't be a moment; I will come and top-up your glasses." Victoria brushed a hand across my cheek before joining the others.

"Did you know of Hans' infatuation?" Claudette asked, tying her hair up with string.

"Yes, as much as I could at that age," I said pulling my braces onto my shoulders with a wince and picked up a boot. "I wish I could say that this absolves him of everything, but he still forced my hand."

Claudette took my boot from me, lifting my leg she pushed it on.

"No-one expects you to forgive so easily." Claudette said, doing the same with the other and sliding my discarded dagger into the ready-made holster hidden within.

"Shall we go and fight my demons?" I said, setting my hat over one eye.

"Everything above board in here?" Nathaniel asked, stepping into the room and brushing his fingers across my cheek.

"Well, we're about to head into battle, you tell me?" My response was a whisper as I wandered into the outer room where the others stood waiting.

"You look like the epitome of cursed pirates, all of you." Victoria grinned, as I gave her a mocking curtsey.

"I've been meaning to ask," I ventured, stepping closer. "Where is Clara? I would have thought you both would be here, did she leave?"

"I hoped you'd forgotten," Victoria sighed, draining a goblet and setting it upon the mantelpiece beside a small frame depicting two women.

"How could I forget the kindness you both showed me?"

"She died Valencia." Victoria's blunt response drew instant moisture to my eyes.

"She's gone?"

"Clara was the one who found Hans' body. You were nowhere to be found, and well..." she paused, bowing her head as she tried to contain her emotions.

"They thought she helped me?" I pressed my hands to my mouth. My whole body shook. Nathaniel wrapped his arms around me as I let the news settle.

"Please do not blame yourself. I was questioned too. Both of us were acquitted, Clara however, she was so changed by his death and your disappearance..." Victoria pressed a handkerchief to her face.

"How can you ever forgive me?" I whispered.

"As I said," Victoria grasped my hands; her eyes stared deep driving the words home. "He deserved all that came to him. No person should have to be forced into what you were. Clara knew and we both wished we could have given you a different life."

"You did the best you could and for that, I'm grateful" I wrapped the older woman in an embrace, my heart heavy.

"Let us try and return to the *Wilted Rose.*" The captain urged, as he cast a weather eye through the window. His furrowed brow gave a different opinion however. I nodded in agreement as I stepped away from Victoria.

"We cannot just wander out there now, we would be ambushed," Butch mumbled, fear casting a greenish tinge across his skin though he tried hard to hide it.

"I can remedy that."

Victoria's eyes widened as Claudette raised her hands creating the protective blue light she had conjured before. Pushing it outward it pulsed around each of us.

"Thank you Victoria, for everything." I said from within the circle.

"It was a pleasure, *Chèrie*, please stay safe."

"And you," I said wiping her eyes. With swift steps, I led the way from the rear of the cabin and out towards the trees.

Sticking together, so we wouldn't step outside of the blue light, we made our way through the now quiet square and back to the beach. It felt strange to see it so empty. Were the townsfolk already there? Or were they plotting? Where was everyone? No-one lined the sand as we returned.

"I don't feel right about this, lads." Captain Rourke

called as we all arrived on deck. "We should prepare for battle, just in case. This seemed a little too simple." Perhaps we could raise the flag and get our weapons ready? Keep a weather-eye, this could turn nasty."

My hand went to my sword as I scanned the still empty sand. It felt too still and calm out there. Where were the angry hoards with pitchforks?

"Would it not be prudent to just raise the anchor?" Butch suggested.

"It would be a coward's way out to leave now," the captain said.

Butch's mouth closed over his suggestion and he stayed silent.

As Butch, began to climb up to the crow's nest I headed for the armoury. Yet, before I made it to the stairs, Rosa began to speak. Her voice stilled us all and we strained to listen to her:

"True bravery is pure of heart."

Though the wooden woman's sentiments were a cry for peace, it didn't stop those who had seen the pirate flag from flooding the beach The captain's feeling had been right as the once empty shoreline now swarmed with people. Where had they all been hiding?

As I gripped my sword, the thirst for the fight grew within me. I didn't want to kill those who I'd once lived alongside. Yet if my comrades were threatened, I would do what I was born to.

"Hold nothing back," I murmured as Nathaniel

gripped my free hand.

"We will be with you," he said brushing his thumb over my knuckles.

"I know."

"Together?" He pressed a kiss to my forehead.

"Together," I agreed as the maddening hoard converged and we raced forward

"We come in peace." A man stepped from the crowd, his hands raised. One held a dagger, its blade sharp and dangerous as it glinted at them.

"Yet you bring hundreds, brandishing weapons?" The captain shook his head.

"We just want the girl. She deserves to pay for the wrong she has done. Sentence must be carried out."

"Everyone has got the notion to knock you off, first the English, now these people." Rupert said with a wink.

"Have you asked yourselves, why would a child need to kill a man she loved as a father?" The captain projected his argument so the group could hear. "Was it pure hatred, jealousy or did he threaten her?"

The speech stilled the crowd. They turned to each other, whispers punctuating the quiet as the throng started to doubt the hysterical fanatics, who saw Hans in a different light. Those few women glared at me, their bodies shaking with anger. The man who had accosted me in the alleyway bared his teeth at me, bringing his finger across his neck. It was that gesture which had me stepping forward. Ignoring Nathaniel's insistences for me to stay by his side, I addressed the crowd.

"I wish to speak to my accusers," I demanded. "My Uncle Hans loved me, of this I'm sure. Despite that love, he forced me into a life of debauchery."

My voice wavered as I continued "I did as he bid out of love, confusion and fear of him. The night he died he turned on me. Something otherworldly took control of my body- something I still cannot explain. I killed him because I loved him."

My lips trembled and I tasted the salt of tears.

"How can you kill someone you love? If you love someone you protect them" A harsh female jeered from the crowd.

"Like Hans protected me?" I shot back. "When you're as cursed as I, anything is possible.

"Lies!" The woman cried again and someone stepped from the huddle. I recognised her from childhood. Bettina, so thin and frail looking, yet her eyes blazed with fire.

"Hans held nothing but adoration for us and you killed him in cold blood."

With swift hands, she pulled a knife from her bosom. Before any of us could act, the blade had lodged itself above my heart. *What was it with this place and knives?* I thought as the pain filtered through me. I knew shock was on the horizon. It was lodged, but not as deeply as my previous skirmish.

"No!" Nathaniel made to retaliate but I held out my

arm. Holding my breath, I pulled out the dagger. Staring at my own blood, I turned it over in my hand.

"Nice shot," I said. "What does this prove? Kill me and Hans will miraculously be resurrected?"

My sarcasm was punctuated by my legs giving way. Claudette reached me as I gulped for air. Just as I predicted, shock was encroaching upon my windpipe and I was fighting for breath. At Claudette's touch the pain eased and I pulled in air.

"I can't heal it, the protection has tired me, but I can mask the pain a little," the enchantress whispered.

"Thank you, can you help me up?" Claudette grasped my arm and hauled me to my feet.

The crowd gasped at my bloodstained form.

I raised the bloody dagger and cried out, anger outweighing the pain. "Hans was the father figure in my life; but he killed me the day I became his whore."

The audience cried out in shock but I called over them, "It was never my intention to kill him, but my love was his downfall."

Pausing I turned to the captain. "Could we leave?"

"Of course." The captain laid a hand on my shoulder.

"A fight with words affects more than one of violence." Rosa's lyrical speech resonated as we climbed back aboard the *Wilted Rose*. As the island grew smaller, I could see the crowd rallying boats. They wouldn't chase us for a second bout, would they? Had my speech riled them?

As I pressed a cold rag to my chest, mopping up the blood, I vowed to keep not only my sword but a plethora of weapons close. A battle with more than just Hadnaloy could be on the horizon.

CHAPTER XXVII
BATTLE

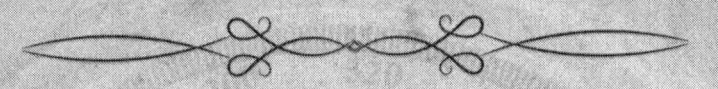

~~~~~~

"DAMN," DAVY CURSED. Glass smashed as the unsettled ocean toppled the table. Davy swiped at his dampened shirt shaking his head.

"Should we reconvene to a drier place?" He suggested, as he righted the fallen furniture.

"I believe that would be wise." Captain Rourke nodded, aiding in the clean-up.

"It is sure to rain, this sky will not abate the storm." Rosa prophesied.

Her prediction put paid to it and the deck-side card game was dismissed.

It didn't take long for the rain to begin its decent. By the time we had arrived below, the sounds of the pelting torrent created an uneven rhythm to our conversations. The portholes were alight with forked lightning, its partner, rumbled in echoes throughout the ship. Claudette entertained us with her own version, blasting light from her fingertips, the multi-coloured masses dancing across the table before erupting into sparks.

"Do you hear that?" Butch asked, turning from the

porthole

"I hear nothing," Rupert said, shuffling his soggy cards.

"Exactly, the storm's passed."

"Was that even worth it?" Nathaniel said.

"There is no better smell in the world," Claudette mused, leading the way upstairs.

I pulled in the scent, I couldn't agree more. My ease faltered however as I took in the damage the short storm as done.

A small torn piece of material floated on the breeze, landing upon the captain's boot. He bent to retrieve it, lifting it up to the light.

"Right men, we need that sail fixed and the deck needs sweeping."

"Are you intact Rosa?" Claudette asked, climbing over the rail.

"No harm befell me, my dear," she replied.

"Me or you?" I asked Butch, pointing to the scattered glass which littered the floor. My young friend bit his lip.

"Well…"

"Go sit in your nest birdie," I teased, grasping hold of his broom.

"Take it easy, Len, it wasn't too long ago that a knife was protruding from your chest"

"Sure, sure – it was only a scratch," I murmured, as I set about my task.

Both my wounds were well covered and whatever

Claudette had done had helped in my quick recovery. As I knelt to pick up some of the larger pieces of glass, I squinted up at the burgeoning sun. Nathaniel and Rupert were holding the sail as Davy sewed the tear. Above me, a hammer drove home nails as Butch attempted to fix the crow's nest.

"For a small storm it did not skimp on the harm it did?" Claudette said piling debris into one corner.

"That is all it takes," Ned said as he and the captain tried to find where we'd been swept too.

"Strangers in the water," Butch yelled from above, pointing north.

I raced to the upper deck, we were being approached on all sides. Growls and readying weapons broke through the silence.

On the left was a boat that looked familiar, on the right, a plain nondescript vessel sailed towards us. I pressed a hand to the hilt of my sword in readiness.

"Steady children," Rosa warned, her view was better than even Butch's. The calm tone put me on my guard, this couldn't be good.

As we awaited our fate, the weak sun hid behind a thick purplish cloud, and spots of rain turned into gushes once more. I knew the fight was coming, the signs were all there. Butch had climbed down to stand beside me grasping for his mop holding it like a shield.

"Is everybody ready?" The captain's voice carried through the wind.

I found Nathaniel as he dodged the intermittent raindrops to get to my side. Reaching me, he cupped my cheek, brushing his lips across my own.

"I love you," he said, touching his forehead to mine.

"I lo-" I couldn't finish.

The strangers converged upon us, climbing aboard the ship like monkeys. Their feral growls and yells were more animal than human. I unsheathed my sword and set to work, clashing it with an enemy. My opponent wore a scarf around his face to hide his identity but I was beyond caring, I wanted him gone.

Surrounding us were a mishmash of Hadnaloy's underlings and patrons of the *'Quart de Plaisar.'* The only way to tell one from the other were their eyes. Hadnaloy's minions were owners of murky iris'. The sounds of blades colliding and their near misses filled the air. I raced to and fro, fighting more than one at times and not caring where I hit. Stepping backwards as I fought against a man twice my size, I stumbled below deck. The gangway was dark yet the glint of the two swords lit our way. He'd garnered more scratches than I had, if I continued to fight the way I was, winning would be easy.

Grunts and scrapes of the fight above, and the echoing shots of the cannon allowed me free reign to battle my opponent. He too was well versed in swordsmanship, flourishing his sword and knowing where and how to step to get at me. I focussed all my strength as the beast pushed his weight towards the hilt of his sword. It caused me to falter. Our blades crossed and we glared at each other, mere inches apart.

As the murky eyed beast bared his teeth, I saw red. Letting out a savage growl, I pulled away from his hold. Staying on my feet, I resumed the duel. This time he stumbled backwards, his body crashing to the floor. As he laid there, I pressed a boot to his chest, the tip of my sword hovered above his throat, the threat of what I could do hung in the air.

"Who sent you here?" I demanded.

"We came to clean out those against our mistress."

At his hoarse answer, I pushed more weight on my boot and he let out a gurgling cry.

"Lennie." Nathaniel looked dishevelled but unharmed as he placed a gentle hand on my shoulder. At his touch my anger ebbed and my lust for blood eased away.

"Send him to the brig," I said, flicking my sword. The action grazed the wretches face. Nathaniel smiled as he dragged the fiend towards the cells.

The war raged on and I returned to the deck to find the fight still rampant. My next opponent was a one legged pirate with a sharp eye. I glared as he clashed his sword with mine.

We fought tirelessly; I felt nothing as my weapon met his. I had hit my partner countless times, more than he had hit me. I swiped at the cut at my cheek as I returned his attack. With another cry we spun and I was face to face with someone new.

A wild eyed youth lunged at me and I twisted, my sword driving straight for his chest. The youth blocked the move, rushing me. I stepped to one side as another sword brushed passed my arm. A thin waif of a man, no bigger than I, grinned in malevolence as he elbowed me in the ribs. I spat at him before hitting him square in the cheek with the hilt of my sword.

He went down as the one legged pirate returned to the throng. I battled the two without fear, knocking back the youth leaving him sprawled across the floor yelling curses as the one legged pirate limped around us. With a swift blow from my sword he too hit the ground and I flicked the hair off my face as I stared at my handy work.

Hadnaloy had bewitched the dregs of society. The poor, useless and dragged along, to do her bidding. They were her puppets to do with as she wished. Their pallor's were sallow and their eyes a murky blend of brown and black. They never remained injured for long, bouncing back as if nothing harmed them. Those from my hometown were easier to defeat, between my own bouts, I could see my crewmates tying some with binds or sending them down to the brig.

"Round 'em up! Hadnaloy's only, Butch, Nate, Rupert, you work on getting the others."

Claudette was stood atop the rail. The storm caused the ship to rock precariously but despite the unstable surface she remained steady. In her hand she held, what looked like a thick white rope. She swung it around her head like a lasso. Focussing on doing as she said, the rest of us corralled the enemy fighters around the mast.

Those from my hometown, who'd not been captured, were forced into a corner. Too entranced by what Claudette was doing, few argued.

"Let us end this," Claudette bellowed throwing her creation at the surrounded underlings. It was unlike any rope of wire or wheat, instead it was cloudy like smoke. Though it looked pliable it kept its prisoners together in a firm hold. More scraps had occurred since the curse had been lifted than ever before.

Had the Sorceress known her request would never be fulfilled? Could this be her subtle way of punishing us? Would we pay for our love after all?

"What should we do with them?" Davy circled the captives, his sword raised.

"Use them as bait," Nathaniel sneered, anger flushed his tanned face. "The other's we can hold in the brig until we decide what to do with them."

"She would not care for these people." Claudette leapt from the rail. "We should arrange a drop off point and—"

"—Release my men," Hadnaloy boomed. "Do as I say and no-one will be harmed."

My sword was gripped tight; I held no fear for the sea-witch any more. Beneath the twelve foot lie, resided a bitter old hag.

"Show nothing, keep calm all of you, she is close by. Who knows where she will appear from." The captain's orders settled us.

I smirked, leaning closer to Butch, "That smoke and mirror attempt to gain fear, holds nothing but an angry toothpick with a vanity problem."

The blond covered his mouth to hide his wry smile.

Hadnaloy spoke again, disdain dripped from every word, "You stole something of mine, I want it returned."

"Where is she?" Davy wondered aloud.

"I demand my men be let go and—"

"—Let you murder us?" Ned spoke up now. He rested his hand upon Rosa's shoulder. He was balanced behind her, more agile than men half his age, his gun in hand.

"Yolandah, I have returned to my rightful place. Please face me and discuss your problems." Rosa spoke now, her voice carrying far across the ocean.

"I have no problems," denied the sea-witch.

"Clearly you do."

A large crash of waves and a whirlpool were added to the torrential rain which pounded down on us. At its centre the false image of Hadnaloy rose. She towered over us, her disfigured face contorted in anger. Her whole body shook as she muttered unintelligibly. Her glaring eyes stared straight through the figurehead.

"Back where you started, *Rosa del mar*?" Hadnaloy mocked.

"Yes, my crew's great honesty, courage and verve saw to that. What will yours do?"

"Enable me to kill those who stand in my way."

"So sad," Rosa sighed. "Perhaps if you had chosen a worthier crew they would have helped you regain your beauty. That is your quest is it not?"

"If a certain magical creature had not acted in such a way—"

"—No man should be killed for love." Rosa's soft voice evolved into something much harsher. "Colt was killed because of your hollow envy; I did indeed kill your love, the love for your appearance."

"Vanity is not a crime," Hadnaloy argued.

"In my eyes, it's the shallowest of sins."

"Enough of this drivel," Hadnaloy snapped, clicking her fingers.

The magical rope Claudette had used to confine our adversary's disappeared. Her underling's grotesque smiles leered but we held firm. There could be no turning back. I didn't want to keep running, not any more. Now the curse had been lifted, I refused to return to a censored life.

"Keep them together," Claudette murmured as the rest of the us complied, tightening our grips on our weapons as we guarded our prisoners.

"Enough." Hadnaloy charged the ship as the surrounding water swirled around us.

The glint had returned to the eyes of Hadnaloy's men upon her outburst. They leapt into action and the fight began again. With their energy returning, the underlings drove Nathaniel, Butch and myself down into the belly of the ship while the rest of the crew battled up on deck.

"Butch," Nathaniel called out and before I could protest, I was shoved beneath the captain's desk. Butch had shed the bottom half of the mop he'd been holding to reveal a blade. Nathaniel and Butch worked together, wearing down their three opponents.

Once their bout was won, Nathaniel knelt to retrieve me. "May I ask forgiveness? I couldn't risk you being hurt again."

"I've fought off worse than them," I muttered.

"I know, I just–" he turned at the sound of a cough.

Butch stood at the door. Nathaniel and Butch stared at each other a moment, something passed between them, something I couldn't fathom. Nathaniel broke their contact turning to face me. He looked into my eyes, searching, for what? I didn't know. He grasped for my hand bringing to his chest.

"Marry me Valencia; let us fight our battles as one," he said with a pleading note.

Before I could answer, the door slammed shut, signalling Butch's exit. I focussed on the shut door, my heart fluttering.

"Yes," I said, with a calm and measured tone, far from what I was feeling. I wrapped my arms around him and he lifted me off the floor as I pressed my lips to his.

"You do not know how happy you have made me," Nathaniel said, setting me back down.

I couldn't contain my smile as I took hold of his hand

and led the way up to the deck.

The scene that greeted us was one of carnage. Many of Hadnaloy's men were lying broken upon the deck. Rupert nursed a wounded arm. Claudette held a blood stained rag to Davy's head whilst Ned bandaged his leg; there was no sign of Butch anywhere. Only Captain Rourke and a masked opponent were left fighting, I joined the others, waiting for the right time to jump in and help. I pressed a kiss to Nathaniel's hand before letting go.

The captain ducked and weaved like a boxer, as their swords came frighteningly close. The storm had abated and the sun peered through the clouds as they circled again. I saw it happen, mere seconds before it did. The adversary crouched, missing the captain's swinging sword. A moment later he rose and without missing a beat, Captain Rourke sunk the blade deep into the fiend's chest. The bewitched devil fell backwards, his eyes blank.

"So much bloodshed," the captain mourned, wiping his weapon.

"Much needed," Rosa said.

"Do you think it would be safe to let our other prisoners go free?" The captain asked, looking to the figurehead.

"Well Brandon, I think that would be an honourable thing, though they do not deserve such kindness, Rosa replied.

"I know that, yet with so much death, I feel something

positive should be done." The captain nodded and the least injured of the crew headed below.

The prisoners were led across gangplanks and back from whence they came, their sheepish faces and platitudes did little to ease the resentment. I knew whatever happened, I still had enemies back in my home town; but returning those who could see our kindness would perhaps cause a new rumour to spread, that we were really more lovers than fighters.

As the last prisoner was freed, I linked hands with Nathaniel again; he remained staring out towards ocean as he brushed his thumb back and forth across my knuckles. The gentleness of his touch sent awareness thrumming through my body. The hairs of the back of my neck stood up as my nerve endings tingled in anticipation.

"Captain." Nathaniel turned, dragging me towards our leader.

I frowned wondering what had caused the sudden change in him.

"It is right that Captains can marry people?" Nathaniel queried.

"Yes, I do believe that is true," Captain Rourke said the strange question drew a curious glance from the man.

"Would you marry us?" Nathaniel punctuated his question by lifting our linked hands. The already quiet ship stilled as the captain blinked in surprise.

CHAPTER XXVIII
UNITED

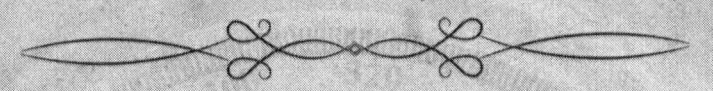

AFTER THE INITIAL shock wore off, the crew erupted with congratulations.

Ned's good eye misted as he exclaimed, "How wonderful."

"Why did you not tell me?" Claudette demanded, as I tried to find my voice.

"I hardly knew myself," I choked.

Beside me, still holding my hand Nathaniel was slapped on the back. The biggest grin I'd ever seen lighting up his face. I didn't have time to revel in it though, Claudette took me by the arm and dragged me away from the crowd.

"We may not be able to dress you up, my friend, but we can sure make you fit to be married." Claudette said, scanning the skies.

"Caw!" She called.

The sound of flapping wings echoed above us and Claudette reached out her arm for the ship's resident bird. His magnificent feathers were vibrant and shone much brighter than any normal parrot.

Following his travel, I watched as he completed a circuit of the crew, before settling atop the Claudette's arm, to await his next task.

"My dear pet," Claudette cooed, reaching to stroke his downy head.

The creature cawed in response.

"We need flowers, the prettiest you can find."

Bowing his head in a nod, he took off, sweeping passed us and out of sight.

"Do you ever wonder where such a creature came from?" I asked, as Claudette stepped behind me and tugged off my hat and headscarf.

"I have. Yet I think of the Sorceress and the countless other mythical creatures we have come in contact with — what are their origins? Where did they grow?"

Before I could reply, the colourful bird had returned. In his large talons, he held a woodland posy. The multitude of smells and colours hit me and I inhaled with gusto. Crocuses, violets, bluebells, hedge parsley and many other beautiful blooms were held in his sharp claws with care.

"Caw — Forever in bloom does love light bring — Caw," the creature said, dropping the bouquet into Claudette's hands. Inhaling their scent, she offered them to me

"Well done," Claudette praised and Caw squawked once more, taking his leave.

As Claudette fussed over my hair, I stared at the bouquet in my hands. Searching the bunch, I found the perfect blossom, a great white trillium. Three white petals with a yellow centre, a pure flower to represent the purest love. Plucking it from the group I handed it to Claudette. She slipped it into my hair through a hair pin she'd conjured up from somewhere.

"Wonderful," Claudette murmured with a smile.

I peered overboard into the water and mimicked my friend's expression. Claudette had pulled the front sections of my hair up letting the rest fall in waves around my shoulders. I felt pretty.

As I stepped back, pulling out the handkerchief Nathaniel had gifted me. Running a finger over the insignia I tied it around my posy. It was the perfect placeholder, the ceremony would be false without it.

"Are you girls ready?"

I grinned as Butch called across the deck. Claudette primped her own hair, quickly plaiting and tying the bottom with twine.

"We won't be much longer," I replied taking from my pocket a sparkling object which glinted in the sunshine.

Maria Davenport's brooch may have held flaws but it was still beautiful. It seemed to represent mine and her son's relationship to the letter.

"Lovely," Claudette murmured over my shoulder.

"Could you help?" I asked and Claudette pinned it to the fabric of my jacket, it may have looked strange, me in britches and braces but it was who I was.

Butch wandered over to us, his hands in his pockets and his scarf tied around his neck like a cravat.

"I wanted to say, I'm so happy for you. I love you, you know?" He said. Leaning forward he pressed a kiss to my forehead.

I blinked up at him in surprise. Butch was affectionate, but never this way.

"I love you too," I replied, touching his cheek.

Sadness flickered in his eyes. It was such a quick occurrence I wasn't sure I'd even seen it.

"I know," he murmured, ducking his head and dashing back to the menfolk.

A strange feeling settled over me, like I had missed something. Shaking it off, I watched my friend race across the deck, nearly colliding with Ned who was on his way towards us.

"My goodness child," Ned gasped, winded. "Both of my girls are a delightful sight."

"Ned." I reached forward to grasp his hand. I turned to look at Claudette who nodded in encouragement, somehow knowing what I was about to say.

"Would you give me away?"

"I would be honoured," he said, offering his arm with a beaming smile.

Pleased he had agreed, I took hold of his elbow and

let him lead me towards my fate. What this too soon? We were barely over a battle and another was sure to be on the horizon.

"Stop fretting, child, this is what is meant to be."

"I don't doubt Nathaniel's affection nor my own, it's just the timing."

"It's the perfect time," Claudette said following behind us.

"Child, please come hither," It was Rosa who spoke and I relinquished my hold on Ned to hear her.

"This is a gift, do not waste it."

"I shan't," I promised.

Returning to Ned, I felt at ease, this was a time for happiness, whatever happened in the future, this was here and now.

The clouds and rain were a distant memory, as the sky projected the clear blue of the water. It seemed to equal the optimism that overrode the tension upon the ship. I looked to the rest of the crew. Like Ned and Butch, they had cleaned up a little. Their smiles genuine under the strain they felt. They all stood within the circle.

My heart soared when I saw my husband-to-be, who stood in the centre. His honey toned skin brightened by the sun. Reaching his side, Ned squeezed my hand before giving it to Nathaniel. At Nathaniel's touch, I held my breath, the butterflies springing to life inside me. I couldn't pull my gaze away from him as the captain began to speak.

"We are gathered here today, to join together Valencia and Nathaniel in marriage. Uniting in this sacred bond does not begin and end in sharing a bed or a dwelling; but in sharing thoughts, hearts, minds and souls. To represent the meaning of marriage we use the elements."

"Air," Claudette said.

She bought her fingers down in front of her and a light breeze surrounded the ship, fluttering the sails and lifting my hair.

"This allows each of you to have room to breathe and trusting enough, for those times to be sacred." She finished, stepping back into the circle.

"Water," Rupert continued, as he stepped forward, a chalice in his hands.

"Drinking this will demonstrate the smooth flow that will pass between you as you journey through life together."

Rupert held out the cup so Nathaniel and I could both could drink.

Once we'd finished, Davy limped over to us, a match in one hand, and a candle in the other. His expression serious as he spoke.

"Fire represents the passion which envelopes you, body and soul, it will unite both body and mind."

Davy handed the large church candle to Nathaniel, before tracing the rune for love into my palm with an unlit match. With shaking hands I lit the wick, then placed my hands over Nathaniel's. Our eyes never left each other, conversing without words. There was so much adoration in the sky blue eyes before me, I felt alight in their glow. This man was going to be mine and I his. We would be a unit, one only divided in death.

"Finally," Captain Rourke said.

"Earth."

The gasps of the crew surrounded the Nathaniel and I, as the Sorceress glided onto the deck. She carried a woven tray filled with dirt. Pebbles pressed into it created the rune for love, spear and mouth. Taking the candle Nathaniel and I held; she pushed it into the earth. Smiling she handed the tray back to us.

"Earth represents the love that is grounded by reality. The passion may diminish, yet the love remains centred."

She nodded for the captain to continue.

"Finally," he repeated as he urged us to join hands again – the tray now sat at our feet.

Butch stood at our side, his inherited scarf no longer at his neck but curled around his fingers. Tears glistened in his eyes as he fastened Nathaniel's hand to mine pulling the knot tight.

"This scarf represents strength. In this instance, it will ensure your vows will never be broken. Your strength will be borne from one another. Please remember this."

He stepped away, a shy smile curling his lips.

"If you would like to say a few words, to one another," The captain said bowing out with a smile.

Nathaniel nodded towards me, a tender look

encouraging me to speak first. I inhaled, surrounding myself in his scent, it brought me back to England and the rescue and how I'd felt in his arms. Pushing out the breath I opened my eyes and as I stared back at him it was then I realised what it meant to truly give yourself to someone. Not just physically but your heart and soul. So I spoke the truth, everything I'd been holding in since we discovered him on that beach.

"Nathaniel, this is a day I never foresaw. This, I felt would never be an option for a girl like me. You allowed me to realise that I am worthy. Worthy to be treated with respect and to be loved. I will spend the rest of my days returning the favour." I pulled in a steadying breath as my emotion overtook me.

"It's such an honour to stand here with our friends – our family," I corrected. "To join together in all that is pure and whole. I've kept my distance but I don't need to do that now. I promise to be faithful, to cherish you and even once we're no longer of this earth, to love you."

Nathaniel wiped away my tears as he cleared his throat. His own eyes glittered, replicating the sea surrounding us.

"The moment I met you, I knew you were the one. Something deep inside me said, keep her safe and never let her go and what could I do but obey?" He said.

His words held such emotion, that the crew drew nearer to us as eager as I to hear more.

"Though you pulled away from me, I pursued you."

Nathaniel continued. "I knew you would come to me in time." His vivid eyes held a spark that had me grinning at his cockiness.

"When we discovered our true feelings, it was like a physical pain, when I could not voice my intentions."

He pressed my hand to his chest, over his heart. It beat with such desire under my touch.

"I vow never to leave you, to take care of you, to be faithful and above all else, love you."

We stared at each other, no more words were needed. I could see my future in his eyes and I so desperately wanted it. Beyond those blue depths was love, family and acceptance. There was no more fighting and no more pain.

"I now declare, before all of these witnesses, you husband and wife,"

The captain's voice broke our private bubble. I'd almost forgotten the crew were surrounding us. Before I could react to our audience, Nathaniel bought his lips to mine and sparks erupted behind my lids like shooting stars. Somewhere around us applause sounded, but I was beyond hearing it.

It was the sound of fingers clicking that ended our embrace. The action, from the Sorceress caused the candle at our feet to change. From the usual blue-orange it transformed into the deepest of reds. We knelt before it to watch the flickering spark.

"This everlasting flame represents your love; it is a

reminder of all you have vowed today. Congratulations my children, I am honoured to bear witness to your union," the sorceress said, bowing before us.

"Please allow me to give you newly-weds, free reign of my forest. There you will have unlimited privacy. I shall remain close by the *Wilted Rose*, to protect your crew mates. Hadnaloy will not return with me here."

"What about your wish for her to be destroyed?" I asked.

"It can wait," she said. "Your love is far more important."

LESS THAN AN hour later, Nathaniel and I were walking towards the forest. My stomach fluttered as my fear and excitement melded together. This was new for me, the emotions coursing through me, excitement, anticipation, love, were entirely foreign to my past. I hoped I wouldn't falter.

As we reached the clearing, the familiar sight of the blue flames greeted us. A scroll lay on one of the logs, awaiting our arrival:

Dearest Newly-weds,
Treat my home as your own, use your time well.
Forever your guardian, R

Nathaniel sat beside me, I flushed at his closeness my

face growing warm and my hands cold. A mixture of nerves and anticipation had me jogging my foot.

"I love you," I murmured as Nathaniel tenderly kissed the corner of my mouth.

The small peck soon consumed us both and I felt myself float away. For the first time in forever, I let go…

CHAPTER XIX
END

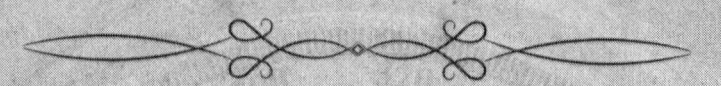

IT WAS THE sunrise that woke me, the rays fell across my face and warmed the grass I lay upon. I let it soak into my skin as I drifted away on the euphoria thrumming through my veins. The soft brush of lips to my forehead opened my eyes. Nathaniel lay beside me, his skin alight under the awakening of the new day.

"How did I win such a prize? I am so blessed," he murmured pulling me closer still.

My eyes fluttered closed once more as his warm lips brushed across my cheek and down my neck. As we lay together under the sheets of nature, I had never felt so free nor so whole. My flawed soul had now been restored. He was part of me and I was a part of him. We had spoken vows before our guardian and our captain, naught but death could tear us apart now.

"I cannot wait for our life to begin," Nathaniel sighed.

His dreams settled around me, conjuring images.

"Nor can I, my love," I said.

I pressed a kiss to his shoulder, laying my head over his heart. The deep, strong thud which greeted me, widened my smile.

"Where do you think we should settle, a house in the country or a cottage by the sea?" I asked.

"The seaside cottage I think," Nathaniel replied; his eyes stared far off, creating our future.

I watched him, my own alight with dreams. As I continued to gaze at my husband, the sound of a bird squawking echoed above our heads.

"Is that Caw?" I was instantly alert. "There has to be something wrong."

"I am sure it is just Rupert or Butch's idea of a joke," Nathaniel said frowning up at the circling bird.

I wrenched on my clothes and thrust my feet into boots. Standing I turned to find Nathaniel dressed and reaching out for my hand. Taking it, I ran with him through the forest and towards the beach.

Our row boat sat waiting and soon we were out to sea. Whilst Nathaniel manned the oars, I took charge as lookout. Nothing surrounded us but Caw flew on, guiding our way.

The sight of the *Wilted Rose* bought both relief and clawing fear. The shouts and sounds of cannon fire made my stomach clench. We hadn't been there when our crewmates needed us. What had happened to the Sorceress and her promises of safety?

Turning to Nathaniel, I saw the guilt I felt etched upon his face too. Rowing as close as we could, we climbed aboard. The enemy ship wasn't three feet away, it was unmistakable. The flag, under which it sailed, showed the symbol of the helm with two crossed blades.

I raced up the ladder, only to be pulled back into the row boat and back into Nathaniel's arms. He kissed me with urgency.

"I love you," he gasped.

"As I love you," I replied, kissing him again.

"Stay safe," he pleaded, as we released each other.

"You too," I shouted as I watched my husband climb the ladder and disappear into the throng.

Reaching the deck, all I could see was chaos. Smoke and sulphur filled the air, along with the mismatch of bodies and swords. Jumping into the fray I pushed forward, my weapon scraping another.

"Foe or no?" Rupert danced around me, pulling his sword away.

I shook my head, "No, dear Rupert, my esteemed apologies."

"Forget that, sister and do what you know," he said with a salute turning to deal with yet another enemy.

I didn't stay still for long; I leapt into action taking on a murky eyed pirate. All around me, I could hear my fellow crew mates doing the same. Claudette threw sparkling flames at her opponent, Butch wielded his mop. My stomach flipped at Davy's frustrated yell, as he battled two at once on an injured leg. Rosa was shooting a substance close to cannon fire at our opposing ship, and from my limited view, their ship was sinking.

Not seeing the captain or Nathaniel, I hoped they were below, manning our own cannons rather than injured somewhere.

"Lennie," Ned called, reaching my side.

"What happened to the Sorceress?"

"She was sent away on urgent business."

"Really? What is more important than the ship?"

"Someone set fire to a part of forest."

I gasped as I sent a small man flying with a kick of my foot.

"We didn't see anything!" I exclaimed.

Ned pulled the trigger on his pistol as the wretch rushed back.

"Claudette tried her circle of protection but Hadnaloy's power managed to push through it. She was weakened by the experience."

"We can defeat them," I yelled, racing towards Davy and kicking out a yet another murky eyed fiend.

As the battle raged on, my muscles burned but I refused to slow down. I carried on regardless, pushing myself through the discomfort. My mind focussed on the battle, trying to take down as many of the bewitched pirates as I could. The sooner we did the sooner we'd get to Hadnaloy.

It wasn't until a piercing scream filled the air, that I began to worry. I let out my own garbled cry as I watched Claudette fall, her body slumped to the floor, blood seeped from her mouth.

Torn between racing to her side and avenging her, I growled. My anger boiled at a dangerous level and my own partner felt the brunt. Ignoring the splash their body made, I raced over and thrashed my sword at the rogue who had taken down our most powerful member. His weapon was blunt and jagged but fear was not an option. My only thought was of my enemy, face down no longer able to fight back.

At least three times he lunged at me, blood seeped from my cheek, arm and torso but I'd harmed him just as much. He now limped as he stepped forward in attack. I refused to play fair, for he definitely wasn't. Using all my strength, I thrust my elbow towards him. It connected with his jaw; the sickening crack ringing in my ears. He didn't seem to notice the pain and lunged forward again. The wretch just wouldn't stall, he kept coming for me.

A cry echoed from behind us, though distracted, I refused to turn. The moment of weakness was enough for my foe to get the upper hand, however. One push and I was sprawled across the deck, spitting out hair. The vile man stepped over me, pushing his face uncomfortably close to mine.

He smelled rancid, like mould, his dull eyes held nothing. Leering he dragged his serrated blade across his teeth. The noise put my nerves on edge. Not knowing where my own sword had fallen, I put all of my strength into my legs and kicked out, the bewitched pirate groaned as he hit the floor beside me. It gave me time to roll and locate my piece.

Nathaniel was there in an instant, his eyes ablaze, as he punched the underling who attempted to stand. The fiend fell backwards, his eyes rolling back into his head. I hid my face in Nathaniel's chest, catching my breath. He stroked my hair as the fight raged on around us, his words of comfort soft as he whispered into my ear.

As I leaned into him, Nathaniel stiffened. I looked up confused, only to stare into his shocked face. The jagged-sword wielding stranger was stood behind Nathaniel, his face held such triumph, it left me cold. He waved a blood soaked blade as his mouth twisted in a merciless grin and I knew what he'd done.

"No!"

My scream filled the air, stalling the battle. Nathaniel's weight fell against me and together we crumpled to the deck. Tears threatened as I brushed his empty eyes closed. Pressing a kiss to his still warm lips I stood. The underling's gloating smile had me grasping for my weapon. His mocking laughter pained me more than the cuts and scrapes across my body. This man held no remorse.

Unable to take any more I raced at the fiend and ploughed my sword through his heart, the force of my anger and pain pushed him over the rail and into the water. Not caring for the battle resuming around me, I curled up beside my love. I pressed my ear over his heart; a dull thud sputtered a few more beats, before silence was all that remained.

"Lennie!" Butch's voice echoed through the dry sobs I was heaving. This was too deep for tears. Nathaniel had grown cold and I'd laid my jacket over his body, yet he'd never grown warmer. His still face was peaceful, as though sleeping and all I could hear was the whooshing sound of my own heart in my ears.

"Lennie!" Butch's voice came though the noise and I turned to him. My head lay upon the still chest of my beloved.

"He's gone, Lennie." Pain contorted my friends face and he reached out to push aside my hair.

"No." I said my voice hoarse.

"Lennie, you need to let us, well, let us get him ready."

"No." I repeated, holding Nathaniel tighter. They would put me in the box and throw me overboard too. I wasn't leaving him. This was not our plan. We were not aged and old and rocking our grandchildren in the seaside cottage of our dream. We were not holding hands in our double bed as we drifted off to sleep in peace together as old, elderly former pirates.

"No," this time hands were on me. I lashed out, hissing like a cat. I knew I hit one person with my clawed hands and another with my leg. I felt the connection and heard the grunt. Was it Davy? The captain perhaps?

"Lennie, this will not help things. You will need to leave him sometime." Ned was beside me, his gnarled hands at my waist. "Please, child, we can do no more for him now."

"You can't take him. He's mine, I'm his. We were one."

"Lennie, you have to go on, be the strength for you both." Claudette's voice had me looking up. Her face was soaked in tears and her hands were outstretched, while her eyes pleaded with me.

"I've had enough of being strong," I said.

"Lennie, get up and fight! You know better than to wallow on the deck, get up and fight or was that just a front for the whore that you are?"

I gasped at the audacity of Rupert's words. My body moved without meaning to and I lifted my sword from its place at my feet"

"Raise your sword, bastard." I hissed. Though my hands shook, I stepped towards my red headed friend. "No one speaks to me in such a way, not even you."

He too lifted his blade, but up and away, the sign of surrender.

"Take him," he muttered to a spot over my shoulder. "Butch, I don't know where or how, just take him."

My eyes widened and before I could return to my place as Nathaniel's side, Rupert had disarmed me and had hold of me, tight.

"Bastard" I muttered into his chest as he held me. His hands smoothing my hair as he whispered stilted words of condolence in my ear.

"Forgive me, Lennie, there was no other way of making you step away."

"He's gone, Rupert. He's gone."

"I know, Lennie."

"Bring her to me," Ned's voice was soft as Rupert handed me over to Ned. The older man sat at the table and began to rock me, his own tears mixing with my own.

CHAPTER XXX
DONE

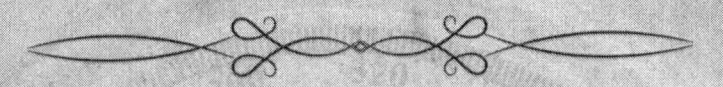

THE DECK WAS cleared, the battle won, and silence danced upon the still waters. Ned tended to Claudette's wounds. The smell of his poultices and potions turned my stomach. They had taken Nathaniel's body below, once the smoke had cleared, and though I wanted to follow, I couldn't. All I could see was a jet hole where my future had been. All the dreams I'd allowed myself to imagine, nothing but torn pages swept away by the wind.

"Come on Lennie, let's get you to bed," Butch said. His voice soft and his touch gentle as he lifted me into his arms and carried to me to my cabin.

Butch lay me on the blankets and I curled up, facing him. Tears had begun to pour silently as Butch brushed the hair from my face.

"I wish I knew what to say to you," he said.

My gaze strayed from his forlorn expression to the earth-lined basket on my bedside table. I lay transfixed by red flame the Sorceress had conjured. The small fire represented the love Nathaniel and I held. My numbness almost broke when the colour seeped away from the flame, turning coal black.

"Oh, who left that here?" Butch admonished taking hold of it.

"No!" I said, my voice pained.

"I'll leave it," he soothed. "Get some sleep Lennie, I shall leave the door ajar, call if you need anything. With a press of his lips to my forehead, he left me alone.

"THERE HAS TO be something we can do," Claudette sighed as Butch aided me to the card table. I squinted over at my lilac eyed friend as she spoke to the figurehead.

"Child, you of all people know the suffering she feels." Rosa's forlorn reply carried.

"As do you mistress," Claudette countered. "Yet, I feel she has succumbed further to the darkness than we could imagine."

I sighed, so they'd noticed. I hated dragging my crewmates into my despair but I felt nothing but sorrow. There was no room for much else.

"How can you be sure?" Rosa asked.

"Her final hope has been dashed. My prayer is that it can be returned to her." Butch had joined them now.

I wasn't so sure my hope could be returned. My entire life had been taken with the strike of that blade.

Four months of numbness had held me captive. On

the outside I looked worn and fragile. I had lost a lot of weight, aside from what Butch and Ned managed, I couldn't find the inclination to eat. My clothes hung loose around my body and my skin was constantly dry. I had nothing to say, and so I barely spoke, I lived like a shadow. Silent and mournful.

Yet on the inside I screamed. They were agonising, blood curdling, gut wrenching screams that could crack glass. Each one cursing the fates for what I'd been dealt, cursing Hadnaloy for the damage she'd done and cursing myself for letting him die. I wanted nothing more than to join my beloved, to be no more than dust.

Yet something told me not to. To let the others nourish me. To make sure I moved outside, so I could see daylight. A voice deep inside me said, 'live Lennie.' I didn't know who it was or where it came from, but I clung to that voice; and listened.

"WHEN DID THAT start?" The crew stilled as I pointed at the jet line darkening the water behind them. I hadn't been lucid long, but the strange sight had worried me enough to speak up.

"Hadnaloy's been following us for a while now," Butch said guiding me away from the rail.

Now the numbness had lifted, my heart raced in anticipation.

"Where are we headed?" I asked.

"Rosa thinks a trip to a certain forest could aid our journey," Claudette said taking hold of my hand.

"I see," I said, wishing I felt something more than empty.

The ship caught speed and I grasped hold of Butch. Clutching his arm tight, I forced the stalling breaths out of my mouth and in through my nose.

"It'll be fine," Butch said disentangling himself and swapping his seat with Ned. "I need to head to the crow's nest," he murmured racing away.

"Will this work?" I asked gazing around at the faces of my crewmen, how long had they been there?

Rupert knelt before me, his mischievous eyes, serious. "We hope so."

Clouds filled the sky as we continued on our journey, the ship slowed but the black veil which followed us, did not abate. We had reached the shallows leading to the Sorceress' forest when the rain began to fall. The waves grew choppy and a simple whirlpool caused our ship to shudder beneath our feet.

"Remain vigilant," Rosa said as the *Wilted Rose* came to a stop. The black stain upon the water surrounded the ship and the maelstrom grew more frantic. The black ink coloured water seeped into the sand, staining it.

"Patience," the figurehead cried and the ship shuddered beneath the crew and a low cackle sounded.

The creature rose out of the swirling water, terrifying

and intimidating. I felt little fear, I'd seen the 'all mighty and powerful' Hadnaloy, in her true state – a withered body surrounding a void soul.

"Come closer, Yolandah." Heads swivelled as I called across the space.

"You dare use...?" sputtered the witch.

I raised my brows. "Is it not the name you were bestowed at birth?"

Hadnaloy's lips twisted into a malevolent smile. I followed the sea witch's gaze and my stomach lurched. The stain on the deck was still crimson with Nathaniel's blood.

"I forbid it," I said, my voice constricted but firm as the crew came to stand beside me.

"You have hurt us enough. No amount of beauty is worth that much."

My gaze moved past the beach to the trees beyond. Evidence of the woodland fire could be seen in the missing clumps but many trees still remained. Memories of Nathaniel threatened to consume me and I fought to regain control. Pressing my teeth into my lip, I tasted blood. The grief was replaced with anger. This woman may not have swung the blade that ended my dream, but she damn well had pulled the strings to make it so.

Stepping from my friends, I stood exposed; I hadn't worn my sword in months but I didn't need it. Opening my arms wide, I gave Hadnaloy clear shot.

"Leave her," Rosa said, speaking to the crew. "She

knows what she's doing."

Did I? All I knew was the anger which burned from the depths of my soul and the fact that I was still somehow connected to the Sorceress. That power hadn't been lifted when the curse had, or at least I hoped not, besides she had to be amongst those tress, hadn't she?

"I'm unarmed and vulnerable," I cried at the sea-witch. "Tell me Yolandah, what happens now?"

"I kill you," came the simple reply

"Stay back!" Rosa cried as the crew made to move closer.

Hadnaloy raised her large withered hand and I did the same. Lightening flashed over our heads and I felt the white hot pain spread through me as the sound of echoing cries shook the ship. Warm dampness dripped down my face, along my arm and I hit the deck with a crunching thump.

Above me, the Sorceress raced through the sky, shooting her own wave of magic at the screaming witch. The creature writhed in the false façade and the Sorceress gave her own cackle as she landed upon the deck.

"Well done child, you have been very brave." The faery touched my wounded cheek, easing the pain.

"Let me continue this," she begged.

My already weakened body had been injured further. I was in no state to fight, I nodded in agreement.

"Well that would have been less than fun," Hadnaloy croaked. "Having Rosa Del Mar the second, on a plate, and here I heard she was the fighter of your crew." Even with her own death staring her in the face, Hadnaloy had presence to gloat and mock.

The pain at my face and arm did not prevent the anger from returning. I sat up, my eyes narrowed on the witch.

Something had happened to her, when she had attacked me, her façade had fallen. The ship's carcasses now littered the water surrounding her frame. Though she was still a large overbearing creature, she was hag-like and frail looking.

"Fighters come in all forms, you forget, Yolandah," The Sorceress said.

She fluttered back towards the centre of the deck, to the sound of Hadnaloy's cackles.

"Now my comrades," she began. The soft words, sent rain pelting through the sky and Hadnaloy raised her hands tossing sparks.

"You will never end my crusade," the creature yelled, amongst the downpour, though the driving rain broke everyone's view.

"End it?" the Sorceress replied "Oh no my dear, you misunderstand me."

With swift hands she tossed a conjured rope of light and lassoed the sea-witch, clamping her arms and ending the opposing witch's attack. The Sorceress' face was the image of power and triumph. While her lips were formed a straight firm line, her eyes held triumph and good humour.

The threads of light were tied at her wrists and she held on tight. Inch by inch, she reeled Hadnaloy in. Bringing her closer and closer to our beloved ship. The Sorceress headed skyward fluttering back towards the beach and dragging the sea-witch with her.

Hadnaloy was infuriated, her growls and struggles proved futile, as she was yanked further towards the shore. One swift tug from the Sorceress and the large wooden witch crashed into the shallow water, floating helpless. Her yell echoed across the ocean, drawing birds from the forest and into the skies. The *Wilted Rose* rocked unsteadily in the already rough water.

With jubilant cries, the crew raced towards the rail to watch the proceedings. Butch grasped me with gentleness and led me over to view it with them. We stilled, as a frail hag the true Hadnaloy emerged from the wreckage of her long lived lie. Small and crooked, the wretch lay twisted on the sand, the magical rope tied at her hands and feet. Fire danced in her red eyes but she only glared.

"Do you wish to say something?" The Sorceress enquired, as she flew down beside Hadnaloy.

Despite the Sorceress' petite stature, no-one would have called her aura small. Yet the witch had the audacity to spit at the nymph's feet, her disrespect drew gasps from the crew.

"Very well," the sorceress said, her eyes narrowed in disapproval. Clicking her fingers, a small group of fae appeared. Three male and two female stood guard whilst the rest awaited orders from their ruler.

"Since gifting my crew with love, I have learned forgiveness," The Sorceress continued, her attention on the writhing prisoner. "Yet the things you have done do not deserve such a thing."

The Sea-witch sneered, but said nothing.

"My friends please fetch the present I have for our esteemed guest."

With mischievous smiles, the remaining faery comrades left the beach and soared into the forest. Laughter and rustling disturbed the trees and I clung to Butch's hand awaiting the surprise. Soon the stream, running the depth of the beach, ebbed and flowed into the seam. The turquoise water hit the ocean creating frothy bubbles along the shore, obliterating the jet water which had tarnished the sand.

The new current bought an old, weather beaten ship. The faeries rode atop it, their delight lighting their glowing faces. They sang a sea-shanty style song in their high bell like voices. The contrast to their merriment and to what had just transpired was jarring.

"Yolandah, I have brought you a gift."

The Sorceress pointed a long finger and the witch was lifted from the ground. Her binds disappeared as her body transformed. Her screeches were muted as she was slammed into the vessel fused to the ship's bow.

"You have what you wished." The Sorceress' once condescending tone turned dark. "You are now the guardian of a ship. I have bewitched it with a magic I never thought I would use."

Disappointment clouded the Sorceress' face as she continued with her explanation.

"Your vessel cannot hold a living creature. With them you shall surely sink; without a loving heart aboard, you will struggle to thrive."

The Sorceress fluttered towards her creation and nudged the boat to the water's edge. A breeze rustled through the trees pushing the worn boat further out to sea. It didn't take long for it to leave, sailing towards the moon.

In my relief, I sank into the ground. My tears fell without pride as the Sorceress broke the silence.

"I cannot confiscate her power, it is entrenched within her far too deep, yet she will find it hard recruiting more followers with a ship as cursed hers. Perhaps in my mercy she will find her own form of forgiveness." The Sorceress turned back to the sea, she glowed in the sunshine.

The crew could not contain their joy, rushing to the Sorceress and dancing amongst her faery friends. Only I remained on the ship, bleeding and crying and not knowing where to turn. Ned found me, concern creasing his scarred face.

"What is it child?" he asked, wrapping me in his arms.

"Sorceress?" I called, hoping she could hear me.

The winged mistress flew over the ship's walls on her

delicate wings and landed before me.

"What troubles you child?" She asked, kneeling beside me. Her small hand brushing away the crimson staining my skin.

"My journey aboard the *Wilted Rose* has been both exhilarating and terrifying. I've made the most wonderful friends and felt the greatest love—"

"—But you do not wish to fight any longer." It wasn't a question, the Sorceress had spoken my truth with such articulation.

"Are you angry?" I asked.

"You, my dear, hold much more courage and depth than you know. I would be a fool to deny you this." She gripped my hand. "But are you truly sure? For once this decision is made; you cannot change it back so easily."

"I know I'll miss it," I said. "But I don't think I could survive much more, one more battle could kill me."

Behind me a gasp sounded, I turned to see Butch, his eyes wide and his mouth agog. I sent him a smile of apology before returning my attention to the Sorceress. The faery cocked her head to one side, thoughts turned and tumbled in her unusual eyes. Her long fingers were stretched out before her, almost aligned with my stomach. I pulled in a pained breath as her blue tinted iris' stared deeply into my face seeing something I couldn't even fathom.

"I am aware of a dwelling, not too far from here. I am sure it would be ideal for your situation," the Sorceress said. "Be free."

I closed my eyes as the Sorceress touched her forehead. Relief as well as warmth flowed through me and she could breathe again. Weight lifted from my heart and shoulders and for the first time, I felt freedom.

The pain in my face and arm too was gone, though the puckered scar lining my skin showed I would carry the weight of my bout with Hadnaloy forever. I couldn't tell what my face looked like. I touched my cheek, feeling the raised welts and dried blood.

"I will leave you to say your goodbyes." The Sorceress said. With the flutter of her wings she headed towards the trees — her friends following beside her, their voices in harmony as they followed their queen.

"I will miss you all," I said my cheeks were drenched in renewed tears.

Ned was the first to approach me and clasp my hands. "I have always felt like a father to two daughters…"

"Papa." I pressed my lips to his twisted knuckles. "Let us not say goodbye, just 'I will see you soon.'"

I pulled him tight and kissed his cheek, his body shook within my arms, I would miss this man. He was my hero, I would have never left the Châteaux had it not been for him.

"Please do not think you can bid farewell to me," Claudette scolded, wrapping me in a warm embrace.

"Here," Claudette said. She pulled a thick leather journal from her pocket and I held my breath as

Claudette handed it to me. The binding showed wear and parchment poked out from the edges. Nathaniel had begun writing his own story within the pages – our story.

"Read this and remember us," Claudette implored.

"Of course, I won't need any books for that."

"Here's something else for you to keep," Davy said holding out a bone handled comb – the one I had pushed at Nathaniel all those months ago. I had been so frightened of my heart, back then, worried of where that journey would lead.

"Thank you," I said taking the token.

I turned it over in my hands and a small smile lifted my mouth. Just as I had treasured his handkerchief, he had held my comb. The fool had been as sentimental as I had.

Before grief could take over, Butch stepped forward.

"I wish you didn't have to leave us," he said, giving me my weapons belt and two bags filled with what I guessed, were my belongings.

"I'm not, not really. I'll always be with you." I said.

His face held such sadness that I touched a palm over his heart before pressing a soft kiss to his lips.

"You're my closest friend, Tobias and I love you. I want you to have this."

It had been a long time since I'd called him by his birth name, but it seemed fitting as I handed him my sword.

"I can't take that, it was your fathers."

"I won't be needing it where I'm going and besides, I need to know it's in safe hands. Taking it from me, he belted it around his waist. Pulling me to him and as his arms surrounded me, I swore he said 'I love you too' as his embrace tightened. He held on longer than necessary, his body trembling.

"It'll be all right," I assured, brushing a hand down his back.

He stepped away from me and without turning back he strode to the mast and up to the crow's nest. Wiping away my tears, I plastered on a smile. This was hard, but it was the right decision. I couldn't fight this battle anymore.

"Boys!" I cried, taking hold of Rupert and Davy.

"I will truly miss you," Davy said, a single tear spilled over. He clasped my hand, tracing the rune for journey onto my palm.

"As I will miss you," I said caressing his tear stained cheek.

"Who will I tease now?" Rupert said thickly as he fought to remain unmoved. His red eyes were telling however. "You will let us visit?"

"As if I could keep you away." I chuckled, squeezing his fingers to draw a smile to his face. "You're the most valued, you know," he whispered, pressing his lips to my injured cheek.

A proud smile brightened the captain's craggy face as he took his turn. "Remember, Lennie, you will forever be part of this crew."

His words were formal but their sincerity was proven by the tenderness in his voice.

"Thank you, Captain," I said. "You all will never leave my heart."

My eyes wandered to the wooden woman who was trapped aboard the ship. Rosa lifted her floral staff in a silent salute.

"Take care and live your life with love, my darling girl," she advised.

I would always be a crewmember of the *Wilted Rose*, but the moment I stepped off the ship I would no longer be a pirate. It was time to find my way, and figure out who this newest incarnation of Lennie was. I pulled my bags higher up my good shoulder and waved as my remaining six crewmates sailed off towards the horizon. I would see them again, I was sure of it.

I'd found solace aboard the *Wilted Rose*, family, friends and love. Now it was time for a new place to rest, and a new adventure…

EPILOGUE
THE VISITORS

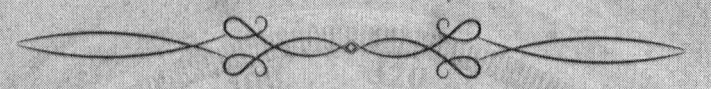

THE WELL-TENDED garden overflowed with wild flowers, the most beautiful of them being the roses. Each colour, variety and size made a protective border around the small piece of land. Much closer to the house, someone had planted a plentiful vegetable garden.

A woman was knelt amongst the turnips and potatoes. Her hands covered in dirt and her basket, filled to the brim. Her bountiful harvest was more than enough for a week of meals. Clenching her teeth at a particularly stubborn root, she tugged hard, yanking it from its home. Without ceremony she tossed it amongst her other edible treasures.

Resting back on her heels, she brushed off her hands. Looking up at the dimming light, she wiped the perspiration from her face. The gesture left mud streaked across her forehead and down a scarred cheek.

"*Ma mère!*" a child's voice cried.

She turned as a boy, no older than five, raced along the uneven stone path. His face was flushed and proof he'd used the hedge as an entrance, clung to his hair and clothes.

"What happened?" she asked, as he skidded to a stop. Her mismatched eyes roamed over him, fearful he'd hurt himself.

"You must come and see," he urged. The boy batted her hands away as she pulled a leaf from behind his ear. "*Ma mère*, you must!"

He gazed up at her, his sky blue eyes making her heart throb with long buried pain.

"Very well," she conceded, satisfied he was unharmed.

Smiling she took hold of his outstretched hand. They hurried back along the garden path and through the hedge. The other side revealed a small stretch of sand. The woman's laughter bubbled at her son's frustration. She travelled much too slow for him. Her smile faded, as she spied the object of her son's excitement.

There in the distance, was the unmistakable silhouette of a large vessel. That in itself was strange, for the beach that backed onto their property was quite anonymous. Their visitors were lost souls or the curious, no more than two or three a year. In her anxiousness the woman grasped at her hip. She found nothing but the fabric of her worn dress.

As the ship sailed ever closer, the half-raised flag hit the setting sun. What it revealed caused the woman's smile to return. The black flag displayed a skull and crossbones, much like any other pirate ship. The difference with this one however, was that it also portrayed a wilting red rose. The thorn covered stem was intertwined with the bones. The scarlet petals falling from the bloom looked forlorn, as though drifting out to sea. The woman's fingertips brushed across its twin, branded upon her own wrist.

Her son beamed up at her before clambering upon a large piece of driftwood, his eyes centred on their approaching visitors. She stopped beside him and pressed a kiss to the top of his head.

"See son, my stories were more than just faery-tales and folklore…"

The End…or is it?

ACKNOWLEDEGMENTS

Inherited has taken many years and experiences to write. There has been a cavalcade of people along with me on the journey to publication so here goes nothing!

Granddad, you were the catalyst to my writing; I would never have put pen to paper without you. You taught me to read, write and imagine, not to mention how to build the best blanket forts! I miss you so very much and wish you were beside me to see my dreams come true. I hope I've made you proud, I wouldn't be here without you. I love and will always miss you!

Callum and Ciaran, my wonderfully annoying pains in my posterior! You came into my life when I was far too young to be an adult but far too grown to be a child. You taught me so much and are still teaching me to this day. No matter how big you get, or how high you tower over me, you will forever be my best boys, Love you!

Claire-ZOMBIES! See I've got your attention now haven't I? You and I connected over our mutual love of books and have never stopped connecting. You've introduced me to some amazing authors and for that I am forever grateful. When I plucked up the courage to share my work with you, you were honest and encouraging – you still are. You are more than a cousin, you're a best friend. Everything I write will be pushed under your nose, you do know that, right? Oh, and special thank you to Hector for having my back and telling Claire off for correcting things LOL as well as giving me house room! You are very special and mean a lot to me!

Anna for reading my first stories at nine or ten years old and for telling me then, that one day my words would be in print! I never imagined your words would come to anything, and look at us now! You were forever in my corner and for that I am dearly thankful! You have been such a wonderful friend and I would never have made it this far without your advice, guidance and support– you know, you too are going to be subject to my early drafts of my other books, right? Much love and thanks to you!

With the size of my family, it would take another novel to thank them all individually. I want to thank all of the *Matthews and Williams families* and their offshoots. Every Aunt, Uncle and Cousin has cared for, encouraged and loved me and for that I am forever grateful.

Special family shout outs for:-

Mum, Dad & Mark- who have no idea what all this is about but are happy for me and supportive anyway- thanks for keeping me grounded guys, I wouldn't function without you!

Mickey, Sally, Auntie Babs, Auntie Eileen, Auntie Eve, Auntie Tess, Vera, Uncle Gus, Uncle John, Auntie Eileen & Emma and Aunt Hilda & Uncle Bill – Thank you all for letting me take up house room and squawk at you about these fictional characters, until I was blue in the face. Your support, help and encouragement have kept me going.

Uncle Den, for gifting me my first computer which allowed me to type up my stories and kick start my writing journey. Thank you for thinking of me, I miss you!

Kirsty (#cousincrew) for helping me with #freedomfriday's and for listening to me, even when I didn't make any sense – I've got your back baby!

Uncle Richard, who we lost just when I was gaining my author legs – I have a feeling you had a hand in all this, I am forever grateful. I miss you

The Willmont/Coles and Shilton/Reading families – I see you all as extensions of my own family. Your unwavering support, love and encouragement holds no bounds – thank you for letting me be a part of your lives, you all have my heart -especially Tracey & Sam

Thank you to *Ann, Amy, Peter, Bea, Kevin, Rachel, Melissa, Cloe, Pauline* and many other friends and neighbours who have stuck by me, listened, encouraged and read. You all know who you are and you all have my thanks and appreciation

A BIG thank you to the *Oftomes Family:-*

Xina, who read my work first and has become such a wonderful friend throughout this journey! Thank you for making my pirates shine! You are the ultimate Emoji, stowaway elongated hashtag queen! *Big frantic waves in your general direction* This journey started and ended with you. Oh and Bruce finally made it into the book #bookishfriendsareforeverfriends
#piratesfaeriesandfiguresheadsohmy
#yohohoandamugofcoffee
#yohohoandanerraticwavingfriendship

Ben, who is so encouraging, patient and dedicated. You championed and fought for my pirates from the get go! Thank you for being so supportive and for taking on a neurotic debut author and her band of misbehaving pirates and faeries – you've made my dreams come true. Thank you just isn't enough! I love you very much, you lovely man! Thank you for welcoming me into this amazing family! I appreciate your guidance and friendship, I'm SO happy to have stumbled upon that Youtube video!

Sara, one the first fellow Oftomes authors I think I spoke to and who is always so encouraging and ready to chat. I adore you! Thank you for listening and letting me into your very cool life! Your book(s) rock and I'm SO very proud to call you a friend!

Laura,- my yarn buddy, who chats with me about the most random of subjects which always comes around to either, books, writing or yarn! I can't wait for Butch to meet Mynta – thank you for being such a lovely friend.

Claire (Mother of Dragon-Boy) – Who was so kind the first time we messaged and continued to be once we had met. Thank you for your advice, for being such a great friend, listening to my rambling waffle and for just being one of the coolest people I know! I just adore you, lovely lady! I can't wait for that coffee and IRL chat!

Gabriella, Esther, Jen and Joel – I look to each of you in awe. You all have said the most wonderful things and helped in a multitude of ways. Your aid, advice and encouragement have kept me sane and made me feel so welcome in our group. I love our comradery and support network – it is such a lovely family and you all rock! I am here for you as much as I know you have been/ will be for me *Esther, Gabriella & Jen*, reading your work has truly made me want to be a better writer, you (and all of the team), inspire me in a multitude of ways. Each of your books have stayed with me, long after I read 'the end.' I am very thankful and honoured to be situated alongside such talented people!

Kim – I am amazed at your talent. You have captured my stories within such beautiful images. I never imagined the cover of my books to ensnare me in such a way, but they do. You have a such a talent for depicting just the right mood, character and feel. I am so very lucky to have your work encasing my words. Thank you!!

Kate – Your sweetness and book recommendations are such a breath of fresh air! Your messages always make me smile. I can't wait to hear your thoughts on Lennie's story and to discuss more about Beauty & the Beast & ACOTAR – thank you for chatting with me, you are the best!

This bookish family is such a wonderful addition to my life- having like-minded people (including all of those I interact with on IG, Twitter, Goodreads & my street team (Wilted Rose Crew), join me on this journey has been the best! Thank you ALL for being there and your continued support. I have grown in more ways since becoming a part of Oftomes than I could ever imagine and I will be forever thankful to all those involved.

My final thank you is to you, the **reader**. Lennie's story isn't a simple romance, where they all ride off into the sunset, but I hope you have enjoyed your journey aboard *The Wilted Rose,* all the same. It has taken me many years and many incarnations but I finally feel at ease, knowing Lennie's story has been told and out into the world. I hope you've finished it with both a smile and perhaps a tear or two, I know I did writing it.

I look forward to reading your thoughts and interacting with you on social media! Welcome to the crew – here's to the next journey!

Much love, faery dust and (imaginary) rum!
Freedom

Made in the USA
Charleston, SC
11 June 2016